DATE DU'

SPA DAYZ

LAWRENCE DALY

8B
D154
2015

For Zhenya

Chapter 1

Margaret:

Spring 2010

A Spa Odyssey

"It's bedtime, Helga," I said to my favorite psych ward patient as I stood by the doorway with one hand on the light switch. *This room would look so much nicer without fluorescent bulbs,* I thought. A gust of cold wind blew open the ugly grey curtains revealing a crescent moon in the sky. "Do you wanna tell me a bedtime story?" Helga was a former professional wrestler who loved to entertain me with tales from her youth. The other nurses called her our gentle giant.

Instead of responding, Helga growled like an angry wolf. *That's weird,* I thought. She stared out the window, squinting her black eyes. Her curly brown mullet, billowing in the breeze, reminded me of a vintage horror movie.

I yanked my tight green scrubs from my butt crack and tried to stay calm. "Is there something wrong, Helga?"

"You know it's not time to go to bed, Nurse Margaret," she said in a thick German accent. "It's ring time!" She leapt across the room with her arms extended, ready to rumble. *Oh my God!* I turned to run but

Helga knocked my legs out from under me and locked her mannish arm around my neck. Unable to speak, I kicked my feet in vain as my pulse pounded like a snare drum in my ears.

What the fuck!?! I dug my fingernails into Helga's muscular forearm and she jumped to her feet, taking me with her. She screamed, tightening her grip around my neck. From the corner of my eye, I watched mascara stained tears drip down my cheek like they were being squeezed out of me. The world went out of focus as my long red ponytail—trapped in Helga's grasp—pulled violently at my scalp.

"Boy, you're a big one," Helga said through clenched teeth. Then she delivered a zaftig girl's least favorite back-handed compliment: "And it's too bad—because you have such a pretty face. Oh well, prepare to die!"

Images flooded my mind at lightning speed. I saw myself blowing out three birthday candles and eating cake with my fingers. Performing a puppet show for my parents as a pre-teen. Smoking clove cigarettes in the high school parking lot.

Helga increased her vice-like hold around my neck, completely constricting my airway. Quickly I sat down, thinking I could wiggle out from under her, but she joined me on the floor without missing a beat. *Does anyone know I'm alone with Hulkette Hogan?*

My brain went into overdrive. *Maybe Tony Germanotta was "the one." I shoulda called my mom today. And what about my dreams?* The room started to go black. *I can't let this job be my legacy!*

I gripped Helga's wrist with both hands, summoned all my strength, and pulled her forearm from around my throat. With millimeters between our flesh, I inhaled, wheezing for a split second before Helga regained control. My body cried out for more oxygen. I opened my mouth to scream, but still couldn't utter a sound.

As I winced in pain, Helga lurched forward and pinned me to the floor face down, forcing the last drop of air from my lungs. I saw a long white tunnel and a feeling of peaceful joy washed over my body. A beautiful man in a cream colored robe, with a chestnut beard and luminous hazel eyes, floated towards me. He said, "Margaret, it's not your time. You must save yourself. If you can't scream, make Helga scream instead."

With all my might, I rolled over, gasping for air and flailing my legs, but Helga stayed attached to me like an enormous parasitic twin. After a montage of positions that would have impressed Jenna Jameson, she curled her right arm around my neck and her left elbow around my leg. *Stop showing off, bitch! This is my shot.* I lowered my chin, squeezed my face under Helga's Popeye-like forearm, opened my mouth and bit down as hard as I could.

"AAAARRRGGHH," she yelled, scurrying into the corner. *Thanks, Jesus!*

The room spun. I reached for the doorknob and tried to pull myself to my feet, but I felt like I was balancing on marbles. I wobbled up on one leg, only to hear that animalistic sound again, "AAAARRRGGGHHH!!" Helga snarled and shot across the room with her fangs out. *Holy Shit!*

The next thing I knew, I was running down the hospital corridor at full speed with Helga in hot pursuit. "Help! Help! Help!" I yelled as semi-sedated patients stuck their heads out of their rooms. I lunged for a dinner cart in the hallway and threw it in her path. *Where the hell is everyone?!* I turned around and saw Helga hurdle the culinary destruction. *The medicine closet!* I was steps away, but she was gaining on me.

Left, right, left. As I fumbled for my key, I turned the doorknob, surprised to find it unlocked. *Another miracle!* I darted into the tiny room, closed the door with my back and wedged my feet against the opposite wall. Helga rammed against the other side. I grabbed a syringe and a dose of Haldol from the shelf next to me. SLAM! My knees buckled. Steadying my shaking hands, I filled the syringe. SLAM! My body turned to Jell-O. I couldn't hold her back anymore.

Helga barreled in, knocking shelves of pills, linens and paper products on top of her. The force of her entry threw me into the corner. *I'm trapped again!* She jumped out of the pile, looking like a crazed mermaid surfacing for air. I covered my face as flying toiletries threatened to blind me. She lunged for my throat. I slammed the syringe into her meaty right ass cheek in the nick of time. *Take that bitchbutt!* "AArrgghhrr..." she moaned and fell onto my lap like a 250-pound baby.

"Match!" I said, rolling her off me. I closed my eyes and took a deep breath. Loud voices echoed in the hallway. Someone shouted, "Maggie?! Helga?!" *NOW you're here for the party?*

JoAnn peeked in the closet and surveyed the strange scene. "Oh my God!" Her hand flew over her mouth. "What the hell happened?" she asked, lowering her palm to her chest.

"That's what I'd like to know! Where did everyone go? I almost just lost my life," I yelled, my legs shaking like a newborn calf when I tried to stand. Helga was sprawled flat on her back, snoring loudly. The smell of her dog breath filled the room. Helga's gigantic feet pointed towards the sky and under her pajamas, two ubangous breasts spilled onto the floor—one on each side. I came out of the closet.

"Helga," JoAnn gasped as she dropped to her knees and placed two fingers on my wrestling opponent's neck. "Maggie, is she OKAY?"

"Fuck her! She attacked me. Now she's sedated." My face burned.

"What?! Maggs, I wouldn't have left you two alone if I knew she was capable of—"

"Now you know," I said striding down the corridor, this time with JoAnn in hot pursuit.

"It's just that we had a code red down the hall. Little Tim stole the key to the medicine closet and he was trying to swallow it—"

"Well I had a code red, too."

"I'm so sorry, Maggie. Should I go get Dr. Gilmore?"

"Please don't!" I kept walking. "He'll just find a way to blame me."

"Are you sure you're not hurt? I'll go with you to the ER," JoAnn said, skipping in front of me. "I feel terrible." I stopped in my tracks as I wiped a waterfall's worth of sweat from my brow. *No one could have predicted this,* I thought. *Why I am yelling at my best friend?*

"I'm sorry too, Jo," I said, sighing. *"I'm* the one who should feel bad. I shouldn't be taking this out on *you.*"

Tears gathered in JoAnn's beautiful blue eyes. "But somehow, I should've known or helped or—"

"It's not your fault." I shook my head and smirked. "You're just not as psychic as I am." JoAnn let out a breathy laugh. "If only you had my abilities," I said.

She dabbed her eyes, attempting to smile. "Then I too could predict the rerun schedule of 'The Office.'" She took a mini flashlight out of her pocket.

"That is a *minor* gift compared to what my dreams tell me."

She shined the light in my eyes. "Just because you dreamt about Tony and ran into him the same week—"

"It was the next day!" I pushed the flashlight away. "I *never* dream about him and we hadn't seen each other for three years."

"Ok, you win." JoAnn grabbed my hand. "Are you *sure* you're okay, Miss Long Island Medium?"

"Physically I seem to be in one piece—emotionally, not so much. Two years is long enough, Jo. I gotta get out of here."

****

I walked to my car in the rain, shivering in the chilly spring air. *Just another day at the office.* I pulled my burgundy trench coat tighter, but I couldn't stop shaking. *They'll have to give me a bed of my own if I don't get out of here soon.*

I flinched when I saw my disheveled reflection in the dewy, dark window of the tan 1999 Honda I had the privilege of driving. Wisps of my hair stuck up all over the place and remnants of make-up discolored my puffy cheeks. I climbed into the driver's seat and caught a glimpse of my bloodshot eyes in the rearview mirror. The redness made them look über-green.

You can take this job and shove it up your ass, I thought, pulling out my cell to call Dr. Gilmore. The seconds ticked by slowly as I held my breath. I stared at the phone's broken screen, and didn't exhale until he picked up.

In times of stress one of two things happen to me: I get *angry* or I get *funny.* For some reason (maybe it was Dr. Gilmore's striking resemblance to Steve Martin), *funny* kicked in. "I won't be coming to work tomorrow or any day after that," I said robotically so I would have a good story to tell later, "because I, um—I broke my arm. Yes, that's it. I broke my arm."

"What?" Dr. Gilmore said.

"You heard me."

9

"Margaret, you seem awfully calm for someone who's just fractured a bone. Are you in the emergency room?"

"Nope, I'm sitting in my car," I continued in a voice we would call a "flat affect" in the psych ward, "but you outta know this parking lot is very slippery in the rain."

"Should we send out a gurney?"

"No, thanks. Besides, now I'm finally able to touch my fingertips to my elbow Gumby-style. I think I'll just go home and put it in a sling, but you will definitely have to replace me."

"You're quite the liar and it's not amusing. In fact, it's absolutely outrageous!"

His anger kept my Catholic guilt in check. *Having a problem with authority is finally coming in handy.* The pendulum swung from comedy to hostility. "In the past week alone, patients have bitten me, punched me and attempted to kill me!" I trembled with rage. "I couldn't possibly fight them off with one bad arm." *You have to calm down.* I took a deep breath. "I gotta go. I have a very difficult one-handed drive ahead of me. I'd say it was nice working with you but I don't wanna give you a big head—too late!"

"How dare you!" My walls went up as he continued in vain. "Now you're adding 'insubordination' to 'quitting without notice.' You will NEVER get a positive recommendation from me."

"I don't need one! Being a psych nurse is a dead end job that I've barely managed to survive and I'm through—officially. This is my last day working at a hospital and you'll be lucky if I decide NOT to sue you."

"Don't be ridiculous."

"Why wouldn't I? This parking lot is a major safety hazard. Ouch! Owww. Another wave of pain—peace out!" I slammed the phone shut and threw it on the dashboard. *No wonder the screen is broken.*

My words to Dr. Gilmore would later prove to be true. I never worked at another hospital again. I thought, *Where will the tides take me next? Maybe someone exciting! Or maybe just to the unemployment office.* The world was my oyster.

And even though the phone rang all the way home, I had no problem letting it go to voicemail. Long before Oprah started her campaign, I had implemented a "No Phone Zone" policy in my car. It was my time to daydream about becoming the star I'd always wanted to be. So I sang like an angel, or actually more like Lisa Stansfield, to "All Around the World." I couldn't find my baby either, but newfound freedom made my song sound twice as sweet—even with a pretend broken arm.

****

Three mornings later I poured myself a glass of orange juice and shuffled to the living room. I sat down on my imitation leather couch and grabbed the remote from the claw-foot coffee table I'd gotten at a yard sale. As I surfed the channels looking for "Seinfeld," I moved a zebra print pillow behind my back, but I couldn't get comfortable. *It's too dark in here.* I got up and opened the heavy red velvet curtains that were blocking out the sun, hoping a little light would make me feel better.

I gazed out the third floor window of my Queens apartment at the bustling city street below. A man in a business suit yelled frantically into his cell phone, pacing back and forth on the sidewalk. Across the avenue, a well-dressed older couple strolled along arm-in-arm. Three Latina girls in Catholic school uniforms laughed in front of

McDonald's. *Everyone else has somewhere to go,* I thought. A palpable wave of jealously took over my entire being. *I should have found another job before I left the hospital. What's wrong with me? Why did I let the anger take control?*

I glanced at the television. "Ain't Nothing Going on But the Rent," played on "Pop-Up Video," mocking my pain. *I don't need a new job, I need a new career. Maybe listing your talents will give you direction.* I headed over to my desk and took out a calligraphy pen with a pretty piece of paper that looked like it had been cut from a scroll. I wrote:

1) Taking care of others (not in a psych ward, though—too scary)

2) Making people laugh (great at parties, but not very lucrative)

3) Applying make-up (highly enjoyable, but I may be a bit heavy-handed based on my love for winged eyes and a strange childhood connection with Tammy Faye Bakker)

4) An uncanny ability to eavesdrop at restaurants (maybe I can parlay this into a career as a private investigator)

Even though the list was pretty negative, I tacked it to my Dream Board on the refrigerator. As I reread my lackluster skill set, I felt deflated. *Get real. An idea for a new career isn't going to shoot down from the Heavens like a bolt of lightning into your pen. You need money now.*

I picked up the receiver of my Roman column phone and dialed the number I knew by heart.

"Hello, VNA," the woman said.

"Hi, are you looking for nurses?"

****

The next morning I arrived at Park Avenue and 71st Street wearing my "first impression" black pantsuit; I knew if it became a regular gig, I'd be in dark jeans and a cute animal print top by the end of the week. What I didn't know was that my job would be on the line before the end of the shift. As the gilded elevator sped to the penthouse, I peeked into my compact and freshened up my Mary Kay Pink Parfait lip-gloss. I applied some extra mascara for a boost of confidence.

When the doors opened, my jaw dropped. The apartment's décor was positively Elizabethan, with 15-foot ceilings and leaded-glass French doors leading to a gardened terrace. I floated onto the balcony in a trance. Before me was a miniature Versailles that looked like spring and smelled of flowers in bloom. When I took in the view of the city skyline from the dazzling full-floor apartment, I thought to myself, *The Visiting Nurse Agency does not disappoint!* But then I wondered, *Why is this client using a service instead of getting permanent help?*

On the terrace, a small Asian woman sat in a chair with her hand to her forehead. I cleared my throat. She noticed me and sprang to her feet. "Thank God you're here." My pulse quickened. *This can't be good.* "I gotta go."

Where are your manners, lady? "Hi I'm Margar—"

"Mrs. Evans is ready to go to her appointments. She's in there." The woman pointed to a room at the end of a long golden hallway. "I have to warn you, she's in a foul mood 'cause she didn't get much sleep. Good luck." My heart skipped a beat. The woman handed me a piece of paper—folded into thirds—and literally ran out the door, leaving me to fend for myself.

Thanks bitch. I felt like I was walking the plank as I made my way to the master suite. I crept into the room, afraid of disturbing the beast. The canopy bed and breathtaking arched ceiling reminded me of the

Plaza Hotel. A tiny woman with blue-grey hair, wearing a pink Chanel suit, was sitting in a wheelchair watching TV. "Good morning Mrs. Evans." She shifted her gaze towards me. I tried to smile.

"What's so damn good about it?" *Okay, so much for pleasantries.* I took off my jacket like I was getting ready to fight.

I unfolded the paper the other nurse had given me. At the top of the page it read: **Today's Schedule.** The first line said: **10am appointment at 10 Central Park West, 8th floor.** *Gee, thanks for the cryptic clue,* I thought. *Hopefully we're not going to meet a hit man.* The second entry read: **3pm Botox with Dr. Loo.** *Seriously? If Mrs. Evans is still looking for love, there's no hope for me.*

"Well, I guess we're off to see the Wizard," I said, putting my jacket back on. I took the brake off her wheelchair and pushed Mrs. E towards the door.

"And step on it, Red. My driver is waiting!"

"As you wish, Blue." I popped a wheelie and double-timed it to the elevator.

****

When we reached the 8th floor of the Central Park West high-rise, Mrs. Evans said, "Over there," pointing to the right. I steered her past black marble hallways with silver trim that screamed 1920's. At the end of the corridor, sparkling clear doors opened automatically, welcoming us to a reception area bathed in amber light. As we entered the room, I heard my heels clicking on glass and looked down to find a tiny brook running beneath our feet. Small schools of colorful fish swam along a stream complete with bedrock, green moss and miniature wildflowers. I gasped quietly. *There sure is a lot of*

HGTV eye-candy around today. I followed the little tributary like it was the yellow brick road until we reached the front desk. The receptionist, standing at attention, could have been Jennifer Lopez's doppelgänger.

"Good Morning," she said through Russian Red lips, a hint of a New York accent counteracting her formality. "Welcome to Von Spa." The candy apple-colored chopsticks poking through her updo brought out the bright hues in her floral kimono. "I'm sorry the staircase is hidden under the scaffolding." She gestured to a fairly elegant construction zone behind her. "We're protecting it while we undergo some renovations."

"What staircase?" I said.

"Oh, never mind then. Will you be enjoying services with us today?"

"Actually, Mrs. Evans has an appointment and I'm here to read your magazines."

"What's wrong?" Mrs. E scowled. "You don't like to be touched?"

Is she having a senior moment? The receptionist looked at me, her eyebrows raised.

"I don't mind being touched, but I'm not exactly sure—"

Mrs. Evans said, "You could use a facial." She turned to the receptionist. "Do you have another appointment available?"

"Let me see," the girl replied.

"No really, it's okay. I'll just read—"

"The magazines here suck!" Mrs. E shouted. "It's on me. Besides, look at your pores. Who wants to stare at those craters all day?"

I shared a knowing glance with the receptionist. "Book it," I said.

"I'll take Mrs. Evans to her treatment room, while you fill out one of these." She handed me a leather booklet with a questionnaire inside. "I'll be back to escort you in a moment."

I filled out the skincare form at lightning speed and reached for a *Vogue*.

Two minutes later the receptionist reappeared. After a quick elevator ride to the 9th floor, she guided me through a maze with bamboo floors and yellow silk banners flowing from the ceiling. Hundreds of votive candles lined the walls and filled the air with a citrusy vanilla.

The girl let more of her New York accent come out. "You actually have gorgeous skin."

"Thank you. Pore reduction is a hobby of mine. And by the way, your magazines don't suck."

She giggled. "True. I think Mrs. Evans just wanted you to enjoy yourself."

"Well now that she is safely fifty feet away from me, maybe I can."

We walked down a long hallway with many doors. The girl finally chose one and opened it for me. "Your therapist will be here in a moment. You can change into your robe and lie down on the treatment table, face-up. Enjoy your treatment."

I hung my clothes on a hook next to a heavily draped window and quickly wrapped myself in the soft terrycloth robe that waited for me. Soothing music played in the little 10 x 10 room where sparkling charcoal mosaics lined the shower, and a shiny contemporary black sink jutted out from one of the silver leafed walls. I sat on the side of the bed and twisted my hair into a Britney Spears-inspired bun atop my head. I heard someone knocking as a shadow punctuated the crack of light under the door.

"Are you ready?" A female voice asked through a thick Eastern European accent.

"Oh yeah!" I said, cracking my knuckles.

A skinny young woman with a white-blonde pixie cut and heavy eye make-up entered the room. "I'm Christie. Is this your first time having a facial?"

"It sure is."

She looked at the questionnaire I had filled out. "Wow. You use some nice products. And sunscreen every day! No wonder you hardly have any wrinkles."

"Aw shucks. You should give Mrs. Evans an etiquette lesson."

"What?"

"Never mind. I've always loved products."

"So have I." Christie smiled. "Lie down and we can get started."

I leaned back, closing my eyes. The new age music was accompanied by the sounds of bottles being opened and hands rubbing together. A gentle breeze flowed over my shoulders when Christie glided towards me on a rolling chair. She massaged my temples for a few minutes, then placed warm towels over my face. I felt her thumbs smooth out the one permanent wrinkle in my brow as the smell of lavender filled the air. Next Christie applied a gritty lotion and gave me a thorough exfoliation. The lemon scented salve was gently removed by a hot washcloth. Steam began dancing over my cheeks, lulling me to sleep.

"Do you want extractions?"

"What?" I said, trying to return to consciousness.

"Do you want me to squeeze the blackheads out of your nose?"

"If I have any, but I probably beat you to it. I love doing that!"

"Me too." She examined my pores with a bright light. "You don't have many." Christie pressed small areas of my nose together between two paper cloths. Afterwards, she applied a cooling mud mask and began to massage my hands. "Very soft," she said.

I slipped into a deep state of intoxicating relaxation. Thoughts drifted through my mind. *How the hell did I get so lucky? A few days ago, I was working in an institution and now I'm getting paid to have a facial. This is the place to be.* I jolted upright.

"Is everything okay?" Christie said, rolling away.

"Are you guys hiring? How do I get *your* job?"

"You have to go to school."

"School?! Oh, never mind."

"The intensive course is only a couple months."

"That's not too long. Is it hard?"

"It would be easier if my English was better, but I made it."

"Hmmm."

"You like skincare, you have soft hands and you speak English. Try it!"

"How much did it cost?"

"About $4000."

"Yipes! Never mind."

"You're American. You have credit cards, no?"

"I'm American. I'm at my limit."

"Think about it. Let's finish you up."

Christie cleaned the mask off my face and gently rubbed astringent over my fresh complexion. I should have enjoyed the facial's afterglow, but I had too much on my mind. *I need to work somewhere beautiful like this. The clients here must love the people giving them treatments. At the very least, I'm sure they don't try to murder you!* The baby Jesus had given me a sign.

****

After Botox, we rode in Mrs. Evans' Lincoln Town Car back to the penthouse. I marveled at my perfectly smooth skin in the rearview mirror. *She's kinda bitchy, but Mrs. E sure is generous.* The wrinkle in my brow was completely gone. *That other nurse must have personal problems. Mrs. Evans isn't so bad!*

"…and my daughter's lousy boyfriend is a gold digger!" she said as we sped along the West Side Highway.

I nodded, pretending to care. I was busy hatching a plan. *Keep working for mean-but-free-handed-old-lady-blue-head, save the funds for esthetician school and parlay my degree into a job at Von Spa.*

Once we were in her apartment, I rolled Mrs. Evans into the kitchen and parked her safely in front of Oprah while I made us a snack. But Mrs. E wasn't watching the TV, she was glaring at me.

"YOU STOLE MY MONEY!" she yelled. *Oh shit! What happened to my new BFF?*

"Mrs. Evans, we've been together all day. How could I have done that?"

She continued giving me the stink-eye when I handed her a cheese plate with fresh grapes. *Maybe she needs some space.* I took out the trash, hoping Oprah's voice would have a calming effect on her. I stepped

19

into the hallway and a moment later, heard a slam, followed by a loud click.

Shut the front door. Did she just lock me out? I didn't even know she could walk. Jesus must be with me—again!

"And stay out!" Mrs. Evans screamed from the other side.

I knocked on the penthouse door. "Open up, *please.*" *What if something happens?* The panic crept in as I imagined Mrs. E grabbing her chest and keeling over. Flop sweats started dripping down the sides of my arms. I ran to the intercom and paged the doorman.

"I'm working for Mrs. Evans in 15P and I've accidentally locked myself out of the apartment."

The doorman bellowed with laughter. "She got you too, huh?" he said with a heavy Brooklyn accent. "Don't worry kid. I'll be there in a flash."

I felt a vibration on my left breast and reached into my jacket for my phone. I inhaled sharply when I saw the number. *Oh dear Lord—it's the agency,* I thought as I answered.

"Mrs. Evans called us to report a problem," the girl on the other end of the line told me. "She said you left early."

The little brat is throwing me under the bus! "No, *she* locked *me* out."

"Oh, that again. I should have briefed you on her behavior patterns."

"Ya think?"

"Anyway, I don't blame you."

"Clearly *you're* the one to blame." Pressure was building in my head. I imagined my face coming to a boil. "What kind of other surprises are in store for me? Did you also forget to mention she's a member of the NRA?"

"There is no need to raise your voice. I'm trying to apologize."

"You know, my last job was in a psych ward and I refuse to work in a dangerous, unpredictable environment again." *Thanks for the Botox, bitch,* I thought. *Peace out!*

"Rest assured, Mrs. Evans has no history of violence." *I've heard that before.*

The elevator opened to reveal the smiling doorman jangling a set of keys. Behind him was the night nurse whom I had met earlier. "Hold on," I told the agency representative.

As he let me back into the apartment, I held my breath, expecting to see Mrs. E's lifeless body. Instead, she was back in her chair parked next to the TV, cackling away at The Three Stooges whooping it up in black and white. She gave me a wink and said, "Where did you run off to?" I rolled my eyes, unamused.

The night nurse smirked. "It's her little form of initiation." *Then you should have warned me this morning!* I opened my mouth to let her have it, but stopped in my tracks. *Don't let your temper get the best of you again.*

I stepped into the foyer to finish my call. "I'm sorry I raised my voice," I said. "I know you're just trying to do your crappy job, too."

"It's okay," the agency rep said. "It's partly my fault since I didn't brief you in advance."

"So, can I get another assignment?"

"We don't have anything else."

I sighed. *If you play your cards right, this could be your last nursing job.*

"It must be hard to get regular help for Mrs. Evans," I said.

"It can be."

"I'll commit to three months on one condition."

"What's that?"

"Pay me the overnight rate."

"Deal."

I closed my phone triumphantly and slipped into the elevator with the doorman.

"Tough first day?" he asked.

Thanks, Captain Obvious, I thought. "It's actually looking up."

"Well, let me know if there's anything I can do to make your job easier."

"If you could guide me to the nearest Krispy Kreme, I would be eternally grateful."

We both laughed. *Time to celebrate my new career trajectory with doughnuts.* It felt good to have a purpose and a plan. When we got downstairs, he ushered me outside and said, "Have a good night, kiddo."

As he closed the door to the building, I put my face up to the glass like a needy puppy. "But seriously, the Krispy Kreme?"

****

That night I fell into a restless sleep and a strange dream descended upon me. I was lost in a steel jungle, thirsty and looking for refuge. An oasis appeared, complete with a babbling whirlpool filled with glamorous women drinking sparkling water. When I reached for a glass, I looked down to see I was naked. The beautiful ladies pointed and laughed, their faces morphing into chimpanzees. As I covered my body—overcome by embarrassment—a knight in shining armor materialized, handing me a Technicolor bathrobe. My savior's face was obscured by blinding sunlight. I cloaked myself in the soft terrycloth, a feeling of pure love enveloping me. I opened my mouth to say thank you, but chunks of the scene fell away like pieces of a puzzle.

I shot up in bed. *That's what you get for eating sugar late at night.* I tossed and turned, then I counted sheep, but no matter what I did, I couldn't get back to sleep.

Chapter 2

Thomas:

Fall 2010

The Yvonne Von Courtland Spa

"Oh my God! I can't pay for this." I imagined the livid girl in front of me spent her college years watching "Sex and the City." *Now she's trying to live the life.* The funny thing was, if it weren't for her enormous boobs, she would have been a dead ringer for Sarah Jessica Parker. Her colorful polka dot jumpsuit and upswept curly blonde hair made me wonder if she'd stolen a page from Carrie Bradshaw's Lookbook. "These prices are insane!" she said, sounding like a used car salesman in a homemade commercial. *Of course it's expensive,* I thought. *What do you expect? This is the best spa in New York. Too bad it feels more like a prison.* "What's your name?" she asked me, narrowing her eyes ever so slightly. "I want to speak to the manager."

"My name is Thomas Haven and I *am* the manager," I said, worried she might not believe me; my uniform's black Nehru jacket and gold name tag didn't project as much authority as a business suit.

I typecast "Miss Golden Globes," guessing she was a fashion house executive assistant who struggled to pay her astronomical New York

City rent. "Since when is a massage with hot stones three hundred and fifty dollars?" she asked.

Well, I thought, *it all started with The New York Times article.* The full page spread made us the next big thing in the luxury spa industry. Money was no object for the majority of our clientele and there was no shortage of them: CEOs, ladies who lunch, movie stars, captains of industry, beauty queens and even ex-Presidents. The harder it became to get an appointment, the higher our prices soared—simply because Yvonne Von Courtland, the founder and director of Von Spa, knew people would pay.

I shifted uncomfortably from leg to leg, leaning on the front desk for support, my eyes involuntarily squinting from exhaustion. Twelve-hour days were winning the battle against my body.

I couldn't think of a good way to answer her question, so I asked, "Would you like to try a credit card?"

She began digging in her white faux Chanel purse. Her skin was flushed and beads of sweat formed on her brow.

How am I going to get out of this situation again? With the economy in the toilet, I knew giving out another discount could cost me my bonus. *Times have changed.*

I felt a tap on my shoulder and turned to find one of my spa concierge girls looking at me with giraffe-like brown eyes. She said in her unusual accent, which was part British and part Audrey Hepburn in "Breakfast at Tiffany's," "Thomas, it is imperalatative—"

"Do you mean imperative?" I whispered from the side of my mouth.

"Yes," she said. "It's imperative I let you know—"

"Would you excuse us for one moment?" I said to Miss Golden Globes. She nodded, shuffling through her wallet. I put out my hand, motioning for Gabrielle to follow me into the spa concierge office.

We ducked inside and I said to her, "You know I love you, but talking business in front of guests is against the Five Star rules. It could ruin our rating." Gabrielle lowered her gaze, defeated; a beautiful woman melted into a little girl. "Why don't you get Ms. Richards her shoes while she settles her account," I suggested. Gabrielle glided away. *Shit! I never asked her about the imperalatative problem.* I returned to the front desk.

Gabrielle retrieved Ms. Richards' purple pumps from the bamboo drawer under the product display case. She bent down next to one of our plush rust-colored couches, placing the shoes on a silver tray. I marveled at her physique. She possessed the figure (thanks to her thyroid condition) of a high fashion model. *If she were two inches taller, I'm sure she'd be working runways all over the world.* I scanned Gabrielle's flawless cocoa face. She wore subtle false lashes, which made her brown eyes pop. Her tiny "ski-jump" nose sported a sun-kissed sheen, supplied by bronzer since summer was already a distant memory. Ebony tresses cascaded down her back in waves like a jet black waterfall. *Oh snap,* I thought, *her hair's supposed to be up. She's breaking another Five Star Rule. What if a shopper comes in?*

Shoppers' reports are a necessary evil in the ranking of luxury spas. An undercover guest books services and records every second of their spa experience from the initial phone call, which should be answered before the third ring, to paying the bill. The final report includes everything from the appearance of the staff (for example, men are required to have short hair) to the quality of the treatments to the overall atmosphere. The more rules that are followed, the higher the Five Star rating.

Von Spa was the first spa in the country to be awarded Five Stars. Although we'd already achieved the highest rating possible, we were always being tested and could lose our standing at any time.

Ms. Richards finally handed me her Visa. "Try this." I swiped her card. The word "Declined" flashed on the silver monitor embedded in our Brazilian rosewood reception desk.

"Do you have another one?" I asked, trying to sound nonchalant. I handed it back to her. "This didn't go through." *Pick a card lady, any card, I have a deadline looming.* Gabrielle gracefully slipped behind me, underneath the staircase, and back into the spa concierge office.

Miss Golden Globe's eyes welled up. *Oh no!* I wondered if her tears were genuine or if she was trying to manipulate me. At that moment, I almost felt glad I could repress my emotions. Where I was from, a crying boy was not tolerated. Compassion and disdain warred within me.

"I just wanted to take my best friend to a spa for her birthday. It's way too expensive here!" she said.

"Well, I'm sorry you feel that way, but we are including a free gift for her." My head throbbed. *Why did I leave my glamorous life and get into the service industry? What happened to my punk rock days?*

She began sobbing. I grabbed a tissue from under the desk and handed it to her. *Can't have someone blubbering away in reception. What if Yvonne walks by? Accept your fate.* I clicked on "Manager Functions," entered my code and selected the "20% discount" option. *This better do the trick, because 50% means it's coming out of my paycheck.* Two clicks stood between me and financial ruin when I heard the sound of footsteps descending the staircase.

Spa guests could enter the reception area from the locker rooms on the main floor but most people went back upstairs to have finger sandwiches in the Tea Room after their treatments. A young brunette with pin straight hair parted down the middle, sashayed toward me in a gorgeous earth tone maxi dress, trimmed in maroon lace.

Ms. Richards quickly dried her eyes. Under her breath, she said to me, "I'm going to step outside and call my credit card company." She turned and sprinted into the building's eighth floor Art Deco lobby.

I asked the Birthday Hippie the obligatory question, "How were your treatments?"

"Oh my God—they were amazing," she said in a spa daze, unable to focus her eyes. "This place is incredible."

Gabrielle whisked out of the office, slipped me a pink post-it, and fetched the Birthday Hippie's cowboy boots. I snuck a peek at the note. It read: **Greetings, my love. There is someone here to see you. ~Gabrielle.** *Um, a name would have been helpful.*

"You guys look like you could be cousins," said the Birthday Hippie. "Are you related?"

I was flattered. Growing up, kids taunted me because of my feminine attributes: big light brown eyes, full dark pink lips, wavy brown hair, and smooth olive skin. *Now I'm being compared to a virtual supermodel.*

"No," Gabrielle beamed at me, flashing dazzling white teeth, "but we are like family."

I smiled back, feeling silly for keeping a mental score card of Five Star rules.

The Birthday Hippie replied, "That's so sweet! You must love working together."

"We do. Gabrielle makes the spa feel like home."

"It's such a peaceful, beautiful place." The Birthday Hippie sounded stoned. "You're so lucky you get to come here every day."

"But of course," Gabrielle exclaimed.

Thank God she handled that one. Gabrielle was the only spa concierge who could respond to this kind of statement truthfully. She wore her title like a badge of honor. I, however, was sick of people telling me I'd won the "job lottery." I wasn't sitting in a hot tub eating bon bons and/or having massages all day. I was working. *But I can't complain about the view.* I'm a sucker for great interior design.

I looked around the grand reception room while The Birthday Hippie put on her cowboy boots. She sat on custom furniture imported from India. Our harem couches were upholstered in deep oranges and dark reds. Gold leafed walls met a mirrored ceiling with crown molding made from real silver. The chandeliers and sconces were whimsical, original Chihulys that resembled yellow paisleys melting into one another. They were more like works of art than light fixtures.

But it was the centerpiece of Von Spa that took people's breath away: the spiraling crystal staircase. It remained unchanged when Yvonne renovated the reception area. I stared at its reflection in the glass wall that opened up to the lobby. The clear steps looked like they were chiseled out of ice. And when the scarlet curtains were open, the railing's twisted prisms captured the afternoon sunlight and sent it dancing in a spectrum of color on the gilded walls. The new decor delighted our guests and filled the room with magic. *It's a shame I can't feel it, anymore.*

Ms. Richards, still red-faced but no longer crying, stormed toward the doors. They opened with a whoosh, blowing her curly updo back in the breeze. She waved to her friend, glared at me with conviction and handed over her credit card. I swiped it once again. *Success!* The printer spat out the receipt. I presented it to Ms. Richards in a black leather folder. Her hands shook when she signed. Gabrielle brought the girls their coats, and they headed out. "Wait!" I shouted, following after them. "Don't forget your complimentary gift." I handed the Birthday Hippie a small candle in a ruby red box, which cost us a mere two dollars total. She let out a little squeal. I enjoyed the moment; I've always felt quite passionate about giving away free shit.

I glanced at the clock on the computer and thought, *Time really flies when you're wiping out people's life savings.* I pictured Ms. Richards eating cat food and living in her car. *At least I didn't have to give out another discount.*

I turned my attention to next week's front desk schedule. *If I don't finish it now, I'll have to skip lunch again.* We were already one person short, which meant I'd have to cover the desk later. The spreadsheet was springing to life when I remembered Gabrielle's note. I peeked into the office but she was on the phone. When I turned around, Yvonne was standing at the front desk.

"May I speak with you?" she asked in a cold voice. *Can you please just tell me what the problem is?* I imagined the possibilities. *Did that fucking Mrs. B complain again? Does Yvonne want to add another shift to my sixty hour work week?* Gone were the days before the economic crisis when I was just the sidekick who made her feel important. I was no longer the gay boy behind the powerful woman, complimenting her on her shoes.

Gabrielle came out of the concierge office and said, "Did you read my note?" Yvonne shot me a look. I opened my mouth to answer and Yvonne began tapping her foot. *I guess I'm not allowed to make you wait for a millisecond,* I thought. I put my index finger in the air to let Gabrielle know I'd be back in a minute. I obediently followed Yvonne out of the spa and across the hall.

The office we shared was more like a large well-appointed closet. It was ten feet long and five feet wide. Directly across from the door, the only window faced an interior courtyard. The sunlight never made it inside. Regardless of the weather, we were caught in the shadow of the building. The forecast was always easy to predict: grey. No one ever turned on the unsightly overhead lighting but we had two colorful Tiffany lamps, which helped brighten up the room.

Our desks were side by side. Mine was within arm's reach of the door and Yvonne's was next to the window. We both faced the same wall covered in sepia-toned pictures of Von Spa. Behind us loomed three enormous black metal cabinets filled with inventory.

Yvonne swiveled her chair toward me and began her assault. "This email is unacceptable. We *cannot* settle for imperfection!" she said, horrified, waving a printed copy in front of my face. She handed it over, looking terribly avant-garde in her charcoal Donna Karan pantsuit. Yvonne played the role of the hot blonde untouchable cougar with panache.

We had a student/teacher type of relationship. I looked up to her, fascinated by her mystery. I gazed at Yvonne's dewy complexion and wondered what was hiding behind her perfect make-up. Von Spa had been an instant success as soon as that *Times* article hit the press. Yvonne had friends in high places, but I still didn't know how she'd *really* clawed her way to the top. *God, I'd love to find out!*

The email she'd thrust into my hands read:

Dear S. Peterson,

I am writing with pleasure to confirm your Ethereal Experience Treatment with a male therapist at 11am on the 20th. Please touch out to me if there is any inquetitude.

Best Wishes, Gabrielle

I didn't even have to read the signature line on the appointment confirmation. *My favorite ESL student strikes again.* With all the mistakes she made, most managers would've fired Gabrielle a long time ago but sometimes her enthusiasm was the only thing that got me through the day. *I have to protect her.*

I shut the oak door. Yvonne continued her tirade. "Gabrielle is wonderful with the guests and her sophistication is innate, yet

English is obviously not her native tongue. This email is an embarrassment. Any spa director in her right mind—"

"That Gabrielle," I said. "I love how she's always throwing in those million dollar words."

"What do you mean million dollar words?" Yvonne narrowed her eyes.

"Like 'inquetitude.' She's obsessed with building her English vocabulary." There was no question in my mind Gabrielle had made an error, but Yvonne thought I was smart, and I knew she wouldn't want to look dumb. *I hope she doesn't look it up on Dictionary.com.* She was sitting right in front of her computer. I leaned back in my chair and saw that her monitor was off. I exhaled. *I have to get out of here before she decides to discipline Gabrielle.*

Yvonne had implemented a "three strikes" policy. When someone made a mistake, she forced the employee to sign a Disciplinary Action Form (DAF) acknowledging the error and documenting the coaching session. After the third offense for the same problem, the employee was fired. DAFs prevented wrongful termination lawsuits, so Yvonne didn't take these forms lightly. Even I had earned a strike when Mrs. B told Yvonne I was "difficult." This system was a glaring example of Yvonne's trust issues. *If I give Gabrielle a DAF for misusing the English language, she'll be gone within the hour.*

"She did say 'touch out' instead of 'reach out.'" I folded the paper in half. "I'll follow up with her right away."

"You do that," Yvonne said like she was starring in her own movie. *Oh my. She knows!* Yvonne turned her attention towards a large stack of mail.

I left the office and let out the breath I was holding.

"Oh Thomas," Yvonne called. I pivoted right back into her clutches. "One more thing," *There's always one more thing.* "Was the girl crying in the hallway one of our spa guests?"

"Unfortunately, yes. She was unable to pay her bill."

"And?"

"She paid it—eventually," I said, exasperated.

"So what is the problem?"

"There's no problem." *What are you getting at?*

"I will tell you what the problem is. You are taking *her* issue personally. It is evident by the exhaustion seeping from your pores while you explain. You know my favorite catchphrase by now, Thomas." Her grin widened.

"Of course: 'Don't take it in.'" *Easy for you to say—you're not on the front lines.*

"Exactly. Under my tutelage, you have already come so far. Your job will be less stressful if you see things my way."

I nodded and rushed back across the hall. *It's hard not to take things personally when you're completely overworked, lady.* I was so not in the mood to give her the gratitude she was fishing for.

Gabrielle stood safely behind the front desk speaking to a tall dark handsome man. Italian words effortlessly dripped from her tongue. Seeing her smiling—happy to be on the clock—made me feel like I was doing something right. Gabrielle handed the man a pamphlet. He nodded in thanks. "Ciao," she batted her eyelashes. He turned and left.

"What was that all about?" I asked her.

"He just inquired me about a brochure." The way Gabrielle crossed her arms made the female version of our "suit meets a sari" uniform, look like haute couture.

"Lucky you!" I didn't correct her English.

I flipped through the spa brochure. Images of Gabrielle covered the pages: Gabrielle sipping tea in the reception area wearing a neon yellow chiffon Valentino gown; Gabrielle receiving a reflexology treatment in the nail room, her toenails painted a glossy tangerine hue; Gabrielle enjoying a facial in the VIP suite, a blue mud mask covering her skin. The photos easily could have been included in an issue of Vanity Fair.

"I can always tell if you're hot for a guy when you give him one of these."

"How do you say?" Gabrielle paused. "I got game, baby."

"I guess so," I laughed. "What were you talking about, anyway?"

"Ah, we got to chatting about my days in Venice as a kept woman." She sighed.

"Gabrielle," I guffawed, "you know you aren't supposed to talk about personal matters with guests. It could cost us one of our Five Stars!"

"Don't be silly, bello—since when do the 'spa spies' speak Italian and look like that."

Stop acting like a corporate drone, I told myself. "You're right." I smiled. "So, if you're fluent in Italian, I'm guessing you grew up in Italy?" *Yvonne isn't the only one around here shrouded in mystery.*

"Actually, I resided in Italy for merely nine months."

"Why won't you tell us where you grew up? We're like family, remember? You just said so, yourself."

"If you tell *me* about your previous profession, I will be happy to enliven you about my childhood." Gabrielle smirked.

"You mean en*light*en?"

"Yes. Enlighten me." She stuck her chin in the air. "Where did you work before you came to Von Spa?"

If word gets out, no one will take me seriously. Better change the subject. I pulled the pink post-it from my pocket. Gabrielle shrieked, "Il mio amore, I completely forgot. I apologize most sincerely! I tried to tell you before, but you reprimated me."

"Reprimanded," I said. "I know, sweetie. Don't worry—it's totally my fault. So who's here?"

Gabrielle anxiously fiddled with the emerald orchid tucked behind her ear. "There's a girl here for her job interview. She has been in the Tea Room for almost thirty minutes!"

"Jesus, I'm late. Call Yvonne and tell her I'm bringing the new spa concierge candidate over right away." Gabrielle nodded. "Thanks, sweetie." I would have to skip lunch again and email the front desk girls their schedules later. *They are gonna kill me.* "And could you do me one more favor?" I asked, winding my way up the crystal staircase. "Just have someone read your appointment confirmations before you send them. Sometimes there are misspellings."

She confirmed with her usual level of extreme gusto, "But of course!"

Chapter 3

Margaret:

Sew What

I was walking down the hall towards my apartment, after another awe inspiring day with Mrs. Evans (this time she locked herself in the bathroom), when I heard my home phone ring. I hurried inside and threw my keys on the table. Despite my fear of the dark, I ran into the living room without turning on the light. I picked up the receiver, half expecting a burglar/murderer to put a gloved hand over my mouth.

"Are you okay over there?" JoAnn asked from the other end of the line.

I flipped on the lamp next to the couch. *Phew, no "bad guys,"* I thought, somewhat surprised by my disappointment. "I'm fine. Sorry I haven't called. How are things at the hospital?"

"Nothing unusual. Paranoia, delusions of grandeur, multiple personalities—you know, your average Wednesday."

"I sure do. I still have nightmares about that place. I just dreamt Helga tried to strangle me. Oh wait, that really happened. Too bad I didn't have that dream *before* she jumped my bones."

"You're losing your powers, Sylvia Browne."

"Maybe the hospital drained me of my infinitesimal psychic abilities."

"Damn you, Dr. Gilmore!" JoAnn shouted.

"Now if I want to know which episode of 'Friends' is on tomorrow, I'll have to check my local listings. How can you still work there, knowing my sob story?"

"Compared to taking care of three boys under the age of eight, it's not so bad. But enough about me, how's the new gig?"

"Life changing."

"That's amazing. How so?"

"Well, my client took me to a spa and I decided to make a career change."

"Wow. Hold on to *that* job."

"Oh, don't let Mrs. E fool you. In addition to throwing money around, she also enjoys faking heart attacks, standing on building ledges and other pranks. Anything that makes me sweat she finds unbelievably hysterical."

"That's not good. But which spa did you go to?"

"It's called Von Spa."

"I love that place!" I wondered if JoAnn's whole family went there. Her father had made a fortune as a Hollywood producer. When she was in high school, he relocated his wife and kids to New York to found an East Coast division of a movie studio. JoAnn, a gorgeous California blonde, quickly became the most popular person in the 11th grade. While she was dating our quarterback, Karl—who she married after he became a doctor—I was cutting class to drink beer with the auto-shop hoodlums. "The crystal staircase is breathtaking isn't it?" she asked.

"It was actually covered in priceless hand carved scaffolding and rose-colored silken tarps," I chuckled. "So I had a facial and I decided I want to be an esthetician." Silence on the other end. "What do you think?"

"Sure, might as well try it."

"Aren't you excited for me?"

"Well, this isn't the first time you came up with a get-rich-quick-scheme."

"Oh this won't be quick. It's not like back in the 90's when I was waiting tables by day and selling vitamins at night. You have to go to school to get certified."

"*You* want to go to *school?*" *Here we go,* I thought. "Well, if it doesn't work out, I'm sure you'll find something else," she said, sounding chipper.

"Jo, you don't get it. I'm doing this."

"Of course you are."

"Do I detect a hint of sarcasm?"

"It's just you're always up to *something.* I guess I'll believe it when I see it."

"I knew you wouldn't understand," I said under my breath.

"What? Maggs, this is me. I'll support you in whatever you want to do."

My walls came tumbling down. "Here's the thing. I know this sounds silly, but I think if I get to work somewhere like Von Spa, I'll feel like I've finally *arrived* in the world." As soon as I said the words I regretted them.

"Oh Maggs, that's silly. You've already arrived. Wherever you go, everyone wants to be your friend. You're so funny!"

She has no idea what you're talking about. "It's not your fault you can't relate, but when you aren't born thin, rich and gorgeous, sometimes you feel like you want to show people you've made it."

"Like people from the past?" JoAnn laughed. "As in 'Romy and Michelle's High School Reunion?'"

"It's not funny. I KNEW you wouldn't get it!" Her amusement incensed me. This was uncharted territory in our friendship. "In high school I had a complexion reminiscent of a Jackson Pollack painting, my eating disorder was bingeing without purging, and I had no friends."

"I'm sorry," JoAnn said, "but the last part is not true. You had me."

"We didn't become friends until the middle of junior year when you discovered me out of boredom in study hall."

"And it was a great discovery. You cracked my shit up!"

A little smile broke through my tense face. I loved JoAnn for being such a "good audience." She laughed at all my jokes.

"Yeah but before you, I only had 'Large Marge' and Tutty, the lunch ladies." I heard her giggle. "Laugh if you will, but when we hit menopause, I will be light years ahead of you with the knowledge they bestowed upon me."

JoAnn said as she chuckled, "See, that's what I'm talking about. But if you ever feel bad, just remember I work part-time in a psych ward to get away from my three beautiful children."

"'Cause you want to, and not 'cause you have to." *Besides, you're really a nurse so you can be a candidate for sainthood,* I thought spitefully. I bit my tongue to punish myself for being negative. "When I do this, I feel like I'll finally be able to leave that high school girl behind me—the one everyone teased." *Oh shit. What are you doing? Stop saying things you'll regret.*

"This is ridiculous, Maggs. You have to let go of the past."

Mama, don't preach, I thought. "Easy for you to say. You can revel in yours!"

"It was almost twenty years ago! I've forgotten most of the details."

"Well I can't forget. Listen, I have to go register for classes," I lied.

"Don't be mad, Margaret. I just don't understand—"

"No, you don't."

"Maggie—"

"Bye." I hung up the phone and started crying. *If your best friend doesn't get you, who will?* I caught a glimpse of myself in the silver mirror hanging on the wall across from the couch. *You look defeated.* I grabbed a Sharpie and marched over to my Dream Board. I wrote violently in big, black letters over all of the affirmations: "Become an esthetician at The Von Courtland Spa or die trying."

****

For the next few months I scrimped, saved and slaved away working overtime for Mrs. Evans. We spent our time together in a strange world somewhere between luxury and drudgery. One day she took me to the Saint Regis for tea, and when I tried to slip the waitress a decent tip, she got pissed—literally—and wet her wheelchair to spite me. The next week, Mrs. E made amends by getting us tickets to "Book of Mormon" on Broadway. She paid a scalper $2000 in cash. Another time she insisted on eating lunch outside at The Boathouse in Central Park. We dined under umbrellas in the rain. As soon as I

40

saved enough money to cover esthetics school and my expenses, I returned Mrs. Evans' keys to the other nurse. Then she locked me out for the last time.

Skincare classes at The Jane Matthew Beauty Institute were challenging and interesting. The intensive course allowed me to earn my license quickly through long hours and few days off. The schedule was hectic, but I really felt passionate about the subject matter. This translated into good grades. I had finally found my niche. Rosacea, puffy eyes and blackheads didn't stand a chance against me. For the first time, I was the teacher's pet. In fact, if it weren't for some of the other English-speaking girls, I might have been valedictorian.

When I passed the state boards, I pounded the pavement and landed a job at a cozy little Four Star spa called Waterlily. The staff was so small, I answered phones if I wasn't booked giving facials. My plan was to lose weight, build my résumé and work my way up to Von Spa. But after only three weeks of steady work, Waterlily became another victim of the economic crisis, closing its doors forever. Once again, rent was due and I was unemployed. Even though I promised myself I would never call the VNA for any reason whatsoever, trying to get another spa job proved as difficult as cleaning a urine-covered wheelchair.

One day I woke up and thought, *Screw the plan, cut to the chase.* I dialed 411 and they connected my call. While I waited for someone to pick up on the other end of the line, I grabbed a fresh, fictionalized résumé off my desk. I started saying a prayer, then heard, "Thank you for calling Von Spa, this is Diana, how may I assist you?"

"Hi, I was wondering if you're hiring estheticians right now." I felt like I couldn't breathe. I was talking to someone who worked at the only Five Star spa in the country. God, did I want to be in her shoes.

"No we are fully staffed."

I literally hung my head. Just as I was about to slam down the receiver, something caught my eye. Under the Waterlily entry of my résumé, I had written: **duties also included answering phones and maintaining the appearance of the spa.**

"Are you hiring receptionists by any chance?"

"We *are* short of staff, but I don't know if they've hired a new spa concierge yet."

"Oh." *Please let it be me,* I prayed.

"You can always fax over your credentials, Attention: Thomas," the girl replied, articulating every word.

After I hung up, I grabbed my résumé, put on my black patent leather coat and hit the door. I ran to Kinko's in the rain, sent the fax and arrived back at my apartment in thirty minutes flat.

The next three days were excruciating. It felt like I was waiting for a guy to call. By the fourth, I'd given up hope. I knew what I had to do. With a tear in my eye, I dialed the number I knew by heart.

"It's Margaret McCarthy, are you looking for nurses?"

"Actually, we only have one position available—with Mrs. Evans."

I threw up in my mouth a little. But I needed the money or I would have nowhere to live. *All of that hard work and I'm back where I started.* My call waiting beeped. The number looked familiar. *Oh my God. It's my landlord!* I guessed signing last month's incomplete rent check "All my Love, Margaret" didn't work. *Shit! Now I have to take the nursing job.* I asked the VNA to hold and clicked over. I closed my eyes as I answered. "Hello?"

"Hi, can I speak to Margaret McCarthy?"

"This is she." I opened one eye a little.

"It's Thomas Haven from The Von Courtland Spa. We've received your résumé and I'm calling to set up an interview for the spa concierge position."

The rest of the conversation was a blur. I wrote down the date and time of the interview, seeing flashes of Oprah and Whoopi crying with joy like they did at the end of "The Color Purple." When I hung up, tears were streaming down my own face.

I was going to call JoAnn with the good news, and then I remembered we still weren't speaking. This sad realization led to another: *Even if you do get hired, you won't last long.* I tried to tell myself, *Wild dogs wouldn't keep me from that interview,* but I couldn't stop thinking, *What if they ask me about my embarrassing secret?* I prayed to God for a small favor. *Please don't let them see through me until after I get the job.*

****

The day of my interview I was beyond nervous. I knew if I was hired at Von Spa I would have money, admiration and maybe even a date or two. At the same time, I was slowly accepting an unfortunate reality. A titanic problem stood between me and my dream—her name was Yvonne Von Courtland. She was the type of woman who scared the B'Jesus out of me. Not only was she wealthy, but she was a member of Mensa and uncommonly regal-looking. Her vortex of power made my head spin.

The rumors surrounding Yvonne's path to success were legendary amongst the estheticians from school. The consensus was that she began life as a Southern belle, became a New York City socialite, and morphed herself into a shrewd business woman as middle age approached, but the details were rife with speculation. Some said, "Yvonne must have slept her way to the top." Others assumed her family was wealthy and had financed her ambitions. No one *really* knew how Yvonne managed to open her "10 million dollar spa," but one thing was clear. She named Von Spa after her favorite person: herself.

When the subway pulled into the station at Columbus Circle, I put on a fresh coat of Revlon Hazelnut lipstick and fought through the crowd. As I exited the turnstile, I had a torturous thought: *What if Yvonne conducts the interview herself?* I took a deep breath. *Just focus on getting through it.* I emptied all negative ideas from my mind like they did at the end of "Ghostbusters."

The Midtown hub bustled with energy. I climbed the stairs, imaging the people around me were salmon swimming upstream. A gigantic metal sculpture in the shape of a globe punctuated the cement above our heads. It seemed to signify that millions of people traveled far and wide to make this city their home. Some of the most expensive real estate in the world bloomed into skyscrapers right before my eyes. I glanced across the street at Central Park. The fall foliage burst with color. *Those trees are like Miracle Grow for condos.*

I looked down at the navy DKNY suit I'd gotten on sale at Daffy's. The long jacket covered a multitude of sins brought on by stress-eating. *You never stood a chance, Jenny Craig.* I reached into my pocket, pulled out my grandmother's pearls and put them on for luck. Then I smoothed down the tight mauve shirt that was suppressing my pendulous ubangous blouse bunnies. *If one of these buttons pops off, anyone within a ten foot radius could surely loose an eye. Lock and load, baby!*

I bent down and picked a piece of schmutz off the best part of the ensemble I was wearing: Moschino black suede ankle boots that made me feel like an urban warrior. My mother always told me to invest in footwear because "the size of your ass may change, but you'll always be a size eight—shoe, that is." I was as scared as Honey Boo Boo at a spelling bee. *God, I need a job—and a drink.*

My phone read 12:45. *Better kill a few minutes so they don't know I'm desperate.* I looked up at the shiny stainless steel building that housed Von Spa, hoping to find a stairway to employment Heaven. Suddenly, I felt like I had vertigo. *Don't forget to breathe and think positive thoughts.* I reached into my purse, pulled out a crinkled piece of paper and recited some inspirational affirmations I'd jotted down:

Your aptitude determines your attitude's altitude!

That can't be right. I must have copied it wrong. I took in a deep breath of crisp air and refocused.

Your purpose has to be backed with perspiration.

That I have. I can feel it running down into my socks.

Nirvana seemed within my reach. The inner strength was building when I felt something else: a button pop off my blouse. The time was 12:47. *Dear God no!* I feverishly scanned the busy streets for a pharmacy. My eyes fell upon a red and blue neon sign heralding "Duane Reade." I sprinted towards it, and as I ran, the twins pounded the bottom of my chin. *Better slow down, can't go to the interview with two black eyes!*

After some creepy ogling from the male cashier, I spent my last five dollars on a mini-sewing kit, and hurried back to the spa, creating a new affirmation on the way: *Walk and sew. Walk and sew. Walk and sew.*

****

Steps away from touchdown, the skies opened up. If a light Hawaiian mist is teardrops from Heaven, this could have been categorized as a monsoon from Hell. On the elevator ride to the eighth floor, I checked out the damage. Alice Cooper peeked back at me from my compact mirror. *When too much confidence boosting make-up backfires—film at 11.* I was about to cry, but then I burst into laughter. *What can you do?* I thought, as the other passengers stole glances at my new look. I decided not to do any repair work until I could access the necessary tools.

"Restroom?" I asked the security guard when the shiny gold doors opened. He pointed robotically. *This is the ultimate "let go and let God" moment.* A sense of relief washed over me. I went into the ladies' room, scaring more unsuspecting victims, but I was on a mission. The clock on the wall read 12:54. *Yipes!*

I took a paper towel from the dispenser and wiped away as much of the "Tammy Faye" effect as possible. After two quick swipes of concealer, the perfect amount of eyeliner remained. *My original make-up was probably a little too editorial, anyway.* I crouched under the hand dryer, focused the heat on my hairline and gathered the damp lady locks into a low chignon. *Not bad,* I thought, taking a final look in the mirror. I threw my fake Tory Burch bag over my shoulder and followed the silver-plated signs to my destination.

Returning to Von Spa was like walking into Oz. *Fountains and candles and flowers, oh my!* The streak-free doors opened like magic. Gone were the tiny creek and the scaffolding. Sunshine streamed through 12-foot windows overlooking the skyline. The clouds had cleared up just in time for my arrival.

There she blows, I thought when I saw the star of the show. *You made Von Spa the toast of New York.* The images that had graced so many magazines really didn't do justice to the crown jewel of the oasis. Right before me, shining like an enormous diamond, stood the famous crystal spiral staircase—an open invitation to relaxation Utopia. Rays of sunlight filtered through the Swarovski crystals casting shimmering little rainbows on the gold plated walls. Transparent glass steps stretched towards the second floor where blissful treatments awaited the spa guests. *I have to work here!* I was surrounded by beauty—including the girl at the front desk. In fact, I couldn't believe we were the same gender.

"Welcome to Von Spa," she said with an inflection that made "Von Spa" sound like "voilà." I imagined her unveiling a soufflé. "Will you be enjoying services with us today?"

"Actually, I have an appointment with Thomas."

"Wonderful. Please have a seat," she purred. "Can I bring you anything?"

My inner child asked for liquor; she was all for underage drinking and Mama needed a stiff one. "If it wouldn't be too much trouble, I'd love some water." *And hurry up. I need to get credit for being on time!*

"But of course," she replied. "Sparkling or fat?"

Did she just call me fat? Don't you realize I'm only visiting this weight?

"Sparking or flat?" she repeated.

"Oh, flat is fine." *What's up with that accent, anyway?*

"If you'd follow me, I will serve your water in the Tea Room." She flittered up the crystal steps like a fairy. I struggled to match her enthusiasm for stairs, but kept up with determination.

The Tea Room did not disappoint. A mosaic wall in shades of beige glittered behind antique tea sets in every color and shape imaginable. Floating on glass shelves, pitchers and teacups stretched up to the vaulted ceiling. *They must've spanned decades and continents alike.*

The spa concierge motioned for me to sit. I perched myself on a futon-like bench attached to the wall and moved a pale yellow pillow behind my back. She left to get my water. As soon as she was out of sight, I ran to take in the view, pulling back layers of pale pink drapes to find a picture window with a postcard quality panorama of Central Park. I looked down at the distant foot traffic, flashing back to the dark moment in my apartment when I'd felt so jealous of all the busy people below. I thought, *Today I've arrived at a destination that's important to me.*

I turned around and saw a large green bottle on the table. The girl had come and gone so quietly, it seemed like the water had appeared on its own. I poured myself a glass and flipped through some magazines.

Fifteen minutes dragged by slowly. *At least my shirt is finally dry.* Half an hour later, I finally finished drinking the last few drops of San Pellegrino. *Maybe they consider this "flat" wherever that supermodel whore is from. If this guy doesn't hurry up, I'm gonna hafta pee like a racehorse.* My inner child made a pouty face.

I was digging in my purse, looking for lipstick, when another tall thin gazelle-like creature appeared before me. He flashed a megawatt smile and extended his perfectly manicured right hand. The ends of his short fingernails were so white they looked like French tips.

"Hi Margaret, I'm Thomas." He shook my hand firmly. Thomas had big light burgundy lips, a strong nose and medium-length wavy brown hair slicked back to dramatic effect. *There must have been someone exotic in his family tree.* Thomas's long thick black lashes created a natural liner for his eyes, which were the exact same color as iced tea. I had one problem with him: He was prettier than me. "I'm sorry I kept you waiting so long," he said.

"I was beginning to wonder. I sent in my résumé at the end of last week."

He giggled. "Oh, I meant to keep you waiting *in the Tea Room.*"

I giggled, too and felt my shoulders drop about three inches. *Bring on the weird interview questions!* I thought. *Thank God Yvonne isn't gonna be the one doing the grilling.*

"If you'd follow me, I'll take you to our office. Yvonne is ready to interview you. No one works at the spa without her approval."

Oh shit. Or at least that's what I thought I might do.

I trailed Thomas down the stairs, through reception and across the hall into a tiny office covered with black-framed pictures of the spa, in depressing yellow tones. When we made our entrance, Yvonne stood up but didn't offer her hand. She was wearing a high-waisted grey skirt with a fitted white button-down shirt. Yvonne looked exactly like she did on Page Six—a tall blonde Upper East Sider as thin as paper. *Doesn't anyone eat around this joint?* I wondered. *I'm starving!*

"Welcome, Margaret." She sat down at her desk. "I'm Yvonne Von Courtland—and why do you want to work at my spa?" She motioned for me to take the chair between her and Thomas. He settled in. *Phew! At least he's staying.* I took my seat and puckered up to kiss some serious ass.

"Well, when I decided to pursue a career in the spa biz, I knew I had to work for the best. If I wanted to go into real estate, I'd try to land a gig with Donald Trump. Besides, you have better hair." *Never hurts to start with a joke. Every politician does.*

Yvonne smiled. Thomas stifled a laugh. *Hopefully the next question doesn't involve my mortifying secret.*

"Why thank you, but enough about me, why should I hire you?" *So I can pay my fucking rent, lady! I'm a woman living on the edge.* It was hard to think of a better answer; her sparkling teeth distracted me. *It's like she's wearing Vaseline.* A memory from a Lifetime movie about beauty pageants popped into my mind. *Before replying, repeat the question to buy yourself time.*

"I believe *you* should hire *me* because of all the skills I've acquired by working at the top spas in New York City." *I'm full of it*, I thought. *If you enjoy reading fiction, you'll love my résumé.*

"Good answer," she said. When she glanced at my embellished credentials, I became transfixed with her diamond earrings. *They're bigger than Usher's.* "I see you also worked as a nurse in a mental health facility?" This usually got me a lot of laughs during interviews. For example, "You'll fit right in!" *Here we go, time to talk about the nut hut.* Yvonne continued, "Why did you leave that profession?"

I knew I couldn't say, *If I stayed any longer, I'd be the one in the straitjacket.* I desperately wanted to tell the story about my "pretend broken arm." Even though Thomas was sitting there as quiet as a mute, I could tell he was a good audience. *Ugh! Don't try to be funny. No one will take you seriously.* I literally dug my heels into the ground for strength. "I decided to go to school for esthetics. I'm very passionate about skincare."

"Ah, so you are an esthetician, too." Yvonne's eyes lit up.

"Yes, you can see on my résumé that I did facials at Mena Brooks' spa."

"Great. I'll have to give her a call. She is a dear friend of mine." *Please don't!* I thought. *She probably won't even remember me.* "You do realize, however, we are trying to fill a spa concierge vacancy?"

"Oh I know," I said. "I was a concierge at Waterlily, too. I prefer working the front desk because I'm interested in spa management." *Where did that whopper come from?* "It can be a great training ground," I continued, surprising myself.

The spark in Yvonne's eyes burst into fire. "Very true. And I see you worked as a nanny for Mary Ann Driver the Vice President of Global Services. It is good to see you can work for powerful women."

Woo-hoo! Yvonne likes me, I thought. *She isn't asking about my secret, either. And she smiled when I made a joke.* As I let my guard down, something shifted inside of me. "Yes! Mrs. Driver had the cutest 5-year-old named Emma and one time..." My mouth started moving faster than my mind. The accumulation of pressure was too much. *Oh crap, comedy is taking over!* "...I took her to the park and this little stray dog kept following us—" Yvonne crinkled her brow, and Thomas's eyes were opened so wide he looked like an Anime character. *What am I doing? Wrap it up!* "The point is, don't ever wear brown corduroys with a leaf-print shirt."

Thomas stifled a laugh. Yvonne looked at me like I had insulted her ladyhood. Then she asked, "And why did you choose to share this story?"

I have to redeem myself. "Because I have a letter of recommendation from her." I handed it over proudly. "From Mrs. Driver, not Emma—obviously." I couldn't help but imagine a picture drawn with crayons, showing us as stick figures, running away from the dog.

Yvonne placed the letter on her desk without giving it a glance. "So tell me, what is your biggest weakness?" she asked.

"Cheesecake," I said. Thomas tried not to laugh again. Yvonne didn't even crack a smile. *Oh no! I think I lost her.*

"I meant professionally," she said.

Disguise your weakness as a strength. "I work too hard."

"And your greatest strength?"

"I work too hard?" *Did I just negate myself?*

"Well, I have all the information I need. Naturally, we are interviewing other candidates. So, we'll be in touch." Yvonne smiled, the light in her eye completely extinguished.

"It was a pleasure meeting you both." We all stood up and I reached out to shake her hand, but she was already bowing like a Japanese businessman. I tried to followed suit. The only problem was, I didn't know whether to bend at the waist or nod my head, so I alternated doing both, and ended up creating a weird modern dance move. *Must save face.* "Your spa is absolutely breathtaking."

"Why, thank you," Yvonne said. "Thomas, would you escort Margaret to the elevator?"

He nodded. "Of course."

I followed Thomas into the hallway. The silence was deafening. *I have to ask him.* "For some reason I feel like I can trust you," I blurted out as we walked down the corridor. "Can we just talk like you weren't part of the interview process? What do you think?"

Thomas pressed the button to call the elevator. His pretty lips frowned. "Look, I really like you. You're funny and quirky and I would love for you to work here." He paused. "The problem is, Yvonne is all business and your interview—well, it kind of wasn't. To make matters worse, my powers of persuasion are usually wasted on her." More awkward silence. "Don't get me wrong, you get high marks for entertainment value, but most people wouldn't have told that story. I don't think Yvonne liked it." The elevator bell sounded like a metronome as it zoomed past the upper floors. "If you don't mind me asking, what were you thinking back there?"

"I don't know! It's my *real* biggest weakness. I can't help but try to make people laugh." *Damn it. Why did I have to be funny?*"

"Did the little dog really try to pee on your leg?"

"No, thank God. He tried to pee on *Emma's* leg." We both chuckled. "Besides, I haven't worn brown corduroys since I was a size six, which was actually when *I* was five." My laughter almost turned to tears.

Thomas grinned sympathetically. "On the positive side, it sounds like humor is your god, which happens to be my favorite quality in an employee."

"Well, thank you. If only Yvonne felt the same way."

"Listen, I would love to hang out with you some time. I know this sounds a little unorthodox, but can we be friends—even if you don't get hired?"

"Maybe, but I think it'd be easier if I got the job." I smiled and shrugged my shoulders.

"Me too. I'll see what I can do."

The elevator opened to take me back to reality. I tried telling myself, *So what? There are 100 other luxury spas in the city,* but I wanted to work at Von Spa more than ever. On the way down to the street, my mind went into overdrive. *At least I won Thomas over. Why did I tell Yvonne that stupid story? My delivery wasn't even that good. Now I failed at funny, too.* I thought, *Thomas Haven, only you can save me now.* I looked up towards the eighth floor and repeated my final mantra of the day, *Thomas Haven, only you can save me now!*

Chapter 4

Thomas:

The Heat is On

Gazing into the mirror, I drank in my outfit—black leather pants, knee-high boots and a shredded grey t-shirt. I counted to ten before stepping on stage. The band began to play a scorching new rock song with electronic undertones. I smeared on some eyeliner and shook out my long wavy hair. The crowd roared and under the guitar, a rhythmic bass pounded: BEEP! BEEP! BEEP!

Suddenly, I was awake in my Chinese-red bedroom. I rolled over to turn off the beeping alarm. The dream's soundtrack repeated inside of me like an internal echo. I patted the nightstand. *Where is it?* I squinted when I lifted my sleeping mask, but found what I was looking for. *What're you gonna do with all these badly sung melodies?* I sang it into the digital recorder, anyway.

I got up, opened the curtains and stretched while sunlight warmed my face. I stared out the window. In front of me, housing projects heralded urban living, but in the distance, City College stood on a hill, looking more like West Point than Central Harlem. Five stories below, in the building courtyard, our superintendent planted bunches of flowers—canary yellow and pumpkin orange mums.

I took a shower, got dressed and walked through the sky blue living room of my railroad apartment, heading toward the kitchen. "Urban Outfitters Chic" best describes the design aesthetic I was going for. I paired things from the past with modern pieces to create a contemporary look: an antique white Queen Ann couch with a purple flokati rug; a glass table top lamp—featuring hanging lanterns—with a nouveau indigo lampshade; my Nana's navy La-Z-Boy with cerulean beaded pillows.

I nuked a piece of leftover quiche and settled into the vintage recliner. I fed two addictions at once by eating in front of my 36" flat screen TV. *God*, I thought, *I love Ellen and everything she's done for our people. If only I had more time for you.* I watched the intro while I scarfed down breakfast, then turned off the television.

Oh how I'd love to stay home. I shoved a freshly laundered uniform into my backpack and let the front door slam. Hurrying down the hallway, I dreaded the long night ahead of me. The elevator took forever so I made good use of the time by putting on a pair of sunglasses. I glanced at my iPhone. I had twenty minutes to get to work. *If the train comes right away, I might still make it.* I arrived at the ground floor of my building, waved to our doorman and hit the street.

This walk needs music, I thought. I dug through my bag, found some earbuds and stuck them in. On my quick jaunt to public transportation, I sashayed down the warm sunny city streets in Ray Ban Aviators, listening to Lady Gaga. While I strutted, I imagined working a high fashion runway in my skinny jeans and open combat boots. Descending into the cooler subway station, I saw the train on the platform so I swiped my MetroCard and hurried through the turnstile. I ran down the stairs to the beat like Madonna in the "Papa Don't Preach" video, and shimmied into the closing doors. An announcement exploded over the train's speakers. I took a bud out of my ear and heard the conductor say, "We are experiencing signal trouble at 59th Street. Expect heavy delays." I cursed the MTA gods. *Damn it to Hell!*

****

A half an hour later, I arrived at the spa, snuck into the men's locker room from the service entrance and put on my uniform in a bathroom stall. We weren't supposed to change in the same area as the guests, but I didn't want Yvonne to find out I was late. *She doesn't notice if I have to skip lunch because we're short of staff, but God forbid I'm delayed a few minutes due to transportation anomalies.* I avoided going past our office by heading directly to the spa's 2nd story, which was on the building's 9th floor. I took the undecorated back staircase that was reserved exclusively for the staff. I scurried past the treatment rooms and descended the crystal stairs. When I saw Yvonne in reception, I stopped dead in my tracks. She finished straightening some products on the shelf and looked up; my refection was clearly evident in the glass doors. *Busted!* I slunk behind the front desk.

"Welcome." She pierced me with her cobalt blue eyes. "Thank God you're *finally* here. Someone needs to assist our other guests while I escort Mrs. Jones. I'm expecting her at any moment."

Mrs. Jones, also known to the staff as Mrs. B (for bitch), was especially important because despite the economy, she still brought in clients. This woman spent thousands of dollars at Von Spa, sometimes more than once a week. She also sent her employees to the spa and bought hundreds of gift cards.

Yvonne joined me at the desk, standing in front of the other computer. After I checked the reservations, I glanced over to find her lost in thought. Yvonne's high cheekbones looked like they were carved out of ivory, her alabaster skin impossibly smooth for her age. I knew she had a Park Avenue dermatologist filling in her creases to perfection. When Yvonne caught me staring, I decided to make small talk so she wouldn't think I was a freak. And Mrs. Jones' wicked ways, while repulsive, were the perfect topic of conversation. *What's her real story?* I had to find out.

"It's great that Mrs. Jones is still coming in so often," I lied. "I'm glad her business hasn't suffered because of the economic crisis." After I spoke the words, I consciously wished Mrs. Jones would permanently disappear from our lives. *The universe needs to know the truth.*

"On the contrary," Yvonne said, scrolling through the bookings on the computer, "she is busier than ever."

"That's surprising with the housing market in the toilet. Isn't she a real estate agent?"

"She is, but her clientele is predominantly European. They are scooping up cheap investment properties like they are playing Monopoly."

"Oh," I said, shocked. *Unmitigated greed! Leave it to Mrs. B to profit from other people's broken dreams.*

Yvonne's eyes sparkled like they were being lit from inside her skull. "And Mrs. Jones is making millions in commissions."

I grinned at her so she wouldn't know I was really thinking, *The rich get richer.* A chill shot through my bones. *They'll never understand what it's like to struggle with money. But at least I have a job—for now.* I looked at Yvonne and felt a little sad. *Maybe it's lonely at the top…HELLO!* I interrupted my own thoughts. *You're wasting your chance to push for Margaret.* "So what'd you think of the spa concierge candidate we just interviewed?"

Yvonne didn't respond.

"I really liked her," I said. "She has luxury spa experience, she seems smart, and she's funny."

Yvonne looked straight at me, tipped her head to the left and blinked several times. "'Funny' is not what my spa is about. Don't you know me well enough at this point? If *I* had liked her, she would be working here already."

"I get it, but the situation is becoming very challenging for me," I said, my voice cracking. *Don't be so emotional or she'll roll her eyes and shut down.* "It's hard to juggle working the desk and supervising the spa concierges. I don't want service to suffer because of my time constraints." Yvonne cared more about *service* suffering, then *my* suffering. *If I keep working like this I'm going to have a breakdown.* I usually spent the whole weekend in front of the TV recovering from exhaustion and sometimes it only consisted of one day off. "Do you think we can just give her a chance and see how she performs?"

"No. At any rate, the point is moot," Yvonne said, scrolling through the bookings. "I have already hired someone else. She is the daughter of an acquaintance from The Benevolent Society." *Oh no. Not again!* The last time Yvonne hired a rich girl, she called out sick constantly. Since Genevieve always presented me with a doctor's note, I could never give her a DAF. I was stuck with her for months until she turned twenty-one and came into her trust fund.

Mrs. Jones approached the glass doors. She must have been in her mid-thirties, but her powerful persona made her seem older. She wore a fashionable, trench-style, black mink coat, even though it was a warm fall day. It brought out the shine in her ebony bob. *I wonder if she killed those minks herself.* Disdain spread through me like poison.

Yvonne finished her thought, "Shane is the name of your new concierge." Then she glided toward Mrs. B, putting on a glorious veneered smile.

Soon after our new hire joined us, the girls at the desk gave her another moniker: Princess Shane.

✳✳✳✳

On Shane's first day, I worked the closing shift, as usual. June, our resident glamazon lesbian, was showing her the computer system when I arrived at the spa. I sized Shane up. Perfectly penciled kohl eyebrows and dark red lipstick contrasted sharply with her pale face. It was easy to tell by her roots that Shane was born with mousy brown hair, but her long straight tresses were dyed ash blonde. Her eyes were dark with unusually small irises, which gave them a beady quality. Although she barely looked old enough to drink, there were permanent creases where her brow met her nose. Shane was far from ugly, but she looked about as warm as a polar bear's balls.

You're intuitive, not psychic, I thought, trying to keep myself in check. I knew how it felt to be judged, so I tried not to jump to conclusions about Shane. It wasn't her fault Yvonne had hired her behind my back. And being born rich was out of Shane's control, too. I shifted my train of thought. *If she's anything like June, maybe I'll be thanking Yvonne later.*

At 6'3", June—whose father was a Nigerian pro-basketball player and mother a German model—towered over Shane by at least a foot. June's black uniform hid her banging body, complete with double D's, an apple bottom and a small waist. Tiny tendrils of light brown curls exploded from June's scalp and fell to her shoulders framing her fantastical features: a button nose, sparkling blue-green eyes and enormous pink bee-stung lips. *It's nice to see June in her full glory, but they both hafta put their hair up.* I approached the dynamic duo.

"You must be Shane. I'm Thomas, the front desk manager. It's a pleasure to meet you." I extended my hand, admiring the free manicure Yvonne had awarded me. It was one of my favorite perks. We exchanged treatments with other spas and either enjoyed the services ourselves, or gave them out as prizes to good employees.

Shane didn't go in for the shake. She was already in motion, grabbing her smartphone from her pocket. "Oh good, Yvonne said I could talk to you about my schedule. I need Saturdays and Sundays off because I spend the weekends with my family in Connecticut. I can work Monday through Friday, nine to five."

Really, Elmira Gulch? I thought. "I'll see what I can do, but those aren't the shifts we need covered."

"Yvonne told me that you could take care of this sort of thing," Shane said in a tone like we'd been friends for years. "So are you going to help me or not?" *Guess I should have listened to my intuition.*

"I'd like to help," I replied, holding in my rage, "but someone already has that schedule because she's been working here longer…" *than five minutes.*

"But—"

Oh my God, seriously? "Why don't you get settled in and we'll talk about this later."

"Listen, Shane," June said, "Thomas is great with the schedule. I'm sure he'll come up with some sort of compromise."

Shane glared at me like a predator, refusing to break eye contact.

I'm outta here. "I have to check my email, so if you'll excuse me. It was nice to meet you Shane." She pursed her lips, held her gaze a little longer then looked down at the computer. Disbelief flooded over me. *What a charmer!* I turned and left. "Welcome back to work," I muttered under my breath.

****

I greeted Yvonne and turned on my computer, trying to ground myself.

"Hi, darling," Yvonne said, smiling, her latent Southern accent slightly audible. *Uh-oh. She's excited about something, which means I won't be.* "Who's working the front desk tonight?"

"June has the closing shift," I said.

"Perfect. I knew you would pick our most capable concierge. So we will leave around seven. June can close up." She turned her attention back to her paperwork.

"Okay, great," I said. *I'm glad we're leaving early, but where the hell are we going?*

I didn't want Yvonne thinking I wasn't on top of things so I scanned my inbox, hoping to solve the mystery. *Is it a boring Spa Directors' cocktail party? Dear God, I hope not.* Last time, Yvonne paraded me around like an old-fashioned secretary taking people's contact information. She loved a good power trip. *Maybe we're meeting with her alleged best friend and fellow Spa-trepreneur, Mena.* Whenever we'd had dinner together, I would sit there silently, bored to tears while Mena and Yvonne talked shop. I checked my iPhone calendar and found the answer to the riddle. *No wonder you're in such a good mood.* Yvonne had scheduled some time with her favorite crush—our accountant. We called him Clark Kent because of his chiseled features, dark hair and blue eyes.

"Did you meet Shane?" Yvonne asked, turning toward me, her flaxen hair flowing around her face like a model in a Pantene commercial.

"Oh yes." I tried to mask my anger again.

"Well, what do you think?"

Have you seen the movie "The Bad Seed?" I thought. But I said, "She seems really smart."

"She is! Shane attended Miss Porter's School and Vanderbilt University. Plus she has management experience." Yvonne gleamed.

"Oh really?" *She must be a liar, too. A former manager wouldn't have complained about the schedule.* "At what spa?"

"I don't remember. The point is she possesses a leadership sensibility. Anyway, I know she will do an excellent job. And now you are fully staffed again, so you can concentrate on tightening up the front desk."

"Definitely." *Ugh! I would rather bomb the desk and run away screaming.* I turned back to the computer, but my thoughts were racing. *Aren't I working hard enough already? You're always so pumped to hire someone with "management" experience, even if all they MANAGED was to avoid stepping in dog poop.* If she couldn't "remember" what high-powered position Shane had left to come work for us, I'd have to find out myself.

****

At 6:45, Yvonne and I slid into the car service's black Cadillac and headed to our dinner meeting. We were less than fifteen blocks away, but the red soles of her Louboutins were not allowed to play on the sidewalk and her golden locks were forbidden to fraternize with humidity.

We sat in silence for the next few minutes. Yvonne took a gold compact out of her Louis Vuitton bag and touched up her nose. She closed the pressed powder with a snap, then rubbed her crimson lips together. The closer we got to our destination, the more she checked herself in the rearview mirror.

I glanced at my iPhone and scrolled through the newsfeed on Facebook. *Who cares what your food looks like?* I was interrupted by an incoming call. It was someone from the mother ship. *Oh shit!*

I answered. "What's going on?" My BPMs doubled.

"I can't talk," June said under her breath. "Just get here right away!" She hung up.

"Yvonne, I have to go back to the spa."

"Why? If we turn around now we could lose our reservation! And you know how I feel about punctuality."

"Let me try June again and find out what's happening." The call went straight to voicemail. I had a horrible thought. *Nothing ruins a massage like a 100 decibel alarm.* "Oh my God."

"What?" Yvonne shouted.

"It's the first Thursday of the month!"

"And?" she huffed.

"They're probably testing the building fire alarms. June must be dealing with a spa *full* of angry guests. I better catch a cab or no one is gonna end up paying for a treatment."

"Fine!" Yvonne threw her hands in the air and turned her face toward the window. "Pull over," she yelled at the driver.

The car stopped. I jumped out. "I'll meet up with you as soon—"

"Don't bother," Yvonne said. "I can't very well have you showing up late." She slammed the door.

What the fuck? I thought. *Are you that nervous to be alone with your Romeo?* I called the spa and left a message. "I'm on my way, but please call me back. I'm totally freaking out and I need to know what's going on." *Damn it, June! Why are you torturing me?*

I stood on the corner scanning the street's horizon for a taxi in the bumper-to-bumper cross town traffic. I decided it would be quicker to run through Central Park. The song "The Heat is On" played in my mind as I made my way off the sidewalk and into the trees. The October air felt surprisingly humid for a fall day. The sunset was magnificent, but I couldn't appreciate the array of golden and lavender hues which set the skyline ablaze, casting shadows on the canopy of leaves. A pack of bikers on the main loop flew by in the opposite direction. *God I wish I was like them. I wish I was free.*

At the very least, you can enjoy your unexpected workout. I selected a playlist on my iPhone, put in my earbuds and ran to the beat of the Black-Eyed Peas' "Rock That Body," followed by Beyoncé's "Why Don't You Love Me," and finally "Sugar 5" by an amazing electronica group called Lamb.

Sweat soaked the armpits of my uniform when I arrived at the spa. I caught a glimpse of my reflection in the glass door, only to see Diana Ross staring back at me. *I just might be talking to angry guests with an enormous new hairdo.* June floated around the desk like a summer butterfly.

"What happened?" I asked a little too loudly for the spa environment.

"Oh never mind, I handled it," June said, gliding into the concierge office.

Did you, now? I stuck my head in the doorway. "June, I ran all the way here. Why didn't you call me back? I'm sweating like a whore in a megachurch!"

"You see—that's what I love about you. Even angry, you still throw in some humor. To answer your question, I was too busy dealing with the situation. She just left. Besides, I did you a favor." June dug in her purse.

"Thank you," I said sarcastically. "You're right. That's what I really needed today—a little more stress."

"But what you *wanted* was to get out of that meeting—you were complaining about it all afternoon. And we both know Yvonne would've made you go out for drinks afterwards, too. Then tomorrow you'd have a hangover and you'd be Les Misérables all day." She applied some pink lip gloss. The smell of bubble gum drifted toward me. "Now you're free!" June smacked her lips together and smiled.

True, I thought, feeling relieved. "Be that as it may, you still haven't told me what happened."

"It's nothing new. This woman didn't like her massage. She thought Tootsie was fake, etc., etc." June coated her long lashes with mascara.

"I'm not surprised." Tootsie's grey hair, glasses and vocal inflection reminded everyone of Mrs. Doubtfire. We found it hysterical that she resembled one man in drag from the silver screen and shared a name with another. "Like I always say, if you don't like a good ass licking, don't book a treatment with Tootsie."

"They are few and far between, but I actually love someone who can see through the bullshit. And don't worry. Gabrielle took care of everything."

I gasped. "Gabrielle? That's like pouring gasoline on a 40-foot-tall burning man! Why?"

"Because she volunteered. She actually did a good job. I reminded her beforehand to 'Listen, Apologize and Rectumfy'—I mean, 'Rectify.'" June saluted. "I packed up some free gifts and waited in here."

"And?" I crossed my fingers for June to see.

"The gifts were enough. We didn't even have to invite her back to 'experience the spa the way it's meant to be,'" she said, making air quotes.

"Great. Because when that happens, *I* experience getting my ass handed to me by Yvonne. It's not like the old days when the money was rolling in."

"You'll be happy to know the lady actually booked a follow-up appointment," June powdered her caramel complexion, "with someone other than Tootsie."

"Of course—good work, but next time, could you do me a favor?"

"Sure!" June feigned über-enthusiasm.

"If you've already solved the problem, can we just *pretend* there's a reason for me to leave whatever event I'd like to get out of? I would like to minimize my stress level."

"Okay. I'm sorry. But you have to admit, my way was more fun."

"For you!" I smiled. "You drama queen."

"You're the queen," she said, playing her gay card.

I headed towards our office across the hall. *Yvonne's gone for the night.* I smiled mischievously. *Now I can try to solve the mystery that's been bugging me.*

"Oh, Thomas—there's one more thing." June took her place at the front desk.

There's always one more thing. I turned back around. "Go ahead."

"After the unhappy woman left, Tootsie was lighting sage again to get rid of the imaginary 'bad energy' and some of the guests were complaining about the smell—you know how sage stinks like burning ass. Anyway, we gave the complainers eye pillows and they were fine, but when I told Tootsie people were whining about the stench, she was like, 'It's very necessary to cleanse the aura of the room,'" June said, doing her best impression. "I didn't want to get into it with her 'cause it's not my place, so can you talk to her? The therapists are always doing shit and then we have to deal with the angry guests when they're leaving."

"No problem. I'll take care of it."

I walked into the 8th floor lobby and felt my phone vibrate. I had a text from my best friend Anthony: **Allow me to introduce, Christopher...** Under the message was a picture of a cute, scruffy, dark-featured guy. Below the pic, the text continued: **My future husband!**

Good to know. It wasn't the first time Anthony was overly excited about a guy he'd just met. He often found his alleged perfect partner, only to discover some unforgivable flaw like a weird crooked toe, a love for show tunes or a small third nipple. *We'll see how long this one lasts.*

I returned to my mission, ducking into our office like an international spy. There was a stack of papers on Yvonne's desk which looked promising. With her trust issues in mind, I gingerly flipped through the pile, careful not to change the order. And there it was—Shane's résumé. "Yes!" I said like a seven-year-old. There was a single post-college entry. Shane had worked as a shift manager for two months at Applebee's.

Chapter 5

Margaret:

Ya Gotta Have Friends

It had been three weeks since my interview at Von Spa. While I waited for them to respond to my myriad of friendly voicemails, I sent my résumé to every spa in the tri-state area. I didn't receive a single phone call in return.

On day twenty-two, I woke up earlier than usual and essentially hit the delete button on the last month. I hobbled over to the mirror and forced myself to beam from ear to ear. During my short college career, my English professor had taught me a trick—he said most days he felt like driving off a cliff, but the power of a smile, even a fake one, fooled the mind into being in a good mood.

With a grin plastered unconvincingly on my face, I flipped on the TV. An ad for Jenny Craig came on. *Those "after" photos look amazing. Better get rid of all the junk food around here so I can start dieting again.* Rocking back and forth on the couch a few times for momentum, I jumped to my feet and shuffled to the fridge. I opened the stainless steel door to find half of a decadent cheesecake that had eased my pain a few days ago. A gooey cherry topping dripped over mouthwatering chocolate and vanilla swirls on a crunchy, salty/sweet cocoa crust. *In these uncertain economic times, I can't let this go to waste.*

The creamy sweetness of the first bite made me forget about everything. I was so high I decided to have another piece. Midway through the second slice, I tasted defeat. My bunny slippers looked up at me with judgment. *What's wrong with you?* I poured water over the rest and threw it in the trash. I was ready for some tough talk for tough times. JoAnn and I hadn't spoken since our fight. I missed her desperately, but I avoided confrontation like the plague. I grabbed the receiver of my home phone and put it right back down. *What if she hasn't forgiven me for hanging up on her?* I was so tired, part of me didn't care. Slowly, I dialed her number.

"I've been waiting for you to call me," Joann said without emotion. *She's holding in her rage!*

"You *have?*" My heart started pounding.

"Of course." There was a long moment of silence. I held my breath. "Listen, before you say anything, I want to apologize."

"Okay." I exhaled. *Thank God!*

"I'm sorry I was so insensitive that day on the phone. Sometimes I forget you don't know how wonderful you are, like everyone else does. I didn't know high school was such a bad trip for you. I thought we were having a good time. Why didn't you ever tell me?"

"Because I was embarrassed. I didn't want you to know how badly people picked on me before you showed up and changed my social status."

"Maggie, you can tell me anything—then, now and forever. I love you unconditionally."

My frozen heart melted. "Oh Jo, I'm sorry I overreacted, and for the record, we *were* having a good time and that was the best revenge, because I knew those mean girls were jealous of us. Speaking of which, I did something back in high school I never told you about."

"You're making me nervous. What'd you do?"

"It's no big deal, but one time when we were walking down the hall, laughing our heads off, I actually turned around and stuck my tongue out at Jenny Shapiro."

JoAnn chuckled and I thought, *It's so good to have you back.* "That's hilarious," she said. "I'm sure she deserved it!"

"Totally. But enough about the past," I said. "How *are* you?"

"I'm fine. How are—can you hold on a minute—get off of your brother or I will call your father at the hospital! Sorry 'bout that."

"Are those kids giving it to you again? I told you to get goldfish. They're a lot less 'me, me, me.'"

JoAnn laughed. "I know. I haven't had a moment to myself in years. Yesterday, I almost called my neighbor to watch them so I could take a shower."

"I'm sorry, honey. That sucks."

"Anyway, are you still working for the VNA?"

"Oh but no. I'm an esthetician now and I did have an interview at Von Spa."

"That's great, Maggs! How'd it go?"

"It went okay. I haven't heard from them yet, but I still have my fingers crossed."

"You weren't funny were you?" she asked.

"Of course not—well not until the end—and maybe only a little."

"Uh-oh."

"I tried not to, but I told them the story about Emma and the little dog—"

"Margaret! The nanny gig?"

"Yeah." I crinkled my forehead.

"Why on earth would you tell them that? Who are you, Kathy Griffin?"

"I wish."

"Maggie, it's an interview, not an audition."

"I know. I know! It's like an illness. I can't explain what happens. I simply must try to bring the funny."

"Hopefully they want to see a second act."

"Let's hope." I twisted the phone chord in my hand. "The front desk manager was kind of into me."

"That's good," JoAnn's voice perked up. "Do you like him? Is he cute?"

"Oh he's cute alright, but I didn't mean it like that. Besides, he already said he just wants to be friends and unless I have gender reassignment surgery, I think it's the only option anyway."

"Well if you ask me, making friends is a good way to get your foot in the door. Maybe they still need an esthetician. You should give him a call."

"Believe me, I've left several messages. And actually, the job they're hiring for is spa concierge."

"What's that?"

"A receptionist position with a fancy name so you don't feel like a loser. But my real goal is to do facials there. Just don't tell them that."

"Got it. And I'm sure they loved you," JoAnn said.

"You have to say that 'cause you're my best friend. It doesn't change the fact they haven't contacted me in three weeks."

"I bet you'll hear from them soon. They're probably still interviewing a bunch of candidates."

"I appreciate the vote of confidence, but once again I am days away from calling the VNA or looking into the New York City shelter system. I don't know which option is worse."

"Remember, you always underestimate your fabulosity, Maggs."

"Thanks, Jo. I'm sorry, too, by the way. You're my best friend and in the future if something is bothering me, I promise to tell you immediately."

"Okay, Iyanla Vanzant. I promise to do the same. DO NOT FART IN YOUR BROTHER'S FACE!"

I pulled the receiver away from my ear. "Seriously? Is that the wedgie of the new millennium?"

"Sorry, Maggie. These kids are gonna kill each other if I don't get off the phone."

"Now I know why some animals eat their young."

"Yeah, they might be onto something. Can I call you back later?"

"Of course, I will be here willing the phone to ring." As I uttered the words, my cell rang. I checked the number as my heart skipped a beat. The caller ID read 1-800-000-0000. *Damn it! Stupid telemarketers.* I let it go to voicemail. "Now get on your striped shirt and blow the whistle on those little bastards."

"Alright, Maggs. Let me know when you hear from them and remember— you're a lion. Take what's yours."

"Will do."

I admired her incredible ability to make me feel better. Before becoming determined to work at the premiere spa in the world so I would have something to brag about, I was pretty much permanently logged onto www.whogivesacrap.com. Luckily for me, I had my trusty co-captain back. She knew this ship just needed a destination and fast. I wasn't getting any younger. In fact, I was pushing forty. How I prayed Thomas would contact me already. My hair had grown a quarter of an inch since we'd first met and I was officially livin' la vida broke-a.

Chapter 6

Thomas:

Spa Babies

The concierge girls were in the reservation office, behind the reception desk, but it sounded like they were standing next to me. *It's hard to get these city girls to speak quietly,* I thought. They weren't Middle America loud, they were New York loud. I couldn't blame them. Living here, amongst so many people, sometimes it feels like you are shouting to be heard; even speaking is a competitive sport.

I popped my head into our messy little office. "Ladies, could you please use your 'spa voices?'" We used the term "spa voice" like a kindergarten teacher would use "indoor voice." Diana, our resident party girl, and Shane were stunned into silence. *At least Shane is finally trying to be part of the team. Maybe the "baby pic" thing worked.*

"Sorry about it." A faux-tanned Diana smacked her gum.

"Not only are you guys wildly inappropriate for our spa guests," I scolded them with a wink and a smile, "but I'm trying to finish the schedule."

"Oh, while you're working on that," Shane said, "I need Saturday off. There's an event honoring my mother at the Westchester Country Club."

"What's the honor?" I asked. *If you're gonna be a snob, be prepared to be called on it.*

"She made a large donation to a charity. My family is kind of a big deal, you know." She flipped her hair.

Was that an attempt at a joke?

Diana rolled her eyes, put on a headset and dialed a number from the guest call log. *Wow, she's getting back to work without being asked.* Like most party girls, Diana considered herself beautiful and special. She was a sweet, cute, Jennifer Lopez type, but sometimes she acted like she *was* J-Lo. One time, I had asked her what her dream job would be. Without missing a beat she replied, "Movie star!"

"I'll look into Saturday for you, Shane," I said. "You know I like to keep the troops happy."

Diana took off her headset. "I was telling Shane if she needed coverage, maybe 'Tick-Tick-Boom' can do it."

"Diana! I told you not to call her that. Her name is Anne."

"Sorry, babe, but the shoe fits. She says she's not angry, gets all passive-aggressive, and then blows up."

"And you think calling her 'Tick-Tick-Boom' is gonna help with that?"

"She deserves it. She ripped me a new one before lunch 'cause I couldn't help her at the desk. I was on the phone!"

"It doesn't matter. If there is a problem, you need to come to me and I will address it. In the meantime, call her Anne." Diana rolled her eyes again and put her headset back on. "Shane, would you mind covering the front desk? I need to go check-in with Yvonne." Shane sauntered to the desk at glacial speed.

I approached our office. The sound of Yvonne's phone ringing stopped me dead in my tracks. She answered, and then I heard Diana's voice on speakerphone. I paused around the corner so I could eavesdrop. Yvonne said, "Who is calling?"

"She wouldn't say, but apparently it's an emergency."

"Very well, put it through." The phone rang once, followed by, "Yvonne Von Courtland speaking."

"Vonnie, I need mon—" the caller slurred. Yvonne picked up the receiver. "I have told you time and time again not to call here when you've been drinking!" There was a pause. "I have already given you your stipend for the month. If you need to reach me, you have my mobile number."

I peeked in to see Yvonne slam the receiver down. I waited for thirty seconds before heading to my desk. "Hi Yvonne," I said.

"Damn it." Yvonne stared at her gigantic, flat screen monitor. She looked perfect (as always) in her midnight blue Gucci pantsuit and freshly styled updo.

"What's wrong?" I asked.

"I've just responded to an email from Michael."

"Who?"

"Michael *Greene*—our accountant," she said, still looking at her computer. *Oh, so you're on a first name basis now,* I smirked to myself. Yvonne turned and faced me. "You have to do an investigation regarding a gift card. There was no receipt attached after it was processed."

"What do you mean?"

"I *mean* someone created a gift card for a full-day package without documenting proper payment. Mr. Greene thinks it may have been stolen."

Oh my dear sweet Gabrielle, what kind of fascinating new errors have you managed to come up with this time? At that moment I knew two things regarding Gabrielle: she wasn't a thief and she needed me to save her. "How am I going to do an 'investigation?'" I asked using air quotes. *That was a stupid thing to do.*

Yvonne flared her nostrils. "Will you please pay attention?" She removed her black Chanel glasses causing a lock of her blonde hair to fall across her face. "You understand the system better than anyone else here. I am fully confident you will figure it out." She paused briefly. Through gritted teeth she said, "If there is one thing I can't stand, it's having an employee pilfer from me when I have provided them with such a good job."

That was true. She had famously fired a locker room attendant for taking a few complimentary travel size shampoos.

"With all due respect, Yvonne, why would a staff member steal a gift card? They'd never be able to redeem it without getting caught."

"I don't know. You will have to look into this detail."

There was a knock on the door. Startled, I turned around. Shane peeked her head into the office. *Uh-oh, we have a leak—from someone's face.* Tears streamed down her red, puffy cheeks. "Thomas," she sniffled, "may I speak with you?"

"I'll be there in two minutes," I said. She disappeared and closed the door.

"After you talk to Shane, this investigation should be your top priority." Yvonne gave her head a nod toward the hallway and put her glasses back on.

Jesus H. Christ, I thought, *I just got here! Could there be any more drama today?* I had a sneaking suspicion the answer was "yes." I grabbed a box of Kleenex, swiveled my chair around, and leapt to my feet. I stepped into the hall and murmured to Shane, "Let's go to the secret meeting place." We hurried through the back corridor, passing boxes of aromatherapy oils next to several bins of fresh linens, which permeated the air with the smell of bleach.

I held open the fire door for Shane and we entered the stairwell. "What's up? Are you okay?" A pang of pity spread through my chest. We sat down in our grey second office, bathed in fluorescent light. The cold cement sent a jolt through my hot ass.

"Nobody likes me!" She exploded into a new wave of tears, causing her eye make-up to run south toward her mouth. "None of the girls talk to me and when I went into the reservation office, they got really quiet like they were talking *about* me."

"But you and Diana were just chatting—"

"She only wants me to get her into the country club," she wailed, her sobs echoing through the empty space.

I hate seeing someone upset, even someone like Shane. *She's no work horse, but at least the desk is fully staffed. We're all gonna hafta learn to get along.* I handed her a tissue and gave her a few compliments so she could handle some honesty. "Listen Shane, you're smart and very capable. You should be proud you needed very little training. Here's the problem, though. I think the girls might have the impression— and it may be a misperception—that you feel superior." I held my breath, awaiting her reaction.

"Are you saying they think I'm a snob?"

Bingo. "No, not at all, but maybe you should steer clear of mentioning your family so much. I know you're proud of them, but stay more on the same level with the other girls. They really are a sweet group in general." Shane didn't respond. "The next time you're one-on-one with a co-worker, why don't you ask them a lot of questions. Everyone likes talking about themselves. Show 'em you're interested. Try to be their friend."

"That would be a great idea," Shane said, "if they would even sit with me in the building cafeteria." A fresh explosion of tears erupted.

"I know these girls. If you approached their table and asked to join them, they would never say no. Then you can ask your questions." Shane blew her nose. "Listen, I'll reach out and ask the others to give you a chance. I won't tell them we had this conversation; I'll just say it's something I noticed." I put my hand on her shoulder. "It'll get better—you'll see." I felt like I stole my speech from a bad sitcom. "It might even start to turn around by tomorrow if you make an effort."

"Okay." She dried her tears and wiped some snot from her nose with the tissue. "I'd be so upset if I lost this job. For the first time, my mother is bragging to her friends about what I'm doing."

"I know how good that feels," I admitted.

"Oh, which reminds me—I have something for you." Shane stood up and dug through her taupe Birkin bag. "My mom found this the other day." She pulled out a picture and handed it over.

"Great. Ya know I did the whole 'bring in a baby pic' team building exercise for you, right?"

"Really?" She smiled even though she still had tears in her eyes.

"I thought it would help everyone bond with you, our new colleague. So there's another thing you guys can talk about."

"That's true."

"Why don't you go to the restroom and take a few minutes to get yourself together before you go back to the desk."

"Ok, thanks," she said. I stood up and opened the door for her. "Oh Thomas, one more thing."

There's always one more thing. "Hit me."

"My cousin Vivien is coming in next week to celebrate her birthday. May I order her a complimentary cake?"

"Of course. You know I love giving away free shit." I winked.

She grinned back. "Thanks again—for everything."

I headed to the front desk. *Doing good deeds does make me feel better about this job.* The morning and evening shifts were overlapping, so Anne, June, Diana and Gabrielle were all standing around, chatting quietly. The candlelit spa looked warm and inviting, especially compared to the stark secret meeting place. The scent of lavender filled the air. *No essential oil is gonna help me relax today!*

"Could you guys gather around? We need to talk."

"But of course," Gabrielle said happily.

"Let's go in the office."

Anne followed the other girls, taking down her curly red hair. "Actually, Anne, would you mind watching the desk? I'll fill you in later." *And talk to you about your temper.*

"Fine," she snapped, and began winding her hair back into a bun. Shane's baby picture slipped out of my hand and fell to the floor. I bent over to pick it up and noticed Anne was wearing open toe sandals. *Great, you're also breaking a Five Star Rule—one more thing to add to your coaching session.* I put the pic in my pocket, slipped into the office and struggled to close the heavy wooden sliding door.

"Does anyone want a Pez?" Diana asked through a mouth full of candy.

"No thanks," I said. "I'm full."

Diana laughed, choking on her saliva. "That's the funniest answer I ever got!"

"I'm glad. Okay guys, here's the thing. It's clear she's made a bad first impression on some of you, but we have to try to be nicer to Shane."

Diana rolled her pretty hazel eyes.

June shook her head. "Everybody knows how easy I am to get along with, but either that girl is a homophobe, or she's a narcissistic sociopath."

I shuddered. "Sweet Jesus, June. Don't you think you're being a little harsh?"

"Not really. The definition of a sociopath is someone who can't empathize with other people's feelings and that's Shane in a nutshell. She told me all babies need a father, she made a comment about my size and you can tell she has no soul when you look into her eyes."

"Wow. Okay," I said. "But I know one person I'm sure she cares about—herself. And I can see she feels isolated. I don't give up on people, because I believe everyone can change." I paused to let my words sink in. "Maybe we can show her how to get along better with others. I have a feeling she's open to a new start. Here's the *other* thing—we need her." I went around the circle, looking each girl in the eye. "All of us, myself included, work hard enough around here and we can't afford to be short staffed again. Will you *please* give her another chance?"

"I really don't believe someone like her can change," June said, "but I'll do my best to get along with her as a co-worker."

"Diana?"

"No problem, babe." She parted her lips and sucked in a mouthful of spit. *That girl is always eating something.*

"Gabrielle?"

"Don't worry, mi amor, I will try."

"Thanks, you guys."

The girls dispersed. I taped Shane's pic on the poster board with the others. Baby Shane sported a white dress with a pink ribbon and a matching hat. Bloomers, white frilly socks and ivory Mary Janes made her completely adorable. She had an expression on her face like she was in the middle of saying, "Ga, Ga!" Hopefully, it would humanize her to everyone. To me, the picture said, "I'm a person, like the rest of you, with a family, a life, etc."

My peaceful moment was interrupted by a sound I would only hear twice in my four years at the spa—screaming. I ran out of the office.

"My foot!" Anne yelled. "You bitch!"

"But it was an accident," said the soccer mom sitting on the couch.

Anne grabbed a bottle from the floor and poured water over the soccer mom's head while soothing spa music droned on in the background. My internal movie reel shifted gears into slow motion. I distinctly remember saying, "Noooooooooo," and thinking, *We can't be short of staff again!* The cold San Pellegrino drenched the soccer mom's rhinestone top so completely she could have entered a wet t-shirt contest. The woman gasped in shock, trying to catch her breath. I looked over at Gabrielle, whose eyes were popping out of her skull like Bugs Bunny.

"Screw this place. I quit!" Anne smashed the bottle on the black marble floor. My hands snapped over my face. I peaked through my fingers and saw Anne pull her hair out of its bun, throw off her uniform jacket, and hit the door in her bra. No one moved a muscle. The sound of peaceful harps continued to play.

Holy fucking shit! This can't be happening. The soccer mom took her hands off her eyes and looked around to make sure Anne was gone. *How the hell am I gonna correct this situation? It wasn't covered in the handbook.* I grabbed a towel from under the desk, ran over to the soccer mom and placed it around her shoulders. "I am so sorry, ma'am," I said, kneeling in front of her.

"I didn't mean to drop the bottle on her foot, it was an accident."

"I know. I'm so *very* sorry. What can we do to make this up to you?" I asked. Gabrielle glided over, handed her another towel and returned to the desk. "Would a free massage help?"

"I don't think so." The woman began crying. *Oh. My. God. What am I gonna do now?*

"Gabrielle, can you bring our guest some chamomile tea and scones?" Gabrielle nodded and motioned for me to come over to the computer. She pointed to the woman's profile notes. This was her third time at Von Spa and she had yet to pay for a treatment. We called this type of guest a "chronic complainer." These people milked the system for free services. I breathed a sigh of relief. *At least she can be bought.* Gabrielle and I shared a knowing glance. "We don't need to tell Yvonne about this little incident. I'll take care of everything."

Gabrielle nodded. "Okay, mi amor. I'll go get the tea."

I turned my attention back to the soaked soccer mom. "Would you enjoy a full day package, ma'am?" She didn't look up, but stopped crying. "For you and a friend?"

"That sounds reasonable."

****

When Gabrielle returned, I headed to the secret meeting place to gather my thoughts. *Did that really happen or was it all a hallucination? How can I make lemons out of lemonade? Think, bitch, think. What is*

Yvonne's weakness? A divine voice said, "She can't handle emotions—hers, or yours." I learned in one of my psych classes that reciting something mundane like the alphabet can activate ideas. I paced back and forth singing, "A, B, C, D, E, F, G…" *If I stage a breakdown, she'll give me what I want. Eureka!*

I ran over to the office, jumped into my chair and said to Yvonne, "So Anne just walked."

"What?" Yvonne stopped typing. I couldn't help but notice her nails were beautifully manicured in coral pink.

"She quit."

"Well, we are probably better off without her. She was a bit passive aggressive, was she not?" Yvonne went back to her feverish typing.

Ya think? "So," I said, "I was wondering if—"

"What did you find out about that gift card?"

"Nothing yet. Yvonne, I'm trying to tell you Anne quit, she didn't give notice and she needs to be replaced immediately."

"Oh, I see. I'll set up some interviews for next week. Did you read the email from Mr. Greene?"

I ignored her question. "If we interview candidates next week, they'll have to give notice at their current job, then I'll have to train them. It could be *a month* before I can put them on the schedule." I furrowed my brow in an attempt to look broken down. "I need someone to start tomorrow. I'm too burnt out to keep picking up the slack at the front desk!" I tried to make my lip quiver, but realized Yvonne's glasses were on top of her head. *Shit!* She couldn't even see the dramatic nuances I was incorporating into my performance. *This isn't working.*

"What would you have me do instead of scheduling interviews?"

"Maybe we can give Margaret McCarthy a chance."

"Who?"

"You know the redheaded woman." Crickets. "She interviewed here a few weeks ago."

"Her again? As I told you before, she is not the right fit for my spa."

"Maybe she doesn't interview well but she's actually a great worker. I will train her personally to make sure she *becomes* the right fit."

Yvonne softened her gaze. "I know work has been challenging for you lately with these staffing issues, and I could tell you found this woman charming, but her personality does not fit our image. Certain things I cannot compromise on. End of story. Now get to work on that investigation."

I nodded without responding, turned on my computer, clenched my jaw and squinted at the screen. *She doesn't give a shit about me or anyone else.* I opened up the email from Michael Greene, hoping I could figure out what had happened, but our gift card program was a disorganized nightmare. The software was full of glitches. Sometimes serial numbers disappeared or names turned into cuneiform. We were forced to keep hard copies of all the transactions in a filing cabinet. They were allegedly in alphabetical order, but a few weeks earlier I discovered some of them were filed by first name.

The only information Mr. Green offered in his email was a serial number. I frantically searched it on the system. *Nothing.* In a sea of thousands of receipts, I would surely drown. *And who would file paperwork after they stole a gift card?* I didn't have a name to look up anyway. *If I can't solve this crime, Yvonne might begin to suspect ME.* At times I hated my job, but I still needed the work. New York was expensive and I had a mortgage to pay. There was only one thing left to do until I could decide on a game plan—pray.

****

The next week, June asked me to meet with her, Diana and Gabrielle. After the spa closed that night, the four of us gathered in the secret meeting place.

"She has to go, Thomas," June began.

"Who?"

"Princess Shane."

"I thought this was a going to be a discussion, not an ambush. Do you have any idea what you're asking me? First of all, we can't be *two* people short at the desk. I can barely cover the gaps as it is!"

"I will work overtime—at no extra charge," Gabrielle offered.

I chuckled uncomfortably and massaged my temples with my palms. "That's a lovely offer, but also illegal. And remember, Yvonne hired her, she's her friend's daughter, and she hasn't done anything to warrant getting fired."

"Bullshit!" Diana pointed her finger. "She orders the locker room attendants around like servants."

June added, "And she walks around the spa with her Birkin like she owns the place."

"What am I supposed to do," I asked, "make her sign a DAF for purse-walking?"

Gabrielle adjusted the purple orchid behind her ear. "Maybe you can give her a DAF for trunacy?"

"Trunacy?" I said.

"Yes, for calling out sick over the weekend."

"Oh, *truancy*. Shane always covers her bases. She emailed me a doctor's note."

"We all know she had that thing at the country club," Diana said.

"It doesn't matter," I told them. "The point is moot. Did you guys even try to give her another chance, like we talked about?"

"Oh, yeah," June said. "Me and Gabrielle had lunch with her and she was all up in our grills asking us these weird questions."

"Maybe she was trying to make friends," I offered.

"Well she has a strange way of doing that," June said.

"Shane told me I was from another planet," Gabrielle tried to explain.

"What?" I asked.

"She asked me where I was from and I told her I was a citizen of the world."

June said, "And Shane goes 'what world?'"

"That bitch!" Gabrielle yelled and slapped her hand over her mouth.

I attempted to reason with them. "Gabrielle, I understand why your feelings were hurt, but Shane was trying to reach out to you, with what limited social skills she has."

"Limited social skills?" June scoffed. "Get this. She asked me where I lived and I told her Spanish Harlem. Then she was like, 'Oh my God,'" June imitated a snotty white girl's voice. "'Has a stray bullet ever gone through your window?'"

Gabrielle said, "And when June told her 'No,' Shane called her a dyke!" Diana gasped and almost choked on her gum.

"What?!" I shouted.

"Gabrielle, that's *not* what happened," June said.

"She might as well have," Gabrielle yelled. "The puta desgraciada!"

"After I told Shane there were no stray bullets in my 'hood, she asked me if anyone ever called me a 'dyke' on the street."

"She had no right to use that word!" Gabrielle screamed.

"She's got a point, Thomas," June said. "Maybe we can get her for discrimination."

My plan completely backfired, I thought. *Time for a reaffirming speech.* "I'm sorry she said those things and I agree with you 100%, but in order to fire someone for discrimination, we have to build a case against them. I'll have a coaching session with her when she gets back and give her a DAF, but that's only the first step." Frustration was etched all over their faces. "I want you girls to know how grateful I am to have you. And what upsets me most about this situation isn't working overtime at the desk, it's the effect it is having on our core team. You guys have been with me since the beginning and I appreciate your loyalty, as much as your friendship. I hope one day soon we'll return to a peaceful work environment. So let's stick together and I will do everything in my power to make that happen."

"Bravo!" Gabrielle shouted. "I feel better already. Sometimes it just helps to be heard. Let's do a group hug." We all went in for the hug, but June only stayed in the huddle for a millisecond.

"The saga continues," June said, opening the fire door and holding it for the others.

"Hasta mañana." Diana grabbed her Kate Spade.

"Meeting adjunct!" Gabrielle exclaimed.

****

Shane conveniently returned to work, after her alleged sickness, on the day her guest came in for treatments. She, June, Gabrielle and I (Diana was off) gathered in our office for the afternoon briefing, my favorite part of the day.

"Alright, everyone," I said. Shane and Gabrielle swiveled their office chairs away from the phones and faced the bulletin board. June leaned against the door jamb so she could keep an eye on the front desk. She readjusted two large bronze clips that were keeping her hair up. "We have a few VIPs today," I said, reading from the printed copy of the briefing on the bulletin board. The poster I had made with everyone's baby pics caught my eye. There was a big "X" over Anne's portrait. "You guys," I stymied my laughter, "who did that?" All three of them looked back at me with blank stares and pursed lips. I took the picture down.

"It's not like she's coming back for it," June said.

"Clearly," I replied. "Anyway, Mrs. Jones's group will be having treatments at 5 o'clock."

"Oh no," June put her hand on her forehead, "not Mrs. B."

"Actually, I should have been more specific. Mrs. Jones will be *sending in* a group today. She won't be here herself."

"Praise be to Jesus!" June threw her hand up.

"We still need to give them the best service ever, so they don't report anything negative back to her."

"But of course," Gabrielle said.

I continued, "And Shane's cousin Vivien is currently enjoying treatments with us." Shane let out a nearly inaudible squeal. *Diana would've rolled her eyes.* "It's her birthday and we've ordered a complimentary cake, so be on the lookout for that. The Five Star rule of the week is about wearing professional make-up. June does an excellent job with this. Would you mind modeling for us?"

"Wait," she said. "Let me put on some more lip gloss." She reached into her pocket, cocked her bottom lip to the side, smeared on a fresh pink coat, puckered and smiled.

"Gorge," I said. "It accentuates your accoutrements, but it's not too heavy. Okay, we'll be rolling out the new four-handed-massage very soon. June, do you have the paperwork?"

"Yes, ma'am! Er, sir." I shot her a look, but smiled. "Extra, Extra, read all about it!" June handed out the Xerox copies, then returned to her station by the door.

"Study up, everyone. This treatment is going to be a tough sell because of its high price tag," I said. "Two therapists will be working on one client at a time so we'll have to pay twice as much in labor costs and guess who will be footing the bill?"

"The guests!" Shane proclaimed.

Is she on something today? "Correct, Shane." *Diana would've rolled her eyes.* "Our featured treatment of the week is The Age Rewinding Facial or as I like to call it, The Youth Inducing Skin Job." The girls giggled. "It's wildly exfoliating, full of retinols and shit like that. Meeting adjourned." I looked over at Gabrielle, who whispered "meeting adjourned" under her breath several times.

Shane bolted to the front desk. *She never does that.*

June pulled me aside. "When are you going to talk to Shane?"

"It's more of an 'end of the day' kind of chat," I said.

"Why?"

"Do you wanna work with her all night *after* I tell her someone reported her for using discriminatory language?"

"Good point."

"Don't worry, it's at the top of my list."

We parted ways, me into the reception area, June further into the office. I hustled toward the glass doors.

"We seem to be running low on spa brochures," Shane said, sounding like a teenager on prom night. "Can you bring me some more?"

"Sure." I turned and saw her swiffering the front desk. Sunlight filtered through the windows while tiny specks of dust danced around the crystal staircase in swirls. Shane flittered around, humming to herself like a Disney princess, perfectly playing the role usually reserved for Yvonne: Von Spa's Queen Bee. I knew it was a limited engagement. *There can only be one reason for this Oscar-worthy performance: Shane can't wait to show off to Vivien.*

Gabrielle poked her head out of the concierge office. "Thomas, my love, Yvonne just called. She said you must go see her right away. It's an emergency."

"I'm already halfway there." I left so quickly I imagined hairpins flying behind me, à la Witch Hazel from Looney Toons. My palms began to sweat when I crossed the hall. I lingered in the doorway to give Yvonne the impression I couldn't stay long, because I didn't want to. She took off her black double-breasted jacket and pulled at a colorful Versace scarf like it had been strangling her.

"What's up?" I asked.

She turned to face me. "Close the door and have a seat," she replied.

Oh my God. This is bad. What did I do? She's angry with ME!

"As you know I have been very upset about the stolen gift card so I have stayed in close contact with our accountant." My heart pounded. I was in full "fight or flight" mode. "Today he has

91

informed me of a new discovery. Only one person could have created a gift card without securing payment, someone who could override the system because they had the master access training." *Holy shit!* "The sole individual who took that course here was you!" She pierced me with an unflinching stare.

My stomach dropped to the floor. I opened my mouth to speak, but had to choke out the words. "Yvonne, I-I would never. You can trust me—"

"I thought I could, but I wondered why you were dragging your feet on this matter. What other explanation is there? You cannot argue with facts, Thomas." She maintained her glare.

I can't believe this. "Give me until the end of the day," I said. "I swear I'll figure out what happened. It's just been incredibly challenging since we started using this gift card system."

"Very well. You have until 10 o'clock, but that is all you have, and do not attempt to deceive me or you will never work in the spa industry again." She swung her chair away from me.

I couldn't get out of there fast enough. I felt like a misunderstood child being scolded by my mother who didn't believe I was innocent. I hurried back to the concierge office, where I found Gabrielle on the phone.

"Thank you and have a peaceful day," she said and hung up.

Perfect timing. I wrote down the digits of the stolen gift card on a piece of paper. "Does this number look familiar?"

"I'm sorry my love, but it doesn't ring bells. I have sold so many."

"It's alright. It was worth a shot."

The tan filing cabinet loomed in front of me like a skyscraper. I knew what needed to be done. The ominous whoosh of the drawer opening evoked the sound of an executioner's sword. There were

92

thousands of hard copies inside. *I'll have to go through every one to find the rogue gift card.* I began my quest, giving success a .05% chance. There was only one hope: that Gabrielle had made one of her terribly creative errors. For the first time, I prayed she had.

****

By the time I came to the last receipt, seven hours later, I looked like I'd been attacked by an office poltergeist. Paper cuts covered my hands and my fingertips were stained with ink. I never found a record of the stolen gift card. My empty stomach grumbled and I could barely focus my tired eyes. Feeling completely spent actually made it easier to accept my fate—*it's the last day I'll spend at the spa.*

I made my way to the front desk, reminiscing along the way. *Nighttime always felt so magical here.* I gazed out the enormous picture window next to the concierge office. The city glistened below me. Dim light from the chandeliers illuminated the room and the candelabras next to the couches took me back in time, reminding me of how excited I was when Von Spa first opened. I could hear people singing "Happy Birthday" from the Tea Room at the top of the famous staircase. *This isn't Five Star behavior—people are having massages. It doesn't matter,* I told myself. *You won't be calling the shots anymore.*

Yvonne strolled through the eighth floor lobby, glancing at her Blackberry, heading toward our office. She usually left hours before we closed. *Message received,* I thought. *You're still here, ready to fire me if I can't prove my innocence.* I scoffed under my breath, "Why don't you go into your den and sharpen your claws?"

Gabrielle glided up next to me. "What's wrong, mon chéri? Are you tired from cleaning out the filing cabinet?"

93

"Yeah, that's it. I'm just tired." I didn't feel like telling her the truth. "But I want you to know how much I've enjoyed working with you over these past few years."

"You're not leaving us, are you?" she cried out. We both knew she wouldn't last very long without me covering for her. *What a beautiful symbiotic relationship we shared.* When I looked at myself through Gabrielle's rose colored glasses, I liked my own reflection. *God, I'll miss her.*

"I'm afraid I am."

"Oh, no!" she shrieked. "Please don't go! What would we do without you?" Tears gathered in her eyes, but the sound of footsteps on the staircase snapped us back into Five Star mode. A group from Marie Claire magazine had just finished relaxing and they were ready to leave. I went through the motions, using the script I had grown to hate: "Did you enjoy your treatment(s)? For your convenience we have included an 18% gratuity. How would you like to settle your account?"

I realized how much I would miss saying those words while I worked beside my fantastic friends—June, Diana and of course, Gabrielle. I wallowed in full dramatic self-pity and nostalgia. My "tragic romantic" came out of repression.

The women finally left and Gabrielle burst into tears, hugging me tightly. I began to well up myself, but swallowed my feelings when I saw Shane's cousin approach the desk. Gabrielle ran to the office, hiding her sobs. I couldn't help but notice how wealthy Vivien looked: her perfect olive complexion; her clear grey eyes; her light brown bob, which boasted a loose finger wave. Decked out in a silver mesh mini-dress, Vivien had landed the part of the chic post-modern flapper. She wore matching stilettos, topped off with rhinestone bows. Shiny eye shadow—the color of a starlit sky—and black-red lips, seemed virtually air-brushed onto her face. Vivien was off to her birthday celebration after spending the whole day at the spa. I wondered, *Does she know what it's like to worry about making ends meet?*

"How were your treatments?" I asked.

"Wonderful, thank you," she said in a spa daze induced by hours of pampering. Vivien gave me her credit card and I swiped it mechanically. She was the final guest to leave that day. *Shane's cousin is the last person I will ever check out of The Yvonne Von Courtland Spa. I'll be off script now—permanently!* I handed her back the credit card.

"Oh, I won't be needing that. It's finished."

What? You're at your limit? I looked down. I was so upset I didn't realize she had actually handed me a gift card. I quickly turned it over and saw the number. In my battered hands wasn't just any gift card, but *the stolen* gift card. *Oh my God!* It all made sense. Shane must have received the master access training at Applebee's and activated the card without paying. *Now maybe I can save myself and get rid of Shane in one fell swoop!*

"Thanks so much for coming, Vivien. It was lovely to meet you. You are a delight! Please take some free gifts." I handed her fistfuls of samples.

"Oh, thank you," she said, surprised by my reaction.

"Let me help you with your coat." I ran over and retrieved her white fake-fur from the closet. "Here you go." She put her arms through the sleeves and I patted her on the shoulders with glee. "Thank you and please come again." Vivien juggled her purse and gifts while I shooed her out the door.

I can't wait to tell Yvonne! Such a feeling of exuberance had come over me, it crushed the anger I felt toward her. I was like Norma Desmond at the end of "Sunset Boulevard," minus the crazy.

Yvonne sat at her desk, staring into space. I slid in the door. My hands shook with nervous excitement. *Oh the drama. Dive right in!* "I found the stolen gift card. Shane activated it without paying and gave it to her cousin, who redeemed it today. Here is the card along with the receipt for you." I handed them over. The paper quivered. *What's she gonna say?* The evidence seemed irrefutable, yet I'd never seen Yvonne admit to being wrong. *Oh the suspense!* I waited for her response and stewed about Princess Shane. *That entitled little brat. She thought she was better and smarter than all of us. I bet she felt like she deserved that gift card. Shane wasn't just showing off today, she was acting like a child getting away with stealing a cookie. But she didn't. I caught her!* Yvonne was still looking at her computer and examining the evidence. *Hurry up. I have important business to attend to!*

"The gift card number matches the accountant's email." *Vindication.* "Good work. See you tomorrow."

That's it? I gave Yvonne a half-mast smile. *Not a very gratifying apology,* I thought. In fact, it wasn't an apology at all. *Oh well, I know exactly what will make me feel better.* I skipped over to the concierge office. An older woman in a pink Chanel suit, whose wheelchair was parked in the corridor, caught me frolicking. Without missing a step, I offered her a salute and let her imagination run wild. *She must think I love working here.*

I found Gabrielle sitting by the phones, wringing her hands while she watched the printer spit out the closing reports. *I hope she's ready to do some overtime.* Gabrielle finally noticed me smiling in the doorway and looked at me with tears in her big brown giraffe eyes.

"I wanted to let you know..." I paused for dramatic effect, "I'm not going anywhere."

"Bello! Thanks God!" Gabrielle jumped up and threw her long skinny arms around my shoulders, nearly tackling me in the process. She kissed my cheek repeatedly, pecking away like a little bird. "What happened? Oh never mind, just don't ever do that to me again. My heart can't take it. We love you too much here. Don't ever leave us!"

I patted her on the back. "And I'm pretty sure Shane will be the one packing her bags, instead."

"Bravo!" Gabrielle gave me a high five.

My internal movie reel went from black and white to Technicolor. *Maybe this job isn't so bad after all.*

****

The next day I arrived at work to find two enormous bouquets in our office, but no Yvonne. *It smells like someone Febreezed the shit out of this place.* I walked over to her desk and reached for the note which accompanied a dozen long stem white lilies in an elegant glass vase. My hand froze mid-air. *Better not. Don't wanna get caught snooping.* A huge arrangement of red gerbera daisies in a bright orange jar blocked my computer. I grabbed the envelope, relishing the anticipation. I pulled the card out slowly to further delay my gratification.

Dear Thomas,

I left early today, due to a family emergency. I will be out of the office for the remainder of the day, so please accept these flowers as a token of my gratitude. Thank you for your diligence in resolving the issue with the stolen gift card. I apologize that I did not trust you—it's something I'm working on.

I am very grateful for all the hard work you have put into making my spa a success and I do not want to increase your stress level now that you are two people short at the desk.

Maybe you can ask Margaret McCarthy, the woman who worked at Mena's spa, if she is still available. See you tomorrow.

Yvonne

My brain almost short-circuited. *Margaret! Joy! Rapture! Comedy! I hope she still wants to work here.*

Then I ruminated about Yvonne. The note actually served both of us pretty well. *This written apology smoothes things over so Yvonne won't have to say "I'm sorry" out loud. And thank God she's finally working on her issues.* I admired her for that. There was another thing I really loved about the message she left for me. Yvonne had told me something priceless. Every employee dreams of hearing these words from their boss: I won't be back until tomorrow! It was nice to finally feel appreciated, too. I grabbed the handwritten note attached to the fragrant lilies on her desk. *Now I can enjoy my snooping.*

Dear Yvonne,

I'm sorry about the gift card. I know that what I did was wrong. I'll pay you back every penny. Please give me a second chance. It's been such an honor working at your spa. There's no doubt it ranks as the best spa in the country, if not the world. I'll do everything I can to regain your trust. If you hire me back, I will not disappoint you. This would mean so much, not only to me, but also to my mother. She was very proud that I was working for you. Thanks for your time and consideration regarding this matter.

Apologetically Yours,

Shane

Jesus, Mary and Joseph! What I loved about *this* note was the fact it contained not only an apology, but a confession. If Yvonne had any lingering suspicion I'd orchestrated the resolution to "Gift Cardgate," Shane's own words were evidence to the contrary. Yvonne could even do a handwriting comparison with Shane's notebook. *She probably already did.*

I sat down and put my head on my desk for a few seconds. *What an insane week.* I knew when I finally got a day off, I'd be spending it in front of the television recovering from exhaustion. I checked my iPhone and saw I had a voicemail from Anthony. He said in a little-old-lady voice, "Hello, is anybody there? Does this thing actually work? If it does, call me back, bitch! Miss you, love you, bye-eeee!" *I'll have to try him tomorrow.*

I fired up the computer to check my email for any pressing matters. I knew I wouldn't do much else; it was one of those days I decided to take an "at work vacation." Only one email demanded action. It was from Yvonne.

Hi Thomas,

I hope you enjoy the flowers. You can have the other bouquet, or shall I say "manipulative gift," as well. Please take them home so as not to inflame my allergies. I am sure you know by now that Shane is no longer with us. While I am not going to press charges, I have informed security not to let her in the building. Since she was escorted out, some of the guards are already abreast of the situation, but there is a picture of her posted at the main entrance to prevent any oversight. I do not want her showing up, begging for another chance. Since you have already read Shane's note...

Holy shit! I gasped. *Does Yvonne know me that well or is she watching me on a live web feed from a spy camera?* I looked above and around, but didn't see anything.

...please file it with all of our important documents. That way, if she chooses to sue us for wrongful termination, we can use the letter as evidence against her.

Damn. She might be working on her trust issues, but not with Shane. She was one of "Yvonne's Most Wanted" with a mug shot and everything. What I liked best about *this* email was the part about using the apology note to prevent litigation. *Yvonne is such a badass.*

The email finished with a bang.

I have one more important task for you, but I am sure you will find it enjoyable. The therapists have completed their training for the new four-handed massage. Please schedule two therapists for each spa concierge so they may practice. You will need to allocate two-hour time blocks for this one hour forty-five minute treatment. Diana, June and Gabrielle should experience receiving the service so they can recommend it to guests. (With a $1200 price tag, even our wealthiest clients may need some convincing.) The concierges must stay after work or come in on one of their days off. We do not want to affect service at the desk. Be sure to schedule yourself as well.

Thank you once again.

Yvonne

The part I liked about *this* final request was the free, two hour, four-handed massages! I couldn't wait to tell the others. I was in the mood to socialize anyway, so I walked over to the reception area where Gabrielle, Diana and June were all helping guests with checkout, products and gift cards. I got three smiles when I entered the room. In Shane's noticeable absence, I sensed the dawn of a Golden Age at the spa. *I hope Margaret is still available to add to the fun.*

The phone rang in the concierge office but the girls were too busy to answer. *I'm not picking it up either. We need a break.* Normally I would

100

never let a call go to voicemail during business hours because of the Five Star Rule, but it was a special occasion. *It's a day to celebrate.* Princess Shane was no more. From that day forward we would call her "Shane-Who-Got-Fired-for-Stealing."

The girls finished at the desk and crowded into our little office at the same time. June stood guard at the door to check for incoming guests. Gabrielle and Diana bombarded me with their eyes, begging me to confirm their suspicions, without making a sound. *I have to choose my words carefully. It's not professional to gossip with the staff.* As my Army dad would say, I "addressed the troops."

"All right ladies. The details will emerge later, but Shane is officially no longer with us. Hip, hip…"

"Hooray!" June, Diana and I shouted in unison. Gabrielle watched us, perplexed.

"I also wanna let you know if all goes well, you won't be putting in too much overtime because we are hiring a replacement immediately. Hip, hip…"

"Hooray!" we cheered, this time *with* Gabrielle. *A cunning linguist,* I thought.

"And finally, free treatments for everyone! Hip, hip…"

"Hooray!"

"Seriously, though?" Diana asked. June and Gabrielle leaned in.

"Seriously. And these aren't just any treatments; they are the new four-handed, two hour massages." The girls squealed with joy. *We're getting too loud.* "In your spa voices, ladies, hip, hip…"

"Hooray," we whispered, our fists halfway up in the air to accommodate our lowered voices.

"How wonderful," Gabrielle said. "Thank you most sincere—"

"Incoming. Multiples," June interrupted. Several people were approaching the front desk. June held out her hand formally, allowing the straight girls to go first. All three of them sported gorgeous, beaming, white grins.

That was fun. I stayed in the concierge office, basking in the afterglow. The poster with the baby pictures caught my eye. Little Shane smiled back at me, holding a pink balloon, wearing her frilly, over-the-top outfit. Someone had written a speech bubble coming out of her mouth.

It said, "Me go bye-bye!"

Chapter 7

Margaret:

Bang! Bang!

"Waa! Waaa! Waaaa!!"

Dear Lord. I had agreed to watch JoAnn's kids; not my dream job, but I needed the cash. The older boys were already sleeping but the baby would not stop crying. I tried to reason with him, "Do you wanna go beddy-by?" I asked, thinking it would be the human equivalent of shaking a leash. He continued screaming. "Do you want to go for a walk?" *Does this baby speak English? Maybe I should call a real sitter and take a loss.*

"Waaaaa, waaaa, waaaa!!!"

"Did you ever hear the expression 'cry yourself to sleep'?" I asked him. Personally, I was already exhausted by the time I'd gotten to JoAnn's house. It was definitely over the river and through the woods. I felt like I'd taken planes, trains and automobiles to get there. *What is it about the New Jersey suburbs that steals all my former city slicker girlfriends?* I wondered. *Is it the outlet malls? The easy access to IKEA? The dream of having The Real Housewives as neighbors?*

"Waaaaa, waaaa, waaaa!!!" *Where is the Suppernanny when you need her?*

I'd read somewhere if you bundle a baby, while making loud shushing noises in their ears, it makes them feel like they're in the womb. This supposedly shuts them up. I swaddled away. "Shhh! Shhhhh! Shhhhh!" Silence. The baby stopped crying. I gave him a little smile. He looked at me like he'd been tricked. I practically heard him say, "Oh, yeah? You think I'm that stupid? Take this! "WAAAA!!!"

My cell rang. *Where the hell is it?* I put the baby down on the couch, quickly creating a fortress around him with pillows so he wouldn't roll off. I dug behind the cushions, but my phone wasn't there. *Maybe it fell out of my cleavage when I picked up the poopy diaper that missed the Genie.* Something told me if I rubbed it, I still wouldn't get three wishes. *Oh shit—literally.* I flipped the lid and I winced from the pungent aroma of dirty diapers mixed with air freshener. *That's what I get for hurling a crap filled missile across the room.* I couldn't bring myself to reach inside so checked behind the Genie first. *There it is. Thank God!* I picked up hoping the call hadn't gone to voicemail. "Hello," I said with a lilt in my voice since I hadn't checked the number. *It could be my long lost recently divorced boyfriend who decided I was the one who got away.*

"Hi, it's Thomas Haven." *There is a God! Or maybe he still just wants to be friends.* "I was wondering if you found another job."

Is this the world's worst courtesy call? "Yes." I wanted to save face. "I'm actually at work as we speak."

"Oh, that's too bad because I'm calling to offer you a position at the front desk."

"No! I'm available. Hey, here comes my boss. I quit! There, now I'm free. When do I start?" I looked up to the Heavens thanking God I'd never have to become a full time nanny, constantly blockading children with pillows and warring with diaper containers.

"Did you really just quit your job? Are you sure you don't have to give notice?"

"It's only temp work. I was joking. My boss isn't really here."

"Oh, okay." He chuckled.

"So, today is my first and last day."

"Great! Can you start on Friday?"

"YES!" *Take it down a notch,* I thought.

"How's 1 o'clock?" he asked.

"One is wonderful." *I can sleep in! This guy is speaking my language.*

"Cool. I'm looking forward to hanging out. To be honest, I've been pulling for you."

"Thanks. You, too," I said.

"What?"

"I mean, I'm looking forward to working with you, too. Not that I wouldn't pull for you or push or whatever you want. See you Friday. Gotta, go! Love you. Bye," I stammered. *Did I just say, "Love you?"* I put my hand over my eyes. Thomas was giggling on the other end of the phone. I breathed a sigh of relief. *He sounds like a good audience already.*

"Bye, Margaret."

I looked over at the baby, who was cooing and sucking his feet. He must've liked the fort. I smiled and sang in a baby Gaga voice (to the tune of "Born This Way"), "Maybe being funny pays!"

****

105

I was so nervous approaching Von Spa on my first day, I worried I might pass out and become "spa road kill" before I even made it inside. When I rubbed a little lint off my jacket, I could actually see my heart pounding. *I can't breathe,* I thought, as I loosened the chunky, bejeweled black necklace that was strangling me. I regretted not purchasing some Depends. *An adult undergarment would've been a total confidence booster.* I tried to stay centered. *Just concentrate on controlling your bodily functions and keeping your secret until the end of the day—then you might stand a chance.* I reached into my purse and put on another coat of lipstick.

As the glass doors opened, I detected a hint of lavender in the air. The reception area's gold walls made me a little claustrophobic; I felt like I might get trapped in Yvonne's genie bottle or, worse yet, ejected immediately. One wish, however, had already come true: There was no sign of her. Thomas was standing alone with his head down, working on the computer. I exhaled, relieved.

He'd been in the exact same position when I saw him on a re-run of "Queer Eye for the Straight Guy" two weeks ago. The cast had visited Von Spa with a client. *This is definitely a good sign from God, or Jesus or at least the Holy Spirit.*

Thomas lifted his head. He wore a chic black uniform with frog closures and a Chinese collar. His exotic eyes, the exact same color as iced tea, lit up when he saw me. "Hi Margaret. Welcome back. I'm really happy you're here." The red curtains were drawn that day, so the soft lighting from the blown glass chandeliers illuminated his lovely skin and full pink pout.

"Thank you. I'm happy to be here."

"And I like your pale lip/smokey eye combo," he said with an ultra-white toothed smile. "It goes great with your red hair."

"Oh, thanks. I always say make-up is a girl's best friend."

"And some boys, too," he replied. "Let's find you a uniform."

"A uniform?" I was so packed into my "goal weight" size twelve black pantsuit that if there were a superhero for undergarments, I'd be known as Wonder-Bra Woman. With the amount of wires and corsetry I had on, I could repel bullets and set off metal detectors ten miles away. I feared any wrong move would cause an explosion. *What if I lift up my arm for a measurement, and I blind Thomas—on my first day? Then I'll never be an esthetician here!*

"Who's going to fit me?" I flashed back to getting weighed in gym class.

"I am. Yvonne assumes every gay person likes to do some sort of work involving fashion. I guess she watches a lot of 'Project Runway.'" I giggled. *This Thomas is adorable.* "In my case she's actually right. It's probably why she chose me to work with Vera Wang when she designed our new uniforms."

Wow. Von Spa might be a little out of my league. I didn't know what to say, so I prayed as Thomas motioned for me to follow him. *Are you there God? It's me, Margaret. Please retroactively give Vera Wang the good sense to make plus-size uniforms.*

"Let's go in the back," Thomas said. "I'm the only one here at the moment, so I'll have to watch for guests while we fit you." We headed into the tiny office behind the front desk. It was the polar opposite of the gorgeous reception area, with ugly beige filing cabinets, crowded bulletin boards and fluorescent lighting. He pulled out a measuring tape and gingerly took my stats, smiling kindly the whole time. Something told me Thomas knew how it felt to be ostracized for being different. I was sure he wouldn't say anything rude, even if he got to the end of the measuring tape and it read "To be continued."

"Okay. You're all set. Let me go see what we have in stock."

"If you can't find anything in my size, I have a tent and awning company on speed dial."

"Oh Margaret. You do know Marilyn Monroe was a size sixteen, right? And she was the biggest sex symbol in the world." I smiled at him and just like that, our friendship began to blossom. "Could you watch the desk while I go grab your uniform? I'll be back in thirty seconds."

"Um, okay." I couldn't stop my eyes from widening.

"Don't worry. The therapists have already started their one o'clock appointments so we aren't expecting anyone. If a guest does come in, you can offer them a bottle of water and say, 'Someone will be with you in a moment.'"

"No problem. I give good desk!"

Thomas chuckled and walked out the door. As I stood in the reception area, my heart began to race while serene music echoed in the background, mocking my pain. *I've barely taken my coat off and suddenly I'm manning the front desk all alone. What in the name of lack-of-training have I gotten myself into? And where the hell are my new co-workers? Thank God I'm only expected to hand out water.* I felt grateful I had experience from volunteering at the New York City Marathon. That vain attempt to meet a guy (runners don't usually stop to chat in the middle of a race) was finally paying off.

Oh shit! I thought as a bevy of extremely tall blonde goddesses approached the glass doors. Every one of them looked so perfect I couldn't help but imagine they'd been genetically engineered in some secret government experiment. All six women possessed flawless tanned skin and legs up to their necks. I wondered if they were flight attendants because they each wore the same grey business suit jackets—punctuated by an official looking patch—yellow scarves and pencil skirts. *Maybe they're not American! Then it would seem like I know more about the spa than them.* I took a deep breath. *Fake it 'til you make it, Maggs.*

"Good ladies, afternoon. I mean, good afternoon, ladies. Welcome to Von Spa. Will you be enjoying services with us today?" I couldn't believe the first words I uttered on the job, twisted my tongue.

"Ja, we are members of the women's Swedish volleyball team," said the woman with the biggest patch. I assumed she was the captain. "You should be expecting us."

"Oh, okay," I said. *What the fuck? I thought we weren't expecting anyone.*

"We want to get massages," she told me.

"Swedish massages no doubt." I thought a little humor would make me appear less terrified.

"No, we need deep tissue. Our hotel concierge told us your spa is number one in New York City."

"Yes, definitely. If you will wait one moment, someone will be back who will be able to help you, in one minute." I felt like Lucy in the Vitameatavegamin episode. *I don't think that's exactly what Thomas meant for me to say.* "Would you like some water?"

"No, we want massages. Why can't you tell us? Don't you work here?"

Are you there God? It's me, Margaret. "Well actually, I'm only the water girl," I said in my best spa voice, holding up a Pellegrino and jiggling it. "Are you sure I can't tempt you?" *What a nightmare! I arrived less than ten minutes ago and I'm already dealing with an angry customer.* Beads of sweat formed on my upper lip, but I knew I couldn't get flustered. This always added another layer of stress to working at a spa; if you didn't act calm at all times, you could be accused of ruining the atmosphere.

The blonde supermodel glared at me and just as she was about to get all up in my face, Thomas swooped in. "Welcome Ladies. I can book three deep tissue massages at one-thirty and three massages at two o'clock. While you are waiting for your massage to begin or waiting afterwards for your teammates' massages to end, you are welcome to use the Radiant Heat Area free of charge. Now I need to get your names so you can begin relaxing."

Thomas effortlessly entered their information into the computer, printed out their itineraries, took their sophisticated array of fairly large designer heels and brought them sandals. The way he presented a tray of hot towels for their hands, reminded me of a magic trick reveal. They sipped acai tea, which he served from a silver teapot so long and narrow, it looked like it belonged to the Mad Hatter. I watched in awe as he held these women under his spell. When they disappeared into the spa, I said, "Wow! You really lassoed those little hussies."

"It's not my first time at the rodeo, kid. Yvonne taught me not to take the client's anger personally."

"That's something I'll have to work on."

"I apologize they got here so early. Maybe I shouldn't have left you by yourself, but I did find you a uniform." He held up the monstrosity. It looked like a long-sleeved black overcoat that buttoned all the way up to the collar, with plain black sashes crisscrossing in the front. The thing was so stiff, the words 'tuxedo straight jacket' came to mind.

"It's not very feminine is it?"

"It's like a suit married a sari," he said.

"It's sorry, all right. And what's this?" I looked closer at the neckline to see a monogrammed name—"Bruce." Not only were they giving me a man's uniform, but what the hell happened to Bruce? I had to face the truth: The girl's top didn't come in my size. Once again, I was relegated to stretchy fabric.

"This one is pre-Vera Wang but it's all we had in stock," he said sheepishly. "I'll order you a new one today."

"No hurry." *I'd wear a garbage bag to keep this job.*

"Why don't you get changed and then I'll train you on the computer."

My heart skipped a beat. I walked into the tiny office and put on the polyester overcoat. At Waterlily, the uniforms were made from the same scratchy fabric because it resists fading. *One more thing that separates us worker bees from the guests.* I looked in the mirror. *This outfit needs help.* I took my flashy necklace, put it on the outside of the uniform and returned to the desk.

"Gorge!" Thomas said when I entered the room. "Work it, own it." I stopped to pose with my hands on my hips. "It looks like you've done some bedazzling. Back in the day, I actually used a Bedazzler to put Swarovski crystals on my costumes."

"*These* are Swarovski crystals! What kind of costumes were you making?" I asked.

"Well, I used to be a drag queen." Thomas promptly turned bright red as the smile disappeared from his face.

"No wonder you were so good at taking measurements." He didn't say anything. "Is everything alright?"

"I'm sorry. No one here knows what I did before I got this job. I can't believe I blurted it out like that."

"Don't worry. I'll never tell a soul. Like my mother would say, 'I'll put it in a safe within a safe.'"

"Thanks. I guess I felt so comfortable with you, that it just slipped out. I always worried if the staff knew, they'd laugh at me."

"Well, from what I've seen, you're very good at what you do. And I promise I won't ever mention your secret past, but to be honest…" I giggled without completing my thought. I wanted to add some drag-inspired drama by keeping him in suspense.

"To be honest, what?" he asked with a crinkled brow and goofy grin.

"I bet you were gorgeous!"

"Oh thanks. I had my moments back in the early '0's."

"Early '0's?"

"You know, from 2000 to 2009. Anyway, I'm an adult now and I have a real job." He tucked a lock of dark, wavy hair behind his ear. "Let's get you comfortable with the system." The Swarovski-like twinkle in Thomas's brown eyes faded under his thick black lashes. *I guess he misses his days as a showgirl.*

"So this is how you check in a guest," he explained, taking control of the computer and demonstrating. "You click on the client's name, scroll through the drop down menu, select 'arrival' and enter the time. Then you copy their treatment information and paste it on the itinerary screen."

"Do you really want to put paste on your computer screen? Isn't that an expensive piece of equipment?"

"Funny, but do you want to try it?"

"Sure," my hand was shaking as I reached for the mouse. *This moment is totally surreal.* I had dreamt of it for so long, but now I felt like a fraud. I looked up at him like a scolded dog. *Oh God!* I couldn't hold it in any longer. I almost passed out when I revealed my embarrassing secret. "I don't know how to use a computer." *There—the truth is finally out in the open.* This handicap made me inherently unqualified and totally incapable of being a spa concierge. I knew I shouldn't have lied on my résumé, and it had been eating me up inside ever since I first interviewed at Von Spa. I'd sold them a phony bill of goods. *Now my first day would be my last!*

"Seriously?" Thomas replied, cocking his head to the side. "How have you managed to avoid them?"

"Fear! I have some sort of phobia." I was beyond mortified. *My granny is more tech-savvy than I am.*

"And how did you function at your other spa jobs?"

"Everything was handwritten. We had appointment books." My lower lip started to quiver.

"So why did you want to work at the front desk?"

God, he's really grilling me. "I needed a job and I really wanted to work here and that was the position you were hiring for." I held back tears. "Guess you won't be needing me then. I'll go take off this polyester dream coat and head home."

"Don't be silly. I didn't hire you for your computer skills, Margaret." Thomas smiled, the twinkle returning to his iced tea-colored eyes. "I hired you for your sense of humor."

"Really? You mean you aren't gonna fire me? Should I just stay the water girl?" I let out a relieved chuckle.

"Of course not. I'll teach you how to use a computer."

And that's what he did. Over the next few weeks, he slowly and patiently taught me everything about technology that I'd been avoiding for the last twenty years. We laughed, I cried, and we became fast friends just like I imagined we would. Thomas was my former-drag-queen-miracle-trainer.

Step one of my plan to become an esthetician at Von Spa had finally been accomplished. I knew if I ingratiated myself to Thomas and overcame my fear of Yvonne, I stood a chance of being promoted. But something was bothering me. The dream I'd had with the wicked women and the Technicolor bathrobe had become a recurring nightmare.

****

A few months later, I felt as comfortable as I was ever going to be doing a job involving computers, entitled people and groveling. I realized that whether the lighting was fluorescent or provided by priceless chandeliers, after a while, a job was just a job, with good moments and all too many tough ones. I barely made it through the holidays without reinventing the words "Christmas bash." My survival strategy included name recognition combined with personality mirroring to make the clients believe I gave a shit. I wanted to quit every time a spa guest yelled at me, which was pretty much on a daily basis, but I still had my secret ambition keeping me there. Besides, working at Von Spa had so much cachet. For the first time, I got rave reviews from people at parties, and my family was totally proud of me.

Thomas had me working 1:00 p.m. to 10:00 p.m. every Thursday through Monday, so we could be on the same schedule. He was my new BFF and we were having a ball getting to know each other. Our brains were wired the same way. Then one blustery January day, he said to me, "Margaret, can I see you in the secret meeting place? Yvonne wants me to talk to you."

In Bruce's ill-fitting uniform, I followed Thomas as negative thoughts percolated in my mind like coffee brewing at Starbucks. *Dear Lord! What can it be? Did some stuck up biyatch—I mean valued guest—complain about me? Did I get caught drinking one of the complimentary smoothies? I only had one; I was starving! Do they have some more men's clothing for me to wear? Maybe they think I should grow a beard. Yvonne rarely acknowledges my existence, but now I'm in trouble. I can't lose this job. It's my new calling card. Jesus this place is exhausting.*

"What's wrong?" I asked, trying not to sound panicked as we entered the stairwell. "Spit it out. Let's get this over with."

"Oh my God. I didn't mean to scare you. It's nothing serious."

"If that's the case, in the future, could you avoid phrases like, 'Yvonne wants me to talk to you' because I go into anaphylactic shock when I hear those words."

"I'm sorry. I should have realized that. I've just been so tired. I'm not thinking straight 'cause she's been working me to death. I'm really only built for a part-time job."

"Me too! What are we doing here, then?" We shared a fatigued, knowing smile. *It's amazing how much we have in common.* The day before, we had talked for hours about our television addictions. We both loved "Sex and the City," "Mad Men," "Ellen," news shows like "20/20," "SNL," "Project Runway" and The Oprah Winfrey Network. But Yvonne was interfering. We were the friendship equivalent of Romeo and Juliet. "What does she want me to know?" I asked.

"You need to wear your hair up like the other girls. A pony tail doesn't count, I looked it up. It's a Five Star requirement. If you don't, it could lower our score."

I inhaled sharply, thoughts once again speeding through me. *But long red hair is my thing. It's my crowning jewel and personal crystal spiral staircase, even though I usually flat iron it. It's bad enough I'm still walking around in an Indian leisure suit without breast darts, and now they want me to look like a dude with man boobs.*

115

"Are you sure? Have you seen me with my hair up?"

"I'm only the messenger."

"I'll look exactly like a Cabbage Patch Kid, but if that's what you want—"

"*I* want you to be happy. This is what Yvonne wants."

"It's okay. I know it's not your fault. Maybe I'll just get bangs."

Thomas gasped. He morphed from my boss, back into a friend. Sometimes I called him my "fross."

"If you wanna stay single," he said, "definitely get the bangs. Guys hate bangs. Bangs are for your girlfriends."

"Really? I'm shocked yet intrigued. What do you mean?"

Thomas twirled a pen in his hand. "Men like long hair; even the hair around a woman's face. Your girlfriends would probably tell you, 'Your bangs look cute.' Some of them might even be secretly happy you won't be stealing as much attention. Guys don't want 'cute' they want 'sexy.' 'Cute' is for little boys and so are bangs." *Holy shit I think he's right. Who is this love guru?* He continued, "Have you ever heard a man compliment a woman on her bangs?"

"I don't remember," I said. "I never noticed."

"It's like that Cher song 'Bang! Bang! My Baby Shot Me Down,' because that's what men will do to you if you get bangs, shoot you down."

"Good to know."

"Think of it as follicle attempted murder. You are nearly killing the hair. Look how long it takes to grow them out again—years."

"It's such a weird word, isn't it? Where did they get the name 'bangs' from anyway?"

116

"I'm not sure. Maybe it's an acronym. It could stand for 'Boys Are Not Gonna Sex' anyone with bangs," he said.

"Ha! But that would be Bangsawb."

"The 'you' of anyone is implied."

Wow. That sounded smart. "But my ex-husband never complained when I got bangs."

Thomas dropped the pen he was twirling. "Whoa, whoa, whoa. What?!" he said. "Ex-*husband*? You were married? I can't believe you never told me that."

"Only for a year. It was an arranged marriage—arranged by desperation and alcohol. Besides, we were young and I needed the wedding money."

"But still! It's kind of a big deal."

"Not really. As my mother used to say, 'The marriage had the staying power of potato salad in the sun.' She also used to say, 'You're not complete until you're married—and then you're finished.'"

"Well I think what you did is genius."

"Really?"

"Yeah! Good job getting *that* out of the way. It's so brutal out there. Now you don't have to be married *and* you don't have to be one of those single girls in NYC still looking for love. It's almost like New York City relationship street creds. You'll always be divorced."

Thomas the love guru had spoken. "Now I think *you* are genius. You're the first person to see the silver lining in my failed marriage. Suddenly I feel so much better about it. Therapy has nothing on you." Thomas beamed at me. "Did I tell you I loved you today?"

"And I love you, too, Margaret McCarthy. If you ever quit, I might have to as well. You actually make this job fun."

"Aw shucks." I blushed.

"But don't tell any of the other girls. I think they're getting jealous that you're my favorite."

"I *am?*"

"I can't answer that. Let's just get back to the desk so they don't suspect we're having a good time."

"Okay, but I have a parting question."

"Hit it!" Thomas said.

"How do you know so much about straight relationships?"

"I think when you're somewhere in the middle of the gender spectrum, you understand both men and women."

"Fascinating. What a gift."

Thomas smiled with his mouth closed. "Now I have I question for you, too. Did your ex-husband ever say anything *good* about your bangs?"

"Not that I remember."

"I rest my case, but if you're dead set on getting them, there's a great wig store on 32nd Street where you can buy some clip-on bangs—just for work. That way there's no commitment."

"Kind of like my marriage."

"Genius!"

Chapter 8

Thomas:

The Shining

I looked out the spa's picture window at the grey February sky, transfixed by the snow falling on Central Park. The building's spires in the distance resembled a winter fairy tale kingdom. Songs from "The Nutcracker" played in my head. Despite this gorgeous scene in front of me, I couldn't wait for the bitter cold to end.

I reached in my pocket to turn off my phone and noticed I had a text from Anthony:

I wanna throw a spontaneous dinner party for you tonight, since we never see you anymore. If you don't come I'll assume I should file a missing person's report, but no pressure. Let me know :-) Luv ya!

We hadn't seen each other in months. *If he's making dinner and I'm the guest of honor, I have to go.* Yvonne popped up behind me and I jumped in surprise.

"Darling," she said, "I'm so excited to share my new idea." *Oh God, what fresh hell do you have in store for us today?* I thought. "Is everyone ready for the amenity launch meeting?"

"Yes, the girls are waiting for us. How was Acapulco?" Her vacation was my *anti*-vacation; thanks to her trip, this was my ninth day in a row.

"It was wonderful!"

I followed her into the concierge office. She took her place at the front of the room next to the coat check closet.

"Welcome everyone…" Yvonne began her speech looking lightly bronzed and extra blonde. Underneath her crisp white shirt, an expensive silver and gold David Yurman necklace sparkled brightly with a pink triangular diamond—an arrow pointing to her breasts. I couldn't help but notice her ageless décolletage.

She's quite the spa Venus today. I glanced around the room. My concierges looked like they'd rather be diving for pig's feet or having an elective root canal. Diana spit her gum into a Kleenex and rolled her bloodshot eyes. *She is definitely hung over,* I thought. June—shifting uncomfortably from leg to leg—stood by the door so she could keep an eye on the front desk. Maggie looked like she was holding in gas, but still managed to plaster a nervous grin on her face. *They must be jealous of Gabrielle,* I thought. It was her day off.

"…and I would like to extend a special welcome to our newest member of the team, Margaret," Yvonne continued. "Would you like to tell us a little about yourself?" *That's weird,* I thought. *Margaret's been here for months—we're all friends at this point.*

"Oh sure," Margaret smiled uncomfortably. "I was raised by wolves." She chuckled. Diana snickered and Yvonne's eyes flared open. "Just a joke there. In truth, I grew up in Scarsdale," Margaret said through clenched teeth, mocking a snotty accent. *Dear God, Maggie,* I thought, *reel it in!* "But I guess you wanna know about my illustrious career. So I used to work as a psych nurse and when the place started rubbing off on me, I quit." I shot her a look. It didn't seem to register. "I've also waited tables and I was a nanny for a while. Never mind about that though. You already know that story."

"Yes, well thank you—" Yvonne said.

Margaret jumped back in. "But my *goal* was to work in the spa industry, even while I slaved away at my last job, taking care of a mean, generous old lady. I'm actually an esthetician, remember? But you were only hiring at the front desk, so here I am."

"Are you telling me you didn't want to be a spa concierge when you applied for the position?" Yvonne asked.

"No, no, no—that's not what I meant. Although you really should let me give you a facial some time. These hands are like butter." Yvonne stared at her blankly. "Anyway," Margaret said, "It's so great to be here. I love it. Bring on the rich entitled women!" Margaret started laughing—alone.

"Thank you once again—for that fascinating information," Yvonne said. Margaret looked down at the floor. Yvonne pressed on, "Let us continue to the business at hand. You all well know we are leaders in the luxury spa industry. Therefore, I am always trying to redefine the word 'luxury' itself. As the owner of this establishment, I am also working to keep our name in the media by creating new tidbits for *Top Spa Magazine* and other elite members of the press. So allow me to introduce Von Spa's latest guest amenity." She reached into the closet and pulled out a contraption with two red, rotating brushes at the base and a plug in the back, like a gay boy.

What the hell is that thing? It looks like a large strange sex toy. Are we going to start pleasuring our clients at the end of each treatment? I smirked to myself. *God knows enough men have asked for it.*

"After our guests exchange their shoes..." *Oh no! Please stop talking. Don't say what I think you're going to say.* "...you simply match the color with the appropriate polish and use this new shoe shiner to buff them to perfection." She gestured to the machine. June's mouth dropped open and Diana's eyes looked frozen in time. Yvonne continued. "Finally, you wrap the footwear in tissue paper, put a signature bow on top and present them to our guests after their treatments. They will be delighted by this unexpected Five Star surprise. It's all theater in the end." She turned to me. "So Thomas, I will leave the details to you and we can roll this out immediately." Yvonne beamed with pride, like she'd just delivered the Gettysburg Address.

"No problem," I said dumbfounded. *Really? Aren't we busy enough?*

The phone rang, breaking the stunned silence. Yvonne looked at Diana and cocked her head. Diana hit the speakerphone. "Thank you for calling The Von Courtland Spa. How may I assist you?"

"Vonnie? Is that you?" A woman slurred. "I need money for a new toaster. This old thing is a piece a shi—"

Yvonne leapt over Diana and hung up the phone. Without missing a beat, she snapped back to her position at the front of the room and asked, "Does anyone have any other questions or concerns?"

This inquiry always amused me. *Hell yes, I do.* I always imagined asking ridiculous things like: *Can anyone on "American Idol" hold a note without putting a "run" in it? Who's the asshole who came up with Daylight Saving Time? The sun is setting at 5:30 these days, plunging the city into darkness. We can spare some light in the summer, shouldn't we reverse it? What if my hairline starts receding Michael Bolton style? Will I be able to afford expensive hair replacement surgery? What about world hunger? Shouldn't we create a charity instead of giving more attention to the rich by shining their shoes? Why aren't drag queens more accepted in mainstream society? We're fun!*

June chimed in to answer Yvonne's real question. "Tootsie is burning sage again, even though the guests and therapists complain about the smell." *Holy shit. I never talked to Tootsie.* June looked right at me.

I can't believe she's throwing me under the bus, I thought. *Better do damage control.* "I'll speak to her," I said in a tone that implied it would be for the second time. *Dear God, June. If you're pissed at Yvonne, don't take it out on me.*

Yvonne grinned. "Well then, I guess the matter is taken care of. I'll check in with you all in a few days to see how the shoe shining is being received before I alert the press. Thank you, everyone," she said, leaving dramatically.

Yvonne's words hung in the air for several seconds while she made her way out of the spa. Then June slammed her notebook on the desk. "And Thomas, *you* can alert the press that I'm quitting!" she yelled. "It's bad enough we have to take people's smelly shoes. Now she wants us to stick our hands in them and shine them. No thanks. I'm Audi 5000!" She stormed out of the office.

"June wait!" I hollered, chasing after her, trying to match her long strides toward the elevator. She was literally out the door, pulling bobby pins from her curly golden locks, freeing them from their upswept prison. "We'll find some sort of solution. Let's just take it one day at a time. You don't have to shine any shoes today. Okay?" She pressed the elevator button repeatedly. "What are you going to without a job?" I pulled out the big guns. "Who's going to take care of Donovan?"

"Fine," she snapped. "You better put an end to this quickly, though. It's *way* too degrading. I won't be shinin' any shoes, masta!" She expertly put her hair up in a few strokes and headed back to the front desk.

What am I gonna do? Maybe I can turn into the shoeshine boy and do them all myself. I made a beeline for the concierge office. Diana was texting madly. Margaret ran up to me.

"About what I said before, I didn't mean it," she stammered. "I'm fine with working at the front desk."

123

"I'm sorry, what?"

"During the meeting, when I said I wanted to be an esthetician and I was only working at the fr—"

"Oh Maggie, don't worry about that. And with the exception of Gabrielle, no one likes working the desk, including me. More importantly how do you feel about the shoe shining?"

"Disgusted and horrified."

"You're not alone, but how am I supposed to tell that to Yvonne?" *This is a nightmare.*

"I dunno, but I do want to give her a facial. If she likes it, maybe I can start filling in when Christie needs coverage, then—"

June poked her head into the office. "Can I get some help out here?"

"Margaret, do you mind going? I need to talk to Diana. I'll ask Yvonne about the facial and I'll fix this shoe shining problem."

"I'm sure you will," Margaret hustled to the desk. *At least someone's got my back.*

I turned to Diana who was texting feverishly. "Diana, you're not supposed to use your phone. I don't really care, but Yvonne would go ballistic."

"It's work related." She sucked some saliva into the back of her candy-filled mouth. There was a thick layer of gold glitter above her eyeliner. *I'll have to talk to you about the make-up rule later.*

"You're texting a guest on your cell?"

"No. It's work related to *me* because I'm texting my friends to look for a new job," Diana said, her New York accent more pronounced than usual. "It's always something around here. Whether it's Shane or Mrs. B or Yvonne—sorry, babe—but I'm over it."

"Did you hear what I told Margaret?"

She looked up at me, her hazel eyes sparkling under the gold shadow. "Um, no," she said, "I was texting."

Sweet Jesus. "Give me until tomorrow, okay? I'll make sure we don't have to shine any shoes. Will you put your phone down?"

"Okay, babe. You have twenty-four hours."

Why can't I just have a normal job? I'm not a queen anymore but I'm still surrounded by drama. My iPhone vibrated. I snuck into the secret meeting place and checked the text:

Are you & Yvonne getting married? If not, you better be coming tonight, especially if you don't want me to file that M.I.A. police report, but no pressure. BIYEEE!

I knew I had to go. *So tired. How am I going to make it to Anthony's and home by midnight?* I'd have to leave work early. June was my only hope. I approached the desk. She stared me down, then turned her attention to a stack of itineraries. *Oh my! She's still pissed.*

"Hey June. Do you have a second?"

"What's up?" She shuffled through the papers.

"I was wondering if you might want to close tonight since you have to be here anyway."

"Gee, I don't know. My back is really tight. I was gonna go home and take a hot bath ASAP. If I hafta close, I'll be here for at *least* five extra minutes. I'm not sure I can wait that long. Unless you have some other solution." She grinned.

"Hmmm." I glanced at the therapist's bookings on the computer. "Tootsie is available. I'll cover the desk if you'd like her to work on your back for an hour."

"Why I couldn't possibly," she said, gliding up the staircase, taking down her hair.

"Thanks, June." I pulled out my phone to text Anthony on the sly:

I'll be there!

I gazed out the window. The sun was setting on the snow-covered park and the streetlamps were starting to glow. Watching the city shimmer into twilight made my eyelids grow heavy. I was excited to see my friends, but there was a giant shadow hanging over me. Tootsie wasn't the only person who got booked that afternoon. Between dinner plans and figuring out how to prevent a mass exodus of spa concierges, I was *double* booked.

$$****$$

I put on my black pea coat, grey scarf and fake-fur aviator hat. Gliding through the revolving door to the street, I braced myself for the cold, but the chilly dry air actually felt refreshing. Outside, the snow on the ground created a calming effect in the city. Cabs rolled along slowly and the sidewalks were fairly empty of pedestrians. It was like New York had taken a spa day. I decided to walk the ten blocks and three avenues to Anthony's place in Hell's Kitchen. *It's good to be in the real world again,* I thought. And the streets looked magical. I passed cozy candlelit restaurants, moody bars with neon signs and little boutiques with fashion forward mannequins in the windows. The soundtrack I played on my iPhone included Portishead, Siouxsie and the Banshees and "Ice Dance" from the "Edward Scissorhands" soundtrack. By the time I listened to "Frostbite" by Delirium, my walk had turned into more of a meditation. When I reached Anthony's building, I felt like I'd just had a massage.

When he buzzed me in, I took off my scarf and trudged up several flights of stairs to his third floor studio apartment. The smell of meatballs wafted down the brick hallway. With a last name like Giovanni, it was no wonder he cooked amazing Italian food. I couldn't wait to binge on whatever he'd come up with.

Anthony opened the door. "Hi stranger!" he said in a high-pitched cartoonish way, his enormous grey eyes beaming. He stepped into the hallway.

"Hi gurl!" I said in a nasal voice like a queen, trying to catch my breath. I hugged his muscular body and rubbed his dark blonde military-style fade. Anthony was the kind of guy all the gay boys liked. He was masculine, funny and cute. And although he was one of the most confident people I'd ever met, Anthony admitted to feeling a little insecure about the hook in his crook. I always told him not to change his nose and mess with a handsome face.

"I have news," he whispered, "but I wanna tell you after Pep and Zhenya leave. Can you stick around?"

"Sure," I said, wildly curious.

"Great!" He grinned from ear to ear. *He's always in a good mood.* I attributed his jovial attitude to the fact that he'd escaped teasing as a child. Unlike many of us, Anthony passed for straight. "Are you hungry?"

"Of corset," I said stealing a line from Frankie Cocktail, a former sister of the cloth—a.k.a a female impersonator. "I'm starving." Seeing Anthony reminded me how great it felt to be loved by a friend.

"Dinner's almost ready. I'm just gonna stay out here and call my mom back. Make yourself at home." He held the front door open for me.

I walked down the long corridor inside Anthony's studio, passing two closets and a bathroom along the way. I entered the main room of his

127

apartment, which boasted a 12-foot ceiling and exposed brick walls, but was barely three hundred square feet. We joked that you could get the salt from the kitchen or the remote from the bedroom without leaving the living room. To my left, glass cabinets hung over a sink, a miniature stove and a refrigerator. To my right was a king-size bed with a navy comforter next to sky high windows. Behind me was a dresser with a 48" flat screen TV on top. Our friend Zhenya sat on the 1980's green couch in front of me.

"Soulnushka! It's been so long," she said in her thick Russian accent, putting her glass of straight vodka on the reclaimed coffee table. "Kiss! Kiss!" she stood up and pecked me on both cheeks. I took off my coat and we sat down together.

Zhenya called herself "Sexy Russian Woman," because she was always in very skimpy, outrageous ensembles. One time she arrived at my birthday party wearing a sequined silver and black Gaultier-inspired dress with an Eiffel Tower running up her cleavage. Zhenya had walked in the door, fluffed up her curly auburn bob and asked me through ruby lips, "Are there any conservative people at the party?" When I said, "No," she said, "Good!" and promptly removed her bolero jacket. The Tower stood between Zhenya's naked breasts.

I drank in her current outfit. While the rest of us were in some variation of jeans and a t-shirt, Zhenya wore pale pink micro fishnets with thigh high suede boots in a beautiful shade of lilac. Her sheer black embroidered dress bloomed with powder-blue and fuchsia flowers. "I love your look tonight," I told her.

"It's just a simple frock." *Thank you,* Zhenya, I thought, *for bringing so much color into the world.*

Peppermint, my gorgeous drag sister, was lying like a Grecian goddess on Anthony's bed, talking on her phone. She sat up, waved at me and mouthed the words, "I'm sorry," tucking one of her long braids behind a silver hooped ear. Pep was a recording artist on the verge of super stardom. Since she was also African-American, people often called her the next RuPaul, but I knew better. RuPaul's public image had a Disney rating of "G," while Peppermint's bombshell persona was more "PG-13." She had several singles out including "Servin' it Up," which was getting heavy airplay on the music program of Logo, the gay cable station. In the video, Pep didn't just work the runway, she worked every inch of her body. She even gave me a cameo.

Seeing her made me miss the days when we got dressed up in drag and hit the town, looking for chasers (guys into girls like us) to make out with. She was too busy networking and I was chained to the spa.

Pep hung up the phone. She joined us on the couch, sandwiching me between her and Zhenya. "Lady!" She squealed, hugging me hard. "How you doin'?"

"I'm exhausted as per usual. The spa is killing me."

"Girl, why don't you just quit? You never have anything good to say about that place."

"I'm open to suggestions if you can think of a 'work-free' way for me to pay my bills."

"Maybe you should open your closet, put on your high-heeled shoes and take to the stage!" Pep shouted, pretending to get up in my face.

"Soulnushka, this is a wonderful idea," Zhenya lightly stroked my arm. "I simply adore you in drag. As a man or a woman you completely captivate me." She uncrossed her legs and stood up. "I'm going to powder my nose. Maybe by the time I come back, you'll be in a skirt."

I let out a breathy laugh.

"Girl, you could grow your hair out, too," Pep said.

129

"That would be awesome, but I can't go from gig to gig, wondering where my next paycheck is coming from, I need to pay my mortgage."

"What you *need* is to be more creative." Pep playfully slapped me on the knee. It stung in more ways than one. "You were so much happier when you were making your own costumes and expressing your female side," she said. "It's kind of like you killed a part of yourself when you stopped doing drag."

"Alright, drama queen. No one killed anybody and I do admit my XXY chromosomes are a little out of balance at the moment—"

"That's right, bitch. You need to dress up or you might go postal and break into a Bebe or something."

"I agree, but I simply don't have the time. I'm an adult now and I've got responsibilities."

"You sound like one of your parents. Ya know, the ones who told you to get a *real* job."

"My parents never said that."

"But all of our parents want us to do some kind of work they can brag to their friends about."

"This *is* a perk of my *current* position."

"It's just like the circus elephant and the stake in the ground," Pep said.

"Okay girl, be careful. Who's the elephant in the room?"

"You are!"

"I knew it, bitch," I laughed.

"So when they're trying to keep the elephant in the ring, they put a stake in the ground attached to a rope and tie it to the elephant's leg.

The elephant quickly figures out how far he/she can go on the leash—"

"Is it a transgendered elephant?"

"Yes, queen."

"Perfect."

"Anyway, after a while the circus people don't even have to tie the elephant up. They just put the stake in the ground."

"Duh-duh-dun!" I said. "And the elephant still doesn't go beyond the original radius."

"Exactly!" Pep exclaimed.

"Learned helplessness."

"What?"

"Did you forget I was a psych major? That's what a shrink calls it."

"So all your life you were taught to be practical and make straight A's so you could get a good job. But for a while, you busted out of prison and did what you were meant to do, something creative."

"And now I'm in a gilded cage again—Von Spa." I paused for a second. "Thanks for the pep talk, Pep," I sighed. "Suddenly, I feel so much better."

"I'm sorry, girl." She put her French tipped hand on mine. "I just hate to see you waste your talents."

"Where did my talent for make-up and drag get me? Into ten grand of credit card debt."

"Is that why you still work at the spa, or did you give in to the pressure?" One of her braids fell across her face.

"What pressure?"

Pep tucked the stray lock behind her ear. "The pressure of living in New York where at every party people ask you 'What do you do?'"

"No, I really quit doing drag because I got dumped by so many gay boys after they found out."

"That's not true."

"We both know it happens, but that's not the reason I made a career change. Life just pulled me in this direction. I discovered something new I was good at and I went with it. End of story."

"Well I think you might have given up something that means a lot to you, and not *only* 'cause you were good at it, but because it's part of who you are."

"Noted. And thank you, I guess."

Zhenya returned and sat next to me.

"Girl, don't be upset," Pep said. "I care about you and I wanna help. I think any kind of creative outlet would be good for you."

"Well, I appreciate your concern." I put my hand on her shoulder. "As soon as I get a day off, I'll look into taking voice lessons or something. Then maybe when I sing my melodies into my digital recorder they won't sound like a dying whale."

"This sounds wonderful, Soulnushka," Zhenya said.

I furrowed my brow. "If only I didn't have an extreme phobia of singing in front of another human being."

"Why don't you take a sewing class, instead" Pep said. "Then you can make yourself an outfit so we can dress up like ladies!"

"One thing at a time, gurl." I laid my head back on the couch, closing my eyes. *This conversation is exhausting.*

132

"Soulnushka," Zhenya said stroking my arm, "Pep just wants you to be happy."

"I know." My defenses crumbled to the ground. I lifted my head, looked into Zhenya's hazel eyes and imagined love shooting out like laser beams. "Well, I'm happy right now—to be with my friends."

Anthony came back inside. He asked, like a mother talking to a baby, "Are you hungies?"

"Yes!" I was glad for the shift in focus. "Let's eat."

Anthony brought me a club soda with lime and a bowl of steaming meatballs covered in so much sauce it looked like red soup. "There you go, little gaybee. I held the pasta, due to your fear of carbs."

I leaned forward and accepted his offering with glee. The warm ceramic dish felt good in my chilly hands. The meatballs tasted like they were imported from Italy, with basil, oregano and garlic blended to perfection. Anthony placed a colorful salad on the coffee table. I took a break from his balls and dug into the mixed greens topped with goat cheese, yellow peppers, cherry tomatoes, candied pecans and pears in a raspberry vinaigrette dressing.

"Thanks, gaybee," I said. "Everything is delish."

"Of corset—I made it," Anthony smirked playfully. "But enough about me. How was your trip, Zhenya?"

"What trip?" I asked, my mouth full of balls again.

"Oh, my pilot friend took me to his beach house in Israel," she replied.

"It looks like you got a little color," I said.

"I was darker," Zhenya told us. "I lost three skins already!" I choked on my balls in a fit of hysterics. "Israel is always good because the men there can't have sex with Palestinians or Christians so they end up making love with me or other guys."

"Wait a minute," Pep said, "let's back up. I thought you were on vacation with your boyfriend. Didn't he get pissed when you hooked up with someone else?"

"No, my pilot didn't care. He was with other women. I was with another woman too, but it was terrible!"

"Isn't girl-on-girl action supposed to be great because lesbians are so familiar with their own equipment?" Pep asked.

"Maybe usually, but this girl was awful."

"Where did you meet her?" I had to know.

"She seduced me at an underground fetish party," *Of course*, I thought, smiling. "I was wearing a chain linked bikini, attached to my nipples and she kept pulling at it." A look of horror spread across her face. "I thought she was going to tear off my titties." Zhenya grabbed her breasts. "Then when we were making love, she bit my clitter!"

"Oh my," I said. "But I like your nickname. It's like 'Twitter' and 'clitoris' had a baby."

Pep laughed. "Facebook for vaginas."

I said, "A status update could be, 'In labor! Feels like someone is driving a Buick through my uterus.'"

Anthony added, "Or 'Getting a Brazilian. I feel twelve again!'"

Zhenya said, "Or it could be having an orgasm like, 'Oh God, oh God! Yes, yes, YES!'"

"Speaking of orgasms, who wants dessert?" Anthony interjected.

From the kitchen, he handed us plate after plate of delectable delicacies. First there were cream filled cannolis, bathed in chocolate and caramel sauce. Then came a red velvet cake with sweet vanilla icing an inch thick. And the finale was Anthony's specialty. We called it 'the best tiramisu in America.' I sampled all three, eating until I was ready to burst, thoroughly enjoying every bite—despite my fear of carbs.

****

After the others left, Anthony joined me on the sofa with a pot of black cherry herbal tea.

"What's the big news?" I asked.

"I'm in love!" he said. "Christopher is my soul mate."

"So that's the name of this one," I blew on my steaming mug.

"You don't understand, Thomas. I've never felt a connection to someone like this before. It's fate."

"How so?"

"He has an irrational fear of scabies, so it was his first time on 'Grindr.' He wasn't even sure why he was using a hook-up app, but something told him to create a profile."

"You *always* think it's meant to be," I said. "Remember how you thought meeting Josh was fate 'cause you were the only gay boys at a straight Goth club?"

"I'm familiar with the story—I lived it. But Josh turned out to be a freak. How was I supposed to know he wanted to wear high heels in bed?"

"Hey! Ouch. Those are my feelings. There's nothing wrong with boys wearing pumps."

"Of course there isn't. At the same time, it doesn't turn me on."

"Me either, but I can't believe you never told me that's the reason you broke up. What with all the love I have for women's shoes."

"Anyway, to make the long story short—"

"Too late!" I said.

"Ha, Ha. So the first time Josh brought it up, I told him I wasn't into that. But every time we were getting busy he'd point to the drawer where he hid his lingerie and stuff. Then he'd say, 'In case you're in the mood.' I was never in the mood for women's underwear and he couldn't accept it. That's when he started feeling ashamed and judged and everything fell apart."

"Oh my Josh!" I said, my mouth hanging open. "I'm totally in shock and I love it. This is the juiciest bit of gossip ever."

"Maybe you could hook Josh up with a chaser."

"Um, FYI, guys who are into transgendered women would never be attracted to him. He is totally butch out of heels."

"I know, right? He had a six pack and everything."

"Maybe it was his way of balancing his inner ying and yang."

"I guess. His yang was really big!" Anthony said. "Enough about him though, I wanna tell you about Christopher. From the minute I met him, I knew he was the one."

Oh big brother, I thought. *Here we go again.*

"Look at this text message." He unplugged his gunmetal blue Galaxy and handed it to me. The text from Christopher read: **I'm ready to set a date ;-)**

"*How* long have you known this guy?" I asked.

"Six magical days."

"Seriously? If this text message were in a gay postmodern fairy tale it would be dreamy and romantic. Unfortunately, this is reality. I think it's a red flag."

"I knew you were going to say that," Anthony said, grabbing his phone. "Can't you just be happy for me?"

"I'm only concerned. Anybody who's sending you a text like that, after less than a week, is probably a little codependent. You're going to end up disappointed or hurt."

"Stop putting your negative energy into the universe. I don't want you to jinx everything," he yelled.

"Anthony, don't you see a pattern here? You've got to get yourself out of it or you're never going to have a decent relationship."

"And what makes you such an expert on relationships?" Anthony turned red. "When was the last time you had one? Alex, the raging alcoholic? Three years ago?" A vein popped out on his forehead. "That didn't even last for six months anyway."

"Thanks for bringing up that painful memory." My heart was in my throat. Anthony had never raised his voice at me before.

"I think you need to examine your *own* behavior instead of judging mine!"

"I'm not judging, you. I'm *trying* to help."

"Why don't you start dating again so you can remember how hard it is to find someone?"

"I date! I just went on a date," I lied. "I forgot to tell you because it didn't work out."

"I don't even believe you. You're too married to Yvonne and that job you hate to have any time for dating."

Tears stung my eyes. "I have to go." *He can't see me cry.* I grabbed my jacket and ran out the door.

Who am I? I wondered. *A miserable person unable to find somebody to love who isn't an emotionally unavailable, alcoholic? The kind of person who wallowed in a crappy job, complained to friends and never took any initiative to change the situation?*

"Oh, it's not so easy when *you're* the one being psychoanalyzed?" Anthony yelled. I walked briskly down the hall, my skinny navy corduroys rubbing together noisily. "Can't you just apologize so we can move on?" There was a pause. "Great. Run away. That will solve everything!"

I was swinging around the corners of the wrought iron staircase when I heard his door slam. *I'm really not myself these days.* My problem stemmed from more than unhappiness. When I started my day at Von Spa, I had to pretend to be someone else. I was not a businesswoman like Yvonne and I certainly wasn't a businessman. I was not a short-haired, formal, elitist spa manager. But that's where I was. That's what I was doing. And in the process, I was losing myself in work. Every day when I took off the clothes that made me feel cool and slipped into my uniform, I also slipped into a role which made me uncomfortable. Now, I was almost out of the 18-35 age bracket and I knew I had to make a change.

The snow had turned to rain and my clothes were getting soaked. I stepped off the sidewalk to cross the street and felt my iPhone vibrate. When I fumbled to check the text, I was startled by a loud horn and flashing lights. I jumped back onto the curb. A taxi swerved by, nearly hitting me. *Jesus Christ!*

Maybe I should tell Oprah about this experience so we can start a new campaign, I thought. *Texting while walking in New York City is highly dangerous to pedestrians.* The temperature outside had actually gotten warmer, but I couldn't stop shivering.

Once I arrived at the subway station, I read the message:

Call me when you get home. I don't care how late. It's an emergency!

The text was from Margaret.

****

Forty-five minutes later, I pushed open the heavy metal door to my apartment, slipped inside and let it slam behind me. I stripped off the damp clothes that were freezing me to the bone, and plopped down on my La-Z-Boy. I dreaded calling Margaret. *I can't deal with any more bad news.* And I knew I wouldn't be able to sleep if I didn't reconcile with Anthony. This was our first fight in ten years of friendship. The thought of facing either one of them was too overwhelming. I felt so drained, all I could do was turn on the television.

Flipping through my DVR list, I found an old news program titled "Happiness." *I sure could use some of that.* My sisters and I used to watch similar shows with my mom when we were kids. I hoped it would be comforting.

Cheerful music accompanied the opening credits. Images of beaming people flooded the screen: couples kissing after taking their wedding vows; children playing with puppies; movie stars walking the red carpet with blinding white smiles. The voiceover began, "The elusive road to happiness. Everyone wants to find it, but what if you don't know where to start? Then stay tuned, because tonight we'll tell you how to unlock the secrets to professional fulfillment, true love and personal joy. If you think real happiness is impossible to find, you might just change your mind. Reporting from Disney World, Jennifer McNally."

I don't need a show to tell me I'm unhappy, I thought, getting pissed. *Maybe I shouldn't be watching this.*

Jennifer, a striking brunette, strolled along the path in front of Cinderella's castle amongst families with skipping children who paused to wave at the cameras. She said, "You might think the employees here at Disney World are good candidates for pure bliss. After all, they are working at 'the happiest place on earth.' So if you've always dreamed of dressing up like Ariel or Donald Duck, and you've landed a job here, you might be on the right track. Research shows that people who are living their passion are the most fulfilled at work." *Thanks for the news bulletin. What if you don't know what your passion is?* The universe was conspiring to laugh at me. I picked up the remote to turn off the TV when Jennifer said, "But don't worry," and stopped me, "even if you still aren't sure what you want to be when you grow up, there's still hope. The second happiest group are..." she smiled and held her breath for a split second, Mickey and Minnie giggled in the background, "...people who have learned to love a job they don't consider their calling." *I wish I could do that,* I thought. "Here's Tom Barry, reporting from Milwaukee."

They cut to the interior of a shiny silver diner where a pretty black woman in a '50s-style uniform was taking orders. The montage showed the chipper waitress laughing with customers, serving burgers with fries and pouring strawberry milkshakes. Tom's voiceover said, "Marion Jefferson has always had a passion for teeth. That's right, I said 'teeth.' She dreamed of becoming a dentist, but as a single mom, money was always tight. So for the past ten years she's been putting herself through dental school by working in a restaurant. Next month she will finally graduate. And that's not the only reason she's smiling. Marion also loves her current job." They showed Tom Barry, a handsome Italian-looking stud, sitting on a bar stool with a cup of coffee in front of him. "Did you always enjoy waiting tables?" he asked Marion, who stood behind the counter.

"Hell no!" Marion laughed. "The hours are long, it's murder on your feet and sometimes the customers get a little snippy, but one day I admitted I was gonna be here for a while, so I decided, I better learn to like it."

"And how did you do that?"

"I made a conscious effort to focus on what was fun about the job. I started making lists and found there was a whole lot of good stuff happening."

"Can you give us an example?"

"I could give you a hundred! First of all, I'm a people person, so I decided to ask my customers about their day. Before I knew it, I had regulars who became my friends—and what's better than making new friends?"

The voiceover began again. More shots of the busy diner flickered on the TV screen. "Marion also enjoys her complimentary meal, and working off the calories as she makes her customers feel at home. She told me she might even keep a shift after graduation, and now says being a waitress is her *second* calling. A calling she discovered when she taught herself how to look on the sunny side of the eggs. I asked Marion what we'd all like to know, 'What's the secret to happiness?'"

"You need to see the light wherever you find yourself. The darker the place, the harder you better look. If you can't remember what you discover, write it down. Oh, and always keep your sense of humor."

Marion continued talking, but the sound was muted. Tom Barry said on voiceover, "There you have it. Attitude is everything. Since I learned so much from Marion, I figured she should have the last word."

141

They cut to Tom taking a sip of his coffee, then asking, "Any final thoughts?"

"Yes, don't forget to floss, or your motherfuckin' teeth are gonna fall out!" Marion slapped her knees, exploding with laughter. Although the network bleeped out the best part, I could still read her lips.

I paused the TV when the show went to commercial. *Oh. My. God. The problem isn't Von Spa, it's my negative attitude. Whatever happened to my Gratitude Journal?* I thought, taking stock of the situation. *I have a loving, accepting group of family and friends. I have a home and a job.* I knew I wasn't living my passion, but I wasn't trying to find it either. *Figuring out what I really love could be a new lifeline.*

I fast forwarded through the ads, sat up on the edge of my chair and pumped up the volume, ready for the next lesson. Jennifer McNally was sitting in a roller coaster as it slowly ticked up a hill. "Welcome back," she shouted over the noise of the ride. "Have you ever heard the phrase 'being in the zone'? It's a mental state of pure focus, which leads to a blissful kind of immersion that occurs when you're performing an activity you love. If you've ever been painting, dancing or even cleaning and the day seemed to pass in a flash, then you know what I mean." The green trees of Magic Kingdom grew smaller in the distance. "If you've ever sat down to write a story or a poem, only to feel like the words were being channeled *through* you, then you've been 'in the zone.' You could call it 'living in the moment.' Madonna might call it 'getting into the groove.'" The roller coaster reached the top of the hill. "Whatever name *you* give it, if you find your 'zone,' you might just find your calling." The car Jennifer was in plummeted down the other side and she screamed like a banshee. I turned off the television. Her wailing rang in my ears, but her words seemed to echo in the air.

I knew what I had to do: enjoy making a living while I explored my options. I needed to find an activity I loved. *Thank you universe,* I thought, *for a moment of clarity.* I decided this would be the first entry in my Gratitude Journal. I also knew what I needed to do next. I had to call Anthony and Margaret.

Chapter 9

Margaret:

Deviled Legs

Thomas was having dinner with his friends and I was stuck alone at the desk. *This place sure isn't much fun without him,* I thought, *but if anyone deserves a night off, he does.* Yvonne was still at the spa, which made me nervous, but it also meant I was bored. I didn't want her to catch me updating my Facebook status or surfing the net for shoes. I had gone from a computer-phobe to an internet addict.

I breathed a sigh of relief when June came out to cover the desk. Once I got back from my lunch break, which was only thirty minutes, I touched up my make-up and the festivities continued. I couldn't believe I had to be on my feet for three more hours. I didn't understand what Yvonne had against sitting. *Maybe she thinks we look more subservient this way.* I still hadn't gotten my "standing legs" as the girls called it. My knees throbbed and pain spread through my lower back like an enormous tramp stamp.

I checked the notes for the rest of the night. The initials "VDG" jumped off the screen. *Oh crap!* I finished reading:

Mr. Kenneth Murry (see pic attached) is an extremely wealthy hedge funder who likes to be recognized. Greet him BY

NAME. He is known for yelling, so resolve all issues in reception, NOT in the Tea Room. Never say "no." Offer alternatives instead.

I opened up his picture. He had crystal blue eyes, ebony hair and a beautiful—yet slightly maniacal—smile. *Black Irish*, I thought. *If he wasn't a Very Difficult Guest, I might just be in love.*

Before I had time to catch my breath, I saw him approach the spa in an Ed Hardy leather jacket. *Really? Does this guy shop for clothes in a "Jersey Shore" time capsule?* His dark mane was slicked back with copious amounts of gel. My tired legs started to tremble. Five attractive young brunettes followed him, champagne glasses in hand. Sweat formed in my armpits. *Very glamorous, Margaret.*

"Hello, Mr. Murry." I put on my 'game face.' "Will you and your companions be enjoying treatments with us this evening?"

"Yes! And I would like a double tequila on the double, darling," he said, his breath already 80 proof.

"I'm sorry, Mr. Murry," I replied, my voice shaking, "we don't serve alcohol here. It can have an adverse reaction with the essential oils. Would you like some herbal tea instead?"

"Ha!" he yelled. "No thanks."

I exhaled.

"So me and these girls are having massages, and I want the best-looking chick you have."

Eww, I thought. *You sexist pig.* My nervousness turned to disdain. I'll have to warn Tootsie about this asshole, or "valued spa guest" as we would sarcastically call him. "Why don't you all have a seat so you can begin relaxing." I made believe I was doing very important work on the computer by quickly typing away. The humor in the "lack of believability factor" was lost on someone so sauced.

I looked at the screen. To my horror, there were no appointments booked for Mr. Murry's entourage. *If he tells Yvonne I fucked up, it's curtains for me—even if it's not my fault.* We didn't have his credit card on file, either.

Uh-oh, I thought, *time to call Thomas.* I knew he really needed a night off with his friends, but I didn't think I could handle the situation alone. June was supposed to be in charge, but she had left to go to the restroom twenty minutes earlier. She had a habit of sneaking into treatment rooms and gabbing away with the therapists. *She better not show up right before we close and blame it on constipation!* We weren't allowed to leave the desk unattended for even a second. I had to buy some time.

"We do have your appointment confirmed, but we don't have any massages available for your friends at the moment."

"WHAT?!" Mr. Murry yelled, sounding remarkably sober.

I jolted from the sheer volume of his voice. I took a deep breath. *You can do this, Maggs. Stay calm.* "While you remove your shoes, I'll look into booking appointments for the ladies. *Or* they are welcome to enjoy the Radiant Heat Area free of charge while they wait for you."

"I'm here with these girls who work for me and I am going to spend thousands upon thousands of dollars at your spa," he said in a high pitched voice that made Adam Lambert seem like he had no vocal range. "*They* want massages and *I* want this fixed NOW!"

"Of course, Mr. Murry. Give me one minute and I'll see what I can do." My heart was racing. I opened up the schedule again. The girl with the biggest hair kept looking at me like she wanted to rumble. *Settle down, Ms. Ogilvie Home Perm.* The only treatments available were for manicures and pedicures. *I don't think that's gonna cut it, but it's worth a shot.* "We do have nail services available."

Ms. Ogilvie Home Perm batted her eyelashes at Mr. Murry, "But I really want a massage, Ken." *And I want to be 110 pounds while continuing to order the entire left side of the menu at IHOP.*

"You heard the lady," Mr. Murry barked.

Think Margaret, you're creative. Spin the situation. "Let me check one more thing." All the nail techs were available. *Thank God!* "Actually, the private VIP nail room is open."

"The *VIP* nail room?" Ms. Ogilvie Home Perm's eyes twinkled.

Or the only nail room we have. "Yes, it's free for all five of you to enjoy. You'll take turns having our Energizing Massage Pedicures. We can serve you high tea while you soak in the jet-stream foot baths."

"Book it!" She looked at the other girls and squealed.

"Wonderful." *Sucker,* I thought. *We serve "high tea" to everyone.*

I heard footsteps behind me on the crystal staircase. *Dear Lord, can I have one moment of peace?*

"Sorry, I was a little backed up if you know what I mean," June whispered and slipped behind the desk. "Is everything okay?"

I said in my best Gabrielle voice, "But of course."

****

Two hours later, I heard loud voices and laughter as Mr. Murry's gang approached the reception area. *Shut up, bitches, other people are still having treatments.* I remembered there was no credit card on file and broke out in a cold sweat. *Now he's really gonna lose his shit!*

He reached into his snakeskin wallet to pay the bill. *Thank you Jesus, I thought.* A rush of relief flooded through me. I slipped into the script.

"For your convenience we have included an 18% gratuity." He looked kind of green in the cheeks. *I told you essential oils and booze aren't a good combo. Please don't puke on me.*

"For *my* convenience?" he shrieked. "Sounds like it's for *your* convenience!"

No one had ever questioned this before. Most of our guests had so much money they didn't care.

"Just pay it, Ken," Ms. Ogilvie Home Perm snapped. "You're embarrassing us."

NOW you're getting embarrassed? He handed over his black Amex and I swiped it. The word "Declined" appeared on the screen.

"Do you have another card," I asked him quietly. He handed me his Visa, which had the same outcome. *Are you there God? It's me, Margaret.*

The ladies' murmurs grew louder.

"What's the hold-up?" Ms. Ogilvie said. "We have dinner reservations."

"I'm sorry, ladies," I replied.

June came out to the front desk. "What's going on?" she whispered. I briefed her on the situation. She took Mr. Murry into the office so he could call American Express.

Ms. Ogilvie Home Perm screamed at the top of her lungs, "No one should come to this spa; they treat you like shit here!" *I can't take any more today.*

"Someone better tell us what's happening," one of the other girls said.

"Or you're gonna be on the front cover of *The Daily News* tomorrow," Ms. Ogilvie sneered.

Seriously? What a strange threat. I stepped around the desk and whispered to her, "Mr. Murry's credit card didn't go through."

"Oh my God, how is that possible? He's friggin' loaded." *In more ways than one,* I wanted to say.

Mr. Murry barreled out of the concierge office with June close on his tail. "Let's get out of here, everyone. Time to go to a real spa!" The ladies huffed and picked up their things.

June's aquamarine eyes widened. Her nostrils flared as she inhaled sharply. "Mr. Murry!" she shouted. "If you do not find some way of paying for your treatments, I will be forced to call the police!"

Oh my God. I froze. *No one has ever yelled at a guest before.*

"Go ahead. I would rather spend the night in jail than give you one red cent. C'mon girls." They all stormed off.

"Oh no he didn't!" June yelled. "Call building security and have them stopped at the door. I'll call the police from my cell and run down the stairs to head them off. There's no way I'm gonna let him weasel his way outta this one." She pivoted back around so quickly she looked like Beyoncé working a Sasha Fierce dance move.

I grabbed the phone and dialed security. "Stop the guy in the Ed Hardy leather jacket. The police are coming for him."

"For reals?" the security guard asked.

"Just do it!" I hung up and stood there dumbfounded. A tranquil piano played over the speaker system. *This place is more stressful than the fucking hospital.*

Minutes later, June ran back into the spa. The second she came through the door, her cell phone rang. She promptly answered, interrupting the Alicia Key's "Empire State of Mind" ringtone.

"Well?" June asked, her eyes darting back and forth as she listened. "Okay, thanks for letting me know." The corners of her mouth turned up. "They got him."

"Who? Security or the police?"

"The cops. He's in custody. Don't mess with a fiery redhead and a tall lipstick lesbian!" June gave me a high five. We were a modern day Cagney and Lacey—complete with polyester suits.

The police ended up collecting money from Ms. Ogilvie Home Perm and the other girls to cover the cost of the treatments, but it turned out Mr. Murry was already a wanted man. When he called Amex, they told him his assets were frozen. He was eventually convicted of stealing money from his clients in a Ponzi scheme. His tiny minion didn't know she had made a startling prediction: Because of Mr. Murry's crimes, we did end up on the cover of *The Daily News* the next day.

****

I heard whistling before I saw Mr. Campbell approaching the spa. *Thank God,* I thought. *Someone I can deal with.* "Nice to see you, Margaret" said my favorite silver fox.

"Likewise, Mr. Campbell. Where have you been?" I asked, smiling.

"Let's see, first I was in Provence, then Monte Carlo, which is lovely in the low season, and when Caroline returns from her tour of Southeast Asia, we'll spend some time in East Hampton. Where do you winter, Margaret?"

I couldn't believe how out of touch he was with my role in this transaction. *I'm the one who takes your shoes at the door. Do ya think I'm here for a sociological study or something?* "Well actually, I'll be traveling later tonight—to my apartment in the beautiful borough of Queens."

Mr. Campbell laughed. "I'm late, so I'll just head to the back." He saluted with his rolled up newspaper.

"Enjoy." *If only they were all like you,* I thought. *Clueless, but sweet.*

As the shift was mercifully drawing to a close, I snuck into the concierge office to sit down for a minute. My body was so out of whack from standing all week that I was literally on my last leg. The second my ass hit the chair, I heard an angry voice coming from the reception area. "Hell-o-oh!" I sprang to my feet, rushing back to the desk where I found a tall woman tapping her chocolate brown fingernails on the countertop. She wore a long black, sheared fur coat. Underneath, she was Nicole Richie skinny in polished grey business attire. A feminine fedora rested on top of her angular, black bob. She looked powerful. She also looked like she wanted to hurt me and perhaps should be kept away from small children.

"Welcome to Von Spa, will you be enjoying treatments with us this evening?" I said robotically. *I'm so over this.*

"No I am not having any treatments and I don't appreciate waiting." She pursed her lips. "I want to buy a lousy gift card, NOW!"

Really, bitch? Is "NOW" the word of the day like on Pee-Wee's Playhouse or Watch What Happens: Live? Maybe we should all scream, jump up and down or do a shot every time we hear someone say, "NOW."

"I will be happy to process that for you." My heart started beating overtime again. I could feel my face burn. Talk about eating your feelings; I had to chew mine up and swallow, I was so enraged, not to mention frightened. *Don't let her win,* I thought. *There sure is a lot of reaffirming self-talk happening today.* "What amount would you like placed on the card?"

"Make it for a full day, all inclusive," she said, jiggling her leg.

"No problem, madam." *Apparently, I sound French when I'm terrified.* I'd always felt learning that language would help me seem more pretentious. Maybe in turn, I would've been more at ease with the clientele. "I'll look up the dollar amount including tax and gratuity for the full day journey. One moment please."

"What in God's name are you talking about? Is this your first day or are you a moron?"

As the words came out of her mouth, I was enveloped by an intense desire to catapult over the counter and pummel her. *Maybe she'll be the one to get me on the cover of The Daily News.*

"No, I've been here for a while now. I just want to make sure I get everything right for you." All the saliva drained out of me like a pool in September. *This dry mouth rivals Snoop Dog's.* I really wanted to ask this pig in pumps, "If you're here with me, who's running hell?"

All my computer skills flew out the window. Once again, I pretended to type away. Then I desperately looked for the gift card "Cheat Sheet" in "My Documents." *It's not under "Cheat Sheet."* Oh Jesus! She tapped her fingers again. I checked to see if it was in the "Gift Card Folder." It wasn't. *Are you there, God? Seriously, is this thing on?* Sweat dripped down my sides. *I knew I should've gotten botox in my armpits for hyperhidrosis. Wait, it's on the desktop!* I clicked on the "GC" icon. While I waited for the document to open, I reached under the counter for a gift bag, then followed the steps to complete the transaction.

"For a Green Tea Scrub, a Deep Seaweed Detoxifying Wrap, a Muscle Releasing Massage and the Age Rewinding Facial the total is $1,152.00."

"Listen, I don't speak spa…" *You sure are fluent in total bitch, bitch.* "Just give me a pen so I can sign and get out of here. I'm in a hurry. I should get a car service home at these prices!"

"Okay, how would you like to settle your account?" I asked sheepishly.

"Don't you know who I am?" *Great, here we go again.* "All of my information should be on file under my real estate agency, Jones and Johnson."

Oh how I wanted to ask her, "Is it unbearably hot where you live?" But since it would be her final resting place, I felt a little better.

I found the profile, copied down her Amex information and entered it into the system. The only thing I still needed was her phone number. "Yes, madam, here you go. Please fill in your number here."

She sighed impatiently, signed the receipt and wrote down her digits on the form with voracity. The evil woman pressed so hard, she actually engraved the information on the rosewood countertop. I couldn't believe she had defaced the spa, but what she did next was even more shocking: She threw the pen right in my face and left.

I was frozen for almost a minute, my nose and forehead stinging; complete demoralization had set in. Again, I was dealing with physical violence in the workplace. *That pen could have blinded me.* Even in the psych ward, if a patient assaults a nurse, arrangements are made to have the offender reassigned. Speaking to Yvonne was something I never did, but if I told her what had happened, I knew it would have fallen on deaf ears. There was an unspoken rule: Unless customers were stealing, they were always right.

That night, on the subway, I did some soul searching. The difficult clients gave all their abuse to the poor spa concierge worker bees on the front lines. We had the honor of dealing with the late, the hostile, and the ridiculously entitled. It was like there were Catholic priests in the treatment rooms conducting exorcisms. Even the most satanic guests came out floating on cloud nine and noticeably kinder. Becoming an esthetician at Von Spa was my Holy Grail. Therapists worked half the hours and made twice the money. *If I can convince Yvonne to let me give her a facial, I know she'll promote me.* Thoughts flooded my head like an angel whispering in my ear.

Von Spa isn't the only spa in the city. You can get a job doing facials somewhere else—somewhere less intense. With Von Spa on your résumé, getting hired will be a cinch. You're waiting in vain for an esthetics position to open. It was true. There was no turnover because Von Spa paid top dollar. If all the guests were like Mr. Campbell, the gig would have been tolerable. But they weren't. *No job is worth your physical and mental health. This isn't about giving up—you've conquered your fears at Von Spa. It's about moving on to a place where you can be a therapist right away—somewhere with a union!* I looked up to the sky. *Thank you, God. Love, Me, Margaret.* The train went above ground and I sent a text to Thomas, telling him to call me. I'd made my decision. As soon as I found another job, I was going to quit.

****

I got home and collapsed onto the couch. I began peeling off my slimming black jeans when the phone rang. *Oh shit,* I thought. *Break it to him gently.*

"What's wrong?" Thomas asked.

All the stress of the day boiled to the surface. "I'm quitting! The way those people treat us is unacceptable. Mr. Murry screamed at me for something that wasn't even my fault and his little girlfriend fucking threatened me!" *So much for breaking it to him gently.*

"What happened?!"

"He couldn't pay his bill and the cops arrested him."

"Really?" Thomas said, his voice an octave higher than usual.

"Yep. Then this other lady called me a moron and we're not even allowed to talk back. I hope you had fun with your friends while you left me in hell with Satan herself!" I burst into rivers of angry tears. *He probably won't care if I quit 'cause I'm acting like a self-centered lunatic.*

"Well, *she* sounds like the moron. Anyone can see how smart you are—look how quickly you mastered the computer," he said.

"And now I'm ready to move on." I blew my nose.

"Maggie, you can't leave," Thomas shrieked. "What would I do without you?"

"You can say whatever you want but I'm not gonna change my mind. After that bitch bought her gift card, she threw the pen at me."

"Oh my God! Are you okay?"

"Physically."

"Did you save the paperwork?"

"Who cares?!" I imagined him pulling the receiver away from his ear. "I should have balled it up and shoved it down her throat, but I filed it away like a good little servant. We mustn't upset Yvonne," I said bitterly.

"I was thinking we could get her number off the form and prank her from a pay phone in the middle of the night."

I chuckled. "I have no desire to go riffling through that disastrous filing cabinet. Besides, I know an easier way. She was so angry she actually engraved it on the countertop when she was writing." Then I said, sarcastically, "Maybe we can put a piece of paper on the wood and rub a pencil over the number detective style."

"That's the spirit, Maggie. In the meantime try not to 'take it in' when a guest is rude. The most important lesson Yvonne taught me is to stop taking things personally."

"Are you drunk?" I sat up and caught a glimpse of my face in the mirror as it changed from white to red. "A few hours ago you felt just like I did. Now suddenly you're all roses and rainbows. When someone yells at you or throws a pen in your face—*it's personal!* I should've known what it'd be like catering to rich, entitled women." Everything I'd been suppressing in front of the guests was pouring out like molten lava. "And now your great mentor wants us to shine these people's shoes? How could she subject us to such degradation? She has obviously never been in *our* shoes!"

"But after the meeting you said you weren't worried about it," Thomas said, panic creeping into his voice.

"Well I'm worried now! That's not what I went to school for. I want to be an esthetician and if I can't do it at Von Spa, I'll have to do it somewhere else."

"I understand, Maggie and I will do everything in my power to persuade Yvonne to promote you. Maybe Christie will need someone to fill in if she goes on vacation."

"She never takes a day off, but *please* convince Yvonne to let me give her a facial. As terrified as I'll be, I know I can win her over. It's my only hope."

"Got it. And I already told you I'd fix the shoe shining problem. Have some faith in me."

"I *do* have faith in you and I'll be eternally grateful to *you*, for mentoring *me*. I'm sorry I went off." I grabbed a Kleenex and wiped the remnants of tears from my face. "It was just a really rough day. The lady from Jones and Johnson was the last straw—"

"Mrs. B!"

"That was Mrs. B?" *Of course,* I thought. "Now I see how she got her name."

"God, Maggie. I'm so sorry. I can't believe I wasn't there to take the blow on your first meeting. She is the worst spa bitch—I mean valued guest—EVER."

"Oh I know! I have the pen marks on my forehead to prove it."

"That woman has made my life hell for the past four years."

"Um, yeah. She is from Hades."

"If I'd known she was coming in, I wouldn't have left you."

"And I would've insisted you go to dinner with your friends."

"Did I tell you about the time she called me 'difficult'—in front of Yvonne?"

"I don't think so."

"Yvonne wrote me up! After I bent over backwards for Mrs. B. I even asked Tootsie to come in on her day off so she could rub that woman and she *still* complained because we didn't have a treatment available for her surprise guest."

"Dear Lord!"

"Oh, and she called me a 'boob' for calling her 'Ms.' I told her, that's how we address all our female guests, so we don't have to pry into their marital status. Then she goes, 'I'm not just *any* guest. You will call me *Mrs. Jones* and if you forget, I will have your job!'"

"Yowza."

"The scary thing is, Yvonne would choose her over me because she brings in so much money. Mrs. B put Von Spa on the map in the high end real estate biz and she could make us passé, too."

I checked my reflection in the mirror. The color in my face was back to normal. "Then how come I've never met her?"

"Probably because her groups usually have treatments in the mornings, before we get to work."

"Oh, thank God. But we haven't even discussed the most disturbing part of this conversation."

"What's that?" Thomas asked.

"Can you believe someone actually married her?"

"Seriously. Poor guy."

"She seems like the kind of woman who'd keep her maiden name, too. Don't ya think?"

"Yeah, I really do think. Maybe Mrs. B needed to change her identity after she lost her temper and murdered someone for cutting in line," Thomas chuckled.

"Probably. She's really impatient. And she showed up the second I had a chance to sit down. My calves are still throbbing because I was on my feet for the *entire* night. So basically, that satanic woman is assaulting me again."

"She gave you deviled legs!"

I laughed. "Now do you see what I was dealing with today?"

"I get it, Maggie. I've totally been there."

"How have you tolerated these people for so long?"

"This is what I like to do—when a guest gets angry, I let them go off and I imagine a force field around me deflecting the rage. While they're flustered, you reply very slowly in your spa voice. The calmer you speak, the madder they get, but you're just doing your job 'cause you have to maintain the atmosphere by talking that way, right?"

"I guess so."

"Secretly you know it's driving them crazy! And they can't complain because you never raised your voice at them. It really is great revenge and it works like a charm. Will you try it?"

"Of corset. It sounds like fun."

"I love that you've adopted, 'of corset.'"

"Let's just hope the throwing of objects doesn't happen again or else I'll have to hurl something back 'Tick-Tick-Boom' style."

"Maybe I'll join in. If I ever saw someone pelt something at you, I don't think I'd be able to control myself."

My heart melted. "Thanks for being so patient with me." I reclined on my couch.

"Anytime. Are you gonna stay?"

"Of course I am, but I still wanna try to get the esthetics position."

"I promise I'll help. And I figured out a temporary solution for the shoe shining dilemma, so don't worry about that."

"What is it?" I sat up again.

"I can't tell anyone. If Yvonne finds out she'll sue and/or fire me for sure. Her loyalty goes out the window if you cross her, but this idea is all I could think of."

"C'mon. You can't put something out there like that and not tell me!"

"No way."

"You know my philosophy: Don't gossip with everyone. Find one person you can trust and do all your gossiping with them. You're my person."

"This is for your own protection. What if Yvonne interrogates you?"

"She would have to beat it out of me. I'm in your corner 100%. Remember how I didn't quit a few minutes ago? I did it for you. *Please?!*"

"Damn you're good. I guess it would be nice to have a partner in crime, and it is a crime by the way. This gives new meaning to the words 'top secret,' though."

"You know me—it's in a safe within a safe—safety squared. What are we gonna do?"

He said slowly, "Let's break it."

"Break what?" My reflection in the mirror went from excited to confused.

"The shoe shiner. We'll find a time when we're alone in the concierge office and smash it to bits. Then we'll put it back, someone else will discover our handiwork and the whole project will be put on hold. If we're careful, no one will be able to prove we were the hit men. Yvonne loves to blame everything on the night cleaners."

"That's a hysterical and terrible idea. I guess you might call it hysterible."

"I know," he said, sounding deflated. "And we really *cannot* get caught."

"I'll say! Won't she just have the shoe shiner repaired or buy a new one, anyway?"

"Probably, but I only need to buy a few days 'til I can come up with a more permanent solution."

"What are you gonna tell the other girls?"

"Oh God, I'm not sure yet. I can't tell them my plan, so I'll have to figure out another way to keep them from walking. We're having a little meeting tomorrow and you know the ultimatum they gave me. I guess I'll have to sleep on it. I'm too exhausted to think right now."

"Well once again, I have complete faith in your management abilities."

"Thanks for saying that. It really helps to have a compadre on my side."

"Anything for you."

"Hey, I forgot to tell you something funny. At the end of a meeting, ya know how Yvonne asks if we have any questions or concerns?"

"Of corset." I put a pillow behind my head and rested my feet on the coffee table.

"Well every time she says that, I go into this whole internal monologue. I imagine asking her about the not-so-great mysteries of life. For example, 'Does anyone else pretend they're working a runway when they walk up the aisle on the way to the bathroom in the middle of a movie?' I put on my iPod and sashayed to Katy Perry's 'E.T.' just the other day."

"I've seen people do that! I got one, 'Whatever happened to peanut butter and jelly in the same jar?' It was a great idea. Your groceries were less heavy to lug home, plus you had more cabinet space."

"Exactly! Or 'Isn't it insane that Alan Thicke of "Growing Pains" fame produced one of the most popular white R & B singers ever?'"

"And 'Whatever happened to coffee in tea bags?' They were so convenient. Was I the only one who bought those? And 'Who came up with the idea of meatless hot dogs?' They might have been inspired by shit in a bun."

"True. They do taste like ass."

"Did you notice all of mine are food related?" We laughed.

"And speaking of things we love. I have vintage TV-related ones, too," Thomas said.

"I love me some TV. Did I ever tell you television saved my life?"

"Oh my God, same here! When I was being bullied freshman year, watching MTV gave me hope that there was a whole glamorous world out there. What about you?"

"'Carol Burnett' and 'SNL' definitely developed my sense of humor, which helped me to win friends and influence people in the cesspool we call high school."

"Awesome. I'll have to write the cast members a thank you note. Your comic abilities have made my job tolerable."

"Aw shucks." I blushed.

"Did you ever consider doing stand-up?"

"In all my pipe dreams, but were you at the meeting earlier?"

"Um, yeah," he said.

"I'm terri*fied* and terri*ble* when it comes to public speaking."

"You might not enjoy it, but you were still pretty funny."

"Inadvertently!" We laughed again. "Now hit me with your TV-related mysteries of life."

"Okay. Here goes: Was I the only kid who wasn't allowed to watch 'The Facts of Life' because my parents thought the title, 'encouraged pre-marital sex?'"

"Oh my gosh! I wasn't allowed to watch 'Bewitched' since it 'promoted witchcraft!'"

"Hysterical," Thomas said through uncontrollable giggling. "My mom wouldn't let me watch 'Diff'rent Strokes' because 'that Arnold has a fresh mouth.'"

I was laughing so hard I could barely get out what I said next, "And my Granny wouldn't let me watch 'Three's Company' 'cause they were 'living together—and they weren't married!'" I gasped with glee and choked on my own spit as tears spilled down my face. I could hear Thomas cackling and slapping his knee. I caught my breath and said, "You are the one person who could take me from crying to *laughing* until I cried in under five minutes. Thanks for that and thanks for convincing me not to quit. I don't want to be unemployed again, anyway."

"My pleasure, on both counts. I need you there as much as you need the job."

"In all the chaos, I almost forgot to ask how your dinner was."

"It was great—until I got into a huge fight with Anthony."

"Really? But you told me you never fought."

"We don't."

"What happened?"

"I thought he was rushing into a relationship, so to make a long story short—"

"Too late!" It was amazing how quickly we'd started speaking the same "friend language."

"Hey!" He chuckled.

"Sorry, I couldn't resist. Go ahead; I really *do* want to hear what happened."

"It doesn't matter. I called him and we buried the hatchet. I wished him a happy life with his new man, and he apologized for retaliating—I still don't think their relationship will last though."

"Thomas!"

"I'm kidding."

"So everything's fine?"

Thomas lowered the tone of his voice, "No," he paused. "Actually, everything is better than fine. I'm turning over a new leaf. And you'll never believe what inspired me."

"Hit me again."

"A show on TV! It convinced me the key to happiness is focusing on the positive things in life, even at work."

"Well then I will, too. Tomorrow we'll make Von Spa all sunshine and lollipops."

"Did I ever tell you I hate that song? It's one of my 'Top Ten Least Favorite Songs of All Time.'"

"What happened to Mr. Positive?" I asked, stretching and stifling a yawn.

"I guess I'll have to give you my list of favorite songs to counteract the negativity. It's on my phone. I'll put you on speaker."

"Hit it."

"'Crying' by Roy Orbison, any track from Garbage's album 'Version 2.0,' 'Princess of China' by Coldplay featuring Rihanna, Nina Simone's cover of 'To Love Somebody,' 'Wicked Little Town' from 'Hedwig and the Angry Inch,' 'The Story' by Brandi Carlile, Sarah McLachlan's 'Possession—'"

"Great song!"

"Right? 'Girls Like You' from The Naked and the Famous, 'Bachelorette' by Bjork, 'Kids Will Have a Blast Probing the Heavens' from SuperMajor, 'Little Miss Understood' by Raeya, and 'Broken Strings' by James Morrison with Nelly Furtado."

"What an eclectic mix. But I think that's eleven."

"At least! And there are a few contenders like 'Love Song for a Vampire' by Annie Lennox, Madonna's 'Express Yourself,' and 'Dominion' by The Sisters of Mercy."

"You sure have put a lot of thought into this."

"Because I really love music."

"I can tell."

"What are your favorites?"

"Gosh, I'll have to think about that one, but I love 80's music and U2 is at the top of my list."

"Cool. Just so you know, there's only one criterion—the song has to stand the test of time. Think about it and tell me tomorrow, right after our law-breaking visit to destruction of property."

"Okay. See you at the orifice."

Thomas giggled, "The orifice, that's funny. Oh, you just reminded me—"

"What?"

"If you have a friend who needs a job, I heard there's an opening!"

"Ha! Goodnight Thomas."

"Goodnight, Maggie."

****

The next day, Thomas stationed one of the female locker room attendants at the front desk with the spa Blackberry in case there was an emergency. He whisked me, June and Diana off to the secret meeting place. Gabrielle wasn't there because it was the second day of her weekend. The grey walls and fluorescent lighting reminded me of the psych ward. We sat down on the stairs and waited for Thomas to begin.

He took a deep breath and said, "So I want start by thanking you guys for standing by me as we get through this challenging situation."

June narrowed her gaze. "That hasn't been established yet. It depends on your solution."

Thomas rolled his eyes slightly. "Would you mind letting me finish before you shoot me down?"

"Sorry."

"Go ahead, babe," Diana said. *Those little diamond hoops really make her look like J-Lo.* I glanced to my right and then to my left. June looked like Beyoncé, Diana looked like Jennifer Lopez and I looked like I had eaten a dozen doughnuts last night. *I should have put on some more make-up.*

"What I was trying to say is, my imperfect solution will only buy us some time…" I was on the edge of my stair. "But here's the good news—no one has to shine a shoe until further notice. We're going to put the shiner in the corner and hope Yvonne doesn't ask about it. She's going to Spa Con this Friday and she'll be gone for six days. By then I'll have a more *permanent* solution."

"Are you kidding me?" June stood up. "That doesn't fix the problem. Yvonne is going to be all over us, asking how it's going!"

166

"Will you give my idea a chance, June?" Thomas fired back. "If Yvonne brings it up, *I'll* talk to her. Just shelf the shiner for now and don't worry about it."

"I'm fine with that," Diana touched Thomas's arm.

"Well, I'm not!" June yelled. "I'm going to be on pins and needles waiting for Yvonne to confront me if she doesn't see me on my hands and knees shining shoes like some kind of slave. What should I tell her—*the truth?* If it comes to it, should I throw *you* under the bus to save myself? It's so unfair of you to put us in that position!"

"My God, June," Thomas replied, "can we stay in the moment? No one is asking you to do anything but not shine shoes." Thomas took another deep breath and said slowly, "If Yvonne confronts you, just blame me. Tell her I said you don't have to do it and I've been meaning to talk to her."

"Fine," June snapped.

"Okay, so we're all on the same page, has anyone used the shoe shiner today?"

"You know I didn't," June said.

"Me either," Diana concurred.

"Margaret?"

"I just got here."

"Oh, that's right." Thomas shook his head a little. "Any other questions or concerns?" Thomas winked at me.

Funny inquiries flooded my mind: *Does anyone else think Justin Bieber looks like Angelina Jolie's long lost lesbian love child? Do Asian people tattoo themselves with American sayings like "Shit Happens?" Why do people say, "You look tired?" Does it make them feel better about themselves to remind me I've got bags under my eyes?*

167

"I have to take my break," June told Thomas. "I couldn't go earlier because of this meeting."

Diana said, "Me too, same reason."

"That's fine," he replied. "Margaret and I will cover the desk." As they left, Thomas motioned for me to stay back. He waited until they were gone before saying, "June and Diana don't know the shoe shiner isn't already broken." His light brown eyes twinkled. "So if we break it right now, Yvonne will assume the night cleaners were responsible. Naturally, they'll deny it. Since she can't prove anything, no one gets hurt."

I was stunned. "What do you mean, *we?*"

"We have to do it while they're at lunch. No witnesses!"

"Okay," I said, trying to be supportive. "You go first though. I'm too scared."

"I gotta find Yvonne and check in with her, but I'll meet you at the desk. You can wait for me, otherwise, pretend you're a rock star smashing a guitar. Have fun with it!"

"I think it's best if one of us stands watch."

"Whatever works for you." He pivoted towards the door.

Walking back into the spa, I could smell the new pomegranate oil burning. *This place smells like a fruit salad.* The irony of the relaxing atmosphere was never wasted on me. Being a psych nurse might have been a dead end job (literally) but "protecting the energy in the room" was slowly siphoning my soul. *At least the esthetics position might be a light at the end of the tunnel.*

As I checked the afternoon appointments, I had a burst of inspiration. *No one is coming in 'til 2 o'clock, so if I start wailing on the shoe shiner now, Thomas would be totally proud of me. When he walks into the spa I*

168

could flatly say, "It's done," like some hired assassin who just bumped someone off. It'd be so gansta and he'd really get a kick out of my delivery.

I slipped into the concierge office and sized up my prey, sitting there smugly with its fuzzy red brushes for feet and beady little eyes made of screws. I checked my sides to see if anyone was watching. It was just the two of us. I grabbed the shoe shiner by the handle. It was about the size of a guitar, but still pretty heavy. I lifted it as high as I could—a few feet off the ground—and started banging it on the floor, thinking, *Die, motherfucker, die!*

Between blows, I thought I heard a voice at the front desk, but the rest of the world went out of focus while I beat the shit out of the shoe shiner. A force greater than me took over as months of spa-rage poured out of my body. *Fuck this place! I don't care if I get fired.* Through the haze, I heard someone yell from behind me, "Abort! Stop!" I came back to reality like a hypnotist had snapped his fingers. I turned around, a wave of shame and embarrassment washing over me. It evaporated when I saw it was only Thomas.

"Oh my God, Maggie—" he said breathlessly.

"I thought you'd be happy. What's wrong?"

"I just talked to Yvonne. That shoe shiner costs a thousand dollars! If it gets broken there will be hell to pay. She will kill the night cleaners and us if she finds out. I'm sorry. It was a terrible idea. It's not hysterical or hysterible—it's dangerous."

"Sweet Jesus!" A jolt of fear shot through my veins.

"Yvonne is totally sue happy. She hits everyone who costs her money with a lawsuit and we sure can't afford this." Thomas bent over to catch his breath, resting his hands on his knees. I was speechless. I looked down at my handiwork, completely overcome by anxiety. *It looks okay, but there's no way it'll still work.* "She even took the laundry service to small claims court for losing twenty-eight towels. I really didn't think this through."

"No problem." I left the office, walking towards the front desk.

"Where are you going?" He followed me.

I stopped in my tracks. "I'm gonna get in my time machine and go back a few minutes before I started pounding that thing on the ground," I said, horrified. "I was only doing what you told me to do!"

"I know. I'm *really* sorry Maggie. I was wrong. I never thought of this shoe shining thing as an act of desperation. Yvonne is trying to keep our name in the press so the business stays profitable. I wasn't thinking and now we could get sued and/or fired!"

"There you go with that 'we' thing again. This was *your* idea. I don't have that kind of money, especially if I lose my job. I'm totally freaking out!" A terrible thought popped into my mind. "Oh my gosh. What if there are security cameras?"

"There aren't any in the office. Don't worry."

"Don't *worry*? How am I going to explain my actions? Yvonne will think I'm a maniac," I said, throwing my hands in the air. "I'll go back to the hospital—as a patient! What I've done makes 'Tick-Tick-Boom' look well-adjusted. And who spends a thousand dollars on a shoe shiner, anyway?"

"Only the best for Yvonne. At that price, it should be durable." Thomas grabbed the shoe shiner. "If it still works, our problems are over."

I waited with bated breath while he crouched down, fumbling behind the copier to find an outlet. He plugged the shoe shiner in and stood up. We looked at each other, crossing our fingers. I crossed my toes and mentally crossed my boobs for good measure. We were in this together. Even though it was his idea, I was the hit man. Thomas flipped the switch—nothing. He gave the shiner a kick but still nothing. *We sure are in trouble.*

Thomas said, "I think it's broken." His eyes were bloodshot.

"Ya think?" I glared at him. "What do we do now?"

"Pray," he said and put the shoe shiner back in the corner. "Do you have any other questions or concerns?"

"Not at this time."

****

The next day I dreaded seeing Thomas. I'd barely spoken to him after the incident and I'd ignored his calls when I got home. My heart had softened overnight, and I was wracked with guilt. *Some friend I am. Now he's probably mad at me for giving him the cold shoulder. We made a stupid mistake, but I should've stayed by his side like Bonnie and Clyde.*

When I came into work, I was greeted by Yvonne's foreboding presence at the front desk. "Welcome," she said in a passive-aggressive tone, looking at her watch. "Please join the rest of your colleagues in the back for an impromptu meeting. We are just waiting until Thomas makes his timely arrival."

"Okay, hi, I mean thanks. Will do. Uh, see you in the orifice. Carry on. Shoes nice. I mean nice shoes. I love you. I mean I love your shoes." *What is it about this woman that makes me babble?* Even the sight of Yvonne turned me into Rain Man on crystal meth. She didn't respond but continued looking at the computer, getting lost in her own fabulous thoughts. It was her planet. We were all just living in her world of aquiline noses and YSL pantsuits. I slipped into the concierge office. The other girls were already there.

"Ciao, bella!" Gabrielle kissed me on both cheeks. We'd developed a little friendship. She thought I was funny, which is one of the qualities I admire most in others.

"Hi guys," I said to Diana and June. "What do you think this is all about?"

"Isn't it obvious?" June snarled. Dark circles surrounded her sea green eyes.

"Is everything alright?"

She threw her hands over her face and started balling. "June, June, it's okay." I instinctively put my arm around her for a moment.

"No, it's not. Andrea got laid off and now all three of us are going to be homeless. That's why I snapped at Thomas yesterday. Everything in my life is going to hell!"

The other concierges gathered around to soothe her. Diana said, "You'll figure something out, babe. Andrea can look for a job on your days off and she can watch the baby in the meantime. You'll save so much money on daycare."

"I know, I'm just scared, though. We live paycheck to paycheck as it is." Tears flowed down June's apple cheeks onto her full glossy lips. *There sure is a lot of crying around here.*

"Don't worry about money either," Diana said. "I'll lend you the cash if things get too bad. I can be your safety net."

"How could you possibly afford that?" June accepted the tissue Gabrielle offered her.

"The same way I afford the glamorous lifestyle I lead—I live with my grandmother and I don't pay rent! I can wear last season if you really need the Benjamins." She shrugged. "It's no biggie."

"You'd do that for me?" June asked.

"Yeah, what the hell," Diana replied, sounding like a true Brooklyn babe. June grabbed Diana as if she were a life jacket.

Gabrielle handed June some more tissue. "I would help, but I owe my citizenship lawyer thousands."

Oh crap, is it my turn to offer? I can barely cover rent. I opened my mouth, "I could, um—"

June blew her nose. "It's okay." She sniffled and tried to smile. "I'm just happy to have you guys."

"We love you, June!" Gabrielle extended her long arms and gestured for us to come in for a group hug. The sound of Yvonne talking to Thomas shifted our collective focus to the door. *Hug aborted,* I thought. Yvonne glided into the concierge office with her nose in the air. Thomas followed, his gaze directed downward. I inhaled sharply. *The lamb to the slaughter!*

"Hello everyone." Yvonne looked over at Thomas. "Now that we are all here, let us begin. I have exciting news." She clasped her hands together. "I have been talking with a reporter from *Top Spa Magazine* who is actually in New York. She would like to write an article detailing the way Von Spa is bringing luxury to the next level. Her focus would include some of the amenities we provide like personalized Bento Boxes, and of course, our newest launch, complimentary shoe shining. How is that going by the way?" She beamed. "Can I see some of the shoes you have shined and wrapped in tissue paper?"

We are so busted. Thomas was flabbergasted, his mouth slightly open. He looked at me. I looked at June, June looked at Diana. Diana looked at Gabrielle. Gabrielle's eyes lit up. She spotted the prize we'd hidden in the corner hoping we'd never have to deal with it again. Overcome with excitement that now she'd be buffing shoes, a feather in the cap of her beloved job, Gabrielle said with her unique brand of unadulterated enthusiasm, "Oh, how wonderful, a shoe shiner!"

She leapt up like a child who couldn't wait to get her hands on a new toy, but just as Gabrielle claimed her trophy, she tripped and fell on the damn thing, breaking it into a million pieces! The way Gabrielle's skinny little spaghetti legs gave out from under her and ended up in the air, exposing her tiny ankles in short black socks, was pure slapstick. I couldn't dismantle this piece of crap by hitting it against the ground, while Gabrielle had accidentally shattered it to bits in the sheer happiness of its discovery.

I took one look at Thomas and our bodies began convulsing with the worst case of stifled laughter there ever was. We were two kids back in church. The tension between us melted like a polar ice cap in a nuclear age. Tears of hysterics formed in his eyes as he backed away from Yvonne's side and into the little coat check room. *After all these years he's literally going back in the closet.*

I kneeled down to help Gabrielle, hiding my own laughter in the commotion. Yvonne picked up a piece of her beloved machine, horror written all over her face. She muttered something about a first aid kit and ran into the reception area. I locked eyes with Thomas. Once we were free to let it out, we laughed so hard, neither one of us could catch our breath. Thomas got on his knees. We each grabbed one of Gabrielle's hands and assisted her to her feet. Thomas looked at me and bit his lip. I followed suit so Gabrielle wouldn't think our reaction was directed at her.

"Honey, are you okay?" he managed to ask.

"Yes, I'm fine—but the shoe shiner!" Gabrielle said in utter distress, crinkling her forehead, her eyes full of innocence. Diana and June smiled sympathetically.

"Don't worry about it, sweetie," Thomas said. "It wasn't the most popular addition to our duties. We'll be busy enough at the desk without it."

Yvonne came back with the first aid kit.

"Thank you, my fair lady." Gabrielle bowed. "I am not injured."

Yvonne nodded to Gabrielle, but seemed like she might pounce. Then Yvonne said, "Well, I guess we will be shelving the shoe shining for now. Thomas, would you mind joining me in the office?"

"Of corset. I mean of course." His smile quickly dissolved. He shrugged his shoulders, whisking out of the room with Yvonne.

Ten minutes later he came back, taking the seat next to me while I finished a phone call. We were alone.

"What happened?" I asked him. "You seem worried."

"Gabrielle is on thin ice."

"It was an accident, though. How could she blame her? I was about to nickname Gabrielle 'Shiny.' I wouldn't be surprised if we saw her buffing shoes at Grand Central on her days off. Gabrielle was the only one who shared Yvonne's enthusiasm about it anyway. I'm sorry, you were saying?"

"She can't fire her 'cause it would make her look too cruel, but Yvonne likes to blame someone when she's mad."

"I know."

"Anyway, she wants to take the money out of Gabrielle's paychecks."

"No! That will ruin her. Are you saying she could get sued and/or fired?"

"I guess so. Hopefully, I can just get it repaired instead, which is what I was *trying* to do last night, without any luck. If worse comes to worse, I'll buy a new one," he said. "It would be easier than upsetting Gabrielle."

"I thought you were with me on the paycheck-to-paycheck budgeting plan."

"I am, but I have this big jar of coins and I need the motivation to roll them up, anyway. Otherwise Diana is going to have too many mouths to feed."

"Wow. How did you hear about that already?"

"Word travels fast around here. June just apologized to me for being bitchy. I guess quitting was an empty threat," he said. "She told me what Saint Diana offered to do for her."

"You know you're a saint too, don't you?"

He grinned sheepishly, "That's sweet of you, but the shoe shiner was already broken before Gabrielle finished it off. And it was all because of my stupid plan. Besides, part of protecting Gabrielle is selfish, like it is with you."

"How so?"

"I love having her around. She's totally happy to be here. Sometimes her positive attitude really helps get me through the day."

"Speaking of positive—how's your new outlook on life going?"

"Fair to average, especially after speaking to Yvonne. It may take a little more effort than I anticipated."

The phone rang. *Time to dig my fun grave*, I thought. *The day has officially begun*. Thomas saluted as he left the room. I saluted back and picked up the phone, answering right before the third ring. "Thank you for calling The Von Courtland Spa. This is Margaret. How may I assist you?"

Chapter 10

Thomas:

Me and Mrs. Jones

After the shoe shining debacle, I basically held my breath, waiting for Yvonne to relaunch the project. The entire incident had bought me a little time but it had also created a dilemma. I didn't have the money to reimburse Gabrielle if Yvonne bought a new shoe shiner and garnished her wages. This became clear when I checked the balance in my bank account, saw how close I was to my credit limit and discovered I only had $67.48 in my jar of coins.

I found out it was much cheaper to have the shiner repaired. I prayed Yvonne wouldn't demand a relaunch until after she returned from Spa Con. The plan was to get the contraption back in working order while she was away, taking special care to make it look as good as new. *Once she's dazzled with its sumptuous beauty, Yvonne won't care that the shiner isn't right off the line,* I thought. *Then I'll just tell her the warranty covered the repairs.* I wouldn't even let myself look further into the future where the bigger problem was lingering: keeping the girls from quitting once the shining began. While I waited to see how things panned out, I focused on my Gratitude Journal. I was even grateful for the distraction.

I remembered to appreciate all the wonderful things about my job and take in the beauty all around me, beginning with the staff. I got to work with one of my best friends, Margaret; my biggest fan, Gabrielle; my substitute spa closer, June; and my favorite philanthropist, Diana.

Then there was Yvonne. She wasn't perfect but she was the first boss I'd ever had who believed in me. My previous employers had mistaken my calm exterior for aloofness or indifference. Yvonne saw this Zen-like attitude as an asset in a business where "calm" is the main objective. She knew I had potential and hired me despite a lack of experience in the industry. With a genuine love of mentorship, Yvonne made me her project and before long I was promoted to second-in-command. I knew without her, I wouldn't have been able to buy my condo. It wasn't always easy to work for Yvonne, but she was far from boring. *It'd be much worse if I worked for some dullard, right?* I thought, *Even in the face of uncertain shoe shining times, I can see the good in everyone. Amazing!*

Two days before Yvonne was scheduled to leave for Spa Con, I began my workday by filling an oil burner in the reception area. I enjoyed the scents of citrus and frangipani wafting through the air. *Gratitude Journal entry number twenty-one!* Margaret and June were busy at the desk while Gabrielle manned the phones with Diana. *Well,* I thought, *if no one needs me here, I'll go eat now. Journal entry number twenty-two!*

I filled my tray in the building cafeteria and charged it to the spa's account. For my main course, I savored a bowl of vegetarian chili topped with avocados and gobs of cheddar cheese. I balanced out this heavy entree by eating a mixed green salad with walnuts, balsamic vinegar and the ripest strawberries on record. For dessert, I devoured a piece of apple pie that tasted exactly like my Nana's. The cinnamon-sugar crumbles became orgasmic underneath melting vanilla ice cream and mountains of whipped cream. *Yvonne may not always verbalize her gratitude,* I thought, *but nothing says "thank you" like free food.* I hoped the rest of her employees appreciated it as much as I did.

I floated through the day laughing with Margaret, giving out free gifts to our spa guests and getting a lot of love in return. Even the boring closing procedures gave me a sense of satisfaction.

That night, after everyone went home, I decompressed in the Radiant Heat Area next to the men's locker room. I liked the women's side better—because it had a better view of the skyline—but one time the cleaning crew caught me after hours and teased me mercilessly. Once that happened, I stuck to the boy's side.

I did some stretching in the steam room. Then I eased into the Tornado pool, reclining in an underwater lounge chair. Effervescent bubbles surrounded me and currents of warm H_2O enveloped my sore muscles. *This job, which isn't my calling, is full of perks! How could I have been so negative when every workday can end like this?* I started getting flushed while the heat soothed my naked body. I sunk deeper into the misty waters, reflecting on the newfound happiness I'd found. My internal movie reel had gone from black and white to full color. *Winter is coming to an end, and I'm experiencing my own personal spring.* I felt so content I knew I'd have sweet dreams when my head hit the pillow. It would be the last good night's sleep I'd have in a very long time.

****

The next day began unremarkably. The doors of the spa opened, revealing a scent that smelled like white chocolate macadamia nut cookies were baking in an unseen oven. *I love our new line of incense.* I grinned to myself. *Cookies for lunch again!*

I checked the bookings. Our least favorite spa guest was already enjoying treatments with us. Mrs. B had brought in a group of her clients. This meant millions of dollars in real estate were on the line and so were our asses; she wasn't the type of guest you could appease with a free treatment. I looked at her appointments. Everything seemed to be in order. The arrival notes were already checked off, but when I took a closer look at the departure notes, the final entry troubled me.

June had reserved a table for Mrs. B and all three of her clients at Akiko, an ultra-chic sushi restaurant. The only menu option was a prix fixe dinner at four hundred dollars a plate. This meal included blowfish, a delicacy that can be poisonous if not handled correctly. The death-defying drama had made Akiko the talk of the town and the eatery was fully booked months in advance. *Houston, we might have a problem.*

I stuck my head into the concierge office. "June, may I ask you about something?"

"Whassup?" June sauntered toward the desk, rolling her curly locks into a bun. She stabbed her new updo with a silver bejeweled hairpin in the shape of a magic wand.

"Why did you make a dinner reservation for Mrs. B? She'll blame us if the restaurant screws something up." I pointed to the notes on the screen.

"Listen Paranoid Patty, the door hostess is a good friend of mine. And whatever happened to 'we never say no to a guest'?"

"We offer alternatives, like serving a Bento Box here, instead."

"It's kinda hard to do that when Mrs. B is breathing fire in your face, but relax, it's all confirmed."

"You're right. I'm sorry." I reminded myself to be grateful. "I should be congratulating you. I know how hard it is to get a table at Akiko."

"It sure was. I had to bribe my friend with some free Radiant Heat time."

"Whatever works. Thanks, June."

"My pleasure," she said, gliding toward the concierge office. June waved her magic wand and her hair sprang back to life. "Let's hope Mrs. B enjoys the blowfish," a wicked grin spread across her glossy lips. "I hear it's to die for."

"Oh my!" I replied.

The whooshing sound of the glass door cut our moment short. Wisps of Yvonne's blonde hair flew back from the breeze when she stepped into the reception area. She opened her eyes widely underneath her black horn-rimmed Chanel glasses. "My office. Now!" She turned and left.

Yvonne usually called it "our" office. If she was annoyed, she might say "the" office, but I'd never heard Yvonne say "my" office. *Here we go....or maybe not,* I thought, practicing the principal of non-reaction. *It might not be what you think it is.* I tried to calm myself down by taking a couple of cleansing breaths. Then I hurried over. *The sooner I know what the problem is, the quicker I can fix it.*

I sat down at my desk. Yvonne was staring straight at her computer. *Is she too angry to look at me?* She slowly swiveled her chair in my direction, "What kind of script are you giving the girls to use on the phone?" Yvonne glared at me. *Maybe it would be better to work for a dullard.*

My heart jumped into my throat. *She's trying to trick me into confessing something. But what?* "The same script we've used since the beginning," I said, masking my emotions. "Thank you for calling The Von—"

"More specifically, how have you been training the girls to describe the treatments?"

I felt like I was on trial and Yvonne was the bad-ass prosecutor. *Beat her at her own game.* "Why do you ask? Do we need to tweak something?"

"Answer the question!" she yelled.

Damn, she would've been a good attorney. "They all have the packet of key words and phrases to sell each treatment. There's a copy in the filing cabinet or I could email it to you if—"

"And were they all tested on this material?"

Stay calm. "Well, during the briefings we still feature a 'treatment of the week,' so after we go over the VIP list, I read them the description—"

"Oh, I have heard you. And I quote, 'It's wild about exfoliating, full of retinols and shit like that.'" I swallowed hard. Yvonne continued, "Once again, answer the question. I am leading up to something."

I know. It was so hard to make the best out of a career you didn't choose when you felt like you were being convicted of a crime you didn't commit and you had no defense team. In truth, I had never tested the concierge girls. I'd coached them as they took calls, but I wouldn't dream of giving them an exam. I wasn't that kind of leader. My leadership style involved treating people like equals. I made people want to follow because they liked me. Yvonne didn't see things this way. No one was *her* equal. She would rather have her answers in black and white so she could keep score.

"They haven't been tested in a while," I said.

"That is quite evident. And out of curiosity, how have you instructed your team to describe the Hawaiian Experience?"

Now she's testing me. I gathered my thoughts. "I have instructed them to describe it like this: The Hawaiian is our restorative island-inspired treatment. First a smooth, thick Koa stick is used to gently knead pressure points along the spine. The rounded branch releases the muscles with reflexology precision, which is superior to the touch of the hand alone. Next the therapist applies undulating wave-like strokes, using firm pressure, to relax the body and soothe the mind. The treatment concludes with a coconut oil scalp massage. It will make you feel like you've escaped to your own personal Kauai."

"Very nice—book me immediately. But just to play devil's advocate, how might one of the concierges sell a guest the Four-Handed Massage?"

How long is she going to torture me? Better lay it on thick. "Naturally I would say, and I'm sure any one of the other girls would say something to this effect. The Four-Handed Massage is our new signature treatment. It is the most luxurious, indulgent spa experience ever created. Each effleurage and petrissage is choreographed. *Two* therapists work in tandem, one on your right side, one on your left, mirroring each other's movements, thus doubling your relaxation. This technique stops the mind from following the normal progression of massage therapy, taking you to new heights of serenity as four hands erase every ounce of stress from your body. Our two-hour treatment escape is not to be missed."

"Well done. I see why I promoted you, but if the spa concierges are saying that every time they pick up the phone, then how do you explain this?!" She took an open magazine from her desk, hoisted it above her head and threw it in my lap. It landed with a loud splat—stinging me in all the wrong places—then fell onto the floor. I picked up the magazine and a headline jumped out: **The Hollywood Bikini Waxing Controversy**: **Is Bald Really Beautiful?** *That can't be it.* I fumbled to find the right article.

"Page 69," Yvonne snapped.

Vagina grooming and now 69? Ordinarily I would have laughed, but when I saw the title of the article, **A Real Day at The Von Courtland Spa: From Head to Toe**, I gasped, scanning the piece frantically. "This looks like a shopper's report, but why is it in a magazine?"

"Oh, that is not just any magazine," she said. "It is *Top Spa*, the leading industry publication. You do remember I was wooing a reporter who wanted to write about our amenities?" I nodded pathetically, like a trained dog. *Don't worry, I'm paying attention.* "Well, after our phone interview, she told me there was not enough material for the article, so she decided to look elsewhere. Naturally I was disappointed, but I knew we would have other opportunities. Unfortunately, *she* didn't. What I am trying to say is she *did* write about our spa— without telling us."

What? "But I thought she was in New York *this week*. How could her article be in the magazine already?"

"Don't you see? The reporter lied—about the subject of the piece and her trip to the city—so she could pump me for information to complete this exposé. She had already been here quite some time ago. That woman basically shopped us and printed every detail. Not so incidentally, some of the details are grounds for termination!" Yvonne shouted.

Dear God! Did she mean MY termination? I'd seen other people cross Yvonne and, once they did, she would kick them to the curb. In my heart, I knew one day I might be on the receiving end of her Koa stick. I glanced numbly at the article, trying to make sense out of what was happening.

"Hand that back to me. We cannot waste a second. Allow me to read you an excerpt." *So you can enjoy my reaction,* I thought, *along with all the drama you're creating.* "Then you need to take care of the problem."

I exhaled, relieved my job wasn't in danger. *Or was it? Don't get ahead of yourself. Live in the "now."* I swallowed hard and handed her the magazine. *But what if the moment completely sucks?* I thought, *I'd rather live in the future. Maybe I'll live in the moment of 11 p.m., when I'm already at home.* It was getting harder and harder to feel grateful.

Yvonne put on her glasses and said, "This is the conversation the reporter had when she booked the appointments." Yvonne did more than recite the words, she actually played the parts of the devious journalist and the inept spa concierge, mocking both women bitterly:

"The first time I called Von Spa, the phone was promptly answered after two rings, exceeding the Five Star three-ring standard. The spa concierge answered in a soothing voice, 'Thank you for calling The Von Courtland Spa, how may I assist you?' A name was not offered.

Top Spa (TS): Good afternoon. I would like to book an appointment.

Concierge (C): Wonderful! What kind of service would you like to enjoy?

TS: I'm not sure. I can't decide between the Hawaiian Experience and the Four-Handed Massage. Could you tell me a little bit about each treatment?

C: I would be happy to. First of all, each treatment can be tailored to your muscular pain and personality.

TS: I see.

C: Because our therapists cater to your personal needs. The Hawaiian starts off with a wood stick. The therapist gently beats your back and then massages your bones. They use small waves to take your stress out to the ocean.

TS: Do you mean out to sea?

C: Yes! Out to sea. The Four-Handed Massage is two therapists on top of one guest.

TS: Oh. That sounds very painful.

C: It is actually superb.

I booked the Hawaiian, somewhat afraid of the beating and bone massage. I was glad the treatment could be tailored to my muscular pain, but my personality? I wondered if someone was going to do a psychological evaluation, and hoped this wouldn't cut into my therapy time, no pun intended. I've heard of having an 'adjustment,' but I've never experienced bone massage. What if I was fuller figured? This is either revolutionary, terribly uncomfortable or a big mistake.

The spa concierge with whom I booked the appointment had a lovely disposition, yet I couldn't believe she was allowed to answer the phone. Part of the problem was clearly lost in translation. Her English—obviously not her native tongue— was good, but her descriptions didn't seem accurate.

Surely, she didn't mean both therapists would really be on top of me during the Four-Handed Massage. If so, would I be able to breathe? Or maybe one therapist is tasked with holding the client down because this treatment gives new meaning to the words 'deep tissue.' The ridiculous possibilities were endless. Maybe they perform erotic massages at Von Spa. Is this what she meant by 'personal needs?' At any rate, I was no longer looking forward to having a treatment. 'Trepidation' is the word that comes to mind.

When I decided to write this article, I imagined calling it 'Redefining Luxury.' I had no idea I would be writing an exposé, but the lily was no longer gilded. My working title became 'Redefining Comedy in the High End Spa Arena.' The concierge who answered the phone was unintentionally hysterical. I don't think this is the image Yvonne Von Courtland is hoping to cultivate."

From the moment Yvonne began reading, I knew two things: Gabrielle had answered the phone and Yvonne was out for blood. She looked up from the magazine. "This article is a national embarrassment with me as the butt of the joke. My spa is my namesake and I am humiliated! How could you have allowed this to go on?"

"These mistakes must have just slipped through the cracks," I said feeling like a shipwrecked sailor being circled by a shark.

"There is no way this is an isolated incident. Gabrielle has probably been making a mockery of me since you hired her."

Suddenly I do the hiring around here? "I'm so sorry, Yvonne. I will retrain Gabrielle and test her before she's allowed to answer the phones again."

"You absolutely will not!" A wicked gleam ignited in her irises. "Now you have confirmed what I have suspected for a long time. You've been covering for her, haven't you?"

"I've just been mentoring her like you've been mentoring me." As soon as the words fell out of my mouth, I regretted them.

"Oh no you don't. Do not you use my desire to mold talent against me! I will not be cajoled so easily. Gabrielle is incapable of avoiding these kinds of errors. It is always something with that one, and there you are, right behind her with a broom to sweep it all under the rug. Even when she displayed excitement for a project, she managed to destroy it, along with the shoe shiner. Gabrielle has embarrassed me enough. It's time for you put an end to this nonsense."

"You mean you want *me* to fire her?"

"That is exactly what I mean," she said, narrowing her gaze ever so slightly.

You can't save her this time, I thought. But I couldn't handle being there to witness Gabrielle's agony. "Don't you want to take care of it? You're always so good at telling them, 'we both know it's not working out' and 'it's best we part ways so you can find your true calling' and everything."

"Since you are so fond of mentoring," Yvonne hissed, "allow me to mentor you. I have always taught you not to take business personally. You have succeeded in this realm when handling angry guests. Now you need to apply that knowledge here. You must perform difficult tasks like this if you want to be successful in the industry. Take your own feelings out of the equation. Gabrielle is bad for the reputation of my spa. I need to protect that—*period.* It's what the business demands."

I felt two feet tall. The lump in my throat was so big, I could barely swallow. The situation was futile, yet I said, "I know what I have to do, but I'll be short at the desk if I do it today. Can it wait until tomorr—?"

"Will you stop acting like a child and start thinking like a businessman? And have you forgotten I am leaving for Spa Con tomorrow?" She pulled off her glasses like she was mad at them. "You need to put her out of her misery before she answers the phone again. The next time, it could be a Five Star shopper on the line! Gabrielle has gift wrapped this opportunity for us. It's time for you to man up."

Ew! I couldn't believe she bullied me with the words "man up." *How passive-aggressive. I'm outta here.* "I'll take care of it," I said and started to leave.

"Wait! You have to tell Gabrielle something else, too. She won't be getting her last paycheck. I will use the money towards a new shoe shiner."

"Can't we just get it repaired?"

Yvonne scoffed, "I don't want some patched up pile of junk touching our guest's expensive shoes. We will continue to strive for perfection. Gabrielle is lucky she isn't paying for the whole thing."

She's not paying for any of it! I thought, vowing that Gabrielle's last paycheck would come out of my pocket. I headed out the door.

"There is one more thing I have to bring to your attention." *There's always one more thing. Jesus—is she trying to kill me?* Yvonne turned her chair to face me. "I had to let Christie go."

"Christie?" I asked, shocked. "I thought she was your favorite. She's never even taken a day off."

"Christie has gotten too many complaints for being short with the guests and now she has crossed the line."

"What happened?"

"There is no time for that now. Just tell Margaret I am making her an esthetician—effective immediately."

I was overcome with guilt. I had never talked to Yvonne about promoting Margaret. Maybe subconsciously I didn't want her to leave the desk. It was Christie's demise, rather than my valor, which had finally made Margaret's dream come true. "Margaret will be happy, but I can't be *three* people short at the desk." *Why did I say that?*

"You will have to be," she turned back toward her computer. "It's what the business demands."

Screw trying to enjoy this place. I hate it here! Leave it to Yvonne to make some good news suck. How could I possibly enjoy telling Margaret about her new position, knowing I'd have to break Gabrielle's heart? *This is only a job to most of us, but to Gabrielle, it's who she is,* I thought. *What is she going to do?*

The fragrance of heavily perfumed candles overwhelmed my olfactory receptors when the automatic doors opened. *I changed my mind. Too many scents give me a headache.* And there was something else in the air. For some reason the spa smelled like shit.

Margaret was manning the desk by herself. This meant Diana and June had gone to lunch. Gabrielle was in the office answering the phones, all alone, unaware of her fate. The evil planets were in alignment. *Let's get it over with,* I thought. *I'll pick up the emotional pieces later.*

I hadn't seen Margaret yet that day. Her eyes lit up when I walked in the room.

"Uh-oh," her smile turned into a frown. "Who's forgetting to take notes for his Gratitude Journal? You are!"

"Actually, there is something to be grateful for, but there's something horrible overshadowing it. I'll have to make this quick, so what do you want first—the good news or the bad news?"

"Hit me with the good news, then tell me the bad news as you leave. At least that way, you can enjoy the theatrics. Give me an existential exit."

"You got it. Guess who's the newest esthetician at The Von Courtland Spa? You are! Effective immediately."

"Oh my gosh!" She squealed, jumping up and down. "Tell me you're not joking," her eyes widened.

"It's true."

"Thank you, God!" She looked to the heavens. "What a relief," Margaret sighed. "I am *so* not cut out for working the front desk. Like Yvonne always says, it's a very clerical job, and I'm totally unclerical. I can't wait to tell my parents!" Margaret embraced me, rocking back and forth. It was a little comforting in a maternal way. I could feel her big boobs pressing up against me and her warm face next to mine. When the hug ended, she said, "Thanks, Thomas—from the bottom of my heart." She put her hand to her chest, tears forming in her perfectly lined emerald eyes. "I never would've survived here without you. You're an angel."

"Oh and I almost forgot. Your new uniform is coming in tomorrow."

"Now I won't be mistaken for Bruce in drag anymore! How much good news can a gal take? I can't remember the last time I was so happy."

"And I'm really happy for you, but it's going to be a delayed reaction. Are you ready for the bad news?"

"Of corset." She tried to dull her smile to a half-frown. "But I think I already have an idea."

"You do?" I couldn't believe she'd figured it out. "Isn't it awful?!"

"It's not that bad. I know you'll be short at the desk without me, so I can wait until you hire my replacement. I'll help you in any way I can," she said with an earnest grin.

"That's another challenge, but it's not the problem I'm talking about." After I delivered the news, I dramatically left the room without seeing Margaret's reaction. I heard her say "yipes," and I imagined her putting a hand over her mouth. My exact words were, "Yvonne has given me no choice—I'm on my way to fire Gabrielle."

****

Gabrielle was on the phone with an extremely chatty guest when I entered the concierge office. *Shut up whoever you are!* Pressure built between my temples while I waited for her to finish. *The universe is conspiring against me.*

She finally hung up and said, "Is there something you need me to do, mon chéri?"

"Not exactly Gabrielle—"

"Good. Then I suppose June told you I have a wonderful idea for when we start shoe shining."

"No, she—"

"We can spray the stinky shoes with herbal perfume! It will be fantastic. Then they won't be smelly when we are buffing and the guests will love it. What do you think?" She beamed.

Do you have to be so cute and excited right now? I couldn't stand the thought of upsetting her. My pulse pounded in my brain, adding fuel to a monstrous headache. *Must get Advil.*

"It's a great idea." I looked around the concierge office trying to come up with the right words to say. "I want to tell you, working with you has always been amazing."

"Oh no! You are not thinking of leaving us again. Please don't! My heart would be broken in a million ashes."

"That's not it, sweetie," I said, wondering if I was making things worse by taking her on an unintentional emotional roller coaster.

"Thanks God! Go ahead. I'll let you finish. I appreciate the compliments."

"Anyway, I love your positive attitude and your pride in working here. You add glamour and fun to the environment." I grabbed her hand. "You make me proud to have this job. The problem is, there are some continuing issues Yvonne finds unacceptable." *Tell her about the article. Gosh this is so hard. Stop stalling.* Gabrielle raised her eyebrows. I felt like I was disowning my beloved sister.

"I know, mi amor. Thank you for being so understanding and coaching me to help me improve. I would do anything you say to get better." She nodded her head and smiled, a soldier ready for orders.

My heart was bleeding. *Get it done. Deal with your emotions later,* my inner record played. Yvonne was right. I took my personal feelings out of the equation, not for me—for Gabrielle. No matter how long she talked, I knew I'd listen. *If she cries for an hour, she'll have my shoulder. Do whatever it takes to make this easier for her.* Keeping her in suspense was killing me. I knew she could read my worried expression. Her lower lip began to quiver. *Does she already know?* I continued, "Gabrielle, I really do love you, but the thing is…" I couldn't get the words out. "Well, we have to let you—"

BEEP! BEEP! BEEP! I was saved by the bell.

Unfortunately, the sound also spelled disaster.

****

I jumped up, so startled I couldn't finish my sentence. The fire alarm was going off. There was no time to explain to Gabrielle the reasons for her imminent demise. She needed my undivided attention, and at that moment it wasn't an option. It would torture both of us, but it had to wait. *Maybe this interlude will help her process everything.*

I had to do damage control in the spa immediately. If I didn't act fast, we'd have to comp everyone's treatments. My mind spiraled into the worst case scenario. *All the angry guests refuse to pay; the spa loses thousands of dollars; we don't make our monthly budget; Yvonne lays off spa concierges; I work overtime until I have a nervous breakdown; I develop such bad anxiety that I can't leave the house; I lose my condo and am forced to kiss my New York dreams good-bye.* I grabbed the phone and dialed the building's engineering department. *The sooner I confirm the alarms are working, the sooner they'll end the drill.* The department's voicemail picked up. *Those lazy fucking assholes never answer the phone! Who's running this drill?*

BEEP! BEEP! BEEP!

"It's Thomas Haven in the spa." BEEP! BEEP! BEEP! "The alarms are working. Turn them off!"

Shit! I decided the security guard on the eighth floor could radio the engineers if they were somewhere else in the building. BEEP! BEEP! BEEP! I ran out of the office, but when I saw what was happening in reception, I stopped dead in my tracks. The alarm was no longer my top priority. A new problem had emerged, which was potentially even more costly. Mrs. B was standing at the desk, screaming at the top of her lungs.

Holy Fuck. I'd forgotten she was in the spa. *Yvonne will destroy me if we lose her business.*

I swung into action, trying to speak over the alarm, but not so loud that she perceived it as yelling. "I am very sorry. Naturally your treatments will be comped—I mean complimentary. When the building does fire safety tests, it's out of our control." BEEP! BEEP! BEEP!

"The alarm is just the icing on the cake," she shrieked. The black and white scarf around her head evoked the Wicked Queen from "Snow White," with locks of her blue-black bob peeking out from underneath. Her guests sat behind us on our harem couches, plugging their ears, waiting to leave.

"Why don't we have someone escort your clients around the corner to Akiko? You and I can go into the office where it's a little quieter to work something out."

Mrs. B's words seethed out of her mouth, "That would be a great idea if you people didn't screw that up, too! They have no record of our reservation." *Oh. My. God.* BEEP! BEEP! BEEP!

194

"I'm sure we can fix this," I said, and muttered to Margaret, "Did you try June on the emergency phone in the building cafeteria?"

Margaret mumbled back, "I did. June called the restaurant but her friend is out sick. Akiko has a group in from Miramax and they don't have any tables available." The wind was knocked out of me. BEEP! BEEP! BEEP!

Mrs. B turned to her guests. "Ladies will you excuse me for a moment?" She motioned for me to step back into the concierge office, grabbed me by the elbow and pushed me through the door. My polyester uniform scratched roughly against my skin. Mrs. B squeezed my arm so hard I knew I'd develop a bruise. *At any other spa, this woman would be escorted out by security.* I felt like I was on the playground again when the boys were calling me a fairy. And she was only beginning.

"This is beyond unacceptable!" Mrs. B screamed. Her face turned purple, making her eyes look impossibly blue. Gabrielle, whose head was on the desk, sat up abruptly. BEEP! BEEP! BEEP! "I ask you people to make a simple reservation and you completely fail." Mrs. B's pungent smoker's breath assaulted my nose. "This is the most expensive spa in New York, and the rest of the country for that matter. At these prices I expect the best service with the most intelligent staff, not some idiots who can't handle a basic phone call to a restaurant." The alarm continued to blare in the background. "We would've been better off going to Chinatown and getting ten minute rubdowns on the street!" Tiny droplets of her spit stung my eyes. "What do you have to say for yourself?"

Hate coursed through my veins. Unlike a normal angry guest, I couldn't help but take this personally. She had violated my space, and treated me like a child, embarrassing me in front of my staff, in addition to her snotty clients. Yet, I gathered my inner strength to do as I had been trained and asked, "What can I do to make you happy?"

195

"What you can do, you incompetent service industry buffoon, is get me a table at Akiko. I don't care if you get on all fours and pretend you're the table yourself. Now I am going to sit in reception until you have done so. This conversation is over. I have to watch my blood pressure. If anything happens to my unborn child because you've made me so upset, I will hunt you down. Remember *that* when you're making our reservation!"

My head pounded with the beat of the alarm. *How could I accomplish this impossible task?* And before Mrs. B broke her predatory gaze, the heavens opened above us. *What the hell is going on?* It was raining in the spa.

****

Mrs. B screamed, "What the fuck?" and looked up at the ceiling. *Oh. My. GOD!* I thought. *The building is on fire!* I shimmied past Mrs. B to get out of the office, pushing her slightly in a subconscious attempt to gratify my disdain. I didn't care about her stupid reservation anymore. This was a *real* emergency. As the fire safety director of the spa, I was responsible for the well-being of the staff.

Reception was in chaos. Mrs. B's guests gathered their coats, scurrying to escape the downpour. Margaret shouted, "What happened?" and dove under the front desk. The therapists filed down the crystal staircase. Clients held newspapers over their heads, speeding to the doors. Two male locker room attendants laughed and skipped playfully like they'd been caught in a sudden thunderstorm.

I ran into the spa. Tootsie hollered as I hurried past her, "What should we do, Thomas?" If the building was on fire, I knew we were all in trouble. In a post 9/11 world, anything could happen.

"Evacuate—everyone evacuate! Take the emergency exit by the secret meeting place. Call me on the Blackberry from outside to let me know what's going on. I need to make sure everyone's out of the spa!"

I sprinted down the main corridor and took the back staircase to the 9th floor. I ran down the hallways, and looked into the treatment rooms, yelling to make sure people were leaving. Fear crept into me like a silent disease, but I was so possessed with my mission, I didn't care. I was the captain. I would be the last person out—even if the ship went down.

Taking three or four steps at a time, I leapt back down the staff staircase and checked the main floor of the spa. Feverishly, I surveyed the locker rooms and heat areas for signs of life, banging on doors, screaming at the top of my lungs, "Follow the staff, down the stairs! Evacuate the building. Evacuate!" I heard an enormous crash, which sounded like an atomic explosion. *What the hell was that?!* A thought shot into my brain like lightening answering the thunder. *The sound came from up front. Oh no! Where's Margaret?!*

I ran to the desk, but she wasn't there. *Thank God! She's gone.* Completely out of breath, I scanned the empty concierge office. Both stories were all clear—or so I thought. The sprinklers had been on for at least five minutes and it was still pouring. I bolted toward the emergency exit but stopped when I heard someone screaming in the background.

Holy shit. This is so surreal! I felt like I was in a movie that was turning into a horror film. I imagined watching myself from outside my body. At the same time, I'd never felt so focused. I had to help, *but where was the yelling coming from?* It was primal, and triggered an evolutionary instinct. A member of my tribe was in danger. I followed the wailing toward the reception area. The shrieking got louder and louder. *I'm headed in the right direction. Oh my God. It's Yvonne!*

197

And then I saw her through the mist, hurrying down the crystal spiral staircase, slipping on the glass in her black Jimmy Choos, clutching to the railing for support. Her navy pantsuit was soaked to the bone, hanging off her skeletal frame. Her blonde up-do was flattened, and tendrils of hair were plastered over her face. She stumbled like a zombie from "The Walking Dead" and looked like Patsy from "Ab Fab," falling in a drunken stupor.

"My spa. My spa!" Yvonne howled, her voice as scratchy as an old record. She was squeezing her cell phone so hard, her fingers were turning blue. When Yvonne's eyes met mine, she bolted upright. "Turn off the water! Turn it off! Security just confirmed there is no fire! THERE IS NO FIRE!" She dropped to her knees at the bottom of the stairs, weeping, banging her fists on the floor. Yvonne's screams paid homage to the Wicked Witch of the West, melting at the end of "The Wizard of Oz." I'd never seen her show so much emotion, but it wouldn't be the last time I'd hear her cry.

Water from my hair streamed down my face, clouding my vision. I was so concerned with everyone's safety, I hadn't even thought about the magnitude of damage occurring right in front of me.

I ran to the back hallway and tried to turn off the spa's main water valve, but it wouldn't budge. I grabbed the Blackberry from my pocket. It was soaked and the screen was blank. The water on the floor was several inches deep. I slipped when I rounded a corner, landing on my wrists and banging my right knee. White hot pain shot through me, yet I managed to limp to our office. I picked up the landline, praying the phone still worked. *Yes!* Even dialing the numbers caused fire to spread through my wounded arm.

"Engineering; this is Daniel." *Thank God someone answered.*

"I need you to turn off the water!"

"What water? Where?"

"In the spa!"

"Alright, let me see who's available—"

"You don't understand. The sprinklers are going off. Come now!"

"Okay, okay."

Sixty seconds later, Daniel turned off the main pipe, but it was too late. The water damage was done. I surveyed the scene. The three-inch puddle was disappearing slowly, which meant it was seeping into the floors below. Our silken Japanese pillows and crimson upholstery in the reception area were soaked. With the slightest touch, they overflowed like squeezed sponges. The splendid gold-leafed walls were back to their original shade of white. A bronze river trickled across the floor. One of the Chihuly blown glass chandeliers, heavy from the weight of the water had fallen down. Broken yellow pieces covered the black marble tiles beneath my feet. Our scarlet curtains leaked dye as if they were bleeding.

I slowly climbed the crystal spiral staircase. Once I got to the top, I discovered what had caused the enormous crash: the pink silk charmeuse window dressing that had once hung in the Tea Room, also heavy with water, had snapped its bamboo curtain rod, which fell onto the glass shelves, starting a chain reaction. Amongst jagged chards, the bodies of priceless antique tea sets littered the floor. It was such a loss, I almost vomited. I ran into one of the treatment rooms and hovered over the sink, but nothing came out. I pulled a moist paper towel from the dispenser, wiped my face and looked around the room. Fragile Chinese paper changing screens, embroidered with cherry blossoms, had turned to mush. The drywall separating the treatment rooms was shedding its magically blue-iridescent wallpaper skin. Mold would be impossible to prevent, and the entire floor would have to be gutted. And this was only the damage that could be seen.

I walked down the sparkling staircase. Despite its delicate components, it might have been the only thing left unharmed in the spa. The railings looked strangely beautiful, glistening and dripping wet.

The computers, copiers and phones had drowned. Both floors would have to be rewired, too. Yet somehow, through it all, tranquil music permeated the air while two magnificent spa stories lay in ruins. What had taken Yvonne over a year to decorate, only took minutes for the sprinkler system—designed for protection—to completely ruin.

How could this happen? Did I just have a mental break and imagine everything? I touched my face to make sure I wasn't hallucinating and became aware of the state I was in. My knees were shaking, my head was pounding, my wrists throbbed. The pain convinced me it was all real. I couldn't believe Gabrielle and Christie weren't the only ones who lost their jobs that day. *Now everyone is unemployed.* The Yvonne Von Courtland Spa was no more.

I didn't have time to think about the future. I had to talk to Yvonne. Von Spa was her child. She reveled in the fact that people walked into the reception area saying, "I want to see your 10 million dollar spa." It was destroyed and I knew she would be, too. I worried Yvonne might be so devastated, she'd do something rash. And I thought, *What on earth is going to happen now?*

****

Our office across the hall was untouched. I found Yvonne staring blankly at her computer. There was only one thing worse than Yvonne refusing to look at you—when she glared straight into your eyes.

"You," she seethed, "*you* are responsible for this!"

Oh my God. Yvonne is in blame mode and she's set her sights on me! I was more frightened at that moment then I had been minutes earlier, when I thought the building was on fire. *You have to defend yourself.*

"I—I beg to differ," I stuttered, imagining the words dribbling out of my mouth, a blanket of anxiety threatening to strangle me. "I followed the proper protocol to ensure the staff's safety."

"You should have immediately investigated the source of the problem and in the absence of a fire, you should have disabled the sprinkler. *You* are the fire safety director but I learned more about proper protocol from reading a brochure!"

"I thought they were testing the building alarm system. It's the first Thursday of the month."

"You *thought*," she said dramatically. "My multi-million dollar spa that I have put my blood, sweat and tears into for the last four years is completely ruined because 'you *thought!*'"

It wasn't that simple. *I have to make her understand.* "Yvonne, the sprinklers only go off if there *is* a fire and there was no auditory indication of that from the alarm. We would have heard the robot voice saying, 'Fire!' repeatedly. The only other logical conclusion is that there was a catastrophic problem somewhere else in the building. That's why I evacuated the spa." I paused. "Something isn't adding up," I said, trying to make sense of the situation. I couldn't tell if she was actually listening to me. Yvonne put her hands over her face. She looked so pitiful. I broke down. "I'm *very* sorry. There's no way I could've known how this was going to end." I felt so deeply sad for all of us, especially Yvonne, that I thought the water dripping from me was my sorrow coming to life.

She snapped back to attention, throwing her arms to her side, and yelled, "Do you know what your apology means to me? It means you are admitting fault. And you are to blame by the way. Because of you, the alarm went off in the first place. What are your *thoughts* on that?!" She panted like a wild animal about to strike and kill.

"I am not admitting anything. I'm simply empathizing with your situation. I can imagine how hard this must be for you."

She looked back at her computer, biting her lip. "You have no idea."

"How could I possibly be responsible for setting off the alarm, anyway? Don't you remember what I was doing when it happened? I was talking to Gabrielle—about to fire her."

"Your actions in that moment are not what I am referring to. It is what you failed to do to prevent all of this." *Now I'm confused,* I thought. *What is she talking about?* She continued, "Do you know what set off the alarm? Because I do!"

Assured I was innocent, I said, "No. Enlighten me."

"Tootsie was burning sage again."

"And why is that *my* fault?"

"How many times have you told her not to burn sage?"

It's over for me. I had *never* discussed it with her. "I don't remember, but I'm sure I did." This was serious and a lie was my only way out.

"Well according to Tootsie, you didn't broach the subject with her at all. Someone is building fires in the spa, which you knew about, and you're surprised the alarm is going off. You should have seen this coming. How could you be so stupid?"

"With all due respect, I think you're grasping at straws. I can't control Tootsie."

"You didn't even try! Did they teach you anything about fire prevention? She could have burned the whole building down, too. Lighting torches of sage, while holding them over her head next to the sprinklers like the Olympic flame! And just so you know I'm *not*

202

grasping at straws, June told me you failed to address this behavior at our meeting. I've never had to coach Tootsie twice, yet she continued saging the spa."

I had to change the subject. "And how in the world did you get all this information so quickly?"

"After I talked to you about Gabrielle, I ran out to get coffee. You can imagine my surprise when upon my return, I saw the entire staff in front of the building looking haggard. They told me about the fire alarm and all eyes were on Tootsie who had smoked out the whole spa with a huge fistful of sage. She gave me the ridiculous explanation that it was necessary to remove the 'bad energy' left by the Jones and Johnson group. When I reminded Tootsie of her coaching session regarding this behavior, she told me there hadn't been one! I defended you, because you insisted you would address the issue."

"Yvonne, I-I—"

"Don't interrupt me! I informed everyone there would be a full scale investigation and anyone who did not provide me with full disclosure would be deemed complicit. June reluctantly admitted she had told you about this problem repeatedly, asking you to put an end to it. Then I realized why everyone looked so haggard. They were wet! I ran upstairs to see my life's work literally going down the drain because of your *egregious incompetence*. So unless you can provide me with the Disciplinary Action Form or the corresponding email documenting your coaching session with Tootsie, I will be forced to take her side!" she shouted, pulling her trump card.

Oh. My. God. There was no form, no email and there had never been a coaching session. *I have to try another tactic.* "Even if all that is true, Tootsie was the one holding the torch." I felt bad for throwing her under the bus, but I was desperate. I remembered the scent of sage wafting through the air right before I went to fire Gabrielle. *That's the reason the spa stunk.*

My head was spinning. *If only I had said something to Tootsie, even in passing, maybe this wouldn't have happened.* I was kicking myself. *But we were lighting incense all the time and it never set off the alarm.* I prayed we were missing a piece of the puzzle, hoping against hope there was some other explanation for the demise of the spa and I was not responsible for this epic disaster.

Yvonne declared, in full melodramatic glory, "As the fire safety director, you have been negligent." And the next few words she said through gritted teeth, "I had to watch my spa melt to the ground while you tinkered away to turn off the sprinklers, but you didn't even resolve the problem, did you? Engineering took care of that."

I didn't know what to say. Then it hit me. *There's only way to get out of this.* I had to call Yvonne on her pattern of "pointing the finger" when she's angry. *Maybe if Yvonne understands what she's doing, she'd realize I might not be to blame.* I decided there was a slim chance Yvonne would hold back her judgment until all the facts were in. *What do I have to lose? My job?* "So that's it, Yvonne. You've done your thirty second investigation and determined I'm at fault?"

"The facts don't lie," she said. Her steely gaze made me shudder.

"The fact is, you like to blame someone else whenever there's a problem. This is your pattern. I've seen you do it time and time again to other people. You've even done it to me until I proved I wasn't responsible for any wrongdoing. I never told you how upsetting it is that you don't trust me."

"I have no idea what you are talking about. And in regards to your 'hurt feelings,' this is your biggest flaw as a manager and a human being. You are too emotional for your own good."

"Whatever, Yvonne. I'm just holding a mirror in front of your face." There was a tremor in my voice and I could feel my knees shaking again. "You don't want to look at yourself."

"What about you, sir? You cannot admit when *you* are wrong or when *you* are at fault—like with Gabrielle. You were enabling her errors because instead of disciplining her, you preferred to cover her tracks. And you didn't want to fire her, even though she was bad for business. You were too emotionally involved. If I *always* need someone to blame when I am angry, I should have blamed you for keeping her around for *so* long and lying to me, TO MY FACE, so she would have the opportunity to make more mistakes!"

"What about the time *you* were ready to point the finger at *me* because *you* were angry about the stolen gift card. You were going to get rid of me unless I could prove I wasn't the thief, whether it was true or not! Even after all my years of service, *you* were so emotional, you let your rage cloud your judgment before the verdict was in. You are such a hypocrite! I can't believe I've worked for you this long. I always had to watch my back. I'm glad I don't have to do it anymore."

"You want angry? You have yet to see my wrath. There *will* be a full scale investigation to prove this is your fault. I am going to sue you for everything you are worth because of what your incompetence has cost me. Kiss your condo goodbye. You will be hearing from my lawyer."

Her words felt like a knife in my heart, but I knew I had to fight back. *She can't see me as weak.* "Why don't you wait until the investigation is complete instead of letting your temper decide? I did nothing wrong. I have a lawyer, too. I will sue you for wrongful termination and use the money to open my own spa."

"Is that what you want to do? Because you're jealous of me?" Yvonne's voice undulated up and down. "Do you hate me because you want to be me?" she guffawed. "You'll never be me!"

"Oh no. I would *never* want to be you, alone in your ivory tower. I have friends, family and people who love me, when all you have is power and rage." I saw the loneliness in her eyes and a strange sense of pity overcame me. I had to look away.

"And if you open your own spa, I hope it burns to the ground."

"That wouldn't happen, because I would be the *real* fire safety director, not someone with an empty title whose hands are tied behind his back because his boss is such a control freak."

"Get the hell out of my office before I have security escort you out!" She stood up like she would have slapped me if we were on an episode of "Knots Landing."

I grabbed my jacket. Nothing else there belonged to me. I dramatically left the room, but before I did, I said, "There's no need. I have wasted way too much time here. Goodbye, Yvonne. See you in court."

My body trembled with fear and anger. *I know something you don't know I know*, I thought. *But I can't play MY trump card just yet.* I wasn't sure exactly when or if I would. Depending on how I used this information, I knew it could save me or be the sole cause of my ultimate undoing. *Wait and see what happens*, I told myself. *I can't believe it's come to this.*

****

It's hard to describe how I felt when I left the building. I was flooded with emotions: anxiety, anger, disbelief, sadness. The funny thing was, I had a nagging question in my mind. A question I never would have expected. The possibilities of what could happen to me were endless, frightening and impossible to predict, but this question almost

206

bothered me more: *What am I going to do now?* Not in the future, rather in that exact moment. *Go home? Sit around my apartment? What will I do tomorrow?* I'd been completely enmeshed with the spa and after it was gone I was lost at sea.

I called Anthony, hoping we could meet so he could help me process what had happened. He didn't answer. I left him a message. *What am I thinking? Where the hell did everyone go?* I tried Margaret. Her voicemail picked up, too. "Where are you? Sweet Jesus—call me!" I said.

I was still in my uniform. My wallet, money and keys were in my jacket, but I'd forgotten the street clothes I'd worn to work that day along with a pair of Steve Madden saddleback boots. *I'm never getting them back. Damn it to Hell.*

Every ten seconds I checked my cell phone. I knew I would feel it vibrate but I kept looking anyway. I was desperate to talk to one of my best friends. *I have to get it out.* If something is bothering me, talking about it, as much as possible, is the key to feeling better. *I'll be gabbing about this one for years,* I thought. Waiting was driving me crazy. I had to do something else.

I headed for Central Park to walk off the frustration, grabbing a newspaper on the way. The clear blue sky did nothing for the rain cloud above me. I was in shock. I was in denial. My thoughts were racing. *Did I just imagine the last hour?* Yvonne's wrath terrified me. *Would she take away my home to satisfy her lust for revenge? What if it really IS my fault? Am I a victim or a perpetrator?*

I sat down on a bench and watched the sunlight dance between the swaying trees. It was an unusually warm day for early March, but I was shivering in my wet uniform. Feeling a little uncomfortable was strangely helpful in its distraction.

Winter is ending soon, but is mine just about to begin? What if I have to move back home? I'll spiral. I'll become suicidal! I can't go to the land of sports where I don't fit in. Shut up. SHUT YOURSELF UP!

207

I looked at the front page of the paper, knowing I wouldn't be able to concentrate. The only solution was to try—even if I had to read everything out loud. First the main headline: **Two Killed in Robbery Gone Wrong!** "A small gang of masked men attempted to rob a liquor store in the South Bronx yesterday...owner activated a silent alarm...staff was held hostage...police raided through the back door...two assailants were shot and killed." *Dear God. At least I'm not dead or being robbed at gunpoint.* Next a smaller item: **Mystery Woman of the MTA** "An unidentified woman fell down a staircase at the northwest corner of the Broadway-Lafayette subway station... approximately 3 a.m....suffering from a concussion and memory loss....no purse, wallet or identification was found at the scene...believed to be in her mid-sixties...blonde hair and grey eyes...if anyone has any information etc., etc." Surprisingly, I felt a pang of jealousy. *I wish I could erase today out of my memory.*

I looked up from the paper and there she was with her posse, standing next to a coffee stand where the park meets the sidewalk, talking on her phone. She had treated me like an animal. And as Sarah McLachlan will tell you on those commercials, animals don't deserve it, either. *Say something. You have nothing to lose.* I walked up behind her and tapped her on the shoulder. She turned around, startled. Her mouth fell open. I thought, *You've earned your name.* I stood before Mrs. Bitch.

I lit into her, "To use your own words, the way you treated me was beyond unacceptable—"

"Well if you'd done your job by providing me with better service, I wouldn't have been forced to. Besides, look at me. Would anyone guess I've just come from a luxury spa? It looks like I narrowly escaped a monsoon."

"Lady, I've had a hell of a day and you are going to listen to me or I'm going to shove that phone so far up your bleached puckered rectum, you're gonna taste it!" She moved her lips, but no words came out. *I'm totally intimidating her.* "I don't know who had the balls, pun intended, to get you pregnant, but I hope for his sake, it wasn't a black widow situation." She backed up, I followed. I was taller than she, looming over her face and looking down on her. I saw fear in her eyes, so I continued, "It's shocking anyone would want to have sex with someone like you in the first place, but for *everyone's* sake, please consider giving your child up for adoption because the last thing this world needs is another bitch like you!" Her clients gasped. One of them stifled a smile.

I turned to walk away and she grabbed me by the elbow again, hurting my injured arm. She yelled at me, inflaming my emotional wounds from childhood, "You listen to me you little fa—"

Oh no! I couldn't let that sociopath call me a faggot. I wasn't on the playground anymore. I interrupted her, barking like the dog she thought I was. I shouted so loudly, I scared her into silence, and grabbed my arm back with such intensity, I nearly knocked her off her stilettos. "Don't you ever touch me again or I will be the one tracking you down!" I stared intently at Mrs. Bitch. She appeared to be rendered speechless again. I headed back to the park.

This might make a good story if I weren't the main character. I should have enjoyed telling her off, yet I felt strangely ashamed; intimidating people really isn't my thing. Guilt seeped into the cocktail of satisfaction inside of me, and ultimately, I found my behavior frightening. *Who am I becoming?*

Mrs. Bitch brought me back into the moment by hollering, "I'll have your job!"

I turned around, walking backwards, while some uncomfortable laughter snuck out of me. What I said next helped me process the truth: "You can have my job, lady. I don't work there anymore!"

Chapter 11

Margaret:

Chapter 11

McMillan's was a bar the spa staff frequented after work, so everyone felt right at home. The décor was typical for an Irish pub, with dark wooden wall paneling and flat screen TVs, usually tuned to ESPN. We had taken over an area with high top tables. The mood was relaxed, almost jovial—one of the building security guards had told us it'd been a false alarm. We collectively decided the spa would be closed until the night cleaners mopped up. People exchanged war stories about escaping the downpour over beer, cocktails and hot wings.

Where's Thomas? I wondered. *Maybe I should text him so he knows we're here.* I opened my phone and saw his barrage of messages. I frantically called him back. He picked up before it rang.

"Oh my God, Maggie. I'm totally freaking out!"

"Why? We have the rest of the day off, don't we? Come and meet us at Mc—"

"I can't," he said, hysterial. "Can you come meet *me?*"

"I would, but Yvonne called June and told her to get the staff together for an impromptu meeting. You'd better get over here—"

"No, I really shouldn't. Yvonne fired me. Now she's going to sue me. I can't even believe it myself, but I really am getting sued and/or fired!"

"Are you serious? *Why?*"

"She blames me for everything. The fire alarm going off, the sprinklers—"

"What?!" I said. "How in the world did that happen? Oh shit. She's here."

"Call me and let me know every word she says. I'll be desperately clinging to my phone waiting to hear from you, but no pressure."

"Will do."

"Actually, can you meet me at the diner afterwards, instead? I really need to talk."

"Of course." I said. *Make it quick, Yvonne. My friend needs me.*

Yvonne approached us with her hair pulled back like she'd just gotten out of the shower. She had a dazed expression on her face. I elbowed June. June nudged Gabrielle as a hush trickled over the whole staff. An elderly couple at the bar abruptly stopped their conversation and looked towards us, confused. I saw vulnerability in Yvonne's eyes for the first time. When she opened her mouth, I couldn't imagine what she was going to say.

"I will begin in a moment, but first I need to speak to Tootsie in private." Tootsie sheepishly slinked past the others and followed Yvonne to a booth in the back of the bar. There were muffled whispers amongst the staff. You could cut the tension with a knife.

A minute later, Tootsie ran out of the room, crying so hard she could barely catch her breath. My heart broke for her. I tried to prevent it from happening, but I thought: *Toot, Toot, Tootsie, Good-Bye!* To punish myself, I bit my lip until I tasted blood.

Yvonne motioned for Gabrielle to come over. Gabrielle looked behind her, pointing to herself as if to ask, "Me?" Yvonne confirmed with a nod. Gabrielle didn't even take a seat. Yvonne pointed to something in a magazine. Gabrielle shook her head and walked out of the bar, averting her eyes. *Yvonne canned our friend like day old tuna. Now we'll never find out where she's from.* I tasted blood again.

Yvonne stood up and took her position in front of the staff. The therapists, front desk girls and locker room attendants sat at the tables or lined the walls. The stench of beer filled the air. It felt weird that two people had just been fired at such a dump. Yvonne smoothed down her misshapen periwinkle silk blouse and began.

"There isn't any easy way to say this," her voice cracked. "The spa will be closed indefinitely."

People gasped. There was no whispering, only voices talking loudly. I froze, completely dumbfounded. She continued, "There was extensive water damage and I'm not sure how long the repairs will take."

June shouted, "Are you serious? I can't be without a job right now."

I thought to myself, *What am I supposed to do with this information?*

"I'm confident most of you will be able to collect unemployment," Yvonne said, her belle-of-the-meeting voice noticeably absent.

"I won't be able to live on half my salary for long." June's angry tone made the whole situation even more surreal. *No one's ever spoken to Yvonne like that.* After pausing for a brief moment June asked, "When is the spa going to reopen? Do you at least have an idea?"

Yvonne clenched her jaw and crinkled her brow. She looked like, just maybe, she was holding back tears and actually sounded human when she spoke. "I'm not sure—six months, maybe a year?"

There was a communal yelp. Then June shouted, "A year? When unemployment runs out, we'll never be able to find jobs with the way the economy is!"

Yvonne snapped into news reporter mode. Without emotion she said, "It's out of my control. Thomas, Tootsie and Gabrielle will no longer be with us. The rest of you will always have a job with me when the spa reopens. This meeting is adjourned." She turned and stormed out, leaving shockwaves in her wake.

****

I waited for Thomas at The Flame Restaurant on 9th Ave and 58th Street. It was a quintessential diner with cozy little booths, a visible stainless steel kitchen and a daisy in a vase on every table. They also had one of those rotating dessert cases with mile high cakes and gooey pastries, but my favorite part of the place was the hanging pothos plant. The vines were so long, they had to be tacked to the ceiling. Green leaves adorned the tin tiles from the door to the opposite corner of the room.

The diner's charm was lost on me that day. Looking around at the people, I kept thinking, *Everybody looks okay, but you never know what someone might be going through inside.* Unlike the other patrons, when Thomas came in, the trauma was written all over him. His hair was disheveled, he was walking with a slight limp and didn't blink. Thomas sat down and I told him every detail of the meeting. He explained what happened after the staff evacuated the spa. I was enraged Yvonne was targeting him. But even though I was finally going to become an esthetician, I was relieved to be free of Von Spa. Thomas, on the other hand, was devastated.

"What am I gonna do?" he said running his fingers through his messy hair.

"Maybe Yvonne will drop the lawsuit after she calms down. This might be just the push you needed. You hated that job. I'm sure you'll figure it out. You're smart and you're a survivor!" I said, thinking of all the difficult things he'd been through growing up.

"Nothing like this has ever happened to me, though. I've never been fired! I feel like I just got dumped and robbed of all my money at the same time. If Yvonne wins—"

"I'm sure it's not your fault."

"But what if it is? She'll ruin me." He looked up from the decaf tea he wasn't drinking.

"My mom used to ask me, 'What's the worst thing that could happen?'"

"Yvonne will determine, whether it's true or not, that I'm responsible for the damage. She will sue me, win the lawsuit and take my condo away. In the meantime, I won't be able to get a job because she'll blacklist me in the industry. I'll turn to a life of crime, spending the rest of my days in prison as the girlfriend of an extremely moody, very well-hung inmate named Tiny."

"Now that's stinking thinking!" I said, pounding my fist on the table. The utensils jingled when they jumped up and fell back down. "Maybe you should write in your Gratitude Journal that no one was hurt today." *What a stupid thing to say.*

Thomas stared at me blankly, holding his tea mug. "I have to go."

"I'm sorry. Was it something I said?" I sprang from my seat to follow him.

"No, don't be silly. It's not you. I just need to go home, lick my wounds and figure out what I'm gonna do. My cousin-in-law is a lawyer. I think I might feel better if I can get someone on my side."

"Well call me if you need to—anytime, day or night."

"Thanks Maggie, that means a lot."

I reached out and put my arms around him, like I'd done earlier that day when he told me about my promotion, before he talked to Gabrielle. Thomas was so upset for her. *He has such a big heart.*

At times of crisis I always look to Oprah. I remember her saying, your life can change in an instant. It blew my mind that a few hours earlier, it was just another day at work. Then without warning, we were all out of a job. So many lives had changed. It was some instant.

Two main characters in my world were playing different roles, too. I couldn't believe Yvonne was no longer my boss. I'd put her on a pedestal of power fueled by fear. After the flood, Yvonne became the villainess who had lost everything and she was only a woman I barely knew, with no connection to me. Thomas wasn't my manager any longer, either. I had always looked up to him, and suddenly he was just my friend in need—facing the vindictive spa queen. He and I were so close I could read him like a book. I thought, *Thomas is hiding something from me.*

****

With the spa under water, I had to figure out what the hell I was going to do. My initial relief had vanished. I couldn't help but wallow in a bit of unrelenting self-pity, sprinkled with an unusual amount of anger.

"Why me?" was the mantra of the day. I'd worked like an eight-year-old slave girl in Mumbai, wasted all that time paying my dues, and just when I had reached my goal of becoming an esthetician (and getting a uniform with breast darts), I lost the job before it started. *What a stupid thing to dream. So what if it was the number one spa in the world? It means nothing to me now.*

I was even more upset for Thomas. He didn't always express to me the pain he was in, but his call frequency was dwindling. In 'Thomas-verse' that meant trouble.

Over the next few days, I emailed my résumé to every spa in the tri-state area. I knew sitting around waiting to hear from someone would drive me crazy, so I decided to get dressed up and head into the big city to wander around aimlessly. *That will make me feel better!* As I picked out my clothes, I had a strange feeling that something special was about to happen. *Better look cute, just in case.* I put on a zebra print wrap dress, black tights and charcoal BCBG knee high boots that I'd gotten on sale at Loehmann's. In front of the mirror, I relined my lower eyelid with a mocha brown pencil and pressed my glossy pink lips together. Before I hit the door, I threw on a grey cape coat and grabbed a violet wool scarf for a splash of color.

When I stepped onto the 7 train, I saw my favorite strap-hanging panhandler. His MO wasn't to recite a typical apologetic speech; he simply made small talk with whoever would listen. I gave him the once over. His dark scraggly hair, dingy jeans and faded black T-shirt made him a great candidate for a makeover. With a smirk, he approached two businessmen. The unsuspecting victims tried to do the subway "look away," but he said to them, "How about the NASDAQ yesterday? Brutal, huh?" One of the guys gave him some change, and shooed him away. He locked eyes with me. *Why not*, I thought, *I've got twenty minutes to kill.*

"Did you hear about the spa that burned down in Midtown?" he asked taking the seat next to me.

I gasped. *Is this a practical joke?* "Do you know something about me? Why are you asking me about that?"

"Nah, I just see you reading those books about facials all the time. In my line of work, my powers of observation have to be very well honed." His less-than-fresh-breath made me squint.

"Oh yeah, what are you getting now?" I glared at the self-proclaimed urban anthropologist. "And for your information, the spa didn't burn down. It was destroyed by water damage." I scrambled through my Balenciaga knock-off bag, which could have housed a family of four, and found a dollar. "Look, here's some money for your time. Now if you don't mind, I'd like to get back to sitting here and staring into space without emotion like all the other subway riders."

"Bag big enough?" he said in a sardonic tone.

"Listen Maury Povich, take a walk and go find a new straphanger to interview." I felt like one of the actresses who storms off the Larry King Show when he goes rogue with his line of questioning.

"Real classy lady—classy with a 'K.'" He sauntered away.

Did I just have a paranormal experience? The train hit a rough patch and snapped me back to reality. I felt a tap on my shoulder. It was a strangely interactive public transportation day.

"That was really funny. Have you ever thought of being a comedian?" A petite tan lady with platinum blonde hair asked me. She held a black bag even bigger than mine, which encompassed her entire left side.

"Just so you know—that wasn't my best work, but I only make jokes on trains because I have paralyzing stage fright and I know I'll never see these people again."

She sat down on the seat vacated by the Maury Povich impersonator. "Well I teach a stand-up comedy class at the New Yorker Hotel, and I think you have 'presence.'"

"Presence? It's been a rough week for me. I could use some presents. Ba-dum-dum."

She chuckled. "And maybe I can help you overcome your fear. But I assure you, you don't need any more presence."

"Thank you, I've always felt more of an absence, but whatever you say."

"See, that's funny!" She reached into her purse, pulled out a business card and handed it to me. "I would love to help you develop your talent."

The subway stopped at 57th Street and 7th Ave. People shoved their way out of the car, and an old man wearing a cowboy hat stepped inside. As soon as the train took off again, he closed his eyes and started singing (if you could call it that) "Stand by Me." The blonde woman and I sat there uncomfortably, waiting for him to finish.

Once he did, he said, "Good afternoon, everybody. If anyone could spare a dollar, I would be eternally grateful. If not, I'm just glad I could share my talent with you today." I dug through my bag again but I couldn't find any small change. When no one else offered him any money, he muttered, "Fucking assholes," and walked into the next car.

"If you call that talent, please don't share your ideas," I said to my potential future comedy teacher. "I wanted him to go stand by someone *else*. Perhaps aggressive panhandling would have been a better career trajectory."

"Congratulations. You're in the class," she laughed and got up to leave as we pulled into the next station. "Be prepared to do five minutes of your best material on the first day. Have a good one!"

I looked at her card, and realized that maybe my entire life had been leading to this moment. Showbiz was beckoning. If the spa had still been standing, I would've been at work instead of on the train. *Maybe it's destiny*, I thought. *Maybe I've been discovered. Or maybe this lady has a pyramid scheme to support and she's just gonna steal my money*. Whatever the case, I'd been ignoring my desire to be a comedian for years. *This is my chance!* Besides, I knew if I stayed home all day in front of a Lifetime movie marathon, they might find me at forty eaten by house cats. An image flashed in my mind like a marquee to the world: Get Ready for the Comic Stylings of Margaret McCarthy!

****

After I signed up for the class, I had no peace. I was constantly looking at life as "one big bit." My new adventure had ignited the creative part of my brain. The only problem was, I couldn't always find a punchline for the common occurrence. *What kind of comic will I be if I can't do that?* This was a perplexing development because I was quick witted in my everyday life. I knew I'd be performing in front of a room full of complete strangers in only a few days, so I jotted down some ideas and prayed for the best. I was losing sleep, peeing every five minutes and eating everything I could get my hands on.

It rained the first night of class. *At least I get to wear my patent leather boots and raincoat*, I thought. The storm howled as I climbed the stairs of the subway station on 34th Street and walked towards the New Yorker Hotel. I pulled up my hood and braced myself. Gusty winds kept changing directions and people on the street struggled to protect themselves from the downpour. Umbrella carnage littered the sidewalks, their broken bodies snapped inside out and abandoned.

When I made my way through the lobby, I felt overcome by fear that was morphing into regret. I stepped into the cold elevator, shivering uncontrollably. The butterflies were so bad, I wondered if I'd been abducted and an alien baby was growing in my belly. *I can't believe I have to pee again.* I arrived on the 3rd floor, followed the signs to the ladies' room and caught a glimpse of myself in the mirror. My heavy bluish-black eyeliner and rain gear made me look like a plus-sized Cat Woman. *You have to stop putting on extra make-up when you're nervous,* I thought as I grabbed some tissue and wiped my lower lid.

I circumnavigated the hallways until I found the classroom. Then I did a walk-by investigation. The walls took me back to the early 20th Century with gold moulding and silver sconces, but the tables and chairs were standard hotel banquet hall circa 1990. There were seven people inside. *They look pretty miserable. They're either going to be terrible comedians, a tough crowd, or both. I think I'll just say I left my notebook at home with all my material written in it. Then I won't have to speak for any reason whatsoever. Perhaps I should be in the pantomime class down the hall.* I put on a fake smile, went inside and took a seat all the way in the back. *Maybe this is all a big mistake.*

A handsome Asian businessman sitting in front of me turned halfway around. "Are you a virgin?" he asked.

"Excuse me?" I said, raising an eyebrow.

"Is this your first time doing stand up?"

"Oh, yes. I guess so. I'm a virgin, again—finally." He smiled. "You?"

"Yep. I just hope I don't hafta go first."

"Preaching, choir, etc.," I said. Another grin spread across his face. Our eyes darted to the door as the teacher walked into the room.

"Sorry I'm late. My cat is in heat." She let out a big sigh, took off her drenched trench coat, and settled onto the edge of the desk. "Good evening everyone, I'm Barbara and I want to help you massage your dreams." *Everyone is reading my mind these days.* "So let's jump right in. I'd like to have each of you come up and give us your best stuff." All

220

I could hear was my internal voice yelling, *Run! You're out of your league. Please don't call on me!* "Margaret, why don't you begin?"

My heart literally skipped a beat. Before I could explain that I'd forgotten my homework, I felt myself stand up and walk to the podium. The room was spinning in dream-like slow motion. *All the fantasies I've had about being a comic come down to this moment.* I couldn't bullshit my way out of this one or cheat off anyone else's paper. Even though I didn't feel ready, when I locked eyes with the teacher, I knew it was go time.

I faced the class and adjusted the new Apple Bottom Jeans that were creeping between my cheeks. *I really expected more ass room in these.* When I looked out at everyone, I felt extremely foolish. My hands shook visibly. I couldn't help but think, *Maybe I should be out doing temp work instead.* The ghosts from my past said, "You're fat" and "You're not good enough." My bladder was about to burst. *I just went!* The doubts crept in like fog. *Who do you think you are? What do I do now? If I give them a disclaimer, I might actually get through this.*

"Hi, I'm Margaret, uh, I, uh, used to work at a spa. Honestly, I'm only trying this out for fun." My level of panic went from a ten to a nine. "I've always had people tell me I'm funny, so here goes nothing." I took a deep breath and opened my notebook.

"I do facials, yeah, one of the most ridiculous professions in existence," I said, the words coming out of me at lightning speed. "You would be amazed at how childish these people are. I mean, how bad can it be to spend your day relaxing? At my first job, a woman asked me if I could make her look like Angelina Jolie by the time I finished her treatment. I told her, 'Maybe Jon Voight.' After all, I was an esthetician, not a magician." I didn't even get a chuckle. I looked over at the teacher and she mouthed the words, "Slow down."

I took my foot off the gas and said, "So I come from a big Irish family and they all want to know when I'm getting married. The other day my mother asked me if I'd met anyone yet. When I told her I hadn't, she suggested I lower my standards. Lower my standards? I said, 'Any lower and I'd have a prison marriage with the occasional conjugal visit.'" An old lady in the front row wearing a funny hat yelled, "Ha, Ha, Ha!" and a few of the others giggled. *What a relief.* "I decided to sit down to write a list of all the qualities I wanted in a man. By the time I was done, I realized he was way too good for me." Not a snicker from the crowd. "I used to want a doctor or a lawyer, but now, if he's got a name tag, a hair net, and the ability to recite the alphabet without singing—he's in!" The other students laughed again. *Oh my God. They like me, they kinda, sorta, like me!*

"I really do think it's a man's world. I mean, my last boyfriend was selling tube socks from his car when I met him, and he actually broke up with me. He said we should see other people because I wasn't ambitious enough—*he worked out of his trunk!*" There was more chuckling. I started to connect with the people who were laughing, while tuning out the miserable scowlers.

"I'm always talking to my friends about how hard it is to meet a guy. We're truly out of ideas. One of my besties named Cindy gets dumped a lot. I think it's because she's a little, um, well—dumb. The only thing she reads besides traffic signs are articles about celebrities with cellulite, and the men who love them. I made the mistake of saying something was surreal. She agreed saying, (in my best New York accent) 'You're right, it is *so* real!'" The Asian guy gave me a full-fledged cackle. I glanced at the clock. *Only three minutes have passed.* I panicked, looking over at the teacher.

"That was great, Margaret," she said. "I can tell you're just getting comfortable up there and you still have some time. Why don't you continue?"

"Um, sure, I guess so. Let me see here." The alien baby kicked inside of me. I frantically flipped through my notebook. Sweat dripped down the sides of my face, but I still wanted to keep going. At the top of page 8, I saw the heading, "Jokes About Weight." *Hmm, I thought, I'm not sure about this. Oh well!*

"So, I know if I lived in Wisconsin I would be Nicole Richie, but unfortunately I live in New York, which has become the new LA. Here, a size fourteen with a nice stretch fabric is considered morbidly obese. I represent the average to above average woman and, in my opinion, you should not be able to buy clothes at Baby Gap when you have a full time job with a mortgage to pay. It's just wrong. Women all over the world need to stop the insanity by having a damn sandwich once in a while." A plus-sized woman in the back row shouted out, "Amen to that!"

"I went to therapy recently so I could talk about my weight and my therapist told me I was way too self-deprecating. I was like 'I know, I'm so stupid.' Then I went to the doctor wondering if I had some kind of chronic fatigue syndrome, but it turns out I'm just lazy," I said, opening my eyes widely for effect. The other students started cracking up. *O.M.G. What is it in people that makes low self-esteem so damn funny?* "I've been on every diet known to man. Recently I went on the toothpick diet. As long as it's your only utensil, you can eat whatever you want. I've been eating 20 ounce steaks, 'cause I found a really big toothpick online." The whole class, that had looked so miserable a few minutes ago, was laughing again. "And speaking of food, have any of you guys had this tres leches cake? It is unbelievable. It actually means three asses in Spanish." The cute old lady cackled so hard her dentures popped out.

Our teacher stood. "Thank you, Margaret," she smiled warmly. "Good work." Everyone clapped except for the senior citizen who was still trying to put her teeth back in. My Asian friend gave me a thumbs up.

I walked back to my seat, feeling as light as a fart. *I just dumped thirty years' worth of suppressed creative frustration on that imaginary stage.* I was in such a state of euphoria that I laughed at everyone's jokes, good and bad, for the next hour.

I'd fallen in love with writing material, sharing my jokes with others, and getting a reaction in return. The process was more than fun, it was satisfying. Even though stand-up was new to me, it seemed familiar—like it had always been there. I couldn't wait to get home and craft a tight act. I was also super excited to tell Thomas the good news. At that very moment, I had found my truth.

On the way out of class I noticed a flyer on the back of the door. The bold print read:

FINAL PERFORMANCE FOR ALL STUDENTS

MONDAY APRIL 6TH AT THE GOTHAM COMEDY CLUB.

It was the final graduation test. I gasped to myself. *There's no way I could possibly do that. A few amateur comics in a room is one thing, but an actual comedy club? I'd surely die.* The alien baby started kicking again. Thoughts of drunken hecklers booing me off stage ambushed my mind. *How in the world will I be able to perform for a real audience in only a few weeks?*

My inner-Joan-Rivers-head-voice screamed at me to grow up. *You do have courage. Look at how you succeeded at Von Spa; you're no size two, but you walked in there with your head held high and your waist cincher on the last rung beneath Bruce's uniform.*

I dug my phone out of my purse to call Thomas as emotions exploded out of me—relief (that I'd made it through the class); excitement (about continuing the process); fear (of taking the next step). *If I don't talk to someone, surely my alien spawn will burst out!* The phone kept ringing. *Pick up, pick up, pick up,* I thought.

"You have reached 212—"

Damn it! I slammed the phone shut and took out my Metrocard.

On the subway ride home, I opened my notebook and began writing like a madwoman. First, I wrote down everything I was feeling. Then, a few stops from home, I decided to make a list.

1) Finish translating my life into a full act.

2) Lose 10 dress sizes.

3) Become completely confident/self-actualized before the show.

I looked at the list. *One of these goals is just wrong. X marks the spot,* I thought as I drew two intersecting lines over my third goal. *Self-actualization doesn't make for good comedy.*

Chapter 12

Thomas:

The Great Depression

Gazing out at the ocean, something didn't feel right, so I headed back toward the dunes, but there were no stairs leading to the boardwalk. I tried to claw up the sandy hill, grabbing at plants and roots to make my escape. It was too late. The shore was moving farther into the distance. The horizon grew smaller. The sea stole from the air to build its monster. An underwater universe of crabs, shrimp and tiny creatures scrambled for cover when they lost the protection of their liquid ceiling. The Atlantic soared to the sky. A tsunami, a tidal wave of biblical proportions, loomed above me. I ran for my life, my legs burning with heat. Before I was engulfed, I shot upright in bed, coated with sweat. I squeegeed the moisture off my chest like a windshield in a carwash, and reached for a Kleenex. *Close your eyes and go back to sleep*, I thought, but my mind was already racing.

This is the third time I've had that nightmare. It's kind of amazing, symbolically. If only it weren't so realistically horrifying. Why are you depressed? You hated your job, didn't you? Not completely, I answered myself, *and the minute I learned to appreciate it, I got sued and/or fired!* I turned over on my other side and looked at the clock. 5:14 a.m.

How could I have been so enmeshed in a job that wasn't my calling? It did give me purpose. I felt like I helped my team in a crisis. At least I was making a difference in their workplace. I was needed there. Now I'm no one to anybody. I reached for another tissue, but the tears never came. *Jesus, I miss the concierges.*

Those girls were like my sisters and Yvonne was the evil stepmother who kicked me out of the house, or actually, banished me to another kingdom. Because Yvonne filed a lawsuit, my lawyers advised me not to talk to the staff. *Fuck it. They could never convince me to stop confiding in Margaret. She helps preserve my mental health. I have to tell her about the "independent investigation." What if they find me at fault? What if I'm not to blame but Yvonne bribes the investigators? Oh GOD! Forget the future, how am I gonna pay the mortgage this month?*

My internal movie reel wasn't even black and white anymore. Life was an ugly sepia photograph.

****

Time stood still while I failed to pull myself up by my bootstraps. With the economy in the toilet, I wasn't able to get a job at a spa or anywhere else. I had endless hours to rest, so the physical injuries I'd incurred healed quickly, but the emotional wounds festered.

I named my depression **It.** No matter what I did, **It** followed me. A massage couldn't help me relax with **It** on my back. Going for a run was a horror movie with **It** chasing me. Watching TV was impossible with **It** standing in front of me.

And then **It** took a wife: **That. That** was anxiety. Because of **That,** I had panic attacks on the subway, when crossing the street and eventually, every time I left my apartment. **That** made it impossible to go on a job interview or shop for groceries. **That** robbed me of my appetite. It was like **That** had given me speed and a resting heart rate of 120 beats per minute. **That** made it impossible to sleep. No wonder I stayed in bed all day trying.

I began to understand the word "suicidal." The surreal state of major depression felt permanent and inescapable. There was no joy in anything. Life itself was pointless. All I felt was pain. To make matters worse, without sleep or the desire to eat, the chemicals in my brain had turned into poison. The thoughts fermenting within me were dark.

What I need is something to do, I thought. But *what?* Anthony was consumed with his job in film production and obsessed with his new boyfriend. We had talked on the phone, but never spent any time together. All my other friends were busy with their lives. I had lost touch with half of them during my marriage to the spa. So when Peppermint called, inviting me to lunch, I jumped at the possibility of distraction.

We met at a gay coffeehouse in Chelsea called Big Cup. The supersized daisies on the purple walls only made me sadder. My eyes fell upon a cute fashionable couple with extreme haircuts laughing hysterically. *Will I ever find something genuinely funny again?* By this point, food literally had no taste. I laboriously shoved a little salad down my throat to stay alive. *I don't even give a shit that I'm back to my fighting weight.*

"I know what will make you feel better, girl," Peppermint exclaimed. "Let's get dressed in women's clothes and hit the town!" The boys looked up from their lattes or laptops. The smell of cinnamon wafted through the air while pop music played over the speakers.

"I dunno. I had a drink a few weeks ago and I couldn't get out of bed for two days. It made it all worse."

"You don't hafta drink, girl. And you know *I* don't need alcohol to have fun," she said. Her perpetual good mood made me even more depressed. "Let's just go out and have a blast."

"Maybe next week—I don't have the energy right now. I feel—" I stopped myself short. *If she knows how bad it is, I'll end up in the hospital.*

"Talk to me." She grabbed my hand across the orange Formica tabletop.

"I've got this feeling I have something trapped inside of me that I want to throw up."

"I think it's your inner lady!" she said, slapping her knee.

"I'm serious Pep. I don't know what to do with myself."

Pep's smile flew away from her face and she softened her brow. She put her other hand on top of mine. "Keep talking to me, girl. Let it all out."

"I just feel so abandoned. It's like Yvonne threw me out with the trash."

"And after everything you did for her." Pep's irises darted back and forth. "You are kind, you are smart and that woman didn't deserve you. You're a wonderful person and that's why we're friends." One of her braids fell across her face. She tucked it behind her bejeweled ear. "Don't you know that?"

"I don't know what I know right now." I looked down and saw she was wearing French manicured press-on nails. Her dark fingers and elegant hands looked so nice against my olive skin, but I couldn't feel it. Normally this would've made me smile. I'd appreciate not only the contrasting colors, but what they meant: that we are all living works of art to be decorated, each of us with a different colored canvas. And people like me and Pep, well, we loved to paint. I couldn't even take in this little happiness. *Nothing on TV or in a book or anything anyone says can get through my wall of despair to make me feel something.*

Just as that thought danced through my mind, a new song began to play over the sound system: Pink singing, "Fuckin' Perfect." I met

Peppermint's gaze. The bustling coffee house around us went out of focus and we became hyperaware of the music. Water formed in my tear ducts, and Pep's smokey eyes welled up, too. She squeezed my hand. When Pink belted the chorus, I finally believed what she was singing about. I saw the good in me, reflected in my friend. I mattered to someone. *Maybe that can sustain me 'til things get better.* Pep moved her chair next to mine and I cried quietly on her shoulder. The song echoed in my ears, navigating its way into my soul. When my astral experience ended, the second I returned to my body, I discovered we were on stage.

"What are you looking at?" Pep said to all the pretty boys staring at us. She stood up, grabbed me by the hand, and we bolted out the door during the final chorus. "Sometimes you just need a song to save your life," she said. I looked at her and nodded, tears quietly streaming down my cheeks.

"Maybe I'm not dead yet after all." Unable to say any more, I mouthed the words "thank you" and fell into her embrace. The bridge to the song played between my ears. Pink screamed, "Yeah-ah-ahhhhhhh!!" and a full orchestra burst into music.

Peppermint and I rode the subway to Harlem together, sitting silently, side-by-side, our arms linked. For the first time in weeks, I didn't have a panic attack on the train. We arrived at our stop and climbed the steps in unison like Laverne and Shirley. Pep caught her breath when we reached the top. "You know it wasn't only me or the music that helped you back there. It was the lyrics."

"I know," I said.

"So the next time you feel like you need to let it out, you should write down how you're feeling."

"Okay."

"If you don't feel like writing, pick up the phone."

"I will."

"And if things get too hard and you need some professional help, we'll find it together." She grabbed my hand again. "Promise me that."

"I promise."

"I love you, girl." She hugged me hard. We parted ways. A few seconds later, I turned around and saw Peppermint looking back, too. She blew me a kiss. The bridge of the song exploded in my mind once again.

The minute I got home, I turned on the radio. "Move Along" by the All American Rejects blasted through my speakers. I thought, *That's what I have to do—just keep moving along.* I took out my laptop and began to write.

****

My raven hair cascaded down my back in long soft dark curls. The ringlets dragged on the ground like a train, covering my ornate flowing lavender gown. I was in another time, another place, a previous life. I was female, beautiful and rich. I looked toward the Heavens, and discovered the sky was really a domed ceiling covered with stars—hundreds of feet above my head. The red mosaic tiles rose to a majestic gilded archway with winding crystal staircases spilling to the floor.

I woke up in a cold sweat. Dreams like this haunted my childhood. I wanted to be someone else—a pretty boy or girl living a glamorous life, thousands of miles from the bullies who teased me. I wished I was far away from the pain and loneliness of being misunderstood, the alienation of being different. I longed to be in a world where I wasn't just accepted, but loved and worshiped for being who I was. If only I were a handsome Hollywood movie star, a rock star in a new wave band, a vamp in a flapper dress, a 1980's video vixen or even a gothic king—anyone other than me. After the life I had known at the spa disappeared, my defenses came tumbling down and these memories flooded to the surface like a tidal wave in a nightmare.

I ran my fingers through my wet hair. I didn't even care that it was finally growing out. What should have been a symbol of freedom, merely reminded me of my torture. I tried telling myself, *Missing the spa is like wishing your abusive ex-boyfriend would take you back,* but it was futile. My moods stayed painted black.

It was 3:00 a.m. I didn't want to write, I wanted to sleep. *It's too late to call Pep.* I grabbed the remote from my nightstand and turned on the TV, bathing my red bedroom in the artificial light I used to find so soothing. The NewYork1 news channel materialized on the screen. An African American reporter with a mustache said, "It's the story that captivated the city. Who is the mystery woman of the MTA?" My ears perked up. I flashed back to reading the paper after the spa was destroyed. "Rumors have been swirling around the case…" "There are reports of a cover up…" "The MTA is not taking responsibility or releasing the surveillance video…" "An anonymous stranger is paying the victim's hospital bills…" "…a media frenzy at Bellevue…"

The information filtered through me. My thoughts raced while the reporter droned on in the background. *Was there an incriminating video of me at the spa, proving I was responsible for its destruction? Maybe an anonymous stranger will save me from my fate! Would there be a media frenzy if we went to trial? Will I be lambasted in the press because I lead an alternative lifestyle? Would they call me a transvestite? I hated that term. I was a drag queen! Queen being the operative word.*

I turned off the television, pulled the covers over my head, and began chanting, "Om Namah Shivaya" in an attempt to silence my inner demons. *If I can manage to "Honor the divinity within," maybe I'll survive.*

****

A requiem played in my nightmare. I was surrounded by men in speedos. They put their hands all over me. I began to get aroused, but suddenly I was being lifted from my underwear. The boys laughed like howler monkeys, submerging my head in the toilet. I held my breath for as long as I could. The world grew dark when a loud flush caused the water to swirl down the drain. I gasped for air choking on my own saliva. I woke up drenched in sweat. *Flashbacks after all these years?*

My sleeping mask had migrated halfway up my forehead, doing nothing to protect me from the sun's rays burning through the window. *It's just another day. Damn it.* I didn't bother singing the melody of the requiem into my digital recorder. *Who gives a shit,* I thought, rubbing my swollen eyes. *How can I possibly feel more exhausted than when I went to bed?* I was sleeping light and waking up heavy.

My iPhone rang. I squinted to unlock the keypad, and hit the speaker button.

"OH MY GOD! You have to go get the paper," Margaret said, her TV on in the background.

"Maggie, you know I don't read the paper." I yawned. "I like to get my news the old fashioned way—through gossip and television."

"Just do it."

"Why don't you tell me what's going on so I don't have to?"

233

The background noise of Margaret's TV disappeared abruptly. "You should have the same experience I had while I was reading it. It's too insane to blurt out over the phone."

"I'm still in bed. I don't want to go outside." I didn't feel like telling her the city's chaos brought on panic attacks.

"What are you, agoraphobic?" she said. I didn't respond. "Open mouth, insert foot. I'm sorry Tom, but it might be good for you to get some fresh air. So if you're curious, you'll have to!"

"Fine. Which paper should I get?"

"*The Post.*"

"I hate *The Post*. It's an unobjective conservative tabloid."

"Exactly!" she said. "The story's on the front page. Call me the second you're done reading."

I threw on some jeans, grabbed my coat and ran downstairs. I opened the door and stepped onto the sidewalk. The sights and sounds of New York assaulted my senses. Cars zoomed by. A vendor at a fruit stand fought with a customer over the price of bananas. The high pitched scream of a siren blared in the distance. *My anxiety's giving me that "not so there" feeling.* I pulled my jacket together tightly, bracing myself from the strong spring wind. *I can't believe the world is turning without me.*

The deli was two blocks away, but it felt like a mile. I opened the door, worrying about all the germs on the handle. *I'm barely surviving,* I thought, *the last thing I need is to get sick.*

My eyes scanned the newspapers for *The Post*. The headline read:

Oh How the Mighty Have Fallen!

There were four smaller taglines:

Mystery Woman of the MTA Regains Memory

Reveals her Identity as the Mother of Spa Maven/Socialite Yvonne Von Courtland

Yvonne's Sordid Past is Finally Exposed

The Truth about the End of the World-Renowned Von Courtland Spa

Holy Mother of God! I thought, my mouth agape. *All those strange, drunken phone calls we got at the spa must've been from Yvonne's mom.* There were several customers waiting to check out, so I threw a dollar on the counter, held up the paper and scurried out the door. *I used to hate it when people did that, but I really don't give a shit right now.*

I ran home, flew onto the couch and flipped through the pages frantically. Inside were snapshots of Yvonne from society events with celebrities and ladies who lunch. The next article featured pictures from the spa brochure. *It's so weird to see things from your everyday existence printed in the press.* I shook my head in disbelief and began to read:

Fall from Grace

Case solved! The shocking rumors are true. The Mystery Woman of the MTA has a name and her daughter has a rather famous name at that.

Grace Schlesinger, 65, has revealed she is the mother of Yvonne Von Courtland, 47, New York City socialite and curator of Von Spa, which was, until recently (see full article), the most exclusive spa in the country. Mrs. Schlesinger shared some of her daughter's rags to riches story with *The Post*.

Public records and our sources, have confirmed her mother's claims. Ms. Von Courtland was born Yvonne Louise Schlesinger on March 22, 1964 and was raised in a trailer park in the tiny town of Pigeon Gulf, Louisiana, outside of New Orleans. Her father, Harold Schlesinger, worked two janitorial jobs to support his small family of three until fate intervened.

Little Yvonne's 7th grade teacher, Mrs. Bonita Sproul, astounded by the girl's high placement test scores, submitted an application on her behalf to The Edmands School for Gifted and Talented Children. Mrs. Schlesinger says that when the private academy accepted Yvonne, "We felt blessed, like Vonnie might make something of herself." Unfortunately, her scholarship request was filed too late and the money Yvonne so desperately needed to attend the academy was given to another student. Her dreams of a brighter future crushed, Yvonne returned to public school. Until, as stated by Mrs. Schlesinger, "A distinguished looking man in a fancy suit paid a visit to our humble home and offered to pay for Vonnie's education." That man was Baron Friedrich Von Courtland, patriarch of one of New Orleans' wealthiest families, who had fled the Vienna Royal Court when Nazi occupation began in Austria. Baron Von Courtland was so moved by Yvonne's story, he felt compelled to help the young girl.

What? I thought. I kept reading, forgetting to blink my eyes. I was completely engrossed. The rest of the article read like an old Jackie Collins novel. The Baron paid for Yvonne's education and over the years, became like a second father to her, molding her into a debutante. But when she fell in love with his dark and handsome son Eric, the truth was revealed: The Baron still looked down on Yvonne's poor roots. He tried to wash his hands of her, but something had already bound them together forever—Yvonne was pregnant with Eric's child. The Baron made her a deal: She would hide the pregnancy until the end of her senior year of high school, give birth to the baby in seclusion over the summer and put the child up for adoption. Additionally, Yvonne was to leave the state and have no further contract with Eric. In exchange, the Baron offered to give Mrs. Schlesinger the sum of $250,000. With no money of her own, Yvonne was forced to comply. The Baron, clearly powerful and used to getting his way, thought he had everything under control. Yet there was one thing he didn't know. Yvonne and Eric, both eighteen, had already been married in secret. That is how she became Yvonne Von Courtland.

She gave birth to a baby girl and handed her over to a loving couple with tears in her eyes. Yvonne was trying to put the past behind her and preparing to go to college when she received devastating news. Eric had been killed in a car accident. In the article, her mother said, "When he died, Vonnie closed off a piece of her heart."

Still, Yvonne moved on, studying business at NYU. Upon graduating, she used her name to join the ranks of New York's high society. Yvonne spent her twenties living the glamorous life. Then with the Baron's bribe, she slowly earned her MBA. But when she met a wealthy investment banker named Perry Copeland, she found an opportunity to make the best business decision ever. They were married by the time she was thirty and Yvonne thought she'd never have to worry about money again.

She spent the next decade as a lady who lunched. Yvonne attended the Costume Institute Gala every May, opening night at the Metropolitan Opera each September and exclusive parties to raise money for the cause of the moment. She donned custom made hats at the Kentucky Derby and even bought a ticket to the Oscars one year. Yvonne wore haute couture gowns and dripped with priceless jewels, yet she felt something was missing from her life. She joined The Benevolent Society hoping to find meaning but uncovered something else instead: her own ambition. She learned that climbing the ranks of the charity gave her the power she'd been missing. Before long, Yvonne became president and finally found her true calling—being in charge.

As summer turned to fall and winter turned to spring, time and time again, Yvonne grew restless. She was tired of giving to the poor and wanted to build a business of her own. She looked to her husband for startup money, but Perry Copeland refused to be married to a working woman. Yvonne felt trapped and unfulfilled. Her sadness morphed into anxiety. And like any woman of means, she was able to throw money at the problem. She found refuge from her panic attacks in the most exclusive spas in New York City. In their treatment rooms and whirlpools, Yvonne decided what she really wanted—to open the most spectacular spa in the country. But for that, she needed millions.

Then one day she saw an item in the very newspaper I was reading. On Page Six, she read:

Banking czar, Perry Copeland, was spotted having a candlelit dinner in the Iris Room of Four Star restaurant, Très Bon. His socialite wife was not with him; however, he seemed very charmed by his companion—a 20-year-old blonde intern from his investment firm.

Yvonne hired a private detective who proved the affair was real, and the day she served Perry with divorce papers, she said, "I guess I'll be opening my spa now."

Holy Mary, Mother of Jesus. I put the paper down, pondering the parallels between Yvonne and her benefactor's life. *She became exactly like the Baron. In her wealth and power, Yvonne thought she could control it all: her mother, keeping her past a secret, and everything that happened at the spa. But she was wrong. When fate intervened, she lost control and everything went down the drain. Yvonne's whole persona was a facade, built on lies and it was bound to crumble. And maybe subconsciously, she felt like she didn't really deserve her success, manifesting her current situation as a result. Yvonne has some big lessons to learn. Dear God,* I prayed, *let her see the light before she ruins me.*

****

I leapt up, grabbed my phone, and called Margaret back.

"Hell-lola!" she said. "Can you believe it?!"

"I'm still in shock. My brain is on information overload."

"I'm sure."

"Why do you think Yvonne's mother told that reporter her life story?"

"Hell-lola," Margaret exclaimed.

"Is that all you can say today?"

"I bet she did it for the cash."

"Probably. It really sucks for Yvonne, though."

"What the hell are you talking about? That woman threatened to sue you into the Stone Age. You should feel vindicated!"

"I guess I feel kinda sorry for her. I know how hard it is to have your life shatter into a million pieces. To add to that, she seems like a lonely victim of her own circumstances. And this is all happening to her publicly." I absentmindedly rolled up the paper.

"Hell-lola! The same thing is happening to you."

"Yeah, but not publicly."

"Oh boy. You didn't read the last article, did you? I'll hold. Turn the page!"

I feverishly scanned the story with the brochure pictures, which explained the details of the spa's demise. When I got to the last paragraph, I discovered what Maggie was talking about. It read:

Yvonne Von Courtland has not made the cause of the water damage public; however, she is suing the spa's manager, Thomas Haven, a former female impersonator.

I dropped the phone.

239

****

"Hello? Thomas? Are you there?" Margaret's tiny voice sounded far away.

My thoughts raced. *I'll be the butt of jokes in the media—the drag queen who destroyed the legendary spa, owned by the socialite, both of us marred by scandal. Yvonne will be more famous than ever and this will put me under the microscope.*

"Hellloooooooooo?!" Margaret said.

I picked her up from the floor and paced around my living room. "Oh my gosh, Maggie. I'm sorry I dropped you."

"Are you okay?"

"No!" I said, my heart racing. "You could have at least warned me about that part."

"What do you mean? You're free of the spa now, who cares about your past? I thought you'd be giving 'em a big 'whatever, I'm a drag queen!'"

"It's one thing to be proud amongst your friends, but most people don't understand. We live in such a misogynistic society that men who dress up like women are ridiculed."

"Elaborate."

"If a man acts like a woman, conservative people think he's lowering himself because in their minds, men are better. Add to that a culture where masculinity is celebrated in sports and action movies and that's when you get discrimination against people like me. The funny thing is, it's all subconscious. They don't even know why they're judging us. They just have a feeling of hatred toward feminine men."

"Wow. This is fascinating and terrible."

"On the flip side, powerful women are looked up to for 'acting like men.' It's seen as male behavior."

"Or people call them a bitch."

"That happens, too. Isn't it all fucked up?"

"I'll say! I still have one more question for you."

"Shoot," I said, trying to keep my imagination from spinning into the worst case scenario.

"How do you think the paper found out about your past?"

"I don't know. Maybe they researched my old MySpace account or a gay boy at *The Post* used to work for a nightlife magazine." I had a horrifying thought. "Oh shit—what are my parents gonna say?!"

"Give 'em some credit. You told them everything when you were eighteen. They love and accept you unconditionally."

"I know. At the same time, they've never explained everything to my religious old relatives. And my Dad's Army friends might make fun of him." Feeling dizzy, I sat back down.

"So what? This is the perfect opportunity to stop caring about what other people think of you."

"I just don't feel like I can do this right now—especially considering the mental state I'm dealing with." The lump in my throat started blocking my airway. "I can't handle the scrutiny."

"Yes you can," Margaret said. "You're stronger than you think. Besides, if this does become more public, which it might not, it's your chance to stand up and be a role model for all the little Thomases out there struggling in middle school."

"You're right. I've always wanted to help kids like me."

"That's the spirit!" Maggie shouted.

"How are you handling all of this so well, anyway?" I unrolled the newspaper.

"Handling *what?*"

"You know—being out of a job, not knowing what's going to happen."

"I'm treating it like a sabbatical. I'm still looking for a gig until the spa reopens, but, well—there's something else I've been doing that I haven't told anyone yet."

"What? Why?"

"'Cause I wasn't sure how it was gonna pan out."

"How *what* was gonna pan out? Spill, lady—the suspense is killing me!"

"Okay, here it goes. It's always been a dream of mine to make people laugh, so I'm taking a stand-up comedy class."

"That's awesome." I attempted to sound excited although I was devoid of normal emotions. "You should be *proud* you took the leap. Most people never face their fears."

"Thanks. It went pretty well last night. I tried to call you 'cause I was so jazzed, but today the old doubts are creeping back in."

"Don't doubt yourself. You're the funniest person I've ever met," I said, trying to forget my own woes. "When can I see you perform?"

"NEVER!" I pulled the phone away from my ear. "I can't handle the scrutiny, either."

"Well, I'd love to *read* your stuff, maybe you can email it to me."

"Um, I'll think about it."

"Don't worry—no pressure." I felt a pang of jealousy. *Would I ever care about chasing my own dreams?* "Wow Maggie, what you're doing is great."

"Even though it's nice to hear some encouragement, don't hold your breath about the sharing part. I put enough pressure on myself and I can't deal with the rejection if someone doesn't like my act."

"Okay, sorry. I won't ask again. I'm still proud of you, though."

"*You* should take a class or something. It *really* helps keep your mind off stuff. I'm so nervous beforehand, I completely forget about everything, including my own name sometimes."

"I dunno. I'm not in the mood to learn anything at this point." I rolled the paper up again.

"I don't mean a boring course on quantum physics, I'm talking about something fun—like comedy. You've got a great sense of humor. You should try it!"

"I don't feel very funny right now."

"Then maybe you should try a more serious creative outlet."

"I *have* been writing though. Peppermint reminded me it's a good way to let things out."

"Perfect. Why don't you take a creative writing class?"

I twisted the rolled up newspaper. "My writings are more like poems." *How cliché am I? Depressed and composing poetry.* My face burned with embarrassment.

"Oh, okay. So let's hear one."

"Sure. Right after you do some stand-up for me."

"Point taken, but I'm already enrolled in a class. If you have the moxie to sign up for something, I'll do some stand-up for you. I have an overwhelming feeling you need to do this."

243

"No way. It's too much."

"I feel it in my gut, but I'll make you a deal. You read me a poem and I will never bring it up again. And maybe—well, eventually—I'll give you part of my act."

The angel on my shoulder said, *Reading one of your poems would be therapeutic.* The devil on the other side said, *You can't be creative, you have to be practical.* I recognized his voice. He was the same one who said, *Fit in, play sports like the others, get good grades and anything artistic is girly. Be a boy.* In all the chaos that was my life, the Heavenly Messenger managed to get the last word: *Those negative thoughts are coming from your old bullies. Find your own voice.*

"Okay, I'll read you something but you'll probably think it sucks."

"Just do it."

"Okay, let me get my laptop." I felt like I was in slow motion. I'd never read anything I'd written out loud—to anyone. My anxiety was so intense, I thought I might have an out-of-body experience. I cleared my throat. "Don't laugh. It's called 'The Beauty in the Ugly.'"

"Good title," Maggie said.

I cleared my throat again—this time louder. Then I bulldozed through what I'd written at lightning speed, my nerves building to a crescendo while I read. By the end, my mouth was so dry I had to choke out the remaining words. When I was done, I swallowed some spit and asked nervously, "Well?"

"It's great."

I exhaled. "It's depressing."

"That's what makes it good. Besides, it's also hopeful. Do you know what it sounds like to me?"

"Poop?" I suggested.

"No, not poop—lyrics!"

"Really?" My inner rock star stirred from his coma.

"My neighbor Auston is a musician, why don't I show it to him?"

"I thought you were gonna stop pestering me if I read you something? I don't want to be judged by a *real* creative person. It would make me feel like a poser."

"I'm just trying to help you. Why do you care, anyway? It's totally anonymous. You don't even know him."

"What's his name?"

"Auston Harman," she said in a sing-songy voice.

"You mean, Auston—the musician?"

"Stop with the bullshit."

"That name does sound familiar." I was half-kidding and half-trying to put end to the conversation. "He plays guitar, right?"

"Good guess, but he plays piano. Email me the lyrics."

"It's a poem."

"When Auston gets a hold of it, it'll be lyrics. I'm not taking 'no' for an answer. I don't have a job, remember? I can harass you all day and all night."

"Fine," I said. Secretly, I did want Margaret to show him my poem.

****

A few days later, I stared out the window from our favorite booth at The Flame Restaurant. It was dinnertime in New York City and for some reason it began at eight o'clock. The smells of bread baking, sauces simmering and coffee percolating did nothing to stir my nonexistent appetite. Under the streetlamps, people of every nationality strolled by. *God, not too long ago I would've found this wildly entertaining.*

Margaret came into view, crossing 9th Avenue. She waved at me through the window. When she opened the door, I felt a rush of cold, moist air against my face. Margaret plopped her enormous bag down and scooted in across from me. Her big boobs brushed against the table, pushing open her leopard print faux-fur jacket.

"Sorry I'm late," she said.

"Don't worry about it. Right now, my time is very unvaluable."

"I have spa gossip. First of all, I found out why Christie got fired, and second, are you ready for this? Gabrielle told me where she's from!"

"No way. Spill it, lady!"

"I will. But before I get to that, I kinda did something."

"Are you trying to make my head explode? One thing at a time. Start at the beginning."

"Fine. I was worried about Gabrielle so I gave her a call."

"How is she doing? *What* is she doing?"

"Engaged to a very wealthy man and working for a lingerie designer."

"That was quick and random."

"I know. Anyway, she's fine now, but right after she got fired she was commiserating with Christie—"

"Sounds like a TV show."

"True," Maggie giggled. "So it turns out Christie was giving a facial at the spa and the woman said, 'Don't touch my tits, they're new.' Then Christie goes, "I'd only do that after dinner and a movie."

"Really?"

"Really."

"Is this a joke? I feel a punchline coming on."

"Listen, this story was filtered through Gabrielle's English, so it was pretty funny when she was telling it, but as far as I know, it's no laughing matter."

"Hmm."

"Anyhoo, the woman said, 'I'm not a dyke' and since Christie is clearly a lesbian, she said, 'Well *this* dyke would never be interested in your fake ugly breasts, anyway.'"

"Holy shit!"

"And that's the story of how I got my imaginary job as an esthetician at the ghost of Von Spa."

"I guess the word 'dyke' really set her off. Not that I can't relate. If someone says the other 'f' word, the one the British use for cigarettes, I'm ready to fight."

"I hear ya."

"Did she tell you anything about June?"

"Yes!" Margaret looked around the diner.

"You, like Hitchcock, are the master of suspense."

"I'm just messin' with ya. Andrea got a great new job and June's happily at home with the baby."

"Any word on Diana?"

"Out partying every night, having the time of her life."

"Cool. So how'd you get Gabrielle to tell you where she's from?"

"I buttered her up by saying how beautiful she is and she should be proud of her ancestry. And she said, 'I am proud, that's why I don't mention where I grew up.'"

"Huh?"

"Exactly. I told her that doesn't make sense and she goes, 'Fine, I'm from Tuvalu.'"

"*Where?*"

"That's what I said. And she got really angry at me because her people '*are* very proud and nobody in the self-obsessed U.S. has heard of my beautiful island country.'"

"No wonder whenever she got cold she said, 'Turn up the heat. I am a tropical woman!'"

"Totally. So I Googled Tuvalu and apparently it's one of the smallest countries in the world. The pics are gorgeous—white sand beaches and everything. Anyway, it's midway between Hawaii and Australia."

"Thank you, Wikipedia. Did you smooth things over with her?"

"Of corset. Guess who got roped into taking Gabrielle to her homeland?"

"No!"

"Just kidding."

The waiter brought us water and asked to take our order. When Margaret told him we needed more time, he rolled his eyes and walked away.

"So what'd ya mean when you said you 'did something'?" I asked, feeling my heart rate rise.

"Well it's something *for* you. I hope you're not mad."

"You picked the perfect time if you're worried about that. I'm basically devoid of all feelings right now. And why would I be angry if it's something *for* me? Unless you did something *mean* for me?"

"It's nice, but it is a little manipulative." She grinned through burgundy lips, which complimented her coat, red hair and winged eyes.

"Now my head is spinning in circles. Give it to me, Ms. Hitchcock."

"Well, remember how you emailed me that song you wrote?"

"It's a poem, but I remember," I said experiencing the one emotion I could count on—anxiety.

"Well my friend Auston actually thought it was a song and you're never gonna believe this, but he takes a songwriting class, so to make the long story short—"

"Too late," I said on autopilot, unable to blink.

In one breath, she blurted out, "Anyway, he forwarded your lyrics to his teacher, she liked them and accepted you into the class, so I just paid her and that's the reason it's manipulative 'cause I can't get my money back, which means you have to do it." Margaret beamed. "Congratulations! You're going to be a lyricist."

"Margaret, I can't do that!" I took off my black skull cap and scratched my fingers through my shaggy hair. "I can barely read something I've written to one of my best friends. There's no way I could share it with real musicians—and a teacher!" I set my flabbergasted gaze on her.

"You can, because you have to. C'mon. You love music. This is your chance to be a part of it."

"It's too scary and I feel so badly about myself. Yvonne dealt me some hardcore rejection." I looked away, on the verge of tears, thinking about what a loser I was compared to all the cool musicians who took songwriting classes. "I can't."

"You just said the magic word. It's the same word I used when I told you about my computer skills—'can't.'"

"I think you said, 'I don't know how to use a computer.'"

"Well, whatever. The point is, *you* knew I could master Microsoft before *I* did. You saw potential in me and brought it out. Now I'm trying to do the same thing for you."

I was speechless. *How can I refuse when she puts it like that? Because you're petrified and you might die from anxiety on your way to class.* I rubbed my scruffy chin.

Maggie softened her gaze and said, "I knew this would be hard for you, so I talked to the teacher. Her name is Debra, by the way. She told me you can just observe at the first session. You don't have to present anything if you don't want to. And if you can't handle it, who cares about the money—screw the class. But I'll be disappointed if you don't try. I want to help you and this is my tough love. Can you accept it?"

I took a deep breath and exhaled loudly, weighing my options. "Of corset," I said. "Although I'm kinda mad, it's the nicest *mean* thing anyone's ever done for me. I also feel a little guilty because it must've been expensive. How can you afford it?"

"I have my ways. Some might call them credit cards. Think of it as a token of my gratitude—for everything you did for me at the spa." She smiled and opened her menu.

"Thank *you*, Maggie."

"Enough about that, then. I'm really excited for you. And if you're like me, you'll be so terrified before class, you'll completely forget about all your problems. You will just love it!"

"Out of the frying pan…"

The waiter came back to take our order. Maggie was right, I felt completely distracted. I was so afraid to go to the songwriting class, I couldn't think about anything else. But I still wanted to go.

Chapter 13

Margaret:

Spa Divas and Spamedy

I sat at The Flame drinking burnt coffee, waiting for Thomas to show up for our weekly rendezvous, and wondering why he didn't want to tell me his 'amazing new idea' over the phone. The booths by the window were taken, so I ended up next to the kitchen. Heat radiated towards me as the lunch rush began. I took off the pink Stella McCartney jacket I'd gotten dirt cheap at Century 21, but still felt hot and a little bothered. I peaked over at my open purse. A bright orange flyer for the comedy class final performance glared back.

Thomas appeared out of nowhere, startling me. I hastily shoved the paper deeper into my bag.

"I didn't mean to scare you," he said. "My bad."

"That's okay, sweetie." His appearance startled me, too. It'd only been six days since our last meal together and he looked thinner—almost too thin. His face was pale and he had dark circles under his eyes. He wore the same outfit every time we met: Grey skinny jeans, a black v-neck t-shirt and a black hoodie. It was like he had lost his flair for fashion, too. Sometimes I went through this myself. I liked to call it my prison issue jumpsuit phase. "How are you doing?"

"I've seen better days, but I have an idea that might help all of us. You look pretty, by the way."

"I do?"

"Sure! I love the grey liner, your plum lips for spring and…" He came in for a closer look. "Are you wearing individual eyelashes?"

God he's good. "I got eyelash extensions." I fluttered my lids. "I like to say if make-up is a girl's best friend, eyelashes are her closest sister. They can take a six to an eight in a few minutes."

"I agree. They look fantastic. How do they put 'em on?"

"They apply them under the lash line so they last for two weeks."

"Two weeks! I've had a lash fall off in the middle of a show. What do they put them on with, Superglue?"

How the hell did he know everything? I shrugged.

"Maggie. It could blind you!"

"But they look sooooo good that I'm willing to accept the risk. And they use tweezers which means there's just a little dab on the end of each lash. Besides, it's only twenty bucks."

"Really?" His eyebrows rose slightly.

"You know how we love a bargain. Anyway, what's the mysterious plan you want to tell me about?"

"Well," he said, taking off his hoodie, "I was thinking we could start our own massage booking service. Since everyone from the spa is unemployed, the front desk girls can answer calls and we'll send the therapists out to give people treatments."

"Genius. How would we make any money though?"

"Commission, which we'd split with the spa concierge who booked the service. The best news is, you can finally do facials and won't have to work the phones," he said, a tiny glimmer in his voice. "Can you contact the staff and see who's interested?"

"Sure, but why don't you wanna do it?"

"I can't right now. In light of recent events, my lawyer told me not to speak to anyone from the spa until the investigation is over and we know what we're dealing with."

"You're making me nervous," My pulse quickened. "What recent events?"

"I'm not supposed to—"

"You have to tell someone. Talking about it will help." I grabbed his bony hand. "We've always kept each other's secrets."

Thomas took a deep breath. "Yvonne served me with papers. She's suing me for 10 million dollars."

"What?!" I felt like I'd been slapped. Rage swelled up inside me. "That evil bitch!"

"My lawyer says she'll never get the full amount, not only because I don't have it—look, Maggie," he paused, "Telling you does make me feel a little better, but I can't even let my mind go there right now. I have to take this one day at a time. If I imagine the possibilities, I'm going to completely break down and I'm on the edge as it is. Let's just finish talking about the booking service. Coming up with a business plan has been a really helpful distraction."

"Whatever gets you through the day." I had to control my anger for Thomas's benefit. *Focus on his ideas and worry about him later.*

"So, there are a few obstacles. The good news is with multiple phone lines, we can work out of my apartment. The bad news is, I would constantly be on high alert because I'm not supposed to talk about

254

the lawsuit, but whatever. I have to make a living somehow. The other problem is advertising. In order to attract the wealthy clientele we'll need to support the business, we gotta think big. It's not like we can post our services on Craigslist."

I squirmed in my chair. My financial problems were nothing compared to Thomas's, but I still hated talking about it. "Well, I'm broker than a headless hooker."

"I know, sweetie. I'm not asking you for money, only inspiration."

"Phew. Maybe you can hit up your folks?"

Thomas hung his head. "No, I'm too embarrassed."

"They won't mind. My mom and dad have given me thousands of dollars over the years."

"There's a reason I can't ask." He looked away like he was searching for words. "The thing is—they've already been helping me pay my bills."

"So what? Don't feel bad about it. That's what families do."

"I'm mortified!" Thomas said. "I'm over thirty and my parents just made my mortgage payment."

"They've only been lending a hand since the goin' got tough. Do you know how many times my folks have paid my rent?" He didn't answer. "Go ahead ask me."

"How many?"

"Fifty!" I exclaimed in my best Molly Shannon "SNL" voice. "When it comes to jobs, I don't like to kick and stretch. I like to quit and ditch!" Thomas laughed. "Thata girl!" I said.

"Needless to say, I can't ask them. They're not wealthy and my little sister is still in college."

"You've got good credit. We can probably make the money back right away."

"I'm maxed out, and I already increased my line of credit for a cash advance to give to Gabrielle."

"For what?"

"Yvonne *did* garnish her wages to pay for the shoe shiner, but I decided to take full responsibility for breaking it in the first place and that meant reimbursing Gabrielle."

"Well, clearly I played a role—" I said, feeling guilty.

"But it was all my stupid idea."

"I can't believe Yvonne still took that money from her. It's like giving someone a parking ticket after a nuclear holocaust."

"Seriously. Enough about the past, though. Let's talk about the future and how we're gonna make some moolah."

"Maybe if you need start-up money, you can borrow from your 401(k)."

"There was only about 1(k) in there anyway, but I cashed it in already. Without my last paycheck, I didn't have a choice A.S."

"A.S.?"

"After Spa."

"And that would make Before Spa, B.S."

"Exactly," he said with a crooked smile. *It sure is nice to see his pearly whites.*

"So maybe we'll have to find an investor. Let's get to the fun part and come up with a name. We could call it Spa Bitches to honor some of the women who'll be our client base."

"Maybe calling them bitches isn't the best way to get their business. And there's already a book called 'Skinny Bitches.' Maybe it's copyrighted."

"True. What about Spa Chicks?" I asked.

"I think there's a nail salon by that name. I do like the word 'spa' followed by a female moniker, though. It should be something glamorous, too."

I searched my inner thesaurus for a word like "chick." Thomas's eyes lit up with the twinkle I'd been missing. "Spa Divas. What do you think?"

"I like it!"

"The best part is, the women who book treatments will think *they're* the divas. In actuality, we'll know *we* are," he said.

"Genius. Maybe it will help my self-esteem."

"I think you mean *our* self-esteem." He smiled, then his lip began to quiver.

We sat without speaking for several seconds. I finally reached across the table and put my hand on top of his again. "I know you don't want to talk about what *might* happen, but maybe you should talk about what's *already* happened. It's not good to keep it all inside."

Thomas closed his eyes and let out a long breath. The silence between us was deafening. "You're right. There's something I've been holding in because I was afraid to tell anyone."

Slowly, to calm his fears, I said, "I'll lock it in a safe within a safe."

"I know, but this is so serious that Yvonne could end up in prison. And if she knows I'm the one who spilled the beans, I'll be looking over my shoulder for the rest of my life."

"I swear this conversation will self-destruct in five minutes." An antsy feeling came over me like I was watching a friend in a play. *Sympathy nerves.*

"Yvonne pays off the fire department," he whispered.

"What?" I said.

"So she could bend the rules without them shutting us down. Right after the spa was destroyed, I thought to myself, 'This is my trump card. Maybe I can use this information against her, if she tries to blame me for everything.'"

"Wait a second. Why would she pay them off in the first place?"

"Two reasons—steam and candles. When we first opened, if a guest didn't close the steam room door, it would set off the fire alarm in the locker room since they're connected. Then we'd have to comp everyone's treatments and—" He stopped abruptly.

"It's in a safe within a safe."

He looked around the room, leaned in and said, "In retrospect, I think she silenced or tinkered with the alarms in the locker rooms, because a few weeks later, the problem disappeared without a trace."

"Why didn't she just put up a sign saying, *Please shut the door when exiting?*"

"She thought it looked tacky."

"Dear Lord."

"Are you telling me she cared more about the toilets getting clogged than fire safety?"

"What do you mean?" Thomas asked.

"There was a tiny waste paper basket in every stall, with a little sign that said, 'discard tissues here.'"

"Oh right, 'cause the toilets used to overflow. Even though the bowls were new, the building's pipes were old."

"So June wasn't the only one that got backed up at the spa."

"I guess not," Thomas smirked.

"Why didn't she just remove the Kleenex boxes from the stalls?"

"It's a Five Star rule to have facial tissues available in every rest room area."

"Do they also have rules about how to wipe your ass and dispose of feminine hygiene products?"

"I dunno. That we'd have to look up. At any rate, I think a sign on a garbage can is one thing, but a sign ruining the décor was out of the question."

"To back it up, no pun intended, to before we started talking about toilets, what's the story with the candles?"

"By law, you're only allowed to have one open flame per room," Thomas said.

"And we had candelabras dripping wax everywhere with votives lining the floor."

"Exactly."

The waiter came to take our order. "I think we need more time," I said. He mumbled and walked away. "And she told you all of this?"

"Of course not."

"Then how did you find out?"

"I snooped." He fiddled with his fork. "It's not right, and it's not okay but I loved doing it. I checked her emails when she left her computer on. I read the note if she got flowers. I went through the papers on her desk and I eavesdropped."

"So she doesn't know you know?"

"I'm not sure. And I don't have all the information, either. But I never saw anyone from the fire department come to inspect the spa. Once I asked her if we should prepare for a surprise visit and she told me they already came on my day off. For some reason, I didn't really believe her. Yvonne might have paid them to look the other way, or never come at all."

"She put everyone in danger to have everything *exactly* how she wanted it."

"Listen, I'm not defending Yvonne, but even if someone tried to torch a steam room, it would be nearly impossible since the heat areas are tiled. And as for the candles, they weren't near anything that could catch fire."

"I guess not."

"And with so many people in the spa, we'd notice if there was a problem. I think she thought the rules were silly."

"She wasn't worried someone might accidently leave a candle burning overnight?"

"Apparently not. The attendants put them out before we closed and I double checked when I did my walk through. I'm sure if we missed one, it'd be more likely to burn out before it set the spa ablaze."

"There's only one thing I'm still confused about. Why did the sage set off the alarm this time? If Tootsie was a repeat offender, why didn't it happen before?"

"I wonder the same thing. I've been wracking my brain trying to figure out what happened. Maybe Tootsie really fumigated 'cause Mrs. B brought in a whole pack of bitches. Or maybe it was something else altogether. For all we know, the therapists could've been lighting their farts after bingeing on Taco Bell. Once the investigation is over, we might have more answers—if Yvonne doesn't pay them off, too." Thomas sighed and ran his fingers through his hair. "Let's change the subject. How's your class?"

"Good. It's almost over." Without thinking I looked towards the flyer in my purse.

"Wow. Congratulations. When's the last day?" His eyes darted from me to my purse and back to me.

"Actually, it's next week, but I can't even go. I'm babysitting for JoAnn—she has a PTA meeting and her husband's been working the night shift in the ER."

"What's that in your bag?" He squinted his baby browns a little.

Thomas was the most intuitive person I'd ever met, but I was astounded. *This is ESP quality investigating.* "It's nothing." I moved my purse off the table and into the booth.

"Let me see."

"It's just a car wash receipt." *Oh shit. Where did that come from?*

"Since when do you have a car?"

"It's my old Honda from when I worked at the hospital. I keep it at my parents' house."

"Come on. Show me the paper."

"No. It's personal."

"A personal car wash receipt?" He looked me in the eye, and without breaking his gaze, lunged for the flyer. I grabbed it, half-laughing, pulling it to my cleavage. *We're acting like schoolgirls.* The paper ripped in two, making a loud noise. Thomas got most of the writing.

I made a baby-pouty face. Thomas moved from side to side, avoiding my little fists as I unsuccessfully reached for the flyer. "I knew it!" he said when he finished reading. "I totally had a feeling you were hiding something from me. Are you gonna do a real stand-up gig?"

"I just told you I can't perform because I gotta watch JoAnn's kids."

"I have to admit that's a good excuse, but I'm not letting you out of this one. I seem to recall you paying in advance so I'd be forced to take a songwriting class and suddenly you're bailing out of your final? You gave me some tough love, now here's mine. You're one of the funniest people in America. Comedy is your gift and you have to share it. If you don't, you'll always regret that you didn't try. This is the first step. You have to take it."

He's right. If only I could overcome my sheer, abject, mortal terror... "I'm just getting comfortable performing in front of the other students and now I'm supposed to get on stage, in front of a room full of strangers—what with their beady eyes and their 'know it all' looks. Your class hasn't even started yet. You haven't experienced how hard it is to put yourself out there with something you wrote."

"Well, thanks to you, I will," Thomas said smiling. "Let's make a deal. I promise I'll go to all of the songwriting classes, even though I'm petrified, if you do this. I hate to be manipulative, but you can't have it both ways."

He's calling me on my own game. I took a deep breath, exhaling loudly. *God he's REALLY good.* "Ordinarily I would, but I gave my word to JoAnn."

"Why don't I babysit, instead? I've always wanted to meet your friend, who happens to be Christie Brinkley's doppelgänger."

"She's gonna love you if you call her that."

"I'm good with kids and it'll give me something to do."

"I dunno."

"Why? Because JoAnn hasn't met me yet?"

"No—she's desperate. As long as you don't have a criminal record, you're in. Plus you have excellent references." I took my napkin and blotted my forehead. *I'm sweating just thinking about performing.*

"So you'll do the show?"

I tried to catch my breath. "Fine."

"Fantastic. And maybe if JoAnn comes back early enough, I can sneak in to see—"

"NO!" I shouted. Thomas jolted, people dropped their utensils and the dining room fell into silence. "I'm sorry, but I can't have anyone I know in the audience. It would make me *even more* nervous."

"Okay," Thomas said, his voice an octave higher than usual. "It's not a big deal. I'll just meet you afterwards to celebrate."

"If I make it," I said. "I might go into cardiac arrest on stage."

"You'll make it. I have complete faith in your comic abilities."

"Let's eat, then." *Hopefully it will make me feel better.*

"I don't want any food. Maybe I'll have a decaf tea, instead."

"If I'm doing the show, you're going to eat. You look emaciated. I'm a little concerned."

"Okay, Mom."

"And whatever you don't eat, I'll finish. That reminds me—I guess I owe you some comedy."

"Hit it!" he said sitting up and leaning in.

"Well, in part of my act I say everyone should have a theme song as well as an autobiographical title. My song is "I'm No Angel," by Greg Allman and my book would be called 'Are You Gonna Finish That?'" Thomas laughed for me, even though he didn't like it when I made fun of myself. "What would you name your memoir?"

"I don't know, Maggie. I'm not very funny these days—or hungry, for that matter."

"Well, I can eat for two. You and me *or* me and my inner child who doesn't want to go on stage."

"You're going to kill, Maggie. Just remember, you're already a spa diva."

"Waiter!"

****

Throughout the next week, I swam in a river of denial that I would have to perform at a real comedy club. The night before the show, I knew I couldn't procrastinate any longer. Even though I *wanted* to conquer my fear for my own well-being, I *had to* because of the deal I made with Thomas. I poured myself a big cup of coffee, and began the arduous task of crafting an act.

All you can do is put your ideas out there and hope they resonate with people, I told myself, but my pen seemed so frozen I wondered if my hand was paralyzed. I paced around my apartment. *It's getting late. Better take out the garbage.* I sat back down. Nothing. The hours were passing and I was running out of time. *1:00 a.m.* Still nothing. *Anyone can write serious, depressing crap. It's so hard to make something funny. The members of the Academy are really missing the complexity of this art form. Why isn't there an Oscar for Best Comedy? I wonder if Thomas is still awake.*

I grabbed my phone. He answered with a yawn.

"I'm sorry, were you sleeping?"

"I wish. What's going on?"

"I'm having a hard time coming up with material." I bit the top of my pen.

"Margaret! The show's tomorrow and you haven't written your routine yet?"

"Don't rub it in."

"Okay let's do a guided meditation. Close your eyes."

"Wow! You just reminded me I already wrote some new stuff on spas." I flipped through the pages of my notebook.

"That's great. I've never heard any spa comedy."

"It's spamedy!"

"Genius. Are your eyes still opened?"

I lowered my lids. "Not anymore."

"So, imagine—"

"Are we doing a past life regression?" I opened one eye. "Because that is fodder for laughs."

"There ya go. Anyway, picture yourself—"

"Thin! Remember when they used to run those ads late at night for weight loss CDs?"

"Not really."

"Well you know *I* bought them. They made you visualize all this delicious food, but as soon as you were about to take a bite, they told you to imagine it was actually covered with maggots."

"That's shocking, which kind of begs the comparison to 'shock aversion therapy for homosexuality.'"

"Totally, so thanks for your help. I better get back to work. I guess all I needed was some inspiration."

"Inspiration through failed mediation. Break a leg tomorrow."

"Oh God. It *is* tomorrow." A chill of fear went up my spine. "Goodnight, Tom."

"Goodnight and good luck."

I put down the phone, picked up my pen, and turned all my nervous energy into fuel for my writing. After Thomas jump-started my brain, inspiration came to me like it was falling from the sky. *I'm on fire!* When I finished brainstorming, I fine-tuned my best ideas to a point. By 4:00 a.m. I felt completely spent, but I had my act. I memorized the material by rereading it until my head hurt. It was the hardest fun I'd ever had. *If I can get one genuine laugh for something I've concocted, I'll be blown away.*

I slept for a few hours until a nightmare woke me up. I dreamt I was on stage, my mind went blank and worst of all, no one was laughing. *I can't let that happen!* The city streets bustled with a new day as I tossed and turned, trying to figure out a surefire way to abate my fear. Finally, I came up with an idea which allowed me to fall asleep again.

By that evening, my palpable anticipation propelled me off the couch and into the jungle. I put on a comic warrior outfit to make me feel skinnier and confident: Tight dark denim jeans, a charcoal cowl neck sweater and black Moschino knee-high boots. When I dabbed on a little extra make-up before I left, I could barely steady my shaking hand. *I wasn't this nervous when I got married. Oh well, I'm as ready as I'll ever be.* Next stop: The Gotham Comedy Club.

Chapter 14

Thomas:

The Beauty in the Ugly

The night before the first songwriting class, I barely slept at all. A recurring nightmare kept jolting me awake. In the surreal bad dream, an unseen voice asked me to read my poem in front of the other students, but when I opened my mouth, only nonsense dribbled out and I sounded like Charlie Brown's teacher. The other students laughed at me, escalating into a chorus of hysterics.

I spent the day in front of the TV, trying to forget my impending doom. I left my place early to minimize the stress of navigating an unfamiliar neighborhood. When I arrived in Astoria, Queens, I scanned the street numbers to make sure I was heading in the right direction. The two family homes and apartment buildings were sandwiched together without an inch in between. I found Debra's building and walked around her block twice to kill time.

Finally—8 o'clock—my personal witching hour, was close at hand. As I completed the last lap to the finish line, my throat was so tight it felt like someone was strangling me. I kept swallowing hard, listening to my shallow breaths. *If I forget to inhale, will I still do it automatically? If I'm not making a conscious effort, I might stop breathing and completely pass out.*

That would be so embarrassing on the first night of class! I went to ring the buzzer and lost my nerve. *You're only auditing this session,* I tried to tell myself. *You don't even have to speak. These people probably play instruments, though. I know nothing about making music. What am I doing here, anyway? Maybe I should leave.* Then I remembered the promise I had made to Margaret and I hit the buzzer. No one responded on the intercom, but the door clicked repeatedly. I pushed open the heavy slab of metal and glass, slipping inside.

By the time I walked up to the fifth floor, I was panting. There was music coming from inside Debra's apartment at the end of the hall. I followed the notes like a snake in a trance, creeping toward the sound of the piano, my heartbeat pounding in my ears. I approached her door, which had a welcome sign hanging below the peephole and a colorful Mezuzah on its frame. I rang the bell and the melody stopped abruptly. Seconds later, the door flung open.

"Hi there. Come on in!" said a tiny thirty-something woman wearing brown yoga pants and an oversized rust colored sweater. Her apartment was cluttered and bohemian. It smelled like spices from chronic incense burning. I flashed back to the spa. A pang of sadness struck me in my stomach. "You must be Thomas. I'm Debra." She threw her little arms around me in a bear hug. "It's so nice to meet you in person." She brimmed with confidence, smiling from ear to ear.

Debra motioned for me to sit on a red velour couch in her living room and plopped down next to me. "You're the first one here." She pulled her wild curly black hair into a ponytail. "So, are you excited about the class?"

"I guess, but I'm a bit nervous. I don't play an instrument or anything."

"Who cares? You're a lyricist. Some of the greatest songwriters of all time don't even know how to read music."

268

"Really?"

"Yep. Dolly Parton for example, who is extremely prolific. And she didn't need an instrument to write '9 to 5.' She came up with the idea by rubbing her fake fingernails together."

My desire to connect eclipsed my fear. "You gotta love her. Dolly says such funny things—she's like a modern day Mae West."

Debra smiled. I breathed a miniscule sigh of relief. "See, you're in good company."

"I have my moments, but I'm no Dolly."

"You don't know that. Maybe all you need is an opportunity to express yourself. Listen," Debra paused, "I'm glad you got here first so we can get this out of the way. The reason I let you into the class is because I see potential in you. For me, it's more gratifying to help a student develop their gifts, than to coach someone who thinks they have it all figured out. So," she smacked her thighs, "will you let me help you?"

"Of course. I'm just embarrassed to be around people who know what they're doing."

"Everyone has to start somewhere."

A fraction of tension dispersed from my neck and shoulders. *Wow, she's great.*

Approaching voices reverberated in the stairwell. There was a knock at the door. The first face that peeked in looked gorgeous. *Oh no. It's Auston Harman.* My stomach dropped to the floor. I had cyber-stalked him on YouTube after Margaret gave him my poem. His songs were brilliant with poignant lyrics and catchy, yet dark, melodies. He made his way into the apartment. The girl behind him came into view. She had glowing ebony skin and jet black dreads. There was a guitar case strapped to her back. *Hopefully her baby face will even out my fear of Auston.*

His confidence intimidated me but his appearance pushed me over the edge. He was a rock star who dressed the part in a military style jacket and distressed leather pants. Auston's long dirty-blonde hair brought out the beauty in his jungle green eyes. *If I let myself, I'd be severely attracted to him.* I looked down at the drab outfit I wore every day—grey skinny jeans with a black tee, newsboy cap and hoodie.

I hot flush came over my face at the thought of Auston reading my poem. *He knows I'm an amateur. Oh God!* Being in a social situation with a straight guy had brought me right back to high school. I was a freshmen again, about to get a swirly, trapped in the insecure state of not belonging and he hadn't even opened his mouth yet. *I think I feel a panic attack coming on!*

"Hi, sweetie." Debra opened her arms, extending her little 5'4" frame.

"Hey." He hugged her. Auston seemed warm, but something about him read as cool as ice. "This is Maya." He introduced the girl with the dreads. "We met downstairs."

"It's nice to meet you." Debra gave her a kiss on each cheek. "I loved the songs you sent me."

"Thank you so much." Maya beamed and modestly tucked a stray dreadlock behind her ear. "I'm really happy to be here," she said in a near whisper. I couldn't tell if she was shy, nervous or just soft spoken.

"And this is Thomas." Debra gestured to me with both hands like she was modeling a Ford at a car show.

I stood up and wiped my sweaty palms on my jeans. "Nice to meet you guys," I said.

"You too, man." Auston shook my hand. "Margaret talks about how funny you are all the time."

"Oh cool," I said. *Well that response certainly wasn't funny and don't expect too much from me tonight.*

I sat back down, looking around the one bedroom apartment. Shelves full of CDs, tchotchkes and books lined the walls. A mini-studio in a crowded corner featured a keyboard, microphone and computer. To my left, a guitar leaned against an amp next to a mixing board. Wires spilled onto the floor like black spaghetti. *I'm so out of my league.*

Maya took a seat beside me on the couch. Auston and Debra sat down on teak chairs from the 70's. The four of us settled in, facing each other. I prayed no one else would join the group. I felt like a watchdog guarding the door from the corner of my eye.

Debra slapped her legs and said, "So, some other people might be coming late…" *Damn it!* "…but let's get to know each other a little better. Auston, this is your—what, fifth class with me?"

"Something like that," he answered.

"Why don't you tell us about your background?"

"Sure." Auston spoke in a low, raspy voice. "I've been playing piano since I was seven, and I wrote my first song when I was about ten, I think." He crossed his legs like a man, resting his right ankle on his left knee. "I did the band thing in high school, then I majored in music at Tisch and now I'm ready to workshop some stuff for my second album."

I have to leave here immediately.

"Great!" Debra said, "Who's next?"

I was on mute.

"I'll go," Maya said in her Marilyn Monroe-essque whisper. "I grew up singing gospel in church and I did show choir until the eleventh grade. I've written lots of music and I play guitar, but I'd really like to hone my skills as a lyricist." She looked toward me. *I guess we're going around the room.*

Sweat was soaking the armpits of my t-shirt. *Did I put on deodorant today? Now Auston is gonna think, 'Who is that feminine, smelly guy and what is he doing here?' Time to get this over with.* I prayed I could speak. *God is hearing from me a lot these days.*

"Hi, I'm Thomas. I'm only checking this class out. I actually studied psychology, not music, in school. When I graduated from college I moved to New York to be a drag queen." *Oh shit! What am I saying? And in front of a straight guy! Now he probably thinks I'm a sex freak.* "After that I worked in the luxury spa industry. Then, well, I lost my job because the spa was destroyed by water damage and the owner is suing me—" *What in fuckery am I talking about? They don't need to hear all my dirty laundry.* I lost my train of thought. My face began to burn. *Now I know how Margaret feels. This is a disaster!*

"So why are you interested in songwriting?" Debra flipped her hair, already free from its ponytail.

"Um, I don't think I could actually write a song—maybe lyrics, though."

"Don't limit yourself. Stay open to the possibility. You're already a good writer and maybe one day you can learn the music part. In any case, I like what you submitted. Why don't you share it with the group?"

There goes my plan to avoid participating. I said, "Oh, I'm only here to observe, remember? You said that was okay on the phone."

"I *said* you didn't have to do anything you didn't *want* to do, but I can tell you want to read it. I'm gonna push you just like the others, even though you're new at this."

Sweet Jesus, no! "Maybe someone else should go first, I—"

"If you don't want to read your lyrics because you really don't want to, I can accept that. If you don't want to read them because you're *afraid*—that I can't accept. So what's really going on here?"

Who is this woman? She had known me for all of five minutes and already had me pegged. I *did* want to share my poem. I wanted to express myself but I was afraid—of being laughed at, of being misunderstood, and not fitting in. I shifted into "get it over with" mode.

"Did you bring copies of your lyrics like I asked you to?" Debra said.

I nodded, pulled the papers from my bag and handed sheets to Maya and Debra. My whole arm shook like a leaf when I gave a copy to Auston, but I managed to avoid looking at him. I had written about what I'd been going through over the past few weeks. It was personal, it was me and like the old cliché says, it was my baby. As unsure as I was of its merits, I knew I couldn't handle anyone rejecting the words I'd chosen and me in the process. I opened my mouth to speak, worried I might have an out-of-body experience. I could barely breathe. *Am I losing sight in my left eye?*

"These are the first potential lyrics I've ever written, so it's probably not very good," I said.

"Noted." Debra threw her hair back into a ponytail and put on the glasses that'd been hanging around her neck from a purple string. "Now read it anyway."

I did:

"The Beauty in the Ugly"

So you're having a sepia toned kind of time

You're feeling out of rhythm

Can't seem to find the rhyme

It's too dark behind the scar

You're too blind to see without your eyes

You've forgotten who you are

You may not feel it

Too stuck in your trap

But this time will pass

It's feeling like forever

But It's not going to last

See the beauty in the ugly

Go ahead it's not too hard

I can already start to see who you really are

So you're feeling numb to the world

It's like no one can get in

You can't seem to feel

Too thick in your old skin

There is time to heal

Got to let yourself win

You may not feel it

Too stuck in your trap

But this time will pass

It's feeling like forever

But It's not going to last

See the beauty in the ugly

Go ahead it's not too hard

I can already start to see who you really are

Grey buildings cast a sunless shadow

Out of the sky comes a blackness explosion

Run for cover, fly toward the light

Your life's not over

A new one is in sight

So I tell you to break through your cocoon

I beg you to claw through your shell

Try to make some room

See if you can tell that

Soon you may look back and say

It's already the dawn of a brand new day

I read it without emotion, my nerves escalating until I finished. I looked up like I'd been caught with my pants down. The sound of two hands coming together broke the silence, followed by a full round of applause. The catharsis was so great, I felt like I could breathe for the first time in weeks.

Debra took off her reading glasses. "Ok guys, tell him what ya think." I tensed up all over again.

Maya said, "If you ask me, it's great for your first attempt at writing lyrics. It's pretty great, period." She put her closest arm around the sofa, turning toward me. "I like the way you acknowledge that the person in the song is really going through something. Then someone else has the clarity to say, it's really only the end of one thing and the beginning of another." I smiled at her.

"Anything else?" Debra asked.

"Yes actually," Maya replied, speaking slightly louder than a whisper. "There's some poetic beauty about sadness in hard times. When I look back at difficult episodes in my life, I'm not upset, I actually feel a little poignant." She put her hand on her heart. "You always learn a lot when you go through something very challenging. You've touched on all of those ideas so it's very relatable to me. I get the message. Is there a story behind it? Did you write this song for someone?"

"I actually wrote it to myself. When I lost my job at the spa, everything fell apart, 'cause the job was my life, although it wasn't my calling. I've been through rough patches before and at the time, you feel like you'll never get out of it, but I did. Subconsciously, I must have written this to remind myself of that."

"It's a great lesson to share with others," Maya said.

Wow.

"Auston?" Debra prompted.

I wanted to hide my face, but instead I looked him in the eye like a normal person would.

"It's good. Have you thought about a melody or what kind of musical genre this might be in?"

"I think it's kind of singer/songwriter, like a Sarah McLachlan song."

"Well if you want," Auston said, "I can play around with it, put some music to it."

"Sure, okay." I was dumbfounded. *Does that mean I would have to talk to you in the real world?*

Debra clasped her hands together "See, that's what we do here. I smell a collaboration! Now we also need to give Thomas some constructive criticism." Tension rose in my chest. "I'll begin with the specifics. So here are my issues. Number one, you go verse, chorus, verse, chorus and then what's this next part that starts with 'Grey Buildings?'"

"I thought it could be the bridge," I said, nervously.

"A-ha! And *I thought* you were new at this?" Debra grinned, my tension drifted away. "A lot of first timers don't know what a bridge is. So, that's great. The problem is with your verses. The ideas are good. However, the rhyme scheme is inconsistent and the lines don't have the same amount of syllables. When you put it to music, you have to be able to fit the words in each verse to the notes."

"Oh, okay." I was so fascinated by what she was saying, I didn't have time to feel bad about being a newbie.

Debra continued, "It doesn't always have to be a perfect match because the interpretation can fill in the blanks, but I'm getting ahead of myself. What you do really well is what we like to call the 'payoff line.' It's the last thought in a stanza that packs a punch, hits you emotionally and drives home what you're saying. It makes you feel. I love it when you say 'Your life's not over/A new one is in sight.'"

"Thank you." I couldn't quite absorb everything, yet on some level, I understood every word coming out of her mouth. I found it hard to believe I was getting so much positive feedback when I still couldn't see myself as a lyricist. This experience called to mind a lesson I had learned from my old Sunday school teacher. She told me not to disagree when someone gave me a compliment, as I had a habit of doing. Instead, if I said, "Thank you," eventually the compliment would sink in and help me feel good about myself. At that moment, it was all I could think of to say anyway.

"Okay, you two," Debra addressed Maya and Auston. "He needs more feedback."

Maya said, "I really like the imagery in the bridge. It's very creative."

"Thanks."

"Do you have any problems with the song?" Debra asked.

"This part where you say, 'Too thick in your own skin/There is time to heal/Got to let yourself win.' Some people might think that's a little cliché."

"Okay," I said. *She's right.* "I actually thought the same thing myself after I finished writing it."

Debra prompted Auston, "C'mon, tell him what he needs to do to improve this."

Auston said, "I agree with what you said earlier, Debra. The structure needs work, which is something you can learn. And also, these are lyrics—it's not a poem or a novel. You want to create concise phrases that are easy to sing." I nodded my head, pretending to scribble notes so I didn't have to look Auston in the eye.

"Excellent advice. Anything else?" Debra asked.

"Let me see what I jotted down." Auston jiggled the leg he had propped up on his knee. "The line Maya pointed out isn't my favorite either. I think it's important to steer away from the obvious with the goal of creating something completely new. I do like the idea of beauty in hardship—overall, it's really nice."

Debra said, "Okay, let's move on." I exhaled. "Who's next?"

Auston raised his hand. Debra nodded. He passed out his sheets, stepped behind the keyboard, cracked his knuckles with a snap and said, "Okay, this is still a little rough, but here it goes." *I can't believe he gave a disclaimer, too.* With all his talent and experience, I saw he was just like me—insecure about what he'd created. Auston took a deep breath. "I wrote this about my ex-boyfriend."

Oh. My. God. All that stressing I was doing about feeling like a freak and he's gay, too! It's really gonna be hard not to fall in love with him now.

Auston sang a powerful, haunting song. It undulated, wrapping around my heart in the verse and then exploding into rock during the chorus.

"A Love Song for Me"

You poured on your heaven

Rescued me from my rain

Filled me with joy

Only covered my pain

How do you write a love song?

Mix a little heartbreak

With some big mistakes

Add a splash of needy

To a dash of codependency

Follow this simple recipe

To write a love song

Just for me

I knew it wouldn't last

Knew you weren't the one

But you drew me to your web

When I knew I shoulda run

How do you write a love song?

Mix a little heartbreak

With some big mistakes

Add a splash of needy

To a dash of codependency

Follow this simple recipe

To write a love song

Just for me

Bridge

Listening to the radio

Unhealthy is the way to go

Desperately seeking magic

Is absolutely tragic

We need a cosmic intervention

A musical revolution

A therapeutic reconnection

Let me be the one

To give you some direction

How do you write a love song?

Mix a little heartbreak

With some big mistakes

Add a splash of needy

To a dash of codependency

You followed this simple recipe

And wrote a love song

Just for me

When Auston finished, there was a moment of silence before we applauded. It was like his music had put us in a spa daze. Debra stood up, clapping with her arms extended like Paula Abdul. Then she said, "Okay, guys—what do ya think? Thomas?"

I couldn't believe she called on me first, but I did have something to say. I addressed the group, alternating eye contact, instead of looking straight at Auston. "I love it. You really nailed what it feels like to be in a bad relationship. And I totally get what you're saying about songs on the radio. They send a fucked up message like 'you complete me.'" I met Auston's gaze for a split second. "This is an antidote to that. It's really cool how the last line of the song is different from the original chorus—kinda like a surprise ending, which tells the *real* story. The recipe symbolism is great, too." The second I stopped talking, I felt a hot flash across my face. *I can't believe I went on for so long.*

"Awesome, thanks," Auston said giving me a crooked smile. My heart fluttered. "You really got what I was trying to say." He captured me in his stare and I couldn't break away.

Debra saved me by shifting our focus, "Okay, I'm the biggest cheerleader in the room and I loved it, too—for all of those reasons. BUT I think the word co-dependency is a bit clinical for a pop/rock song. Maybe this is the reason I've never heard it used before. Thoughts?"

Auston said, "Damn. I mean, I don't know. That never occurred to me."

Debra replied, "In my opinion, it destroys the beauty of the lyrics."

Immediately I thought of a song that featured the word 'co-dependent'. I shook my head slightly without realizing it. "What do you want to say, Thomas?"

"Nothing, I, um—"

"C'mon—say it!" Debra belted.

"I'm only a novice, but that's my favorite line. It's very psychological and I think a lot of people will be able to relate. The other thing is, the word 'co-dependent' is actually in an amazing song by Garbage called 'Medication.'"

Debra looked stunned. Then she slapped her palm on her knee. "Ya see! That's what I love about this class. You just pulled that information out of the lyrical library in your brain. And you call yourself a novice? Oh no, my friend, you know music and I'm guessing it's because you've loved it your whole life. Your opinion gave me, someone who's been working in this industry for years, a new perspective. I'm so glad you're here."

Goose bumps spread across my arms and the hairs on the back of my neck stood up. Debra had given me the best compliment I'd ever received about something I'd said. I really began to *feel* her accolades. My opinion of someone else's work was helpful. And the reaction I had gotten from reading my lyrics was proof that I had something to offer. *I'm a creative person. This is who I am. Now I know it in my soul.*

There was something else I'd realized, too. Although I was only allowed to watch one hour of TV a day when I was growing up, our house was always full of music. My mother listened to Motown, my father loved everything from The Beatles to opera, and together, they bought me a boom box for my 9th birthday. We played "The Top 40 Countdown" every Sunday on the stereo in the living room and both my sisters were happy to dance with me to our favorite songs. All five of us sang along to pop classics when we traveled cross country in our green station wagon. I came to this conclusion: My family was responsible for giving me the musical education I didn't know I had.

Listening to everything I could get my hands on after I flew the coop—including alternative, country, industrial, rock, hip-hop, techno and every genre in between—was my master class. Even without a fancy degree, I knew more than I thought I did. It was my ultimate Gratitude Journal entry. I was so grateful my parents had given me the gift of music. Debra had shown me this and it meant the world to me. Still, the only word I could utter back to her was, "Thanks."

****

Before we left, Debra gave us an assignment for our next session: Write a top ten hit for Leona Lewis.

On the subway ride home, thoughts of Leona Lewis's songs filled my head. *She's always so heartbroken in her lyrics.* Even the titles are sad: "Bleeding Love," "Better in Time," and of course, "Broken." I thought about people who ended a relationship by saying, "It's not you, it's me." For some reason, I kept reversing it in my head, thinking, "It's not me, it's you." *Eureka!* Leona needed an empowering anthem—not another gut-wrencher. The lyrics came to me in chunks like divine inspiration. I finished before I got home, incorporating what I'd learned in class. When I was writing, I forgot about everything—the lawsuit, money, if and how I was going to start a new business. *This is what they were talking about on the TV special about happiness.* I was having a transcendent experience. It felt like the words were flowing through me as a higher power helped me write a masterpiece. I wasn't afraid to go back to the class anymore. I was so excited I couldn't wait—for more than one reason.

That night I had a sex dream about Auston that was more like a music video. We were making out in the rain as it turned to snow, which was blown away by a spring wind morphing into a summer sun and finally becoming autumn leaves, spinning in a circle. Our long hair, caught in a dust devil, swirled around our faces. The wind stopped abruptly, the point of view changed and I was looking right at Auston's jungle green irises. He grinned back at me, tucking a blonde lock behind his ear, while the ethereal world spun around us—a Pierre et Gilles photograph coming to life. An electronic rock ballad played in the background making me feel like I was in love. I woke up and sang the melody into my digital recorder, my heart still fluttering. I thought, *In one week, I'll present my song to the class and I won't be afraid to look you straight in the eye.*

Chapter 15

Margaret:

Like a Virgin

When I arrived at the Comedy Club I implemented the back-up plan, which had allowed me to fall back asleep that morning. I wrote tiny notes on the palms of my hands with a ball point pen, just in case I lost my train of thought. It may have looked like I was paying homage to an Indian bride, but I needed a little security blanket.

I took a deep breath as the announcer said, "Ladies and Gentleman, please welcome, your next virgin, Margaret McCarthy." I walked onto the stage. Heat from the bright lights was beating down on my freshly reapplied MAC war paint. The room stirred with energy. Clinking glasses and the audiences' hushed conversations made me acutely aware of my absolute terror. *There are real people out there!* I hadn't been this excited/scared since the Cheesecake Factory opened steps away from my apartment.

You hafta think of a way to calm yourself down. I stepped into the spotlight and imagined being at home with my big Irish family. I was transported back to a time when our parents let us stay up late so my siblings and I could do shows for their friends. I always began with the Carol Burnett Tarzan yell. Then I told jokes in the Irish accent I copied from my granny. The kids competed against each other, while the adults sipped Manhattans on the back porch, pretending to be 'The Gong Show' panel. Even though they gave me the hook a lot, I didn't care. We were together and all was well. It didn't matter then; there were no repercussions.

This show, however, is real life. I concentrated on my breathing like I was in childbirth doing Lamaze. *All those little performances you did were leading up to this moment, so being on stage should remind you of home.*

"Hello, I'm Margaret," I said into the microphone as my heart pounded, "and I'm a comedian." No one laughed at my AA reference. *Maybe someone's used that before. Better move on.*

"So, I started a new diet recently, but the portions were kind of unrealistic. I was so hungry, I went into a feeding frenzy like a shark and accidentally ate the box it came in, a metal fork, and two inches of my own hair." I grabbed the mike from the stand to give myself a second to catch my breath. "I lost a few teeth, but also .67 pounds. Success!" A loud burst of laughter echoed through the room. *Thank you God!*

"I had to lose the 'lbs' man. I mean, how many undergarments can a gal wear? The other night, my spanks and corsetry were so thick, I was actually bulletproof. I walked right into the Boogie-Down-Bronx without a care in the world." I heard chuckles in the first few rows so I continued in the same vein.

"I gave up carbs for a few months until I went to the doctor and he told me it was affecting my mental acuity. This was solidified by the fact that I accidentally brushed my teeth with Preparation H. I had to ask a neighbor to call poison control because I'd lost all feeling in my mouth. Toothpaste in your butt is more than tingly, too." I opened my eyes widely and heard some snickering. "I was in a permanent bad mood without starch. After cutting carbs for too long, even Gandhi would yell at a limo driver to give him a fucking cracker."

They laughed again. I even heard some people clap in the distance. I died a little inside, but was reborn immediately. Even though the spotlight was blinding and I couldn't see the whole crowd, the auditory response was intoxicating. *I've definitely found a replacement for my food addiction. This is a high like no other.*

"The doctor also told me weight loss would help my self-image," I said trying to own the stage by pacing from one side to the other. "Personally, I think people really need to get over themselves. High self-esteem is so overrated. I much prefer insecure pleasers as friends. They give longer back rubs." I only heard some polite giggling, but I'd learned in class, you have to treat a low response like a segue.

"And speaking of which, does anyone ever go to spas?" A group of girls applauded and screamed. "That's what I do for work. I give facials so I have to deal with some pretty fascinating people. We get a lot of celebrities and they're never like you expect them to be. Recently, I worked on someone who claimed to be one of the biggest animal rights supporters in Hollywood. At first I thought I should call PETA because she was covered in leather from head to toe. Then I realized it was just her skin."

There was an exceptional amount of approval from the back row. "I hate it when I'm working on a client and she starts twiddling her thumbs. It's all I can do not to throttle them, and explain if you have one day to live, spend it doing facials, because it will feel like an eternity. Veal has a better time than this." There was no reaction from the audience. *Maybe only another esthetician can relate. Better switch gears.*

I opened my mouth to skip to the next joke and that's when it happened. My mind went blank. I glanced down at the cheat notes on my hand, only to see sweaty pools of blue ink. *Oh crap! That nightmare was a premonition.* A deafening silence fell on the room. I glanced stage left and saw my teacher smiling enthusiastically at me. There was a mop in a bucket next to her. It sparked a memory. *Dear Lord! I'm saved.* I played it off, like I didn't miss a beat.

"So I was wondering if anyone here has ever thought about who they were in a past life." A few people applauded. "I know you'll probably say you were a great leader or royalty of some kind, but buildings have always needed cleaning. How come nobody was ever a janitor?" The crowd laughed louder than before.

"Why are we all so sure we were someone special? You think you were Napoleon, I think you probably, I dunno, made cheese. *You* think you were Cleopatra, but *I* think you were a wet nurse." The people in the audience were laughing and clapping, too. "You think you were Marilyn Monroe? Well, I'm guessing you worked," I paused, "in a store." The music started playing like my time was up at the Oscar podium. "Thank you, good night!" Thunderous applause erupted as I put the mike back on the stand.

I walked off the stage imagining I was swirling through a cloud of opium; the sound of laughter literally mimicked the feeling of being on drugs. At that moment, I decided being your best self is what really heals your wounds from the past, not having a fancy job or a perfect body.

The announcer asked for another round of applause. The spotlight dimmed, and I could finally see into the auditorium. People were clapping feverishly. Then I saw a beautiful man with eyes the exact same color as iced tea and a woman who looked just like Christie Brinkley jumping up and down in the back row. *Oh my God!* Thomas and JoAnn were the loud cheerleaders I heard in the distance. I blew them a kiss after I took my final bow. I was shocked and delighted they had been there to see my debut.

For the first time, I decided to focus on what I'd achieved. Not only did I get through my maiden voyage in front of a live audience, but I was actually successful. The fact that people laughed was proof. I overcame my fear and discovered what it felt like to be a performer. When you create something and share it with other people during a show, you feel a symbiosis taking place. You're not just entertaining people, you're telling them about yourself. If they respond, they're relating to you. I never thought I would find this kind of affirmation for something I'd written. It made me feel understood, validated, appreciated and maybe even loved, especially because Thomas and JoAnn were there to see it all happening. There was no more time to waste; I had to go see my two biggest fans.

****

JoAnn and Thomas presented me with a huge bouquet of yellow roses when I greeted them under the flashing lights of Times Square. "You were great, Maggie!" JoAnn hugged me with so much momentum, we almost fell over.

"Thanks, sweetie," I said, a little teary-eyed.

"You're not mad we came?" Thomas asked.

"Not at all. It's the perfect situation. I got all your love and support without the extra nerves 'cause I didn't know you were there. So who's watching the kids?"

"Who cares! I've had two dirty martinis," JoAnn said as she swung her purse over her shoulder. "Did I tell you, you're hilarious?"

"You did. And right now the feeling is mutual."

"Cool. I'm gonna go flirt with a strange man so I can bum a cigarette." She wobbled away in her little black dress and sky high stilettos.

Thomas chuckled. "We decided if she had a reality show, we'd call it *Moms Gone Wild.*"

I threw my head back with laughter. "Be careful what you say or I'm going to make you join the comedy class."

290

"Oh no, Maggie, it's your night. And you really were amazing."

I grabbed his boney hand. "Thank you, honey." We gave each other the war buddy look we always reverted to. "I really couldn't have done it without your support and I want you to know I love you. I'm so glad you're my very first and very best gay friend."

"Aw shucks, Maggie."

"I'm serious. Every woman should experience this kind of friendship. It's all the fun and glamour of a girlfriend without all the petty girl crap. You also get the added bonus of a male-ish perspective, which leads to the most insightful advice I've ever been privy to."

"And it's free of charge," he said.

JoAnn returned, puffing away on a cigarette, her hand up like Bette Davis. "I hate to break up the love fest, but let's talk about the show!"

"Totally," Thomas agreed.

"Do tell us about your creative process," JoAnn said.

I blushed. "Well, Thomas gave me some ideas and the baby Jesus did the rest."

"Really, Maggie?" JoAnn said, exhaling a puff of smoke. "Baby Jesus?"

"What I mean is, a lot of it just came to me," I explained. "Something took over my pen last night when I was writing—like it was coming from above."

"Oh my God!" Thomas said as JoAnn wandered off. "The same thing happened to me when I was writing a song for class."

"That's amazing, honey," I beamed at him. "See, it was meant to be."

"From the bottom of my heart, Maggie—thanks for making me do it. I didn't say anything last night on the phone because I wanted to

291

tell you this in person. We've only had one session and it's already given me a new lease on life."

"I'm so glad." I grabbed his hand again. "I was getting worried about you for a minute. And speaking of worried, where's JoAnn?"

"Here I am!" JoAnn popped out from behind a handsome man and stumbled back towards us.

"You guys never told me how you pulled this off," I said, trying to take the cancer stick from her as she spun around avoiding me.

"We just happened to be in the neighborhood, killing time," Thomas said, smiling.

"Let the vodka do the talking," JoAnn shouted. "When I called Thomas to make babysitting plans, we hit it off, so I decided to ditch the PTA meeting and crash *this* motherfucking party. Woo-hooo!" A startled passerby on the sidewalk jumped back.

Thomas looked at me with wide, amused eyes, as JoAnn made love to her cigarette. "I saw the name of the comedy club on your flyer," he said, "and I called to get us tickets."

JoAnn took another puff, "We sat in the back row so we wouldn't make you nervous." Smoke billowed out of her mouth. "Thomas figured if you bombed, we could sneak out. That way you wouldn't have to feel bad. You'd be none the wiser."

"JoAnn!" Thomas laughed uncomfortably. "You didn't have to tell her that part."

"But it's true," JoAnn said through slightly slurred speech. "Besides, she was great."

"You really were."

"So JoAnn, who's actually watching the kids?" I asked.

"My neighbor's daughter." She took a final drag and flicked her cigarette haphazardly into the street. I imagined a cartoon zipping noise punctuating the action. Then she whispered loudly into my ear, "The only reason I asked you is 'cause I thought you needed the money."

"Thank you, vodka. Let's go get some food in your stomach—shall we?" I offered JoAnn one arm, and Thomas, who grabbed my bouquet, the other. As we walked down the street, I felt like I had all the armor I needed to face the world.

"And speaking of food," JoAnn said, "did Thomas tell you we came up with our *own* biography titles?"

"No, do share." My spirit soared at the thought of my two bestie bookends talking about my material and becoming friends in the process.

Thomas said, "My book is called *Spa Dayz* with a 'z'."

"Very clever," I smiled.

"Mine is called *Nut House*," JoAnn said. "I have a husband and three boys at home and I work in a psych ward." She stopped us in our tracks as her knees buckled with laughter. "I don't know which house has more nuts!"

Chapter 16

Thomas:

Your Anthem

Three days before the second songwriting class, I was at home printing copies of my lyrics when the phone rang. I let the call go to voicemail because I was too busy marveling at the fact that creative people were like blenders: You put in your favorite influences and whip up a concoction of your own. I gathered the pages and absentmindedly glanced at the iPhone screen. My eyes flared open. I couldn't bring myself to listen to the voicemail. We hadn't spoken since the spa closed. There was a message from Yvonne.

Why is she calling me? It had been weeks, and the only communication—if you could call it that—had been through our lawyers. The information exchanged was strictly about the case. It gave new meaning to the words cold and impersonal. I didn't know what to do so I called Margaret.

"Yvonne left me a message."

"Oh my God," Margaret gasped. "What did she say?"

"I have no idea."

"Well hurry up and listen to it! I can't take the suspense."

"No way. I'm too scared."

"Why don't you call me from your home phone and play the voicemail on speaker." I could practically hear her smiling. "We can listen to it together. This way if you're too in shock to call the paramedics, I can do it for you."

"That would be kinda funny if it wasn't a distinct possibility. Okay, here we go." I dialed Margaret's number. Waiting for the phone to ring felt like an eternity. Finally, I heard Maggie's voice. "Ten-four, good buddy."

"You're awfully jovial. Could you at least pretend you're a *little* freaked out for me?"

"Sorry, I mean yes. If we were on Skype, you'd see I'm biting my nails."

I played the message. **"Thomas, this is Yvonne. Please contact me as soon as possible. I need to speak to you directly."** Click.

Margaret broke my stunned silence. "Well that was anti-climactic."

"I don't think so! What should I do now? I can't talk to her. I should call my lawyer. What if she's trying to entrap me to admit fault?"

"Then you keep your mouth shut."

"What if I slip and she's taping the conversation? What if the investigation is complete and she paid someone off to frame me?"

"I think you're getting a little paranoid."

"A *little*? Some days I don't even leave the house!"

"Just hear what she has to say. You don't have to speak at all. If it starts getting uncomfortable, tell her she needs to go through your attorney. You can do this."

"Okay. I'll let her do all the talking."

"Thata girl. Call me right back."

"I can't do it *now*," I blurted out so she wouldn't hang up. "I don't trust her. She still might be trying to trick me."

"You've got a point—Yvonne had a lot of people fooled for a very long time. She is wildly devious. You think you know somebody."

"That's the thing. I never felt like I knew Yvonne."

"Me either, but I assumed you were somewhat close to her."

"Not really," I admitted. "She was very guarded, even with me. And sometimes she even seemed a little two-dimensional—kind of a work-lady robot. It's not like we were friends."

"I don't think she's the kind of person who has real friends."

"Maybe not. She was so competitive with her alleged BFF, Mena Brooks. It always seemed as if they were trying to outdo each other."

"Interesting, but now you're totally procrastinating," Margaret said. "Call her. Get it over with. I'll be waiting so if you don't do it immediately, I'll be sitting around for hours, unable to leave my couch, on pins and needles, lonely, while dying for the phone to ring."

"Alright, alright. But just so you know, I get some of my best work done while procrastinating. My dorm room was never cleaner than when I had a term paper due." I hung up. Sweat began to soak my t-shirt. I flapped my elbows like a baby bird, trying to cool down.

I called Yvonne back. Her phone rang. Swallowing hard, I hoped she wouldn't pick up. There was another ring. Then I changed my mind and prayed for her to answer. *I don't wanna hafta do this again.* Another ring, followed by silence. *Is it going to voicemail?*

"Hello, Thomas." My heart was racing faster than an IndyCar.

"Hello." *Don't say more than one word at a time.*

"I'm sure you are wondering why I am calling instead of my lawyer."

"Yes."

"I wanted to tell you this personally." There was a long pause.

"Yes?"

"It's rather good news—for you anyway." It seemed like she was having a hard time getting the words out.

"Okay."

"I'm dropping the lawsuit against you."

What? "That's it? No apology?" Confusion and rage engulfed me so quickly, I thought I might burst. "I have been in mortal terror for weeks and now you're just gonna drop it without even a simple 'I'm sorry?'"

"I *am* sorry."

"Well thank you, I suppose. How can I even be sure you're telling the truth? What if you get mad again and change your mind?" I knew this wasn't the time to provoke her, but I couldn't help it. All my bottled up emotions were spewing out of me.

"My lawyer will be sending you some paperwork. It should arrive at your place by the end of the week."

"It's over?" I tried not to yell. "What the hell happened?! Can you have the common courtesy to tell me that?"

"You were not negligent. In fact, you acted responsibly, even bravely. The investigation determined there *was* a small fire in the spa. It started from a cigarette left burning on a toilet in the women's locker room. It fell into a waste paper basket, ignited some tissues and set off the alarm. The report is more detailed if you have any other questions or concerns."

"I have replayed that day in my mind so many times," I said, clenching my fist, "trying to figure out if there was something I missed, hoping I could make sense of the disaster that washed away my life along with the spa. Now you're casually telling me I'm off the hook?"

Yvonne didn't say anything. Normally I would be so happy I'd want to kiss her, like after the gift card debacle. But by this point, I had been through too much. Relief didn't come easily.

A memory flashed through my brain: Mrs. B had the worst smoker's breath emanating from her mouth when she screamed at me on that horrible day. *It was probably her. And how selfish—lighting up while pregnant.* Now I had someone to blame. Anger ignited in my chest like fire in a hot air balloon. I began to understand how Yvonne felt right after the spa was destroyed. Yvonne had a visceral reaction, not a rational one and she directed her anger at the person she *thought* was responsible: me. I softened ever so slightly. At the same time, I still wanted to know the whole story. *And I deserve a little vindication.*

"So how do you feel about what you've done?" Silence on her end. "I gave you four years of my life and this is how you repay me—by threatening to take away my home. Suing me before you had all the facts—trying to destroy me!" More silence on the other end. "I've had nightmares every time I managed to go to sleep. I've endured panic attacks, depression and hopelessness." Still nothing from her. "I couldn't even get another job to support myself because you bad-mouthed me in the industry, and now you flippantly, in your detached voice, tell me it's all over? What kind of monster are you?!"

Yvonne whimpered softly. I'd never heard her cry this way. The familiar feeling of empathy mixed with awkwardness, made it impossible for me to hate her. *This might be the most vulnerable she's ever been.* When Yvonne finally spoke all she could choke out between her sobs was, "I understand. I am *so very sorry.*"

With those seven words, she said everything and to my surprise, her apology actually sunk in. I thought about what she'd been through since the spa was destroyed. I tried to put my own feelings aside. On some levels, I could relate to her. I had been living in fear of losing everything, but Yvonne had, in her mind, already lost it all—her spa, her place in New York society, even her name. A pang of regret hit me in the stomach. I wished I hadn't called her a monster. Once I felt compassion for Yvonne, relief crept in. It was over—the lawsuit, being trapped in a miserable job, and the fear of the unknown. I was free. For several seconds neither of us said anything.

"You were right." Yvonne breathed in deeply. "I did want someone to blame. It's what I do. I was devastated and now I'm filled with regret. I know how you must have felt with your life crumbling around you because that's where I am today." She inhaled and exhaled loudly. "I was so wrong, and too blind in my own power to see myself objectively. I want to thank you for everything you have done for me over the past four years. I hope one day, you accept my apology and I will be able to make this up to you." She broke down again, after a futile attempt to hold it in.

I knew what I had to say. "I forgive you, Yvonne."

"How can you forgive me so easily?" she asked.

"To be honest, I have to—for my sake as well as yours, even if it's *not* easy." I've always known forgiveness isn't just something you give to the other person; it's something you do to move on. The anger would have eaten me up if I didn't let it go. I couldn't continue to hate Yvonne for the epic mistake she'd made. Maybe the joy of relief had taken over, because, while I still wanted closure for myself, I actually wanted to help her, too. I could never dismiss someone without giving them a little resolution. There were also a few things I was dying to ask Yvonne. *I have to start a dialogue.* "What are you gonna do now?" I asked.

"I'm not sure. I've lost so much," she said quietly.

"I want you to know something, Yvonne. Your status as a socialite, the director of a world-renowned spa, the glamorous persona you've created, you know that's not *really* who you are, right?"

"What do you mean?"

After reading Yvonne's story in the paper and analyzing our time at the spa, I pieced together a greater understanding of her as a person. She, like so many people, was desperate for love. But without it, she survived on the crumbs of her power, the jealousy of others, and her own reflection—instead of finding love within herself. Yvonne didn't like her *real* image in the mirror. She preferred to see the dazzling creature she'd created, reflected through the eyes of others. Yvonne had lost her identity along with the spa and now she was starving. There was only one way to pull her out of the darkness—to help her see the light. If I gave Yvonne a goal, I knew it would give her hope. I choose my words carefully, "I mean it's only an image we create, a way we want people to see us. Madonna even wrote a song about it, called 'Substitute for Love.' It's just a role we play in a certain arena."

"But I *lived* for the role I was playing," Yvonne said, a hint of hysteria in her voice.

"Well, now you have the opportunity to figure out who you really are without it—who you are without your spa."

"I thought I knew who I was, but at this point, I don't even know what that means."

"Hardly anyone does. People search their whole lives to find the answer. It's the million dollar question that we're all here for, isn't it? Personally, I think it's a combination of what you believe, what you're passionate about, what you feel, and who really matters to you in this world. Then you have to ask 'why,' to all of those questions. It's a complicated lifelong process. But as we figure it out, the key is to love and accept ourselves." I hoped it didn't seem like I was preaching. It was, however, what I believed.

"My passion *is* owning a spa and now it's all gone!"

"You still have the ability to run a business. You didn't lose your life or something irreplaceable. You just lost the spa. You enjoyed building Von Spa the first time and you'll enjoy doing it again."

"That is true."

"You made a contribution to the world when you opened your spa and in the process you gave people glamour, excitement, escape. That's what's really important about living out your purpose— creating something for others. Your passion for the industry is a big part of who you are, but it's just one part. Now you have the opportunity to explore other aspects of yourself. Von Spa was a reflection of who you were, and you can always design a new spa to reflect who you've become."

"I guess that's what the insurance money is for." I imagined her smirking on the other end of the phone. I knew Yvonne. She wouldn't just patch the place up and reopen. Von Spa had to be the best haven for relaxation in the country and after this it would have to be even better. Yvonne would settle for nothing less.

She paused. "I could build another spa, but I don't know if I'll ever get over the pain of the scandal. People I thought were my friends, reveled so unabashedly in my demise."

"This is when you find out who your real friends are. Screw the others. Do you have anyone here to support you, who loves you for you and not what you've accomplished?"

"I have Mena and my mother."

It was nice to hear she considered Mena a true friend. I didn't understand the real nature of their relationship because I'd only heard them talk shop, but I couldn't believe Yvonne had mentioned her mother, who aired the family's dirty laundry in the press. *How could Yvonne, the queen of blame, sweep this under the rug?* It was the first time I'd ever asked Yvonne any personal questions, and this inquiry was especially nosey, yet I had to know. It amazed me how this catastrophe had shifted the balance of power. We were just two people—equals in our humanity. Yvonne was no longer my boss and I had nothing to lose. So I fired away. "You're not angry at your mom? Didn't she tell your story to the papers?"

"Yes, she did, but she was high on painkillers at the time. She would not have done so, otherwise. Ever since my father died, she has had some substance abuse issues. My mother needs help and I owe her so much. She gave me confidence and told me I could do whatever I dreamed. Even though we didn't have any money, she never made me feel poor. Instead, I felt limitless. I have nothing but love for her. My mother believed in me when no one else did."

"Just as you believed in me." *We're more alike than I thought.* Yvonne didn't respond. "It's nice to see how forgiving you are." She remained quiet. "So what are you gonna do until the spa reopens?"

"I'm going to take a long trip to Europe and visit some other loyal friends I have there. It's too hard to be in New York. The media made me feel like I was really hated all along. Everyone seemed to get some sick satisfaction out of the exposé."

"It just made them feel better about their own lives."

"I know."

"And wasn't it hard to carry around those secrets? Weren't you always afraid of being exposed?"

"Of course I was. It's another reason I'm no longer angry with my mother. In a way, she set me free."

"That's true. Now you don't have any skeletons in your closet to worry about. You can *own* your story of the Southern girl who grew up poor and made it big. People aren't really so bad. Everyone loves a good American success saga and a comeback, too. When you open your new spa, they'll be happy for you. You'll see. It will give them hope."

"Thank you, Thomas—for everything; especially your hard work and forgiveness. One day I promise to make it up to you." She inhaled like a quiet machine gun. "I have to admit, I feel foolish for not being more appreciative of you when I had the chance. And I can't believe I missed out on getting to know you better. Regrettably, I was too wrapped up in myself. I have to ask, how on earth did you become so enlightened?"

"I guess I'm naturally curious about people and I have a knack for under-standing others, like you have a flair for the spa industry. Which reminds me of another great thing that makes you who you are—your love of mentoring people. You've taught me a lot about business."

"And who taught you so much about life?"

"Mostly Oprah and a little bit of Chopra. Oprah would say this is our holy moment. When you lose it all, you're forced to examine your own behavior."

"I have been. And it haunts me that I was so quick to point the finger at you. I think I'm done blaming other people. Even though the insurance company might have other ideas, it's the reason I'm not suing Mrs. B." I couldn't believe Yvonne used our nickname for Mrs. Jones. "According to the DNA test, she was the one holding the smoking cigarette."

"DNA test?"

"I invited her to dinner and when she went out to smoke, the investigators took the butt and matched the DNA to the cigarette that caused the fire." *Still a badass to the core*, I thought. "But in a way, I know I am the one to blame."

Her words dangled in the air. *What the hell is she talking about?* "There's something else I wish I could undo. I knew Mrs. Jones was abusive to the staff, yet I looked the other way because she was such an important client. I should have been more concerned about my loyal employees than this wicked woman. If I had banned her from the spa in the first place, maybe none of this would have happened."

Wow. I couldn't believe she was capable of such honest self-examination. The old Yvonne stood on her pedestal, where no one questioned her about anything and she didn't even question herself. *Maybe she'll see things differently now.* I felt a twinge of sympathy. "I'm sure you'd never let anything like that happen again. Although it wasn't easy, I think we've both learned a lot from this experience."

"I can't believe it took a catastrophe for us to open up to one another. We've known each other for so long. It's a shame we've never talked like this before."

"We really weren't being ourselves when we were together at work. Now we're just two people stripped down to the bone." I knew this was the real reason Yvonne was able to talk about her emotions; she was an open wound crying to be healed. I could relate. Everything poured out of her, and I, an unlikely candidate, happened to be on the receiving end. Then it dawned on me—maybe I was the perfect person for her to confide in: I was forgiving and I could see her objectively. It felt good to finally show Yvonne who *I* really was. Something told me to continue sharing what I really believed, so I said, "Sometimes it takes a crisis to strip away all the bullshit—before we were too busy playing our roles of boss and employee."

"Well I hope one day we can play the role of friends."

"I hope so, too."

After I hung up the phone I ran to get my Gratitude Journal. I wrote about how thankful I was to be ending this arduous chapter in my life. I wrote about the conversation I'd had with Yvonne and how I should heed the advice I'd given her, by being true to myself in every way. I wrote about the time I'd spent at Von Spa and what I'd learned there.

Although the spa world hadn't been my calling, I still discovered how to spread my wings as a leader, and it'd given me purpose to try to be a good one. My self-esteem had grown by leaps and bounds in the past few years.

I put down on paper the gifts Von Spa—and even Yvonne—had given me. Because she believed in me professionally and because I'd worked hard, I had been able to buy my own little piece of New York—my condo.

But maybe the greatest assets I gained were measured in friendship, especially with Margaret. And the fruits of our friendship were support, laughter and creativity. I was so grateful to Margaret for forcing me to become part of the songwriting class. Not only did she help me find my calling, but sharing the words I'd written with the other students helped me remember this: There are more happy days in the future, and I've had more good days than bad, in the past. My heart almost burst when I realized, *the lyrics I wrote helped me pull myself up by my bootstraps. And maybe one day, I can give a new song to the world.* My internal movie reel exploded into Technicolor.

I called Margaret with the good news about the lawsuit. She seemed happier for me than I was for myself. I thanked her again for making such a big difference in my life. This time, I was the one who began to cry.

****

For a while, I suffered from Post-Traumatic Stress. The nightmares continued. At times when I was half asleep, I thought the conversation

I'd had with Yvonne was just a dream. Lingering remnants of sadness reared their ugly heads at sunset. This seemed strange since most of my daytime depression had lifted. Symbolically, I guess I didn't like the darkness. I prayed the paperwork from Yvonne's lawyer would come quickly. I hoped a tangible document might help me move on, but eventually I accepted the truth: It was going to take time to get over this harrowing experience and getting some extra help wouldn't hurt.

I called my old therapist and made an appointment. Having a breakdown had reminded me I was still a work in progress. Friends used to ask me, "Why do you go to a shrink?" My answer was always the same, "If you want to move past all your pain from long ago and learn how to forgive your bullies, if you want to be happy and fulfilled, if you want to be more enlightened, if you want to understand yourself and others, figure everything out with someone who knows how to help you—a good therapist."

There was one thing my psychoanalyst couldn't give me—a source of income. I decided not to think about it and focus on the positive. Living in the moment wasn't so bad anymore.

I woke up on the day of the second class, feeling more rested than I had in months. My chest was dry when I stretched my arms. *No night sweats!* Something else had taken their place—a beautiful dream of a distant lavender land with long-haired sirens who gazed across the oceans from soaring cliffs, wind in their lovely pastel locks while they sang, "It's Not Me, It's You." *Holy shit!* The notes still lingered. I hummed the tune into my digital recorder. I hadn't just been dreaming, my musical mind was composing as I slept. The universe had given me a gift. For the first time, a melody accompanied my lyrics. What I'd written had the potential to become an actual song.

That evening, I put in some extra effort when I got ready for class. Although I wasn't ready to admit it, I wanted Auston to think I was hot. I did a mud mask, shaved my neck, which defined my scruffy jawbone and flat ironed my hair. The tendrils grew longer as I burned them pin straight. After I was finished, I grabbed a pair of scissors and cut off the dead ends into an angled bob, pointing at my cheekbones.

I sprayed my fitted grey T-shirt with Sake perfume and enhanced the gingery, androgynous scent with a touch of lime extract. I put on dark denim skinny jeans and gathered them at the ankles. Then I slipped on my boots, which I left unlaced. Although I was developing a major crush on Auston, I didn't want to dress as hardcore as he did. My esthetic was really more "rock star light" and it was an expression of me. The clothes made me feel cool, but also approachable.

I couldn't wait to present my lyrics to everyone, but I was too scared to sing the melody, so I decided, *I'll keep it just for me.* I left my apartment thinking, *La dee da, la dee doe, it's off to class I go, will I sing my song, the answer's no, la dee da, la dee dee, la dee doe.* Even my thoughts were turning to rhymes. *I'm on a roll!*

Sprinting through the lobby, I waved to our doorman.

"Wait, Mr. Haven. You have a package." *Thanks for noticing,* I thought. He held up an envelope. *Oh, THAT kind of package.*

I walked over to the front desk, my palms sweating. *Please, let it be what I hope it is!* Feverishly, I ripped open the cardboard tab and pulled out a stack of stiff, white papers. The top of the cover letter read: **The Law Offices of Elizabeth Cordell.** I pored over the document. My knees gave out as I processed the information. I held onto the wall, and began to kneel. Tiny black and white letters confirmed the lawsuit was officially over. Relief spread through me like a drug. Our doorman looked on in surprise when I shook the papers at the sky, thanking God and the Baby Jesus and the Virgin Mary and the Buddha and Mother Theresa and my Sitto and my Nana, my dog Daisy, and anyone else who was up there listening.

****

Findings of the investigation were included in the paperwork. A lit cigarette, forgotten by Mrs. B, was left hanging on the side of the toilet's water tank. This was evident from the nicotine stain on the porcelain. The investigators determined that closing the restroom door moved enough air for the cigarette to fall into an adjacent garbage can. The discarded tissues inside smoldered for several minutes, and created a lot of smoke. The sprinklers took care of the potential problem; security came to the spa during the incident and told Yvonne the building was safe from threat of fire. *It makes sense the problem started in the locker room—where Yvonne tinkered with and/or silenced the alarm system. No wonder we never heard the robot voice saying, "Fire."*

The cigarette butt later found in the garbage can was not smashed and, therefore, not extinguished by hand. The only other smoke seen in the spa was created by the sage, but according to the video, Tootsie had finished fumigating the hallway a full fourteen minutes before the alarm sounded. *Burning sage had never set off the alarm in the past, anyway.*

The report made sense, but some of it seemed speculative. How did they *know* Mrs. B left the cigarette dangling on the toilet? Just because there was a stain doesn't mean it was abandoned. Obviously we didn't have cameras in Von Spa's beautiful frosted glass stalls or this would've been an open-and-shut case. I came up with me own theories. Maybe Mrs. B tried to throw the cigarette in the toilet, but missed and it ended up in the trash. Or maybe a spa daze left her so disoriented, she *did* leave it behind, still burning away. Some might find this hard to believe, but countless guests were so relaxed when settling their accounts, they actually forgot their shoes, leaving Von Spa in our comfy slippers. Then it hit me. *It doesn't even matter. Mrs. B was careless with a cigarette. Her actions set off the sprinkler system. I have been exonerated.*

I put the papers in my bag and pulled out a copy of my song. I walked down the empty street singing the lyrics to myself and as Margaret would say, it sounded twice as sweet. The ordinary subway ride that followed was colored by the music playing between my ears and I wasn't even wearing headphones.

The nervous butterflies didn't take flight until I turned onto Debra's street. I really didn't want to read my lyrics in front of the new class members. Standing outside, the cold breeze caused my teeth to chatter. I hit the buzzer, the door clicked and I slowly trudged up the stairs to the fifth floor. I peeked into Debra's open apartment praying there were no strangers in the room. Auston and Debra were sitting in the 1970's teak chairs. My heart fluttered when the corners of Auston's lips rose to greet me. *One day, I'm going to make those lips mine!* I thought. *Wow, suddenly the voices in my head have more game than Gabrielle.* There was someone sitting on the couch, their back to me, wearing a red and yellow striped ski cap. *Oh no.* My fears had been confirmed. *It's someone new!*

The girl turned around and removed her hat, freeing her dreads from their knitted prison. *Woohoo!* It was Maya. She grinned and patted the seat next to her on the sofa. I took off my vintage brown leather coat and sat down.

Debra caught my eye. "Welcome back, sweetie. I'm glad we didn't scare you off."

"Of course not." I smiled. "I've been looking forward to tonight."

"Great! So it's only the four of us," Debra said. I became drunk on a cocktail of emotions—unspeakable joy, sweet relief, still nervous, but excited. "Who wants to go first?"

"I will!" I shouted, startling myself.

"You must have something you're eager to share with the group."

"Or I just want to get it over with…" I raised my eyebrows, passing out copies of my lyrics, "…so I can enjoy the rest of class."

"Don't worry, I'll be able to tell the difference," Debra replied.

"You are kinda psychic like that," I said feeling like my old self and even a little bit better.

Debra beamed while she put on her glasses.

I began to read:

"It's Not Me, It's You"

You were all I wanted

When I fell for you

Deep down I knew

It's too good to be true

Still you came on like fire

And put out that flame

But I heard you're a liar

Can't say I am the same

<u>Chorus</u>

Don't wanna bleed anymore

Or let myself heal in time

To wait for a cure

For no reason or rhyme

Before this goes further

Let me tell you the truth

This time it's over

And it's not me, it's you

Verse #2

I found out about her

I should let you know

It's too much drama

I gotta let you go

You think you have someone

All figured out

Then you see clearly

What they're really about

Chorus

Don't want to bleed anymore

Or let myself heal in time

To wait for a cure

For no reason or rhyme

Before this goes further

Let me tell you the truth

This time it's over

And it's not me, it's you

Bridge

Heartache made me stronger

It taught me a lesson

I'm better off alone

Without your affection

Chorus

Don't want to bleed anymore

Or let myself heal in time

To wait for a cure

For no reason or rhyme

Before this goes further

Let me tell you the truth

This time it's over

And it's not me, it's you

When I finished, the crowd of three went wild. I'd found my people. I wasn't an outsider anymore, I was one of them. I was contributing, expressing myself. Unlike the first class, I was comfortable enough within the group to remember why it felt so good to be a creative person. When you shared your work with others, you showed them a piece of who you are and if it resonates with them, they let you know—by reacting, applauding, or even telling you. Not only is it incredibly rewarding, but in the best case scenario, both parties might feel less alone in the world.

Maya asked innocently, "Did you get the title of the song from the book?"

"What book?" I asked.

"The one called *It's Not Me, It's You.*"

"Oh shit. I never heard of it before."

"It's also the name of a Lily Allen album," she said.

"Oh, double shit." My heart sank.

"That doesn't matter though," Debra said. "I've never heard of a *song* called, 'It's Not Me, It's You' until today. Besides, you can't copyright a title. Haven't you noticed how many songs have the same name when you're looking for something on iTunes?"

"And don't get me wrong, the lyrics are great," Maya put her hand on my shoulder.

"What do you think, Auston?" Debra asked.

"I fucking love it!" *And that's all that matters.* Auston leaned back in his chair.

"Clearly it's very clever," Debra said, "but we still need to give you a critique. The big problem I have is this—the assignment was to write a song for Leona Lewis. You allude to some of her biggest hits, which is fine, but you're putting them down. No artist would want to insult their own catalog."

My excitement flatlined. Then a light bulb came on inside my brain. "What about Britney? In 'Stronger,' she alludes to 'Hit Me, Baby, One More Time,' like she's moved past that part of her life. I think Leona should graduate to the next phase, too. She's the heartbreak victim in all of her popular songs. I'd like to see some female empowerment."

"True dat!" Auston exclaimed. *He's kinda funny, too.* I looked at him and smiled.

Debra stared at me, wide eyed. I felt guilty for challenging her. "But what do I know?" I said.

She took off her glasses and looked straight at me, "It sounds like you know pop music better than I do and you don't need to go to music school for that—all you need to do is listen. Thanks for reminding me." Her compliment gave me a little frisson. She looked at my lyrics. "So, I love how you applied what you learned in class. Now I can explain what I meant last week when I was talking about interpretation. As Leona is singing, she can hold the corresponding note of a lyric longer or shorter depending on the placement of the word. That way, even if there are slightly different amounts of syllables in each verse, everything will still fit together. With that in mind, you can easily match these lyrics up with the notes of your melody." When she said the word "melody" I could feel her glimpse into my soul. "Let's just start with the chorus, though. If you put it to music, how would it sound?"

Damn this chick is good! But there's no way I'm gonna sing a note in front of these real musicians and my new crush. "I dunno. I got nothing."

"We're going to do an exercise. I want you to look at the lyrics you've written, imagine you're all alone, and sing whatever tune comes to you."

"I can't sing."

"Who cares?!" she bellowed, throwing up her right hand.

"I mean, I don't think I can physically sing in front of anyone."

"If you really don't want to sing, you don't have to, but if you're *afraid* to sing..."

I was starting to have an out-of-body experience again, so I figured if my vocal chords were singing while I was floating around the crown molding, I really wouldn't be doing it anyway. Very quietly, I sang the lyrics with the melody I'd written in my sleep. When I finished, Debra stood up and clapped. She sat back down and began to preach. "Now that you have all the accolades of your peers, and in one week you have managed to write a song with a melody, do you believe?"

"Believe what?"

"That you're a songwriter. That this is important!"

"I guess. Thanks." I was happy, but a bit overwhelmed, too. I couldn't quite absorb what Debra was saying. At the same time, I felt like I'd reached the light at the end of the tunnel. *This is my calling.* It *was* important. It mattered to me. *And it might matter to other people if I share it with them.* Then Debra gave me the payoff line that cemented what I was feeling. She asked, "Hasn't a song ever saved your life?"

Absolutley, I thought, and this time, maybe it wasn't just a song I was listening to, maybe it was a song I'd written. So I let myself 'take it in', and said, "Yes, I do believe!" like I was answering the call in a Baptist Church.

When class was over, I stayed to talk to Debra. She made me feel safe. I wanted her to know me. I told her everything I'd been through. After I was done with my spa story, I told her about growing up as a boy who sometimes felt like a girl, and how people were cruel. Toward the end of my epic, I admitted I used to wish I was someone else. But if that meant I had to give up everything about myself, especially my ability to write, I wouldn't choose to be anyone other than me. I couldn't imagine going through life the same way after finding the gift of creation, again. Writing songs made me more than happy, it made me feel fulfilled. I told Debra how grateful I was that she'd helped me discover a part of who I was meant to be. We hugged. Usually she was very vocal; this time, all she could manage to say was, "Thanks."

I turned to leave and she called out, "Oh Thomas, one more thing!" *There's always one more thing.* I chuckled. *But tonight, I can't wait to hear what it is.* "I forgot to give you guys your assignment for next week. I was gonna ask you to write a cosmic tune, like "Major Tom," but you've given me a better idea. What I want is an inspirational song— something with a message."

"I know just who to write it for."

****

I didn't care how long I waited for the train after class. It didn't matter that it made all the local stops. When we were stuck between stations, I was okay with getting home late. I was having such a fantastic time writing lyrics, I never wanted the feeling to end. I penned an anthem for all of the little Thomases out there, and the grown up ones, too. This time, a song for our people would come from within the community, using our language, written by someone who knew exactly how they felt. Let the song inspire everyone to see the beauty in themselves and remember what makes them special. Because as my Dad used to say, "We should all celebrate our differences." *And one day, I will perform this song myself.*

"Your Anthem"

Walking down the street

Your hair is super queer

With music in your feet

And extensions down to here

Belting in your car

Or strutting down the aisle

Looking like a real girl

The epitome of style

Dressed to impress

People stop, People stare

But you're not a hot mess

So you just don't care

Doesn't matter what they think

You've got style and wit

So you halt and give a wink

Wonder why they give a shit

Then you're writing on the train

Lyrics pouring from your brain

Words are falling from above

Full of hope and love

Feels so good that it's insane

But just wait for the refrain

<u>Chorus</u>

This is an anthem for all of you

You're special, unique and beautiful, too

When you stand up for you,

You stand up for us

Feel the joy, spread the love

Feel the joy, spread the love

<u>Verse #2</u>

Reading is for books

You'd never read a look

Only beat a face

With make-up or base

They think your life's a sin

But He said don't judge

So with Jesus you'd fit in

It's the preacher who's the thug

Full of hate

When it's God who made us great

You speak your mind

Only if it's kind

Don't need money in the bank

To sing or paint, design, create

People tell you who to be

They say you won't go far

Write your own song 'cause you're free

And you know that you're a star

If you feel misunderstood

Now you know, it's all good

Chorus

This is an anthem for all of you

You're special, unique and beautiful, too

When you stand up for you,

You stand up for us

Feel the joy, spread the love

Feel the joy, spread the love

Walking home that night, I felt different. I took off my cap and enjoyed the cool air while my longish hair blew in the breeze. I looked at the cars whizzing by, the skyscrapers full of light, and the charming tree-lined streets. There was magic in the air, but I knew it was coming from me.

I thought about the past few months and how hard it had been to get to this place. I'd heard Margaret say, "Your life can change in an instant," and mine did, but for me, the life changing event was just a catalyst. The metamorphosis that followed was a slow growth. This might be true for Yvonne, too. I knew it would be interesting to watch her evolve after the dust settled. *She may become a completely different person.*

In my opinion though, sometimes the lessons we learn don't come at a fair price. I hate hearing someone say, "Things always work out for the best." The sentiment is positive but it seems to me, people who believe this, have never experienced something catastrophic. Did everything after 9/11 work out for the best? Not for the families who lost loved ones. This expression downplays people's suffering, especially if they're currently going through the fire.

If a magician told me she could cast a spell that would put me into a deep depression, like the one I had just been through, and in return, she'd make all my wildest dreams come true—I would decline her offer without a moment's hesitation. The true evil of being depressed is that the expiration date is not guaranteed. And even worse, it *feels* like it will last forever. You don't relate to your old self, you feel nothing but pain and you can't imagine feeling any differently. This is what puts people in mortal danger.

I had made it safely to the other side. I wasn't sure if the sadness was worth the payoff. Yes, it helped lead me here. What I learned about myself was good. I could appreciate the moments of happiness which had come to me, yet I subscribed to a different philosophy. I thought to myself, *It's impossible to know where the tides will take you, but if you look at the world through positive eyes, you can expect wonderful things to happen.* In times of trial, we always have to remember there are more great things to come.

Deeply in philosophical mode, I replayed coming out to Debra. I had told her part of me was obviously male but part of me was female, too. After sharing my story, I was reminded that I had to live the words I spoke to Yvonne. I needed to love and accept myself unconditionally. And one major component of the equation was this: I had to stop worrying about being judged for my dual gender identity, which is no easy task, because in our culture, challenging your biological sex is just that—challenging.

I thought about being exposed as a drag queen in the newspaper. Although the story never broke, I decided if it ever did, I couldn't be afraid of being misunderstood. Instead, I would tell my tale to help the majority understand people like me. I would no longer be a victim. I would become an advocate. By letting everyone know who I am and what I think, hopefully I could help the little Thomases out there in the process.

I believe the gender spectrum is much like the spectrum of sexuality and everyone falls somewhere on a sliding scale. I'm in the middle. I found an outlet for my feminine side when I discovered drag. For me, dressing up was enough. Making like-minded friends helped me complete the puzzle. I learned to have fun with both halves of myself. Once I did that, I began the process of self-acceptance. And A.S., I was taking it to the next level.

But I would also say this: None of us are really male or female, black or white, gay or straight, anyway. Deep inside, we're all the same. Some call it the soul. Maybe it's our consciousness, but the rest of us is external. It's easy to see why folks identify so strongly with their station in life. Our upbringing affects the way we're raised, what we're exposed to and how we're treated by others. It may be hard for some people to overlook each other's differences because they make the mistake of thinking they should be proud of their roots. But pride separates us and allows judgment to sneak in. Suddenly we're all on a scale of who is better or worse. If everyone was open to embracing our *humanity* over our *identities* instead, there'd be a lot less strife in the world. There'd be less "me" and "them" and more "us." Less judging and more understanding. Less cruelty and more kindness.

Long ago, I'd seen the power of, and learned to practice, the golden rule. I've always believed, when all the great spiritual teachers like Jesus said we should 'love thy neighbor,' they simply meant we should be kind to one another. Looking out for other people has always been my top priority. I want everyone around me to feel appreciated and supported, whether at Von Spa or in my living room. Margaret once told me she didn't care what people thought about her as long as they thought she was funny. I don't care what people think about me, as long as they know I care.

Some people say you pay the price for being different, and in a success-driven place like New York, this may have been even more true for me; caring and cutthroat are not compatible. So at times I'd daydreamed about being like the majority. If I were a straight male or conservative female, I would have the automatic acceptance of society and my family, but that isn't who I am. And if I could change my stripes to fit in, I'd be giving up too much in the process: my empathy, my uniqueness, my creativity, and maybe even the love I have for others, which is returned to me ten-fold. I had found my place in the world, even though I had to work at accepting myself the way I am. My family and friends did the same. I guess when things are hard won, you have a greater appreciation for them, anyway.

My conversation with Debra helped me realize I already had what most people, including Yvonne, searched for their whole lives: love. Although I didn't have a boyfriend, I had found self-love. The people in my life loved me, too. I felt so lucky to have a fantastic biological family, an amazing New York family of friends, with its newest member, Margaret, and a great spa "work family." Hopefully I would see them all again soon.

That night, one of my wildest dreams did come true when I became a songwriter. It was the brass ring I never even imagined I could grasp. I was ready to live the artist's life. All I needed was a way to pay the bills while I pursued my creative interests. I no longer felt the need to define myself by my profession and I didn't care what anyone else thought about it, either.

I had an overwhelming urge to share the evening's festivities. I pulled out my phone to call Margaret; I couldn't wait to tell her the class had actually changed everything and how lucky I was to have found a friend like her. Unfortunately, it would have to wait. My phone's battery was drained. But I saw the bright side of the situation. *We can talk when I'm relaxing at home. That way I can enjoy every minute of our conversation without distractions. And after I catch up with Maggie, I'll call Pep so we can plan a drag night out!*

Our doorman buzzed me into the building and told me I had a delivery.

"I already got it," I smiled.

"Then what's this?" he asked, holding up a manila envelope.

"Oh!" I said. "I guess that's *another* delivery. Thanks. My bad."

When I got upstairs, I plugged in my phone, and reclined in my Nana's La-Z-Boy. I opened the envelope and pulled out a bound booklet with a cover letter. It read:

Greetings from Saint-Tropez! I heard you were starting your own treatment booking service…

Word travels fast!

…I should have given you a medal for getting everyone out of the spa safely on that fateful day. So here it is, better late than never. Thank you and good luck. Best Wishes, Yvonne."

The packet contained the contact information and treatment history of every guest who'd ever been to Von Spa. I gasped dramatically, imagining I was in a movie. It was like receiving money in the mail. The final obstacle to launching our business had been hurdled. At the bottom of the first page, Yvonne had handwritten:

Keep my clients close at hand until I open my new spa.

Yvonne had "made it up to me," just like she'd promised. It was the unofficial launch of Spa Divas. Once again, my life had changed in an instant, this time for the better. I called Margaret to tell her the good news. She answered right before the third ring.

"We're in business!"

End of Book One

Look for "Your Anthem," performed by Lawrence Daly's alter-ego, Evangeline on YouTube (channel LawrenceDalyLTD) and iTunes. If unavailable, it's coming soon!

Acknowledgements:

Two editors helped me mold Spa Dayz into what it is today. Thank you, Jason Black, for showing me I had to take out the weeds and find the story. And thank you, Jane Young, for being amazing. Your patience, kindness and expertise gave me a master class in editing. You are detail-oriented without losing sight of the big picture and your wealth of knowledge about everything from grammar, to storytelling, to pop culture trivia is priceless. Face it; you're kind of a genius. Let's meet at Merchants for Nachos and Peanut Butter Pie—it's on me. And if anyone out there is looking for an editor, she's the one!

My early readers taught me so much about this book and myself. Thanks to: Jesse Volt, a real sister of the cloth. My dear friend Bryan Marsee. My enlightened, accepting Dad—a true renaissance man. Christie Tan, a great partner in cultural crime. And Charlie Brody, my fross.

Much thanks to: Cynthia Savage, you gave me confidence when I was at the end of my rope. Lola Anava, you reminded me to have fun. Amy Buckley, you showed me the artist's way and championed all my creative endeavors.

Gretchen Larsen, thanks for your help at every turn, always seeing the best in me and laughing at all my jokes. To my kindred spirit cousin, the multi-talented Jennifer McNally, thank you for encouraging me when times were tough. Amy Huntington, thanks for everything. I've learned so much from you it's not even funny. You are an incredible writer, a generous friend and the best audience a boy could ever hope for.

Special Thanks to: Heidi Kole, your knowledge of self-publishing was invaluable. You're an inspiring person who showed me what could be achieved. Everyone reading this should buy a copy of Heidi's book, The Subway Diaries—it's absolutely fascinating! Sontino Scrimizzi, your expertise in branding and marketing is top of the line. The cover is just gorgeous, as are you. Ryan Prado, your incredible photography really made the project sing! Sheafe B. Walker, the advice you gave me was fantastic. If anyone needs an Intellectual Property Attorney, he's your guy. Aunt Ginny, your continual contributions to my personal "endowment of the arts fund," were greatly appreciated. You are the best Godmother ever!

Thanks to Mercedes Ribicoff, Kenwyn Dapo, Rebecca Ferguson, Tom Barry, Frankie Cocktail, Bianca Leigh, Matthew Parker, Phillip Carrol, Luanne Surace, JoAnn Roberts, Maryrose Murray, Brooke, Lorraine, Denise, Peppermint, Richie, Gigi, Mark Colin, Starlene, Desi, John G, Yolanda, Kathy, Laura, Colleen, Jen, Zack, Renee, Liz, Moisés, Patrick, Ariel and all the girls at Lips.

Thanks Mom, for being the best Mother in America. You are the first person I want to call if I have good news and if I have bad news, you always make me feel better. You have saved my life a million times. And really, the food is just awesome.

Thanks again, Dad. I won the "father lottery."

Christy and Beth, I couldn't be luckier to have you as sisters. Thanks for always being there for me. You are both superstars. Thanks also for procreating and giving the world such great children.

And thank you to my whole family, especially for having a sense of humor. I love you all! You're great friends as well as relatives. You have supported me in whatever I've chosen to do over the years and as we all know, I've done some crazy stuff.

51377538R00182

Made in the USA
Lexington, KY
22 April 2016